THE *B*ERLIN ASSIGNMENT

❧

ADRIAN DE HOOG

An exchange between the members of international Green Mafia.
Oct. 07

THE BERLIN ASSIGNMENT

❧

ADRIAN DE HOOG

BREAKWATER BOOKS LTD.

BREAKWATER BOOKS LTD.
100 Water Street · P.O. Box 2188 · St. John's · NL · A1C 6E6
www.breakwaterbooks.com

Library and Archives Canada Cataloguing in Publication

De Hoog, Adrian, 1946-
      The Berlin Assignment / Adrian de Hoog
ISBN 1-55081-218-1
      I. Title.

PS8607.E482B47 2006   C813'.6   C2006-901462-0

Cover Image:
Reichstag nach Mitternacht, acrylic, 40 X 60 cm, 2002, Rudolf Stuessi

Editor: Jocelyne Thomas
Design: Rhonda Molloy

The Canada Council   Le Conseil des Arts
   for the Arts   du Canada

We acknowledge the financial support of
The Canada Council for the Arts for our publishing activities.

 We acknowledge the financial support of the Government of
Canada through the Book Publishing Industry Development
Program (BPIDP) for our publishing activities.

Printed in Canada.

For Regina, Ariane and Julian, who were there.

PATERFAMILIAS I

*Y*ears later, members of the Service still drew on the Berlin fiasco. Few stories embellished their gossip in quite the same way. As Service scandals go, it might have been a small event. After all, minor lapses are common in diplomatic outposts. But this was different. A lid had been slammed down on Berlin. Not a scrap of information was ever put into the records. Nothing on file explained why Anthony Hanbury, serving there as consul, was unceremoniously yanked out. Hanbury was neither aggressive nor ambitious. He wasn't a difficult man, nor overly pedantic. No undermining Service animosity seemed to have been at work. How, then, did his assignment end in an atmosphere of intrigue? Were the knives out for him? And, if so, why?

Some thought Irving Heywood, senior staff member in the personnel department at the time, *priest in charge of Investitures* (to use Service jargon), might have started one of those sub-surface suspicions and kept it fuelled until Hanbury finally fell victim. Enough members of the Service have met their end through *that* ploy. But people on good terms with Heywood discounted it. They were confident the Investitures priest had told them everything he knew, little as that was. Moreover, when Hanbury's assignment fell into place, Heywood was priest in the Disarmament Priory. Only later did he move to Investitures. Hanbury was Heywood's deputy in the Priory – had been for years – and as far as anyone could tell they got along. Their long liaison might explain why Heywood gossiped fervently about Hanbury, but it was an unlikely cause for the bizarre end to the assignment. No, the fiasco did not arise from within the Service. If knives had been out, they were external. And the place of their unsheathing had to be Berlin.

Only two facts were known. One, that the *high priest*, top man in the Service, suddenly and personally tore asunder the assignment that Investitures had lovingly created scarcely one year before. The other was that there had been some prodding by the spooks. All else was obscure.

Gossip-mongers agreed the Berlin event had to be a nugget. And they kept it polished. One day a file would come to light; such files always do. And past experience told them the story would have a lustre, a delightfully tainted glow.

❧

Recalling the defeats of colleagues has always been a pleasant by-product of longevity in the Service, but few could match Irving Heywood's store of knowledge, or zest for gossip. Temperamentally unsuited for law, or medicine, or commerce, Heywood in centuries past would have been destined for the Church. His type is not unusual in the Service. Moreover, Service members – like churchmen – are trained to perform solemn rites. And so it was that a metaphor – the Service as a religious order – developed. Cheeky recruits used it first. It caught on, expanded, deepened, and finally became commonplace. The Personnel

Department turned into *Investitures*, policies towards Asia were formed in – where else? – *The Asian Temple*; *The Zealots* looked after Europe; the spooks inhabited *The Crypt*; and Irving Heywood, when Tony Hanbury worked for him, was priest in charge of *The Disarmament Priory*. Their task was to promote the cause of international peace.

⚜

Irving Heywood enjoyed few things more than reminiscing on the porch of his cottage in the Gatineau hills on summer weekend afternoons. Looking out over one of the countless, water-filled dimples in the Canadian Shield, maintaining a subconscious tally of his alcoholic intake (as diplomats learn to do in lifetimes of excess), Heywood conversed with friends – other members of the Service on home duty – about the world and its political disasters in the way others might swap notes on the season's produce ripening in their gardens: tales of encounters with Idi Amin's secret police, phlegmatic accounts of UN cease-fires ending in failure, stories of trade negotiations gone awry, suspicions about diplomatic double-crossings by close allies. And, of course, the endless delight in the snafus created by colleagues.

Today, as usual, talk on the porch is drifting from one Service character to another, but always comes back to Hanbury and Berlin. "He had his limitations." Heywood recalls. "He wasn't exactly a world-conquering type. But still, why accept Berlin? Naturally I asked. Hanbury didn't explain; he just shrugged. He had a strange, I would say a *fatalistic* way of shrugging. Three years ago that was. Christ, Manny, how time flies." Irving Heywood's sidekick today is Manny Stepney, Trade Commissioner. Heywood has known him for decades, ever since they served together in junior positions in Lagos. Stepney is a man of few words, which is why Heywood likes him.

The lake shimmers through the trees. In another hour, the sun will sink behind the solid wall of green on the opposite shore. Loons will start their lament. The mighty insect world will arise out of slumber and fish will splash out a ballet. When Irving and Manny stand, legs heavy with the drinking, they'll pause a moment to dispel lightheadedness before moving to the dock, stripping down, sliding into water which is deep and cool and bites the senses. Take your pick for distance: half an hour to the middle, twice as long around the island, where boulders just beneath the surface provide cover for bass. The wake left behind by a slow breaststroke sounds loud in the stillness. Beneath the evening's iridescent sky, the water's curative effect clears the mind. The world and its affairs shrink in importance, while the appetite for steak expands.

But the swim is still an hour off. First, on the porch, the gossip must run its course.

"Maybe Hanbury wanted Berlin. Maybe he was in luck," speculates Stepney.

"Hanbury didn't *need* to go to Berlin," Heywood repeats, eyes half closed. "He proved he could handle being number two in Kuala Lumpur. And the years he spent with me in the Priory were, with a few exceptions, not that bad. So, he could have gone out as number two again, to some place challenging. Manila, for example. He had options." Heywood sounds as if he's sorry his former deputy went to Berlin.

"Didn't Anderson go to Manila instead?" asks Stepney.

"Yes," says Heywood, "and he didn't last either. We know why with Anderson. But Berlin and Hanbury..." he sighs "...it's a riddle. I'm still looking for the key. So far nothing, Manny."

"Maybe, it's locked away with the Cabinet secrets," observes the trade commissioner.

"In that case, Germany's Cabinet. Not ours."

"And what was Anderson's problem?"

Heywood draws in his breath. He sucks until his great frame balloons. A long slow exhalation follows, and a heave to his lips of a tumbler filled with iced rye whiskey. Telling tales out of school, using alcohol's soft workings to render them a little taller, is pleasurable for Heywood. "Manila, number two and head of chancery," he begins. "Not a bad deal for Anderson. We had lunch the week before he left. My God, he was conspiratorial. He spent the whole time whispering. 'They want me to turn the place around,' he said. So I asked, 'what's wrong with Manila that isn't wrong everywhere else?' He looked around to make sure no one was listening and said *Godinski* was the problem. Naturally I wanted to know from whom he had that, but he wouldn't say. Then he said – you'll like this one, Manny, it's sort of your style – he said, 'fish always stink from the head down.'"

"So Godinski *was* a suspect ambassador," a nodding Stepney concludes.

"Frankly, I didn't believe Anderson," Heywood continues lightly. "We've all been through briefings before assignments. They tell you what's wrong with an embassy when there's a mess down below, never if there's one higher up. Ambassador Godinski *could* have been a problem, but Anderson would have been the last to know. Still, he said he had a mandate. Off he went, like a knight, lance at the ready, and visor down. Every one of us has had that urge. But you know how it gets tempered once you hit the ground. Not so with Anderson. He accused Godinski of wrongdoing the moment he arrived and they went at each other like Rocky Mountain goats. I can categorically state – *that* wouldn't have happened with Hanbury."

"*Gentle* Hanbury, eh? You think with Hanbury, Godinski would have cooed?" Stepney's voice has a sudden touch of vitriol.

Heywood snorts. "Godinski as dove! I like that, Manny. That's good. Speaking factually though, we know Godinski liked being surrounded by yes-men. Hanbury could have handled that. But not Anderson. As you'd expect, Godinski pulled rank. Anderson got sentenced to silence and meditation. What happened next? You guessed it...diplomatic drift. Hit him like a ton of bricks. For months on end, nearly a year in fact, he arrived at the embassy every day around noon with a head like a football, then knocked off in the early afternoon, heading straight back to the club. A textbook case. His zeal took him down for the count in Manila. He's still down. Turns out his mandate was nothing more than a loose remark by someone in accounting that Ambassador Godinski had double-counted the cost of a couple of lunches."

The trade commissioner shakes his head. He doesn't show it – Manny Stepney never shows much of himself – but he enjoys Heywood's stories. Heywood has a knack for making the Service sound Gothic. And the stories are better, more detailed, now that Heywood is the Investitures priest. Heywood, Stepney knows, is incapable of forgetting an anecdote about failure. He reflects on what it must be like to fail and can't help thinking of Hanbury in Berlin.

Heywood's thoughts have been leading in that direction also. *Is now a good time to begin Berlin?* No, the Investitures priest decides, not yet. He doesn't like to start Berlin too quickly, not on lazy summer afternoons. The Berlin file is flimsy. It hasn't that much overt failure in it, not like Manila. Hanbury was on his own in Berlin, and gossip from fellow travellers, the colour commentary from the sidelines, is missing. The Berlin file, Heywood sometimes thinks, is a Teutonic file – colourless and blunt – and if deployed ineptly it would stop a conversation, not promote it. Stick to Manila for a while. Dredge up one more Godinski tale.

The Investitures priest raises his gaze towards the tree tops and says, "The question has been asked, Manny, why Godinski didn't save his new head of chancery. Why didn't he notice that Anderson was suffering from diplomatic drift?" Stepney lifts his glass of whiskey, tilts his head back, finishes it and sits forward, leaning over the porch railing, staring into the forest in the pose of a hunting dog. Stepney smells game. "The point to make about Godinski," says Heywood, "is that he tuned out long before Anderson arrived. The ambassador went to work all right, but mostly to do crossword puzzles. He went out for lunch early so that he could get back early to play cards with the clerks on their break. He was generally sullen, except when he played cribbage. Every point he pegged was a triumph. He'd show his old spark then. It seemed cribbage allowed him to relive the negotiations of the Nuclear Non-proliferation Treaty. That's where he made his reputation."

"Bad for business, that treaty," remarks the trade commissioner gravely. "Cost us reactor sales all over the world." He continues peering dolefully into the distance.

Heywood knits his brows together, as if he's an oracle now, ready to predict chaos. "Once, a delegation of prairie school-board types was visiting Manila. Godinski loathed receptions, but since one of the visitors was a childhood chum from Wawanesa, he felt compelled to have one. The usual mix attended: expats on World Bank contracts, diplomats from second-tier countries, local heavies keen on a few free drinks. The residence was full. It was a wonderful place, you know, a sweeping driveway lined with blooming hibiscus, stately steps up to a grand entrance, marbled hallways, flowering plants everywhere, the air filled with the busy sounds of the tropics. Someone told me that arriving at that house was like entering paradise."

Heywood leans far back. Paradise. He reflects on it. For him paradise is more than a stately mansion. For him, it's a state of mind. That's what the Service is – his paradise. Each movement of the whisky tumbler to his lips quickens a feeling of heavenly affection. Anderson, Godinski, Hanbury, all souls with blemishes. He loves them like kin. On afternoons like this, love cascades around inside Irving Heywood.

He is overwhelmed by love for Hannah too. With her help he did a decent job, he believes, spread over several continents, to raise four precocious sons.

He clears his throat to shake off the emotions. "Back to Godinski. The educational administrators from Medicine Hat, Fort Qu'Appelle, Neepawa, Wawanesa – places like that – flew out of Calgary just as a blizzard was coming on. You can guess they were overwhelmed by Manila. It's a fair distance from snowdrifts up to your kitchen windows at minus forty to Godinski's palace in the tropics. The party started well enough. The Canadians liked the moist floral air. Everyone else liked Godinski's free booze. But half way through Godinski commandeers his third secretary to play cards. This goes on for an hour. The visitors from western Canada are embarrassed, the Filipinos amused. At the end, slurring, Godinski tells the third secretary to *get these damned people the hell outta here!* You can imagine the shuffling that started towards the front door. By the way, he seldom lost at cribbage. He'd just taken the poor kid for ten bucks." The Investitures priest inhales deeply through his nostrils, though it's unclear whether he's signaling admiration or disgust.

"There's a saying," Stepney interjects. "It takes three generations to make a gentleman. I bet Godinski's old man was an immigrant, straight from some place like Minsk." In a fading voice he adds, "Let's hope he's got a son." Heywood raises his ferocious eyebrows and breaks into a grating laugh, which clashes with the stillness of the forest. He appreciates how Stepney sometimes puts things. Coming out of a slouch, he takes the thermos with chilled whisky and reaches over to Stepney who, glass in hand, responds with a practised sideways swing. Heywood pours a generous amount, then treats himself. "Speaking of sons," he says, "Lecurier holds the record in that department. I asked him about it once. We were on a jaunt through Europe to lobby for our position on North Atlantic fish. *Paterfamilias globalis.* That's what he called himself. He always became animated when asked him about his children. He was fond of all of the ones he knew. There were plenty and their skin colour varied."

Heywood thinks of his own children. He waited patiently in his youth for someone to come along to match his New Brunswick genes and Hannah, British-born, was the one. He met her during his first assignment, in Lagos, in the Stepney drawing room. Stepney's wife Laura sang with Hannah in a local Anglican choir. She brought Irving and Hannah together. As happens to foreigners in far-away places, a romance developed, and quickly led to marriage. Manny was Irving's best man and Laura was Hannah's maid of honour. Hannah became the type of wife who once sustained the British Empire: unfailingly cheerful, an imaginative cook, an enthusiastic gardener, lively at receptions. In short, a perfect mate for an ambitious Service man. Everyone instinctively flocked around Hannah at parties. Irving usually stood around helplessly for a while – a backwoodsman's habit he never shook – until the alcohol took hold. At a certain moment, expertly chosen by Hannah, when he was ripe, she'd throw him an opening and Irving would barrel forward with his stories. Their success on the cocktail circuits had no limits, save those posed by Heywood's liver.

Now that the reminiscing has gotten around to Lecurier and his children, Heywood's pride surges over his own offspring. He is thinking that he, also, is a *paterfamilias.* Unlike Lecurier however, his boys are legal. Apart from number three, a problem child, they take after Hannah. A curious coincidence, Heywood sometimes mused, that all but number three were fathered in his favourite conservative position. In contrast, number three was the product of a wild night on a Cuban beach. They had been on vacation. A tempest was raging and nature's violence carried him away. Perversely, he insisted on penetrating Hannah from behind as she, legs astride and feet firmly planted, leaned forward into the tearing wind. Number three had been restless and adversarial – a stormy boy – from the moment of his birth, perhaps from the moment of conception. Heywood always kept this speculation to himself, but he did occasionally think, if indeed undiscovered forces arising from the style and energy of the reproductive act determine personality, that all the world should marvel at Lecurier's imagination, given his rambunctious brood.

Stepney, interested to hear more about Lecurier, prompts Heywood. "Sorry, Manny. My thoughts wandered. Where was I? Lecurier, right? Well, I'll say this about Jacques, he managed his assignments with biological adroitness. He had always left a place by the time the paternity accusations were ripe. You know, after the fish talks in Europe, I was put into Investitures for a spell. Lecurier had dispersed his seed pretty widely already by then and it fell to me to ask him to slow down. What happened? Naturally, he claimed we had no business digging around in his personal affairs. I couldn't reprimand him too severely, because to his credit he did his best to support the mothers."

"I heard there was something with a princess in the Saudi royal family," says Stepney. "That must have been a tough one to have paid for."

Heywood answers smoothly. "I discount that story, Manny. It arose out of the sheer momentum of his reputation. Lecurier developed a pattern of holding back in high-cost countries. It's true there was a princess of sorts in Jeddah, but she was English. She did a veil dance in a secret basement suite in the residence of the Ambassador of Argentina, who would invite his friends to watch. Lecurier didn't stay there long. Not Jeddah, Manny. Kuala Lumpur, Nairobi, Bogota, Peking, those were Lecurier's hallmarks. The last one was the diciest. He took up with the great-granddaughter of a member of the Central Committee.

Somehow he got around Chinese security. It proved his most remarkable characteristic. He could go local, like a chameleon. Disappear. Needless to say, when this happened in China, the complainant was apoplectic."

"Did he have some trick to turn himself into a slant-eye?" asks the wily trade commissioner, "or did he pose as a missionary?"

Heywood doesn't bite. "He just knew how to go local," he insists. "And he did brilliant reporting. It makes you wonder whether paternity and political insight are opposite sides of the same coin. Lecurier had a special knack for getting through to the bare bones of a culture and an uncanny ability to predict political decisions."

Talk of Lecurier pushes Hanbury once more into Heywood's thoughts. Hanbury also had chameleon qualities. He disappeared into Berlin the way Lecurier vanished in Peking. Like Lecurier, Hanbury wrote some acceptable reports. Heywood remembers the Berlin reports. They caused a stir. But similarities ended there. Lecurier and Hanbury diverged, as Heywood often pointed out, when it came to flair. Hanbury plodded, whereas a worldliness propelled Lecurier. Yet despite Hanbury's lack of flair, Heywood always liked him, as he did Lecurier – perhaps even more.

Shifting his great frame, Heywood slaps at a mosquito on his thigh and wipes his forehead on a shoulder. He's been sweating profusely. A pungent odour is developing. "Ever read one of Lecurier's reports?" he asks, knowing Stepney hasn't. "They were special, they really were. He created an extra dimension, a sense of history in the making. He started off in Athens when the Colonels ran the place, then he was in Latin America, the Middle East and Africa, but he really came into his own in Indochina. His work on Cambodia was gripping. It even circulated in Washington. His style was to take a few telling facts, then draw a big picture. His syntheses had energy and ease. I suppose that characterized his night work too, I mean, when he lay down with local ladies. He lived in an enviable world, always injecting order into what seemed all screwed up and crazy. From Cambodia he was sent to South Africa. The issues there were immediate. The business community was squealing about our apartheid sanctions. The Government needed someone who could charm the captains of industry, yet convince them the sanctions would never come off. There were fewer questions in the Commons once he stared down the bankers."

"We were much too holier-than-thou with those damn sanctions," says an annoyed Stepney, beginning to drum his glass. "The Brits and Krauts left themselves more manoeuvring room."

"They had more historical investment," Heywood replies dispassionately.

"We have a habit of misunderstanding investment generally," counters Stepney, "so no wonder we never get around to having any that you could call historical."

Heywood is not inclined to be drawn in, not on investment and especially not on sanctions and apartheid. He fills his lungs for a dramatic finale. "Lecurier's end was tragic. His vehicle was rammed by a rhinoceros while on safari and he sustained mortal injuries. That was the official line. Actually, early one morning he was stabbed in a lung as he left a public house in one of the townships, whereupon he drowned in his own blood. We were concerned, of course, that the embassy would be wobbly at a crucial time. Hanbury turned out to be a passably good chargé. After Berlin, who would have expected it?"

The truth about Lecurier stuns Stepney. "Holy shit," he swears softly. "So it wasn't a rhino?"

"No," Heywood confirms harshly. For a moment he thinks he may have gone too far. The real version of Lecurier's death was always closely held. The trade commissioner is melancholy for a minute, then says, "I've heard Hanbury was a tower of strength managing the funeral arrangements. Sounds almost unbelievable."

"We've all heard that, Manny. There could be some exaggeration."

"I guess so. Did you know, I worked with him once. We were on a task force investigating the impact of high sugar prices on the economy." This link, though decades old and tenuous, allows the trade commissioner a judgement. "When I knew him he gave an impression of treading water. He worked, but he never progressed." The Investitures priest approves of the analogy. In the Priory, Hanbury routinely had a look about him that suggested he was about to sink, and Heywood often had a paternal urge to throw his deputy a lifeline.

"Wasn't he with you for half a dozen years?" Stepney asks. "How did you put up with him that long?"

"Five years and three months," Heywood says possessively. Is this the time to open the Berlin file? He decides yes and plunges in. "Disarmament was hot. We worked our tails off. I have to say it, Manny, Hanbury treaded a lot of water, sure, but some things he did fairly well. He once had to produce a crisp piece for the PM who wanted profile at a security conference in Vienna. Hanbury knew the subject. He might have been meek, but he was smart. SS20's, Minutemen, throw-weight equivalents – he understood the material as well as anyone. All we need-ed for the statement was some hard analysis and a paragraph or two of great prose. He had no problem with the analysis. It was the style, the elevated tone for the PM that eluded him. So that part I did. What I'm saying is, that after he treaded for a while, I always pulled him in." Heywood feels a surge of sympathy. His eyes turn moist. "Funny thing is," he confesses, "Hanbury combed his hair like his mind worked, a part right down the middle."

"I found him secretive," Stepney says. "He never seemed to come or go. He was there, and suddenly he wasn't there. Stealth, that's what he had. Well, what happened in Berlin? How did he screw up?"

"Nobody knows. Just like nobody knew why he went. The Wall was down; the Cold War over. The German Government couldn't make up its mind to move back from Bonn. Berlin had become uninteresting. An outpost. No self respecting political officer would go. But Hanbury snapped it up."

"A marriage made in heaven," sneers Stepney.

"At first it unfolded fairly well. It took a while for things to go off the rails. Not like Anderson in Manila."

"You mean he consummated the marriage," says the trade commissioner sarcastically.

"Well...partially. You know, after Hanbury left the Priory, I did too. They needed me to run Investitures. One day there was a minor blow-up. Seems he hadn't done any reporting. The high priest asked me. Told me to talk to him. Said he wanted reports from Berlin. I called Hanbury. He was surprised, but began sending reports. The next thing, Manny, a couple of months later – I swear there was no advance warning – the marriage was over. Annulled. By the high priest, not me. I just arranged his next assignment. I sent him to Pretoria. Number two to Lecurier."

"Weird," says Stepney.

"It was."

"So the high priest held the dagger."

"All done in the inner sanctum. I was nowhere around."

"When's the last time that occurred?"

"It was unprecedented."

"Nothing on the files? Not even in Investitures?"

"Not a scrap. I swear to God. I looked. I'm still looking." Heywood's heavy eyebrows lift. A look of innocence unfurls around his mouth. "Pretoria is working out fine for him. Maybe it's on account of the woman he brought along from Berlin." Heywood slaps at another mosquito, this one on his cheek. He sighs and reaches for the thermos.

"A woman?" The trade commissioner is surprised.

"It happens, Manny."

"Well sure, but Hanbury?"

"The same thing happened to Pochovski," Heywood says with authority. "He was a changed man once he got a steady woman. A few weeks after finding her he was on a delegation to a UN Conference in Montevideo. Everyone knew something had happened because no matter how desperate the mood in the financial committee, he came out whistling, even in the dead of night."

"Wasn't Burns the head of that delegation?" asks Stepney.

"He was. Now *he* was someone you'd go to the wall for. I recall how in New York he'd regularly stonewall dozens of countries with his brilliant interventions. Back home the papers said he was callous, rough at the edges, but he knew the national interest…"

※

The talk continues. From the Andersons and Godinskis, the Lecuriers, Hanburys and Pochovskis, on to virgin territory provided by the Bradsworths, Lavallees and Careys. The stories, like rivulets, link up into a brook that meanders through the world's affairs and discharges into a vast sea, an infinite receptacle which holds all unwritten Service legends. The afternoon on Heywood's porch ends when the air stirs. A breeze picks up. Forest smells of resin and rich earth waft past, a signal that the heat is moderating. "The girls'll be back soon," Heywood says, stretching and yawning and rubbing sweat around inside his jersey. "By the time they've told us what they bought, we'll never get a swim in. What do you say, Manny? God, I've gotten stiff sitting."

Halfway through the swim, Hannah and Laura return from their afternoon of visiting auctions. They stand on the dock laughing and waving at their men in the water. Afterwards, steaks sizzle and mosquitoes attack the cook. Then they huddle tribally inside a screened-off portion of the porch. Imprisoned by the insect world, the table talk again turns to the Service. With the women, the slant is different: raising children in African outposts, managing servants in New Delhi, finding decent dentists in the Middle East. A night-cap follows and it is then that Stepney says, "I've been thinking about Hanbury. Since nothing's on the file, maybe it's on account of that German woman. Maybe she played a role."

Heywood contemplates this. "Could be," he says slowly. "Interesting angle, Manny. You know, rumour has it she's quite the fireball."

THE PERFECT MATCH

efore Berlin, Hanbury didn't figure much in Service gossip. He had an instinct to hang back, to stick behind cover. But for Berlin he changed. Coming out into the open, he preyed on the assignment. He even penned a memo to Investitures reasoning he was their man.

When Heywood learned of this he bluntly advised his deputy against Berlin. Shunning the limelight was one thing, the priory priest argued, but why calcify your brain? "There's nothing there. It's a dead end," he said. Hanbury didn't reply. He stared back as if he and Heywood lacked a common language.

What Heywood didn't know – and couldn't have – was that Hanbury's note to Investitures had nothing to do with career advancement. It sprang from something deeper…from unvoiced irrational longings. At one time or another most members feel something tug at them. A faint bell chiming deep inside tells them time is passing. They'll try to keep this secret, for a while, but the day comes when they'll agitate for assignments in out-of-the-way places, ones known to spell career disaster – Costa Rica for example, where the collection of rare seashells from two oceans can give great satisfaction, or Addis Ababa, where, in the nearby highlands, a retracing of the footsteps of the early explorers searching for the headwaters of the Blue Nile generates true philosophic contentment. But such self-indulgence passes quickly. Reality comes surging back. Soon enough the prodigal children return to the relentless competition that marks life in the fold. Such mid-career symptoms – Madame Tass, the Service career counsellor, once wrote an erudite monograph on the subject for a psychoanalytic journal – came to be bundled in a phrase: the *For-Once-Something-For-Me Syndrome.* It was this feeling that drove Hanbury when he pushed his interest in Berlin.

Having sent his memo he next went to see an Investitures cleric in person. Unfortunately, when he used the well-worn phrase the inflection in his voice must have been poor, because immediately he got an earful back. It had to do with the first two words. "What do you mean, *for once?*" the icy cleric asked. Hanbury shrugged. He said the last five years in the Priory had been like going through a wringer. "That's the way it's supposed to be," the cleric said severely. He held out no hope for Berlin. "And don't bother going higher," he warned. "I've discussed your memo with Borowski. He backs me." The reply went into Hanbury like a dagger. He argued back, saying in twenty-five years he had accepted every assignment he was given and had never quibbled. He'd paid his dues. Furthermore, as explained in the memo, he spoke German, surely not a trivial consideration. But the cleric was adamant. In his view, Berlin required someone with more presence.

Yet, less than three weeks later, having been overruled by someone somewhere, the cleric called back in a voice brimming with poison. "Damn you, Hanbury," he hissed, "and damn Berlin. Just so you know, as far as I'm concerned, you and the Krauts, you deserve each other."

The uncharitable words rang in Hanbury's ears after the call, but only for about a second. Putting the phone down he leaned back in his chair, put his feet up on the desk and sat without moving for nearly an hour. Deliverance had come. No more Heywood. An end to purgatory in the Priory. Not only that, but the chance had come to look after unfinished business. He had olive branches to deliver. The opening had come to atone for acts committed in his youth.

❧

The final days were hectic. The movers were the only ones that had it easy. They explored Hanbury's apartment like eager crows, but the pickings were disappointing. They found an enormous stereo, and shelves and cabinets filled with ancient records and new CDs. But after that it was all downhill: some scrawny household items, a dearth of clothing, no fancy glassware, no splendid silver, nothing much by way of works of art. "He ain't like the others, Tiny," the head packer scowled to his assistant. What he meant to convey was that they were expecting the materialism of a bishop, but had run into the asceticism of a monk.

Getting ready to depart, Hanbury spent hours waiting outside the doors of overbearing clerks. He got a new passport which identified him as *consul*; changes had to be made to insurance policies; financial matters required updating; he worked his way through an endless list of things to cancel and filled out a form describing the location of his will. He even crammed in a few minutes of briefing on Berlin with one of the European Zealots. But the worst of the ordeal was the office good-byes, some from characters he considered worse than crows. Not until the aircraft door closed – that moment of finality, that sealing off from all that went before – did he experience release. The Priory days were over – even if the unctuous farewell speech by Heywood still rang in his head. Hanbury grimaced as bits of it replayed, as if a demon force was making one last attempt to haul him back. *Tony was brought up in Indian Head, so I was not surprised to find that he can be a fighter and fortunately for me, from time to time, he was.* Painful remarks. Heywood was the only priest Hanbury knew who could turn short and peppy words of appreciation into a funeral oration. Heywood droned on and on at the staff lunch, inventing his deputy's biography as he went. He even managed to include a reference to a dream: he and his deputy shipwrecked on the way to a disarmament conference; *together* they cling to a chunk of driftwood; *rationally* they discuss improvements to an intervention which he, Heywood, the country's highest ranking delegate to the meeting would make. The dream – disaster striking, the will to survive, fellowship in adversity, a commitment to excellence while suffering duress – symbolized, the priory priest claimed, what he and his deputy had experienced. In an awful show of emotion Heywood had used a table napkin to wipe his eyes.

Now, above the clouds, the new consul tried to dispel all thoughts of Heywood. He ordered champagne. His ritual. He always drank champagne when change was happening, when a fresh assignment was hours away. Studying the rising bubbles made him feel he, too, was bursting free.

That was the good thing about such passages. Not only were they prominent boundaries drawn on Hanbury's map of time, they also spelled renewal. He had served in six cities in five countries on four continents over twenty-five years. But this time felt especially heady. Not only was he leaving behind a suffocating bureaucratic mantle with its pockets full of worn out issues (not to mention people), he was going to a place that was also embarking on a new beginning. Berlin, he sensed, would be a kindred spirit.

Despite the champagne, Hanbury's thoughts oozed back once more to the Priory, to the heated discussions over the years on theoretical issues now destined to remain unresolved forever. The merit of MAD – *mutually assured destruction* – was never clearly demonstrated. The world left MAD behind to embark on fresh forms of lunacy. Forty years of Cold War ended in collapse. The issues simply went away and his work on esoteric disarmament subjects had not been worth finishing. The files were now collecting dust. As the relentlessly merry bubbles continued rising in his glass, Hanbury saw that the priory years had been wasted.

He drank and sank into himself a little. Heywood's former deputy tried to form a picture of more than just the Priory. He fought to see his twenty-five years in the Service as a set of neatly interlocking pieces. Did the six cities, the six packets of experience, add up to something larger? Was there a connecting thread and, if so, where was it leading? Hanbury occasionally marvelled at how some Service men treated the progression of their assignments – their careers – with a ghastly posses-siveness, as if it allowed them to gain some warped form of immortality, while others treated them as a collection. But of what? Of a batch of urns stored and ignored in a necropolis vault? For Hanbury, well, his career has been too random to amount to a collection. All he'd had were disconnected lunges, like Brownian motion which leads nowhere and just is. The elements of his career were not worth keeping. They were mostly worth forgetting. The priory farewell lunch had been just like that.

It took place in an Indian restaurant on the second floor of Ottawa's covered market. Inspiring smells of fresh vegetables and flawless beef sold in the stalls on the ground floor, mingled with exotic oriental fragrances coming from the restaurant's kitchen higher up. Inside the Taj Mahal, tall-backed chairs stood in formal lines along the tables. The advertising postcards at the cash register, where after-dinner peppermints were available in a teak bowl, said each guest would be pampered like a Maharajah. But despite the postcard, the tall chairs were uncomfortable, as if in the mixing of Indian and Canadian cultures some key ingredients had gone missing.

All twelve members of the Priory were present. Each one was a master in some policy area, or reigned supreme in some eccentric corner of knowledge. Expertise in the Priory ranged from the illicit trade in surplus eastern European tanks and MiG fighters, through to the secret places in the Middle East where chemical weapon drums are cached. Several were brilliant at procedural manipulations, so they wielded power. Routinely they would get whole groups of nations to accept their personal point of view.

Heywood, presiding with trademark smugness, sat at one end of the table with the office girls, Diane and Sarah, one on each side. Hanbury was next to Sarah and the rest of the Priory was lined up, monastically, on the two sides. The conversation at first had the texture of a thick pea soup cooking slowly – a periodic breaking of the surface followed by a re-establishment of tension. Luckily Zella, the chief secretary, sitting near Hanbury, was the type who liked parties to be lively.

Zella came from Yellowknife, starting out there as a waitress in a bar, though she knew she had it in her to aim higher. She saved up for an Edmonton secretarial college and from there found her way into the Service. This background gave Zella mental toughness. She combined it with boundless optimism and an ability to see good everywhere.

Deciding it was time to get Hanbury's good-bye party going, Zella made some spirited remarks about the wonderful decor of the Taj Mahal, the incense, the beauty of the carved chairs. It reminded her of a holiday she once had in Thailand. Then she turned to Tony. "I've never been to Berlin," she said, "but I've always wanted to go. You know that feeling?" Zella had a singing voice with a hint of western nasal twang. Her smile was quick and wide and cast in solid gold.

"I do," Hanbury replied earnestly. From the day Zella joined the Priory, he admired her northern directness, her way of saying things simply and making people feel warm. In a burst of generosity he added, "Why don't you stop by in Berlin on the way to *your* next assignment, Zella? Berlin is fabulous. We'll paint the town red."

"Not a good expression to use for Berlin, Tony," interjected Jerry Adamanski sombrely. He was sitting opposite. "Red is a political colour in Europe. They're trying to get away from it. Using words like that you're likely to be misinterpreted and cause yourself a bit of trouble." Jerry Adamanski liked to challenge. Presented with an opening, he loved nothing better than to nail a colleague to the wall. His role in the Priory was to promote cooperation on ridding the world of the material remnants of wars, such as unexploded land mines. Before that he had a stint in The Crypt, a secret place with controlled access. He wrote a paper there on the political use of colour in recent European upheavals – East Berlin in '53, Budapest '56, Prague's Spring '68, the shipyard affair in Gdansk. He considered himself an authority. If pressed Jerry could go back further, claiming some familiarity with the role in history of Rosa Luxemburg, though he hesitated to go beyond saying that she had been *a Red*.

Even though for years they had offices next door to each other, Adamanski and Hanbury seldom spoke, like monks in a real priory observing vows of silence. Hanbury couldn't help but look inquiringly across the table, wondering why suddenly he was receiving so much unsolicited advice. "I think Berliners are up to their town being painted red," he said peaceably. "What they don't like is someone telling them what their taste is, especially if he's never been there."

Adamanski stiffened. "And you have?" he said aggressively. "You think you know Berlin? You think you're an instant expert after one session with the Zealots?" He had a big head with a hooked nose, straight hair falling down and a pock-marked face. Sometimes he looked like a snarling dog. After years of scarcely acknowledging one another's presence, Hanbury and Adamanski were finally exchanging a few words, yet immediately it was threatening to get out of hand. Zella drew on her Yellowknife experience in the bars where she often prevented brawling miners from pulling knives on each other. She reacted quickly. "Back off, Jerry," she ordered. "This is a family lunch. Keep your poison for the enemy." The rebuke worked. Jerry turned to Madeleine MacQuary-Ellington, an expert on controlling military exports who sat next to him. Madeleine had children the same age as Jerry and they began to compare the challenges of parenting.

Hanbury had never been a match for aggressive young bulls like Adamanski. Even his delicate appearance – Zella once told him he looked *artistic* – undermined his role as deputy to Heywood. Whenever Heywood was away and Hanbury was in charge, he usually arrived at work with his stomach in a knot. Jerry Adamanski, but others too – Roger Chung, Deepak Ekbote and even the women like Madeleine MacQuary-Ellington or Louise Tetrault – they wouldn't cooperate. Hanbury knew that in a sudden crisis, when alarms go off at the highest levels, his colleagues would abandon him. They simply wouldn't pass him the needed information, hoping maybe to take his place should the high priest want a personal briefing. When an emergency struck the high priest demanded proof that within twenty, maybe thirty minutes it would be in hand. It left Heywood's deputy at everyone's mercy. He often looked ignorant, even indecisive. One time the decibel level went way up. *Balls, Hanbury! Show the world we've got balls!* Hanbury blamed Heywood for being shouted at. Upon leaving for an international junket, he never announced to the priory staff that in his absence his deputy would issue the orders.

Duplicity from Heywood, humiliation dished out by the likes of Adamanski, five years of belittlement. All that remained, Hanbury thought, quietly steeling himself, was to survive this final lunch.

The drinks were served and the curries ordered. Heywood struck an empty glass with a spoon. Rearranging a few long strands of hair from the back of his head across the front, and sending a meaningful look towards his deputy, he began. "Not often," he intoned, "does the Service make a staffing decision that is, well...yes...*benign*. Today we are celebrating a remarkable development, one that's opportune for everyone. We have a perfect match. Tony, our congratulations on Berlin. You've done well, you deserve it and you'll do well."

For several members, trained to unearth the possible meanings of language in international treaties, Heywood's words became instantly memorable as a brilliant example of Service doublespeak. Should the reference to *celebrating* be read as a backhanded reference to Hanbury's imminent departure, something everyone was glad to see? Adamanski, the lines around his mouth tightening, looked about and met the eyes of Deepak Ekbote who promptly signalled he was reading it the same way. Ekbote had a masterful ability to sum up complicated thoughts in a single word. He once confided to Adamanski that he found Hanbury's deputy stewardship *spongy*.

Heywood looked towards the guest of honour for a sign that his words were appreciated, but his deputy sat trance-like, hands on the table, fingertips touching, eyes cast down. Heywood thought he must be reflecting on their wonderful years together and the nightmarish bureaucratic battles they fought. It was enough to turn him mushy. In florid detail he recalled the Priory's accomplishments. There was the day they learned the Soviets had made adjustments to their Siberian radar systems, thus opening up the possibility of air strikes deep into the Yukon. Tony, he said, did the calculation of the longitudinal and latitudinal extent of the area under threat. The Canadian Ambassador in Moscow, Heywood remembered, drew on this analysis to make an informal protest. In fact, if the Cold War hadn't ended, Heywood opined, one could safely say the radar issue would have elevated into a documented violation of the Strategic Arms Limitation Treaty – SALT II.

As Heywood droned on, his deputy made his own, silent evaluation of the five years in the Priory. Some things, he thought, he had handled well. The Soviet radar episode was a highlight. But more could have been accomplished. The problem had been Heywood, who on occasion had thrown good work out the window. The loftier the Priory's client, the pettier Heywood became, as if wanting to prove that only he – *The Priest* – had the right touch for the papers needed by the highest levels. Take the Prime Minister's trip to a summit in Vienna on a new European security pact. Hanbury developed an initiative, a proposal that Soviet SS 20 missiles be dismantled in return for an American slowdown of the development of the Stealth bomber. The idea was checked out with the ambassador to NATO, the PM's security advisor, as well as a batch of generals sensitive to such issues. Everyone was eventually on side. But Heywood, fresh back from a conference in Helsinki, hit the roof. He said the proposal would be too ambitious for the Soviets who were keen to have ever more SS 20s, while a Stealth slowdown would hit the aerospace workers in San Diego. *Don't you know who the current senator for California is?* he shouted in a rare moment of apoplexy. *Do you suppose the American Senate will love this?* Nearly beside himself, he ordered Hanbury off the file. Matters became confused. In the end, Hanbury's idea was reinstated, because domestically there was nothing to lose and everything to gain. *Fuck the Californians,* was the way one of the PM's advisors summed it up. *And screw the U.S. Senate.* Heywood did an about-face. He slaved for a week to reinvent the wheel. He also managed to attract all the accolades. Hanbury was startled when Heywood, back from the Vienna conference, said, "Sorry to have been brutal a couple of weeks back, Tony, but you weren't explaining the idea clearly. Still, all's well that ends well. No hard feelings."

As Hanbury contemplated this and other priory injustices, Heywood's valediction took a different turn. "Tony grew up in Indian Head. A hundred years ago that was frontier country, so I wasn't surprised to learn he can be a fighter. He brings to all his assignments – how many have there been over the twenty-five-odd years, Tony? – that expansiveness of mind and gritty determination that opened up the West. I've never been to Indian Head, but I've flown over prairie towns like it. That's a big country you come from, Tony. The roads out there just go on and on, in straight lines to the horizon and beyond. All I can say is that such vastness, if it forms part of a personal outlook, is something to which we should all aspire."

The lines around Jerry Adamanski's mouth became ever tighter. He'd heard Heywood sermonize like this before. A wonderful – a priestly – gift. Rhetoric so pure that truth falls by the wayside. He looked down the table to see how others were taking it, raising his eyebrows twice in quick succession at Louise Tetrault at the far end.

"Tony stands poised to make a mark," Heywood continued. "Consul in Berlin, a high appointment, his greatest career challenge." Once more he addressed his deputy directly. "The grapevine whispers you speak German, one of your many unsung attributes. I'd like to say, Tony, that I am personally delighted that you're progressing – if I may put it this way – from prairie elevators to the Brandenburg Gate."

Heywood, sensing restlessness growing around the table, ended quickly with a wish the assignment would go well. Glasses were raised in a toast. Zella, bridging the awkward moment that follows table speeches, asked Tony rapid-fire questions: about his departure date, would there be a visit to his family out West, did the works of art in the official residence in Berlin have historical importance, what kind of chauffeur-driven limousine would be at his command. Adamanski then injected fresh energy into the discussion. "Tell us about your briefings, Tony," he sneered. "What did the Zealots tell you? What are you going to be doing out there on your own? Issuing passports and not much else?"

As usual, Adamanski hit a nerve, but Hanbury scarcely needed to reply since the questions launched a spontaneous, table-wide discussion. Energetically, sometimes heatedly, the priory members debated the preparedness – that is, the lack of it – with which they were sent abroad. They relived the disasters they endured for lack of training on local sensitivities before arriving in strange places. When the lunch broke up, Hanbury was relieved the discussion took this turn, for he would have had no answer had Adamanski persisted with his questions. The new consul didn't really know what he would be doing in Berlin.

⁂

Hanbury did have a session with the European Zealots, but it shed no light on his new role. He had flipped through some of their files on Berlin, but there was little in them apart from some amusing accounts of the dismantling of the Wall. One of the notes described Berliners hacking away at the communist concrete to stock up on souvenirs. A humorist had slipped the term *wallpeckers* into one paragraph. This word had prompted a crude, graffiti-like sketch in the margin – a small bird with a long beak rounded at the end resembling a phallus.

After surveying the files, Hanbury spent a few minutes with Hilda Chambers. She had become a Zealot two years before with responsibilities for Germany, immediately acquiring the nickname *Krauthilda* which she bore with humour. Krauthilda was small, her lips were painted fiery red, and she had oversized glasses sitting high on a pert little nose. Newspapers were piled up in her office, beside the telephone, on and under a small side table and in slanting columns on the floor. At her desk, surrounded by so much paper, Krauthilda radiated an image of being a no-nonsense woman.

"There isn't a great deal to be said, Mr. Hanbury," she answered in reply to his question about priorities in Berlin. "Central Europe has changed, sure, but I doubt it'll affect you. Listen, I've only got a couple of minutes. Is there anything you think you really ought to know?" Hanbury sat still, carved in stone. The thin Berlin file on his lap was a sorry excuse for troubling the busy Krauthilda. He took a moment to collect his thoughts. Krauthilda looked him over. "I saw somewhere you're from Indian Head," she said. "I was born in Moose Jaw."

"Moose Jaw? That's just three hours up the road."

"My family left and came East when I was a baby. What did your father do? A farmer?"

"A scientist."

"On the prairies?"

"Soil scientist, at a research station in Indian Head."

"That's freaky. Well, what do you want to know about Berlin?"

Hanbury was still thinking. He recalled a magazine survey on Germany he'd read. He'd made some mental notes of the headlines and these came back "With Germany reunified" he said, "there could be a shortage of capital to put the East on its feet. Interest rates could go through the roof. Is that of concern? And what about Berlin and its new role as German capital? What are the long term geopolitical implications of that?"

"That's several questions all at once, Mr. Hanbury. I'll answer them one by one. For interest rate developments, we use the *Financial Times* and the *Wall Street Journal.* Anything they don't get around to reporting on we get from the IMF. Don't try to compete with that. As for Berlin, it may be Germany's capital, but that's on paper only. As far as I can see, it sits out there all by itself in the middle of a former Communist rustbelt. Frankly, who cares? Listen. It's important for you to remember your consular territory is East Germany. That was a whole country until not too long ago and you're there by yourself. So my advice is, don't extend yourself. Keep lots of flex in case some Canuck gets into trouble and you need time to get him out of jail. I'm sure the local staff will brief you on what's left. And don't forget, if we don't hear from you, the assumption is everything's fine. My sense of upstairs is that that's the way they want it. Our real interests with Germany are pursued elsewhere." Krauthilda paused to view him through her great spectacles. "Okay? All set? Well, gotta go." As she got up, Hanbury saw slim hips pushing out against a tight skirt which fell in straight lines to the ankles. Krauthilda grabbed a fierce briefcase – out of proportion to her slender figure – and lugged it out. At the door she turned. "By the way, where *did* you acquire German? It was on the piece of paper I saw, but no mention of how you learned it." Hanbury shrugged. "What's the best place to learn a language?" he asked, also rising.

This broke the ice. She laughed with unexpected earthiness. Her red mouth spread wide. "I get the picture, Mr. Hanbury. My taste runs towards Italian. Enjoy!" With trim hips swinging, and the huge case forcing her to walk lopsided, Krauthilda swept away.

Hanbury watched her go and knew then who had drawn the obscene wallpecker hieroglyph on the Berlin file. Emboldened by the way she drew (and walked), he scribbled a note suggesting she drop by Berlin if ever she was in the neighbourhood. He signed it, playfully adding a replica of her bird, and placed it in the centre of the cluttered desk. Krauthilda's conclusion about the place where Hanbury learned

German was perceptive. Had she probed, she would have found that he lived in Berlin in the late sixties, attending the Goethe Institute for one year and going to lectures the next at the Free University. He would gladly have revealed other experiences: being temporarily arrested as a bystander at a student demonstration, and being shadowed by the Stasi during visits he made to East Berlin. Had someone asked about this when he joined the Service, he would willingly have written a long essay on his stay. But, like Krauthilda, the Service hadn't inquired, and he hadn't bothered to volunteer the information. That's how these two years in his late youth – formative for him, but insignificant for his employer – were accounted for in his personnel file by two vague words: *travelling overseas*. His Berlin experiences had no paper trail which meant, officially, they did not exist.

❧

Some months after his deputy's departure, Heywood was himself transferred from the Disarmament Priory – to Investitures – where he indulged in his boundless curiosity for the unseen particulars of other people's lives. In the first few weeks he went on a binge, snuffling through documents every day, his large frame hulking over the cabinets like a bear going through offal. Hanbury's file intrigued the new Investitures priest as much as the others. Questions still nagged him. Did Hanbury get the nod because he spoke the language? Had he been tested and, if so, what was the result? Desiring answers Heywood repeatedly went back to the confidential records room.

Hanbury's short memorandum to Investitures, setting out his reasons for the assignment, was there. Next to Hanbury's claim that he spoke German was an annotation. Painfully small writing in the margin in red ink said: *Language capability not essential. Nothing speaks for this request. Refusal strongly recommended.* Heywood recognized the troubled scrawl as the sour cleric's whom he sent packing the day he became Investitures priest. Beneath the cleric's scribble, in neat printing from an expensive fountain pen in a radiantly happy, mind-expanding, almost transcendental blue that ran down the margin and continued along the bottom of the page before petering out, was a detailed presentation of the pros and cons of assigning Hanbury to Berlin, written by Elmer Borowski, then Investitures priest. *So in the end I am forced to agree,* Elmer summarized like a high court judge, *even though he is the only candidate we have and we don't know where else we could send him...*

Then came a question in crisp green from an unidentified source, addressed to the Zealots. Underneath it yet another very prominent contribution in a thick black marker pen. The answer to the question was signed *Hilda C.* and it magnanimously concluded, *No damage can be done if he's assigned to Berlin.*

The final entry on the memo was another green-inked line, this one in capitals and addressed to Elmer. *MR. BOROWSKI: BERLIN IS OK. PLEASE ACTION.*

Heywood whistled through his teeth. It was there in all the colours of the rainbow. Nobody wanted Hanbury and nobody, except Hanbury, wanted Berlin. The match was perfect. The Investitures priest looked deeper in the file, but found nothing that corroborated Hanbury's claim that he spoke the language. This little puzzle, however, was overtaken by a larger one. Who, Heywood dearly wished to know, had been the new consul's green champion? He searched in vain. He looked in other files too, to try to find more green. Yet nowhere else (and never after) did he find another example of the decisive matchmaking that had instructed Elmer Borowski. All the same, inspired by the succinct elegance of the appearance of the phrase – *BERLIN IS OK* – the Investitures priest decided that, henceforth, he too would promulgate his views in green.

OLD FRIENDS

*B*erlin's delights fade quickly when the summer ends. Autumn's darkness sets in with a vengeance. Dull skies hang low; storm winds drive the rain. The carefree young families that romped on the sandy shores of the city's lakes disappear into their dwellings. Will their psychic reserves built up by the summer sun last the winter? They wait anxiously for the first school break, when they trek to the airports, boarding flights to Mallorca, or the Canary Islands, even the Florida Keys. They're like a tribe on the move then. They seek a hasty, final week of sun, a last opportunity to top up. Light as a holy grail.

Berliners in middle age are hardier. Until well past the equinox they continue their daily ritual of swimming in the forest-surrounded lakes. Still, at some stage in the year's decline, even they acknowledge defeat, and the waters are reclaimed by shivering, forlorn, sporadically quacking ducks.

Not long ago things were different. Communist patrol boats on the Havel provided year-round company for the waterfowl. The guards on the boats acted like outdoors sportsmen. They shot away happily – not at the ducks – but at people trying to get to West Berlin. Now that the eastern files have opened, it is known they did their casual killing more often than was commonly supposed.

The autumn's gloominess never failed to affect Sabine. When daylight began disappearing like water down a funnel, when the skies assumed their dreaded, lead-grey hue, and when the fog crept in to claim the trees and veil the rhododendrons in the city's inner courtyards, Sabine's reaction was predictable. She brooded about the inequities of geography. She yearned, not for other places, but for Berlin to have more summer. A twirl of the globe in Werner's study, with a finger tracing a constant line of latitude, showed Berlin is up there, more or less, with Hudson's Bay and the Kamchatka Peninsula. She once mentioned this depressing fact to her husband. The heating season had barely started, but the city's sombreness had already taken on its peculiar force. Werner laughed, not jovially, more dismissively. "Well," he said, condescendingly, "make sure the sun shines in your heart.", knowing full well that with her in a brittle mood, this would aggravate. "Personally," he added, "I like the darkness. It helps me think."

The effect of light, or rather, its lack, was evident everywhere. Most people experienced some sort of inner collapse without the summer's pumping force, much like the fountains at Schloss Charlottenburg which, having fought gravity since spring, one day simply stopped struggling. But Sabine's friend Martina had a different solution. In the autumn she switched from chilled sparkling white wine to Spanish red at their weekly lunch at Café Einstein. "It helps me feel the South," she murmured as the wine went down. "God, give me daily hallucinations – Andalusian earth, orange groves, olive trees, southern men…" Martina was psychologically more robust than Sabine. Physically, too, she was a show of strength. Her body, once curved and ripe, had swelled with the years, though it hadn't slowed the throughput, as she said, of *meine lieben Kater*, her darling tomcats.

The waiter attending them Wednesdays in the Café Einstein library was called Gottfried. Martina liked teasing him, calling him a heavenly tomcat, *mein himmlischer Kater*. Gottfried had a heavy mustache and long hair at the back which touched his shoulders – like General Custer. With his large nose, high forehead and muscular neck, he was imposing: a man at ease with women. Gottfried would tease Martina in return when he passed the menus, referring to her as *ein süsses Gänseblümchen* – a sweet daisy – causing a telling smile to form on Martina's scarlet lips and her eyes to fill with a fresh hallucination – she and Gottfried on daisy-filled summer meadows engaging in extravagant acts. "It is a dreary season", she would agree with Sabine once Gottfried disappeared with the order. She might twirl her long, pearl necklace then and eye Sabine's faint facial lines. "But you complain too much my little dove. Learn to use your body to drive the darkness off. I use mine at every opportunity to create *spiritual* light."

Contrary to Martina, whose body temperature went up when outside temperatures plummeted, Lisa, the second of Sabine's girlhood friends, became coldly censorious with the annual ebbing of the light. The impact on her was a redoubling of the struggle against vaguely-defined dooms. Lisa never really relaxed, not at any time of year. Having married early and now approaching middle age, and with her children gone, she had time but nothing much to do – except listen to her conscience. Her interests ranged from lofty causes, such as teak trees felled on Java, to mundane problems like the high incidence of double-parking on the Hohenzollerndamm. Pacing like a restless vixen, she'd go back and forth from one citizens' committee to another. Only once had she been in a steadily happy mood – three years before, during

Berlin's most frenzied and euphoric moment ever when the Wall came down. Wearing black jeans and a worn-out flak jacket, she'd been hoisted by strong young men onto the Wall in front of the Brandenburg Gate. Lisa's normal melancholy – her deep conviction that the human species was hell-bent on self-destruction – had been swept aside by the utter joy then reigning in the streets. "It's fantastic," she said breathlessly on the day following the opening. She had dropped by *Bücher Geissler* to report to Sabine. "People from both sides are hugging each other at Checkpoint Charlie." But the moment passed. The embracing stopped. The dismantling of the Wall became routine and Lisa, and for that matter Berlin, was not blissful much longer. After the high came the low. The city, after forty-five years of division, now finally reunified – though on paper only – faced a tougher grind than before.

Bücher Geissler, the place Sabine worked, was ideal for catching your breath when global crises closed in on you. It served as Lisa's periodic haven. Amongst the timeless stacks of books rising in disorderly dignity to the ceiling, her thin, tense frame was out of place. But the books soothed and Lisa relaxed. The thought of so much learning waiting to be teased out from between the covers made her feel slightly mystic, that there was another world, another dimension behind the one she knew, a place characterized by perfection. Sensing this was a pleasant change from the political battles in the neighbourhood committees.

The bookstore's respite and Sabine's sympathetic ear were the reasons Lisa liked to loiter. True, Geissler, that old buzzard, bombarded her with evil glances. Inevitably he stood on guard near the front of the store, his head continuously moving back and forth like a mechanical monitor. Depending on how light struck the lenses of his glasses, they alternately flashed like beacons, or became a pair of tunnels going deep. Lisa found it impossible to decipher whether he was sullen because she was keeping Sabine from her work, or because she'd come in wearing her tattered military jacket.

☙

On the morning of the day when the new consul arrived in Berlin to assume his duties, the streets were being pelted by a cold, persistent downpour. That day, about the time Hanbury stepped off the plane, Lisa was entering *Bücher Geissler*. She took off her jacket and standing next to the philosophy section, warmed her hands by cramping them under her arms in a tight self-embrace. Sabine ceased tidying up the shelves and looked at Lisa's soggy garment on the floor. Thinking of what happened to a neighbour the night before, she said with resignation, "Maybe the rain will stop the Poles stealing our cars."

The remark had a vague link to the testy subject of Berlin traffic and Lisa seized on it. Straightaway she expounded her current cause, though her hostility was not directed at the Poles, nor the routine disappearance of cars from desirable neighbourhoods. "I won't stand for it," she said heatedly. Wet strands of hair stuck to sallow cheeks as she began talking about a new, kilometres-long traffic tunnel under the central park, the *Tiergarten*. It had been announced in the morning paper. The article had been accompanied by a map with a double dotted line that showed it snaking from West to East. "A disaster! Is that what we wanted when the Wall came down…more roads, more bridges, more pollution? Of course *not*! We must stop it, Sabine."

Lisa made her fighting remarks in a loud voice. By the front door Geissler stopped the rhythmic swaying of his head and directed his lenses in the women's direction. Lisa continued. "Everyone knows the more you pamper cars, the more you feed traffic jams. Appeasement doesn't work. As for the Poles, as far as I'm concerned they can't steal our cars fast enough." Sabine, although nodding sympathetically, hadn't really listened. She was worried that with the chilling wind and rain, her father, who would be out on his bike as he was every morning, might catch a cold. Colds develop into pneumonia and pneumonia can be quickly fatal for someone over eighty.

The weather, Sabine had noticed, also affected the public's taste in books. She believed that on dreary days customers preferred novels with mystic plots and tragic figures. More of that genre, she sometimes argued, should be displayed on the shelves. But Geissler, with a trivializing motion of his left, his *only* arm – the right one having been severed by shrapnel and left behind in Africa at the time of Rommel – disagreed. With a few almost-swallowed words he'd say the store was his, implying he'd decide the titles that should be moving.

According to some old photos pinned on the wall of a little office at the back, Geissler's forefathers, all of them booksellers, had been well-groomed and correct. But this Geissler was different. He dressed slovenly and seldom shaved. He stooped and his mouth stood slightly open. Then there were his eyes, magnified behind the wire-rimmed glasses, which made him look primitive, even possessed. In short, he didn't have the appearance of a bookseller. The politics of the thirties and forties did this to him. He had no choice then but to fight in a war from which he returned physically maimed and with a mind as badly scarred as his body. The result was silence, decades of haunted silence. Sometimes days went by without him saying a word. He would stand at the front of the store, inspecting the street, pushing back the memories of horror, engaging only in a sweeping motion of his head.

The bookstore went back to Bismarck's time when Berlin boomed. *Bücher Geissler* flourished, then, and through the succeeding generations. But under this last Geissler the business turned static. An ancient bell jangled when the door opened. Customers entering made the wooden floor boards moan. The lights, partly bare bulbs, partly flickering fluorescents, hung down from electric cords, or makeshift metal chains. In the narrow aisles, where the rows of books on the shelves were always tending to disorder, the air was stagnant, smelling like a cave.

Bücher Geissler was run down, yes, but at every turn it offered delightful gifts – literary gems – hidden in amongst the volumes on display. Gremlins, it seemed, had been at work to put them there. Rare first editions were always coming out of the cellar. The old books from below had gone through hardship obviously – some kind of upheaval – because often they were scratched or dented, but inside they were new. The pages had not been cut or turned. A vast collection had to be down there, seemingly thrown together in a random pile. When Geissler went into the cellar to rummage around he grunted and groaned as if he was at work in a mine. The cellar door was permanently locked when he wasn't below. Sabine had never, not in twenty years, gone down the stairs. Geissler sometimes referred to his *stock* there, saying it was *difficult to find things*, referring to *awful light*. With a queer, sad shuffling noise he would descend, returning half an hour later with several dozen rare volumes in a basket slung from his sole arm. Geissler positioned the new arrivals erratically amongst the other curiosities, plugging gaps on the shelves where sales left openings. Judging from the antiquarian reinforcements coming up year-in, year-out, from down below, Sabine suspected there was more than a pile of books in the cellar. It had to be at least a mountain, or, as she once told Werner in a moment of dark humour, maybe a book factory operated by history's ghosts.

Geissler's painful ceremony with the cellar books, especially its unpredictable timing, provided Sabine with secret excitement. The inexhaustible supply of classical works – German translations of Greek philosophers, of Russian histories and Czech plays, Hungarian trave-logues or, for that matter, Roman poetry, American frontier novels, not to mention the full, rich German literary tradition itself – had an addictive effect. Like other book lovers who picked through the shelves with eager, probing fingers and rocked on their feet in the narrow aisles, reading glasses stuck on the tips of noses, Sabine was mesmerized by the printed word. She appreciated complex plots, fiery characters, elegant dialogue, subtle innuendo. She loved the way books exposed the inner workings of real and imaginary things, the way they allowed life to be suspended, or spent in a different world.

Lisa's visit had not helped Sabine's mood. Shortly after the tirade against the outrageous Tiergarten tunnel, she left for the weekly lunch at Café Einstein. Marching under an immense umbrella, her shoulders knotted up, Sabine felt imprisoned by the weather. Shaking the water out at the café's front door, she saw Martina, smiling overwhelmingly as always, already at their table with a carafe of red. When Sabine had settled, Martina asked how the book business was doing. "Your charms are wasted there, sweetie," she added cheerfully. "I've told you that before."

"It's going nowhere," Sabine answered. "The rent from the apartments upstairs keeps Geissler going. Two people came in this morning and one wasn't even a customer. It was Lisa. She dropped by to tell me about some new social problem. A traffic tunnel somewhere."

"Well my business is booming," Martina said nonchalantly, "all over town. Everybody in the West wants to put up advertising in the East. All those run-down buildings with exposed fire walls left over from the war – we're going to cover them with colour. I've told you before, I've got a sales spot waiting for you. You could start tomorrow. You've got a perfect figure for the job." She padded the back of her platinum-streaked-blond fluffy hairdo.

"Geissler has fewer customers all the time," Sabine continued. "People are looking for bargains outside Berlin now, though you couldn't get old books cheaper than from him. Some he lets go for nineteen-thirties prices."

"I don't know much about book prices," Martina replied, "but the good thing about money nowadays is that Berlin is once again attracting it. Did you know? Fresh men loaded with cash are arriving by the dozens. They're buying everything that's going. Dahlem villas are hot items. I'm very optimistic."

"I doubt it's for the better. Everything is getting worse with the Wall gone."

Sabine watched Martina finish off a first glass of wine. She often wondered how someone outwardly slow and slightly eccentric like Martina could be so lightning-swift in business. When Martina talked business her eyes filled with excitement. Disconcertingly, however, they focussed in slightly different directions, as she suffered from an eye problem. When the prospect of business animated Martina, one eye would fix on the person opposite and the other on something in the distance. This could be unsettling. Sabine noticed Martina's eyes began to wander when she talked of layering East Berlin in colour, but as she poured herself another glass of wine, a degree of synchronisation filtered back.

Martina disagreed with Sabine's view that Berlin was in decline. "Nonsense," she said. "Your problem is those books and that creepy one-armed Geissler. It clouds your vision. He's a frustrated man if ever there was one. It's his right arm that's gone, am I right? I'm sure it interferes with his stroking of the flesh."

"Martina!" Sabine was partially amused and partially shocked. "He was injured in the war. It's done things to his mind. You can't hold that against him."

"Maybe. But he landed on his feet right afterwards. In that respect others suffered twice as much as him."

Gottfried brought the orders, marinated duck breast for Martina, a Greek salad with black olives for Sabine. "For you two healthy orchids," he said. A titter escaped Martina. "Thank you, Gottfried. So insightful. Orchids have such splendid inner workings." When he was gone, she said, "If I were him I'd go East. There isn't a decent waiter in all of Mitte. He'd be famous overnight. How's your papa?"

"Out on his bicycle I imagine. As always. Why he goes out on days like this, I don't know. He races around as if he thinks the end is near. He won't slow down."

"He's an example," mused Martina, "for young men everywhere."

But Sabine wasn't sure her father should be an example, at least not the side that caused his non-stop cycling. In her opinion it was overdone. The professional side of him – the lawyer – everyone (not just the young men) would benefit from imitating. But when he left his practice he metamorphosed. Professional conformity was left behind and out stepped an idiosyncratic old man. When it came to cycling he was really quite obsessed. Although Sabine quietly adored her father's unpredictability, she was convinced the world would be a chaotic place if his non-conformity were to be copied widely. Who would sail into a pub and order champagne in a litre mug, or show up at social gatherings with his necktie knotted backwards? She complained too, as she was now doing to Martina, about his sporting ambitions. She couldn't fathom them. She knew no precedent. Nowhere in the world of literature, not even in the fairy tales, was there a character like him. Why would an eighty-four year old desire physical competition? Not only that, but he wanted victory too. The annual cycle race for seniors was not far off and all he did was talk of winning. Given this eccentricity, it was all the more surprising that his professional side was so conformist. The law firm – *Albert Müller, Notar und Rechtsanwalt*, a one-man operation – was known for punctuality, meticulous work and crisply-argued opinions. Immediately after the war, back from being an American POW (the Italian campaign), Müller found a niche. He worked non-stop at settling claims by Jewish families stripped of property by the Nazis. Only in late middle age did he allow himself the luxury of sport, returning to the things he loved most in his youth.

At age sixty Müller decided to become a marathoner. West Berlin, although walled off from the world, wasn't a bad place for running. With a careful choice of route a marathon could neatly take you from one end of the city to the other. After four hours on the pavement, Müller boasted, he'd had a good run. *Did it again. Went Wall to Wall.* Müller ran the marathon throughout his sixties and seventies (the century's seventies and eighties) and would have continued had the Wall stayed up. But when it collapsed, and the cosy, enclosed *Wall to Wall* feeling disappeared, Müller turned to cycling. A great hinterland had opened up. The dream – one day to win a marathon by running into the Olympic Stadium – had been replaced. He now planned to win a yellow jersey just like the greats who do it on the *Tour de France*.

"Three years ago he was featured in a national runners magazine," Sabine said while Martina worked at her marinated breast of duck. "He was the oldest in his club. Have I told you this? *The Hares.* When the wall came down he switched to cycling. *The Eagles.* They race in Brandenburg. It worries me." Sabine said this with exasperation and pointed her fork over a shoulder into the general direction of that new eastern state, a place of mortal danger. "The traffic is terrible there. Ossis don't know how to drive modern cars."

"Ossis have élan," Martina interjected. As she said this she thought of Professor Kraft, her latest *Kater*, a renowned Ossi philologist. Kraft was more corpulent than herself, but despite his size he was remarkably agile in short bursts.

"He's training for a race," continued Sabine, still thinking of her father. "From the Polish border to Berlin. Through Brandenburg! At eighty-four! Why? I asked him. He said, *Either I push myself on my bike or you push me around in a wheelchair.* What can you say to that?"

"I advise against outdoor exercise at any age," Martina said, sounding like a medical advisor. "Strength should be conserved through the day so that it's available at night. I must say, with your papa wasting so much energy, it's a wonder you exist. Maybe his focus was better back then. Didn't he wear out two wives?"

Sabine's mouth dropped and began scolding her best friend for this tasteless remark. Her mother and father had been a loving couple. She never knew her mother, but one could tell it was true from photos. As for the second wife, the stepmother, she'd been high strung. She wore *herself* out. No one mourned her passing, not even, Sabine suspected, her father.

Martina began fiddling with her string of pearls and Sabine recognized this sign of boredom. Her father shouldn't be a topic of conversation too long. This was even truer of her husband, whom Martina didn't like. Nor should she dwell much on her ten-year-old son Nicholas. Family life generally held little interest for Martina. Sabine changed the subject. "What makes you think Gottfried should go to Mitte?" she asked. "As far as I know the restaurants there aren't very good." A report in the paper about dining in the East had concluded it was still a disaster.

"Go sometime. You'd be surprised," Martina suggested calmly.

"I did once. It was awful. The place is full of former communist party hacks. You can tell them by the way they dress and the lifelessness in their eyes. After all the misery they caused, how is it they're running around free?"

"Try to see the bright side of the East, Sabine," Martina said nonchalantly. "Think of all the fine bodies that won medals in the

Olympics." She was reducing the last strips of duck breast to small pieces with her knife. Martina liked the eastern districts, and not only because her billboard company, *Ravensburg Creations*, was doing a brisk business there. She came from East Berlin herself. In the fifties, before the Wall went up, when she was twelve, her family escaped. She had been old enough at the time to know what was happening, but too young to experience the terror as her parents had. After a pause and in a softer voice, she continued, "There are fewer communists than you think. You know, if everyone had got out as I did, they'd have turned out different. They'd be like me. A few might even have turned out like you. That's what I mean. Look at the bright side."

A fresh burst of rain rattled against the windows of Café Einstein. Sabine, continuing to feel assaulted by the season, wasn't ready to see the brighter side of anything, least of all the eastern boroughs of Berlin. She grew up distrusting the place and nothing convincing had happened yet to switch forty years of suspicion off. "The difference between you and them is that they *didn't* leave," she argued. "That's the point. They could have before the Wall came, but they didn't. That's what's strange."

"You try it sometime, leaving behind everything you own except a handbag with maybe only your grandmother's jewellery in it. It's not as easy as you think."

Sabine shrugged. "So they stayed. For what? Look at what the communists accomplished. Nothing anybody can be proud of. And guess who'll have to pay to put it right." This last sentiment was borrowed from Werner. He had strong views about the hike in taxes everyone knew was coming.

"Pass the butter, sweetie" Martina said curtly. Naysayers were everywhere – she knew that – but being reminded her best friend was one was mildly irritating. "It's early days. Things are changing for the better. Everywhere. At Rheinhardt's they now serve Brandenburg butter. Very creamy, better than these clumps from Denmark. My company has a contract for a dozen signs to say just that."

They continued talking in this way about the fallout from the Wall's dismantling, Sabine provoking, Martina defending: the traffic tie-ups spreading in tidal waves from the former border checkpoints; the chaos on the underground with Eastern trains mixed in with the Western ones so that the whole system was breaking down; the stench in the air from the exhausts of socialism's cars; the Poles buying up Berlin's entire stock of stereos and TVs; and the beggars from Eastern Europe transforming the city's sidewalks, turning them into obstacle courses. Martina acknowledged all this was true, but countered it was wonderful too how East Berlin was responding to freedom. "Take cabaret," she said. "It's razor sharp there. They really know how to cut us up. I mean *all* of us, from East *and* West. It's exhilarating. You ought to go."

After Gottfried delivered two cappuccinos, Martina said, "Have I told you about Helmut? What he says about the universities is remarkable. Students in the West want to study in the East, and vice versa. Young blood is so versatile. Some days I think we should all have a transfusion."

No, Sabine had not heard of Helmut. "Oh…Doctor Kraft, professor at Humboldt University. An elegant man. He survived the recent academic purge. He's a linguist, a wonderful English speaker, but more than that…" Martina dropped her voice to a confidential whisper, "…he admits he's always desired Western women. The Wall stimulated his fantasies. He says that even now he finds thinking of women from the other side as erotic. What an invitation! And he's not the only one that thinks like that. We need to take advantage of such sentiments, Sabine, before they disappear. I could help you with some introductions."

As she described Professor Kraft's longings, Martina placed her hand on Sabine's, a token of their bond. Whenever Martina described a new lover, she took Sabine's hand this way. There was never an old lover, a fading lover, or a problem lover in Martina's life. There were only new lovers. And at their corner table in the library of Café Einstein, Martina would talk about them with the enthusiasm of a child.

The rain had eased when they finished lunch, although the leaden clouds continued racing eastward, as if on a seek-out-and-destroy mission. "Next week?" asked Sabine. "Of course," Martina replied, jabbing her umbrella at a passing taxi. Delivering airy kisses to each of Sabine's cheeks, she solemnly remarked, "If by then I've had a chance to cheat on Helmut, you'll be the first to know."

On Wednesdays, Sabine did not return to the bookstore after lunch, a concession won from Geissler when Nicholas was an infant. When she first asked for a shorter working week – Wednesday afternoons off – the discussion faltered before it began. Shaking his head, he had lumbered away into the store's dark recesses, hiding there until closing time. But on her third attempt he relented, even though afterwards he sulked for weeks. Even now, ten years later, Geissler could still be strange on Wednesdays. When her stepmother died, Nicholas being older by then, Sabine transferred her few hours of free time each week from her son to her father.

Müller was suspicious at first. "I'm too busy," he said when his daughter called to say she wanted to come around. She tried to make light of her plans. "Children have a right to see their parent."

"You think you have a right to see me?" the old lawyer grumbled. "That's different. Your generation thinks mostly about inheritance rights. But visiting rights? They exist. Of course they do. In prisons. What are you trying to say? That I'm a prisoner of old age?" The daughter laughed. The father continued. "I can't keep track of all the rights nowadays. Soon there will be a law that creates a right to die. Then someone will claim it has to be balanced with the right *not* to die. The world will then be divided into two camps – those that want to live forever and those that want to die forever. But if you insist, I suppose you can come. Don't stay long though. I'm very busy." Although he tried not to show it, her father was delighted by the visit. Sabine could tell. It was the first afternoon they spent together since she was a girl and he was as playful as he used to be. It was because he was free, she thought, with her stepmother gone. Müller muttered complaints about each Wednesday afternoon that followed, whether they went walking in summer or visited museums in winter, but he was always on time.

Sabine's route from Einstein's took her down Kurfürstenstrasse, past the Urania in the direction of Charlottenburg. At the end of the last war, this area consisted of bombed-out, black shells of buildings rising out of piles of rubble. Since most were not worth salvaging, they got levelled. The new hurried blocks of flats replacing them were square and grey, hardly better than bunkers. In a way it was the war's destruction continuing. Sabine had long since ceased seeing the architectural dreariness. She preferred to focus on the old baroque Berlin that remained. A few of the apartment blocks had been faithfully restored. Their façades were decorated with sculptures of nymphs or other exotic figures, had balconies propped up by classical columns, and stood guarded by centaurs hewn from stone, one on each side of the great doorways. Sabine loved such buildings.

Huddling under the umbrella, she hurried to just such a house, on Fasanenstrasse, where she and Werner and Nicholas lived in a spacious apartment. Wet leaves drifted around. A smell of organic decay rose from the gutter. Wind blasts tried to steal her scarf. She was late. In the apartment, she scribbled a note to Nicholas telling him to take some cookies and to be sweet to his papa. She called her father. She felt relief when he picked up the phone. "You're fine?" she asked.

"Of course not," the bothered lawyer complained. "Work is piled up sky high."

"I'm leaving now," she said. "The Pergamon?"

"Sabine!" the father replied wearily. "We were there last year. No more Greek vases. Please. The cracks in the glazing remind me of myself." He sounded raspy, as if he had sand in his voice. A flu coming on? It worried Sabine.

"The Egyptian Museum then?"

"Worse," declared Müller. "Those mummies make me think I should have a cremation. And that bust of Nefertiti with the bad eye looks too sad. Would you like to be remembered for all eternity with an eye off like that?"

"The National Gallery? Casper David Friedrich is showing."

"Him? Pictures of departing ships? You sure we can cope with poetic painting?"

"I'll meet you there," Sabine told her father. She looked forward to it. Casper David Friedrich was a favourite.

As she balanced, first on one foot then the other, to pull on boots more suited to the weather, the phone rang. Annoyed, she hesitated, mentally running through a list of acquaintances who liked to talk. The ringing continued as she took her coat. It planted a seed of doubt. Geissler's store was full of books with characters whose lives were changed forever by tiny twists of fortune. Maybe Nicholas had been in an accident in school. She gave in. "*Ja?*" she said brusquely. A voice said her name. It was not quite German and she couldn't place it. She thought back to recent vacations, someone British? Or American? "*Wer ist da?*" she asked, impatience growing. She stiffened. "*Ich kenne Sie nicht,*" I don't know you, but she did. More words of explanation came at her. Walls, floor, furniture, the world began spinning. She experienced a stressful, split-second of absolute inactivity, the same as when Nicholas frightened her with a trick. Finally she said, "*Wo bist Du?*" Where are you? It was a reflex only; she didn't want to know. Her mind, flung back through time, became disconnected from the present. Explanations kept arriving. She snapped, "*Was machst Du hier?*" What are you doing here? Then, as still more words pummelled her, she slammed down the phone and ran out.

Street noise wrapped around her like a blanket. She fell in with the crowd. Years ago, readying herself for this moment, she had practised a lecture, a bitter monologue. But now, with the opportunity there, she was dumbstruck, as if the intervening years had gagged her. As she walked, the shock subsiding, anger flooded in. The old monologue was coming back too. She couldn't help rehearsing it. Stepping into the U-bahn, a pimply boy with a bike cut her off. Sabine bared her fangs. He snarled back. "*Halt die Klappe,*" "shut your trap", he told her. "We all pay the same fare." She almost wrung his neck.

ADDING CLASS

*I*n a Berlin hotel room, Hanbury on the end of a dead phone connection sat numbed. Sabine's questions had come at him like a volley of punches. The parting words – *Go away!* – were a hard left hook that sent him to the canvas.

He did his best – fresh off the plane, a few hours rest, a deep last breath before dialling – and hoped for a good conversation. He melted when she answered. "*Was dann?*" That tone of impatience! When they lived in the Savignyplatz apartment, when Sabine had sunk away inside a book, she'd sting back just like that if he broke her concentration. Sometimes he sought her attention solely for the pleasure of hearing that instinctive indignation. *This is a great piece of music, Sabine,* he'd say, taking off the earphones. *You sure you don't want me to play it through the speakers?* The answer? A cold *Nein danke.* Though soon enough, as befits two lovers, it was followed by a pacifying smile.

That was Hanbury's purpose: reconciliation, offering her an olive branch. He had planned to be enthusiastic, to tell Sabine her voice was *wonderful*, hoping similar words – *It's marvellous to hear from you!* – would echo back. But the exchange didn't get that far. The hostile rapid-fire questions gave it no chance. Her transition from *Sie* to *Du*, from formal to familiar address – when she seemed to want to know his location – it was momentarily encouraging. *I'm here. In a hotel*, he answered eagerly. But the Du must have been pure reflex, something from the past meaningless in the present, because when he passed her the news that he was planning to stay – *I'm in Berlin for good* – she became silent and the phone went dead. In those initial seconds, knowing he had miscalculated, Hanbury recoiled. A cold hand reached in. It squeezed his heart and soul until the hopes of the preceding weeks were crushed. The hand stirred some more and placed a dead weight in his gut. Disorientation, pessimism, failure. Feelings he knew from the other places.

※

Earlier in the day at the airport – Sturm, the consulate driver, attending – the arrival had gone smoothly enough. Sturm didn't know exactly what to look for, but the solitary figure marching through customs was easy to pick out. After introductions Sturm took the suitcase and asked politely about the flight. The new consul replied in German. He claimed the language had become rusty, but he looked forward to bringing it back. We'll speak German, he proposed. *Wir sprechen Deutsch.* It came out sounding like a ground rule.

Sturm deferred. "*Wie Sie wollen, Herr Konsul.*" As the consul wished. Sturm didn't want to object to anything at the very start. All the same, he was a little piqued. Half his working life had been spent in England chauffeuring Lord Halcourt around, and Sturm's mimic of an

Oxfordshire accent wasn't all that bad. The regulars in Sturm's local banged their glasses on the table and laughed until the tears flowed when he pronounced *tea time,* or *port, please,* with Lord Halcourt's upper class, crusty intonation. Sturm liked to show his English off. Outside the terminal the new consul remarked that during the descent the clouds turned black. "How long has it been like this?" he asked. "I expect it will improve, *Herr Konsul.*" Until the day he died Lord Halcourt expected optimism from his chauffeur.

The official vehicle was an ageing Opel gleaming in a fresh coat of black paint. Sturm opened a rear door to stash his human cargo, then placed the luggage in the trunk. Away from the terminal they joined a traffic crawl which would continue, he said, the whole way into the city. "It's the rain," he added. "It frustrates people. They do strange things. It slows things down." He believed it was not too early for a briefing on Germany's capital. "Berlin is full of idiots, *Herr Konsul,* and most of them are behind the wheel."

Rain carried by gusts of wind streaked the scene diagonally in grey. It beat down on the Opel's roof and obscured the road, the signs, the vision of drivers. It wore out their good will. Impatient motorists jerked their cars from lane to lane. Sturm shook his wise head at the futility. In a running commentary on the hopelessness that lay ahead, he compared this traffic jam, this Stau, to other recent fine examples. The slower the traffic, the faster Sturm talked. He compared the autobahn in its current state to a glacier, *ein Gletscher,* that froze all life and scoured the marvels off high tech cars. *Stau,* Sturm said, rendered all cars uninteresting. It made them common, indistinguishable, like ground-down pebbles in a moraine. "I propose, *Herr Konsul,* at the next exit we get off."

Sturm explained that more than rain was causing Berlin's endless *Staus.* The Wall – that is, its absence – was a major factor. When the Wall came down, the traffic went bad. Some days the city was nothing but a

Stau. "It's not healthy. Look around. Ever seen so many people ready for an institution? See that woman? See her drumming the wheel? She's going catatonic. Women like that shouldn't be allowed to drive. They lack the necessary inner peace. But the mayor says not to worry. He says we're becoming normal. Soon we'll be like Paris." Sturm changed lanes with several unusual manoeuvres, causing horns to sound and other drivers to tap their heads. Off the autobahn, winding the Opel through narrow back streets, his commentary picked up again. "*Siemensstadt, Herr Konsul.*"

Hanbury's tired eyes took in red-brick city blocks, much of it industrial. Sturm narrated the company's history. "Thirty thousand workers lived here once, a company neighbourhood. Is there anything like that in Canada?"

Hanbury was trying to stay awake. "Not really," he said in a voice that sounded flat. "We've got some mining towns. Uranium City. Flin Flon." He yawned.

"Flin Flon? That sounds nice. Melodious." Sturm became interested in Flin Flon. He pronounced it repeatedly, fast then slow, the emphasis sometimes on the Flin, sometimes on the Flon. "Are you sure it's a place? It sounds more like a rock band." He sang *flin-flon* a few more times, making it sound like the ding-dong of a doorbell.

"I saw this area once before, but from a different angle," Hanbury remarked.

"You could have, *Herr Konsul.*" Sturm was racing through narrow streets in an alert, stiff posture, scanning intersections for signs of danger, but his voice remained detached. "There's a view of it from the autobahn over there." He paused. "You've been to Berlin?"

"It was a while ago. The Wall was just up. I remember climbing an observation platform to look over it. The city on the other side looked dead. Empty space, soldiers with machine guns, dogs, ruins in the distance. Things like that."

"That would have been Potsdamer Platz. Well, the communists put the East into a coma, but that's over with. In most places you can't tell now where the Wall was. And there's big plans to rebuild Potsdamer Platz. It's exciting. Except the traffic. The mayor should do something about it. We don't want to be normal like Paris."

"The excitement seems to be a secret," Hanbury said, laying his head back. "Where I come from people don't know much about it."

"A good thing, too," the chauffeur argued. "We don't want anyone to know what's going on. We don't want the story out. The traffic's bad enough as it is."

Hanbury couldn't help thinking of Krauthilda and being told that where he was going nothing much would be important. His question – *What's expected of me in Berlin?* – had gone unanswered. Sturm's chatter forced the question back and on impulse he repeated it. The answer was quick and practical. *"Zuerst sollten Sie schlafen, Herr Konsul."* First you should get some sleep.

Hanbury nodded; he knew he needed sleep. Yet, stubbornly, he pursued the bigger question. "And then?" he asked.

"Today nothing. Don't bother with the office. No one is expecting you, not today. Herr Gifford asked me to tell you that."

"And then?" the consul persisted.

Sturm's correctness faltered. He raised an eyebrow. "Tomorrow? That's when you meet the staff." Sturm didn't like being asked to prophesy the future.

Hanbury began to think of what he might say to the staff, but his eyes fell shut. When the Opel stopped at the hotel Sturm nudged the consul's elbow to wake him up.

❧

Somewhere during that first, jet-lagged and mostly sleepless night with Sabine's clipped phrases reverberating in his head, Hanbury regrouped. He had gambled; he had lost. In retrospect it wasn't that surprising. Giving in to an insomnia, he left the hotel before dawn and walked to Savignyplatz. The neighbourhood was the same, a little shabbier maybe – though it could have been the light, or his imagination. He stood before the building where they'd lived. He sauntered through their haunts. With a fatalistic resolution he then blanked everything out. Allowing Savignyplatz to live on, to stay with him through the intervening years, had been a bad mistake.

Sturm pulled up to the hotel some hours later. Hanbury, no livelier than the day before, gave a muffled answer when the chauffeur inquired how the night had been. "So, so," he said from the rear seat, staring blankly out the window.

The office was located behind doors draped with security devices. Hanbury's first impression was of the three smiling women. "*Guten Morgen, Herr Konsul!*" they sang with warm, friendly, almost expectant voices. Sturm marched him past them into the consulate's inner chambers. A figure as wide as it was tall and with a fleshy paw extended, scurried forward from behind a desk. Words spilled off an impeccable British tongue. "Honoured to meet you, Sir. Have a good flight? Still a bit under the weather, I should think. Beastly they are, nights on airplanes. I know. Welcome to the Canadian Consulate. We're so pleased you're here to take the rudder."

Hanbury would forever remember the moment he first met Earl Gifford.

Jovially they shook hands. The new consul announced he was pleased to have arrived, made a small joke about transatlantic passages, linked it to seafarers and managed to end up with the importance of a steady hand on the rudder. He didn't think it came off well, but

Gifford giggled and Sturm beamed. Gifford had a triangular head, narrow at the top, widening to broad cheeks with a massive hanging chin and eyes standing close above his nose. A caricaturist would have drawn him as a squirrel.

Hanbury knew Gifford's record. He'd read it in the Zealot files. Top administrator, hired years ago, first came to Berlin as a clerk in the local British Council office, applied for a slot with the consulate when his term was up, disclosing in his letter of solicitation he wished to stay in Berlin because he planned to marry. The woman, Hanbury had read, was from Kreuzberg. He even recalled her first name. Frieda. Might Kreuzberg Frieda, the consul speculated, match the dimensions of her British Earl?

"A family sit-down's planned," Gifford said. "Introduce you to the ladies then. Inspect your office first?" Hanbury nodded. "Splendid," Gifford went on. "I had hoped we might have a chat first, you know, *entre nous.*"

"By all means." Hanbury followed the administrator through more doors hung with security hardware. "Once in, no one gets out," he joked.

"Five combinations is all you need," Gifford reassured him. "I've given them easy sequences. Your safe begins with your birth year, 43. The second number is 23, the last 33. Get it? Don't overload grey matter unnecessarily. My motto."

Photos of Canadian landscapes decorated the consul's office: a Georgian Bay shore in stirring autumn colours; a forlorn prairie elevator in an ocean of yellow wheat; Vancouver from the sky, the mountain backdrop lit up orange by a sun setting over the Pacific; a giant iceberg in Davis Strait with a lazy polar bear staring menacingly in the foreground. "My choice," Gifford grinned, watching the consul studying the pictures. "Windows on home for you, I hope. Like them?"

"Lovely. Very nice. Thank you." The office set-up – a small table and two chairs in a corner, a desk opposite – did remind Hanbury of home. He once obtained a student loan in Saskatoon and visited the manager of a campus bank. The furniture in that office had been the same.

Gifford sat down at the round table, hands on top and clasped like someone praying. Hanbury saw he was a prolific sweater. His forehead was covered with countless droplets. "We got a fax from headquarters," Gifford said, "which indicated you speak German. We were pleased to read that." The consul replied his skills had become rusty, but he looked forward to polishing them. "Yes! Do!" said Gifford with enthusiasm. "Make them shine! Many things could use a polish here. We do hope you will enjoy yourself with us. It's a fine consulate, small but fine." He broke into German, repeating the phrase, *klein aber fein*, and laughed.

Before Hanbury could give a suitable reply, the administrator began that most universal of excuses why things were not what they should be. The failings of the predecessor. He lamented that the previous consul hadn't spoken the local language. That meant he had no profile and that made him languish. Gifford explained that the predecessor, being out of touch, had disappeared into a hole, like a burrowing mouse – from where he tried to run the office. He hadn't made best use of his administrator, who should have been left alone to run the office. A consul's time is used optimally when he's out meeting people. A consul should be attending the glittering openings of cinematic world premières; he should be seen chatting to music critics at operatic intermissions; he should assume the place of honour next to the Governing Mayor at formal dinners. "It's a high calling, that of consul," Gifford said, hands still clasped, streams of sweat tracing lines down his face. "My role is to free you to engage in it full-time. May I call you Tony? Call me Earl. It's an advantage we Anglos have. We are quicker at relaxing than the Germans."

Visions of dallying with art critics in marble foyers and conversing elegantly with the producers and directors of the performing arts wasn't something Krauthilda had prepared Hanbury for. "Is there a lot of that?" he asked casually, masking doubt.

"Of what?"

"Openings. Premières. That sort of thing. I was told the job here would be checking passports, getting Canadians out of jail, that sort of thing."

"Tony!" exclaimed Earl. "That's quite delightful. Your sense of humour is like mine. I'm pleased you're anticipating your official duties. There is a great deal of *glitz* indeed. You won't be able to accept all the invitations. There can be five or six a day. There are boat rides hosted by bankers on the Wannsee, Sunday afternoons at the races arranged by the Rotary Club, late evening performances at variety houses paid for by insurance firms. There's the Press Ball, the Military Ball, the Postal Union Ball, balls in the summer and balls in the winter and garden parties without end."

"Amen," said Hanbury, unsure of how much of all that he wanted.

"*Of course* you needn't concern yourself with the passports! *I* do that. *I* deal with the Canadians in jail. *I* ship the bodies back to Canada. All *you* do is exercise authority and sign documents. This is how *I* free *you*. Think of this office, Tony, as the Berlin Philharmonic Orchestra. The players are so good they function without a conductor. The conductor's main role, his *sole* purpose is to add class. And that is yours."

The new consul nodded. "That's helpful. Thank you, Earl."

Gifford's vision of Berlin's diplomatic life forced Hanbury to retreat. He'd never considered himself classy. In fact, the last thing he wanted to be was classy. Classiness had driven him to break his ties to Indian Head. *You're in a class of your own*, his mother had drummed into him throughout the years of childhood. The school principal also extolled the unique excellence with which Tony played the piano. The only recourse open to him back then – once he became intent on shedding the limelight – was to run. The role described by Gifford gave him the same misgivings.

"Everything all right?" asked Gifford. "You look pale."

"Fine, yes. Thanks. First day. Coming to grips."

"Entirely understandable," consoled the administrator. "One or two weeks and you'll find things settling down. A few points on the administrative side, if I may." Gifford leaned forward. "Your predecessor – excuse my being frank on this point – wasn't interested in an efficient operation. It is quite true that we are not a large office, but all the more reason really to take all steps possible to make it very smooth-running indeed. I have not been able, over the years, to obtain a green light for improvements. I raise the issue now, Tony, in the event it is mentioned by the staff at the sit-down. You may wish to express a commitment to modernization. That would go down well. They look forward to the place being guided by a man of action."

The new consul, having to digest this too, won time by nodding.

"One final point," Gifford pushed on, "after the sit-down you may wish Sturm to take you to your domicile. It's normal to want to see it."

Apart from Zella's interest, no one at headquarters had said anything about the residence. "Is it ready to move in?" Hanbury asked. "I hope it's got good acoustics."

"A marvel, Tony. We constantly catch each other on the same wavelength. I would say, yes, the house is ready to move in, but at this stage I won't say more. The neighbourhood is quiet, no acoustical problems. After you've seen it, give me your views. Speak to me frankly. I am quite certain, if improvements are needed, we will find a way. I hope we can work productively on many things. Need I say more?"

The consul weighed the meaning of this. "I support change," he said calmly. "Of course I support improvement." "Thank you," a smiling Gifford said. He unclasped his hands. "Perhaps we oughtn't to keep the family waiting."

An alcove off a hallway, a holding area for visitors, served as meeting place. Some leather chairs were pushed against the walls and the largest and lowest of these, an oversized black throne, was the consul's. The ladies were on typing chairs rolled in from their desks. Sturm sat slung forward on a stool in a thinker's pose. The consul murmured excuses as he stepped over legs. The chair engulfed him when he sat down and gave way under his weight until he was nearly on the floor. From there he looked up at five expectant faces.

"*Ich bin begeistert, hier zu sein.*" I'm thrilled to be here, he started. He had rehearsed a short speech over breakfast. But his confidence as public speaker was never high and he was worried he would not remember the main points. "I've always wanted to serve in Berlin," he said humbly. "It's like a dream come true." He halted, struggling to generate the drift of his remarks. "It'll take me a few days to settle, naturally. I'll be asking some questions. Some could seem basic, but please bear with me." His worry was becoming self-fulfilling. Before getting to the most important observations he'd planned to state – his admiration for the quality of the staff, their high reputation, his desire to work closely with them – Hanbury's mind went blank.

Like an actor on a stage whose brain refuses to come up with the next line, the consul waited for a prompt. As the silence thickened, Hanbury thought of Zella and how she'd bridge the moment. *I'm more than willing to answer your questions, Mr. Consul. Let's have 'em!* she'd probably be saying to dispel the silence. But these ladies were not Zellas. In the stillness, the women silently observing him, perspiration formed on unseen parts of Hanbury's body. He felt it trickling down inside his shirt. Then a comment from Krauthilda jumped at him – *I'm sure the local staff will brief you* – and he seized on it. With fierce calm he said, "Perhaps you could now tell me some of the things I should know." The quality, not the depth, of the silence transformed. It became brittle. The consul tried once more. "Herr Gifford," he said, turning to the administrator, "why don't you start?"

Gifford remained immobile, wondering about his first impression. Had yet another master of inaction from overseas been dropped into his lap? He believed the agreed script for the sit-down was that announcements would be made about change and modernization. He tossed the ball right back. "We had hoped, *Herr Konsul*," he said, coldly pleasant, "since you have come from headquarters, that you might bring us answers, not questions." There was a soft rustling as the ladies shifted in their seats and crossed and re-crossed their legs. Sturm rose from his thinker's slouch.

The words bit. The damp spread from the inside of the consul's shirt into his jacket. He looked at Gifford who, with a rodent's ruthlessness, stared back. Hanbury felt transported back to the Priory days when Heywood was travelling, when the high priest called wanting immediate answers to complicated questions. His mind had raced then too, searching for a credible reply, a workable point of departure. In this defining moment he needed one fast. He blamed Krauthilda for not having given him a decent briefing, for not even having hinted at some useful questions. Yet, courtesy of Krauthilda, relief arrived. She was growing on a side track in Hanbury's mind, developing, transforming – going from nemesis to saviour. With a survivor's ingenuity he decided to repeat what she had said to him, except he'd turn the tables. Turn her negatives into positives, he thought. Krauthilda, bent through a hundred and eighty degrees, began giving him substance. Looking Gifford in the eye, the consul charged.

"You should know Berlin has a very high priority in headquarters," he said. "A political redefinition is taking place in Europe at this moment and we – you, I, all of us here – we are expected to make sense of it. Germany is reunified, but at what cost? Spiritual *and* financial deficits are setting in. What are the social and security ramifications? What is the geo-political significance? I know this office isn't large, but much depends on our analysis of the issues." The consul looked around at awed faces. "Geo-politics," he repeated. "In Berlin, one feels it. It's in the air. The challenge for us is to think the new Germany through."

On the outside the consul remained flat, unemotional, but inside his self-doubt was ebbing. He was edging close to believing what he had just said. The dynamics of the family sit-down were changed too. Meat had been put on the table and Sturm sunk his teeth in first.

"That's different from what we're used to doing, *Herr Konsul*," he said bluntly. "Thinking Germany through? Where do you want us to start?"

"The world is changing," Hanbury soothed. "We must move with the times. We have to acquire new skills."

"With all respect, *Herr Konsul*," Sturm continued, "that sounds woolly to me. I change the light bulbs, open the mail and stick stamps on letters for the post office. And I know my way around Berlin, even if the street names in the East keep changing. Then take Frau Koehler. She answers the telephone and monitors the papers. Frau von Ruppin does the passports and Frau Carstens is responsible for scheduling appointments. We provide a service. We've been doing it for a dozen years and no one's complained. Why not keep it up? Let others worry about Germany's future. I don't think we're up to it." The three ladies, thorough women of the kind that once made Prussia great, nodded agreement.

The meeting was not yet clearly on the track Gifford wanted, but with a few more switches thrown he believed it might just get there. "Herr Hanbury is right," he said. "Berlin isn't static any longer. We *should* be moving with the times. The consul and I discussed this earlier. He shared his thoughts with me. Wise thoughts. We can change, and we will, but we need new tools for our work." Gifford began to explain how offices everywhere were modernizing.

As the administrator was setting out his vision of the future, Hanbury had a sudden *déja-vu.* It had to do with the phrase *new tools.* It had been his father's favourite. As head of soil science at the research station in Indian Head, Dr. Hanbury was always advocating new tools. "I want to measure three things all at once," Hanbury remembered him saying at the dinner table. There was something intense, almost vengeful in the way the great man held up his fork, like a weapon. Outside, a dry hot wind was blowing; the prairie sky was black with sucked up soil. Tony's mother, whose frilly white blouse had turned grey that day, quickly disappeared into the kitchen. *Je m'excuse*, she said to avoid having to listen to science. So Tony was the audience for a man whose sole interest in life was to stop topsoil from drifting. "I want to measure the rate of disappearance of soil moisture as a function of temperature and air movement," the scientist continued. "At the same time I want to determine the adhesion loss between the drying soil particles as well as the lifting forces exerted by the wind." The boy didn't understand a word. He was uncomfortable being alone with his father. He wanted to go to his mother. "If I could measure all that, simultaneously, at a defined point," the sun-scorched, diagnostically-deprived head of research claimed, "we'd be taking a big step. New tools, that's what we need." The son hadn't liked the father's use of the word *we.* He had no desire to be associated with the violence of soil science. He slipped away at the first opportunity and took cover at the piano by playing a Chopin *étude.*

Odd, Hanbury now thought, how the phrase jumped through the intervening decades. He eyed Gifford warily for a minute, but relaxed. The administrator wasn't ominous. He wasn't remotely like his father. When Gifford finished describing changes to the consulate, Hanbury supported what he said. "I'll be pushing hard to make change a reality. I do want to create a more efficient office. I look forward to advice from all of you on how to achieve it."

"And what exactly do you mean with more efficiency?" a testy Frau Carstens asked. For her, efficiency was more than a way of life, it was a form of art about which she had little left to learn.

The consul wanted to answer, but the administrator cut him off. "Computers," he said, "modems, laser printers, the works." The consul's predecessor, frightened by technology and horrified at the costs, had kept Gifford bottled up. But Hanbury was different. Gifford smelled a chance to break loose. "Data banks at our fingertips," he continued, "linked to a computerized phone system. Cyberspace sitting on our desks. That's what we'll have. In a modern office, typewriters are out."

"But my typewriter is not so old." Frau von Ruppin argued.

Frau Koehler, fidgeting with a handkerchief, agreed. "Computers seem very modern," she said.

"I've heard it's easy to learn to use them," said Sturm. "I'd try." Frau von Ruppin looked at him with bewilderment. "My cousin in Cottbus uses one, and if he can, I can," he told her.

"It could be exciting," Frau Carstens speculated.

Gifford's dream was taking on momentum. With the staff nodding, the consul proclaimed the decision to modernize was unanimous.

As excitement sloshed around the alcove, an emboldened Hanbury rose above the murmur with another question. "Whom should I be meeting in the next few weeks? It's standard to make some introductory calls." This question, so practical, so different from the first, ignited fervour.

"Yes!" cried Frau Carstens. She saw her chance, as Gifford had seen his. She quickly recited a dozen names, well-known personalities with important public functions. The other women chimed in. The Chief of Protocol, editors of newspapers, ranking politicians, heads of financial institutions, cultural figures, leaders of think tanks, chairpersons of clubs, presidents of social science institutes, police contacts, senior officials in the departments of justice and the economy. As the list of the local elite grew, so did the staff's exhilaration. The Priory, Hanbury thought, had never been like this.

Gifford eventually declared the waterfront had been covered. "We've never gone at this so thoroughly."

"Or systematically!" agreed Frau Carstens. It would be her job to stage the consul, feed him his lines, shape his part.

Gifford summed up. Between four and six appointments per week, Frau Carstens to arrange and keep the master list, Sturm to work out the logistics, closely consulting Frau Carstens. Arrivals to be punctual – between three and five minutes prior to the set time. He himself would take the debriefings, write up the notes and ensure a system for follow-up. "Once we have computers, all this will be child's play," the administrator added, winking at Hanbury. From deep down on his dark throne, the consul, happy as a school boy, grinned back.

Hours later – the consul having visited the house he would live in and now returned to his hotel – Sturm came back to the office. The ladies had gone. Gifford was waiting in the hallway. "What's the verdict?" he asked quietly.

"It destroyed him."

"He didn't like it?" The chauffeur shook his head. "Didn't think he would," said Gifford indifferently. "He's had third world assignments, Sturm. Third-worlders have inflated housing expectations. Saw that in the British Council. Even so, the house isn't much, no matter what the standard. We admit it." The administrator rubbed his neck with frustration and once more heaped scorn on the predecessor. "Why didn't he ask for innovation? Creative financing for real estate is child's play for a diplomatic mission." He shrugged at the years of wasted opportunity. "A free hand and a few weeks, that's all I needed. I could have arranged a deal for villa in a fine neighbourhood, maybe even in Dahlem. But this one seems capable of enterprise. A curious chap all the same, Sturm. Can't make up my mind. Is he clever? Is he slow? Several sides to him. Makes you wonder. And his German, how did he come by it? He never said."

"Maybe here." Sturm said.

"You think? He said nothing about that to me."

"He's been here before. He recognized Siemensstadt."

"Did he say more?"

"He doesn't say much at all. Yesterday he slept. This morning he was like a corpse. Just two words came out. That's all. When I drove him to his house he was an extrovert. Said he wants me to take him to Spandau tomorrow. I asked why. He laughed. A long story, he said. Then he inspected the house. It shattered him. So he was back to playing corpse."

"Tell me what happened. The details."

"Nothing happened, not in the car, not at the house. He walks in, looks around, looks into a closet, the bedroom, the kitchen. Stands in the living room, spreads his hands and says, *I can't believe it!* He walks out. I drive him back to the hotel. Not a word said. When he got out he said, *Tomorrow at eight.* That was it."

"When was he in Berlin? Which year? Did he say that?"

"No."

"And why does he want to go to Spandau? Did he say that?"

"No."

"Odd, Sturm. He's odd."

"Not too odd, I hope. I wouldn't mind if he said more. A corpse in the back seat? It gives me the shivers."

❧

In its day the British Officer's Club in Berlin, tucked in behind the exhibition grounds, had the same nostalgic atmosphere as similar institutions sprinkled around Africa and Asia. In Berlin, the pool could only have been better had attention been given to the water by finicky Asian servants. And on the red clay tennis courts, alive before the dinner hour with restrained exclamations of a game in heat – *Well served old boy* – the one ingredient missing was Africans scampering after stray balls. Inside the club, more anomalies: waiters with Teutonic names struggling with the Queen's English. But some universal props kept appearances up. The pictures on the walls were of horses stumbling in the steeplechase and of the English hunt. The sound was genuine too: a hush, as in any Oxford senior common room.

Randolph McEwen was a club regular. With his upper lip motionless, he would describe his line of work, if asked, as *meta-diplomacy.* His corner table, appropriately, had a sweeping view of everything going on. The club was McEwen's anchor. It afforded continuity. It substituted for family. For four decades establishments like it around the world, the vital outposts of his civilization, had been provisioning him. In Berlin he particularly liked the local peculiarity of Teutonic tongues addressing him as *Sir*. Given the century's events – Britain being the persistent winner of the wars – it was fitting, McEwen believed, that the Hun address him with reverence.

McEwen and Gifford met at the club routinely. Their interests had overlapped when Gifford worked for the British Council, where he watched and listened, reporting observations to McEwen. After he jumped ship from the Council to the Consulate, Gifford soldiered on, continuing as a McEwen contact and receiving a modest stipend for the effort. So now too, an hour or so after concluding in front of Sturm that the new consul was an oddball, Earl was joining Randy for a pint. Their talk seemed gossipy and random, but was in fact quite purposeful.

"Your new chap arrived safely, has he, Earl?" McEwen asked, his lips scarcely moving. His eyes did all the moving. Every drink served in the club was registered. Outwardly, motionless and grandfatherly, the white-haired meta-diplomat radiated peace, but inwardly, he churned with uncontrollable suspicions.

In McEwen's presence, Gifford didn't rest his elbows on the table as in the consul's office. With McEwen his hands were humbly squeezed between his thighs. He freed one only when he sipped his bitter. Nor did he look into McEwen's attacking eyes. His attention was fixed on the Union Jack, that is, on a little pin in his host's lapel. It was always like this when they drank – McEwen restless as a bird of prey, Gifford stationary as a salt pillar.

Gifford dutifully informed McEwen that the new consul had arrived safe and sound, but so far he had seen rather little of him.

"What's he like? Any early conclusions? Married I suppose."

"No, not married."

"I say. A wilting pansy?"

"Don't think so, Randy. An odd chap in some ways all the same."

When McEwen asked why he thought so, Gifford presented a few thin facts between sips. "He appears to be acquainted with Berlin. And he speaks better than passing German. Might have lived here once, though nothing mentioned on his CV. Begs a question, I think. Don't you? Not sure why he's odd. One moment he sort of sleepwalks, hands stretched out, feeling his way, that sort of thing. Soon after he's seems fairly sharp. Most odd, Randy. Hiding something?"

"Lacks transparency, does he?" asked the veteran observer of other people's lives.

"Rather. I shall keep an eye on it. Sturm will help."

The random gossip moved to other subjects. The meta-diplomat asked Gifford about recent news in other diplomatic missions. The spectator listened to McEwen repeating hearsay about the scaling back of foreign military units in the city. The military withdrawal bothered McEwen, Gifford could tell. When he talked about it, McEwen's eyes turned lifeless and cruel, like a fish. He loathed all signs that his empire was disappearing. As the session ended, McEwen put in a last word. "I'll inquire into your new consul," he said. "The world is full of wanderers. If he's one it's best we knew."

SPANDAU

"What's in Spandau, *Herr Konsul?* Sturm asked pleasantly as they neared Berlin's western district. He was trying hard to be amiable, but the whole way the back seat was deeply silent. It made the task formidable. Chauffeuring a sarcophagus around, Sturm thought, would be more convivial.

"A citadel," answered a voice, unexpectedly, like an echo from the far side of the grave.

"I know that!" Sturm countered with irritation. "I mean, why are you going? There's nothing there, not for a consul. They've torn down that prison where they kept the Nazis."

Sturm was following instructions. *I would like to know why Spandau,* Herr Gifford had instructed. *Keep him talking. Sooner or later, he'll drop a hint.* Keep him talking? Sturm carried the conversation, the whole way down war alley: Bismarckstrasse, Kaiserdamm, Heerstrasse, past the Commonwealth War Cemetery. He tried topic after topic, but not a peep from the back. Trabis as investment, he tried that first. "Little stinkers, those GDR cars," he said. "Belched like power stations. When the Wall came down Ossis switched to western cars. That cleaned the air fast. Not many Trabis around now. Becoming collector's items. Buy Trabis, Herr Konsul. Store them. Last year you could get one for two hundred marks. This year, they're up to five. In a few years they'll be worth a fortune." But nothing from the back, not a word, not even a grunt. When Sturm saw in the mirror that the consul looked out the window at a bus, he tried public transport. He described how Berlin's U-bahn lines were being reconnected after decades of multiple dead ends. And what a joy to see the trams again. Trams went out of fashion in West Berlin, but not in the East. The East maintained traditions. "I love those trams," he said. "I hope they'll come back everywhere." A wait by Sturm. Bait taken? No. More silence. He next explained the problems of the city's electricity supply – why electric clocks in West Berlin had gone berserk when the two grids were connected. "Powerful stuff, that Eastern juice," Sturm concluded.

As this and other East-West subjects floundered in the shoals of taciturnity, Sturm gave up. It was then that he decided to ask a straight-forward question: *What's in Spandau?* He considered the answer – *a citadel* – more than condescending and in a huff he fell silent too. "Take me there. Take me to the citadel" the back seat suddenly commanded. "Then you can stand down." "No I can't," argued Sturm. "I have to take you back to the hotel." When the voice, resonating as if from the inside of an urn, answered that wasn't necessary, he could not suppress derision, "And how will you get back? It's getting dark. And look up. Those are rain clouds, Herr Konsul. A downpour isn't far off. You visit the citadel, I'll wait." "I'm not here to visit the citadel," the voice informed the chauffeur. "I have other things to do. To the citadel, Sturm. Then let me out."

After the citadel stop, the Opel lurched back into the traffic with tires squealing. Pedestrians looked up. Had the driver seen a ghost, or was he in the grip of a catatonic fit?

❧

Hanbury, in contrast, was serene as he left the car. Gripping him was nostalgia. The citadel, the river, the locks, the foot paths, Sabine's sunny voice instructing him in Spandau history. He recalled how, when it came to the history of her own time, her voice hardened. She described the day the Wall went up around the western edge of Spandau not far from where she lived. Through barbed wire they watched the torment of neighbours on the other side. Then came concrete blocks and the view – and sense of neighbour – disappeared. The sinister permanence of the Wall made everyone feel violated. The communists, Sabine said bitterly to Tony, had sealed her in. "Maybe not sealed in," he replied, pointing at a bright side. "Maybe the other side got sealed out." Sabine didn't argue. "Sealed in. Sealed out," she said with resignation. "Sealed off." Hanbury wasn't much affected by such local history. He enjoyed Sabine doing the talking as they walked along the river. In their cocoon he liked the feel of their arms around each other and of their hips moving as one. And now, walking through unchanged streets to where she then lived, still hearing their past merriment, he was thinking of phrasing an apology.

At a gate with a familiar, small bronze sign, *Albert Müller – Rechtsanwalt und Notar*, he pressed a bell. At first, no answer. He pressed again, longer. A speaker built into the gatepost crackled. "*Schon gut. Schon gut.* Alright, alright. No need to bring the house down. Who is it?" Hanbury leaned forward to the gate. "*Albert? Tony Hanbury hier.*" There was a silence, then Müller came back on. "*Mensch! Tony! Alter Knallkopp. Was machst du hier?*" Hanbury didn't recall being called a knucklehead in the early days, but he recognized Müller's tone as a warm hello. The old man hadn't changed. An electronic release buzzed. Hanbury went forwards. The front door opened. A ramrod figure lit up from behind hovered in silhouette. They viewed each other in the darkness. When Müller said, "You expect me to serve drinks in the cold? Come in. Come in." Hanbury knew that at least the second of his olive branches had been delivered.

The furniture stood in the same places; the house still smelled of air that should be changed. Müller was timeless too, except his voice had a little more sand in it, an old man's net of tiny veins had crept to the surface of his cheeks, and the eyes stood deeper, though they were undimmed and vigorous, as full as ever with impertinence. Müller was as Hanbury remembered him. Unable to suppress his feelings, he took Müller by the shoulders, as if their roles had been reversed, as if the old man was the prodigal son unexpectedly returned.

"So," Müller said, looking him over, "there you are. Resurrected from the dead. Did the devil send you with advice for me on what the after-life is like? You almost came too late. A lot of people think I'm at the end." But the old man's shoulders felt solid, far from ready to give up. Other elderly people Hanbury had known, not as old as Müller, but weaker, were long gone – a mother, a father, a neighbour called Keystone, a colleague or two. "You're looking fit," he said.

"Exercise and alcohol. Plenty of both. That's the secret." Müller led Hanbury into his study where a lit desk lamp showed he'd been working. "What are you doing here?" He asked, motioning to a sofa. "You should have written."

"I was worried if I wrote you wouldn't open the door," Hanbury said. Nothing had changed in the study either. He'd spent hours here listening to Müller.

The old man opened a cabinet and took out a bottle. "If you had, I likely would have arranged to be away. When you stopped sending me birthday wishes, I wrote you off. You're still written off, but that could change. You haven't answered me. What are you doing in Berlin?" He poured two brandies. "*Prost.*" When Hanbury described he'd been assigned to Berlin, Müller raised his glass in genuine surprise. "*Konsul? Ich gratuliere.*" But the voice was already acquiring a familiar undertone and an eyebrow began rippling with irreverence. Hanbury recognized the signs. He experienced them first when he scarcely knew Sabine's father, when he had brought her home after a party and she had invited him in, first into the quiet house and, half an hour later, from the carpet on the study floor into her accommodating bed. In the middle of the night he went to use the bathroom. Tiptoeing back to the comfort of Sabine's warmth, Müller came out of his bedroom. The two collided. Both were naked. "It's you," the father said, scarcely taken aback. "Staying nights now too? Lovely pyjamas. See-throughs, I see. Present from a girlfriend?" He disappeared into the bathroom. Sabine giggled when her devastated lover described what happened. "He likes you," she said. Tony was worried that Sabine's stepmother, a shadowy figure that stalked the family from a distance, would learn he was spending a good part of the night a mere two walls over, but Sabine assured him her father wouldn't tell. The stepmother found out all the same. Some days later she read telltale signs on sheets going in for washing. A violent scene followed, the stepmother shrieking, the stepdaughter shouting. Sabine moved out, into Tony's Savignyplatz apartment.

Back then Müller took it all philosophically, and he was philosophic now. He asked where Hanbury's last ten years were spent. "Your last letter was from some place on the edge of the known world. Kuala Lumpur I think. I assumed a snake got you, or a revolution, or that you fell into the clutches of an Asian woman." He tipped his brandy glass convincingly, emptying it with one smooth gulp.

"It was tough going," agreed the diplomatic adventurer, "I was lucky to survive. Sorry I stopped writing, Albert. No good reason for it."

"Don't have a breakdown over it," the prickly old man said. "I didn't consider it a loss."

The letter writing to Berlin went on for fifteen years. Hanbury wrote his mentor more often than home. Müller's replies were short and factual – a legal tone – except when he described his marathons. Details were always included on the last and the next race. Claiming he'd soon win, he'd write: *It's in the bag. All I need to do is train.* A postscript in one letter informed Hanbury that Sabine had married. Hanbury recalled it gave him a shock, a sense of loss, a dull ache that lasted weeks. He had studied the postscript closely. *One never knows, he may turn out to be a stand-out as a son-in-law, but I won't hold my breath.*

His own letters had been long. He wrote about being third, second and finally first secretary. He had interesting things to write about: other continents, pathetic countries, squalid cities. He reported visiting Inca shrines, sailing in a dhow on the Arabian Sea, walking in the Himalayas. He described music pouring out of stereo speakers into his tropical garden in Malaysia. When a Mahler symphony was playing and the kettle drums began, he wrote, all birds big and small took flight. A spectacle! Music and nature in a clinch.

Hanbury was unable to write home in the same way. Letters there were short. His father's only interest was to bring an end to prairie dust storms while his mother was slowly going insane. Writing Keystone, the family neighbour was easier. Keystone, a railroad engineer, liked to hear about trains. It didn't matter where the trains were – Asia, Africa, Indochina – anywhere. Hanbury made trains the subject of those letters. In Japan he rode the Bullet Train. *I think we touched 200 miles an hour,* he wrote Keystone. *Was that baby moving!* Keystone wrote right back: *Imagine doing that here! There's a dip just before Broadview and with that speed…on the way up…I sure would love to see a fast freight get airborne. Keep riding them bullet trains, son. We always knew you'd be a fast mover.* Keystone retired soon afterwards. The next time Hanbury was home he saw the railroader wasn't adjusting well to doing nothing after forty-eight years working for Canadian Pacific. During that visit Hanbury realized it was a toss-up who would be the first to go, his mad mother or the retired neighbour.

"There were advantages," Müller was saying slowly, "not getting letters from you anymore. It saved time. Wading through them sometimes ruined my schedule. Uwe wondered what was keeping me. What was I supposed to tell him? That I was delayed on account of reading a letter? He would have barred me from *The Tankard*. Also it took pressure off my shelf space." He gestured to the rows of legal files crammed up to the ceiling. Hanbury looked up and down and noticed two framed photographs on the far end of a middle shelf. He didn't recall seeing photographs in the Müller household before. Two women in their prime. He recognized Müller's second wife. In the picture she was staring into the distance at something, an intangible devastation, just as she did when he first met her. The troubled look dominated an otherwise pretty face. The second woman could have been Sabine – blond hair, high cheeks, moody eyes, a slight pursing of the mouth – an exquisite, smouldering beauty. "You had lovely wives," Hanbury said.

"Usually the women outlast the men," shrugged Müller. "Bad luck for me. Number two passed away four years ago." He paused, nonchalantly sipping brandy. "I can tell you about her now since she's no longer with us. I married her after Sabine's mother passed away because the infant needed care. From the beginning they didn't get along. I knew early on marrying again was a big mistake. By the way, I seldom saw Sabine after you left. Only when her stepmother was gone did she start coming around again. Now it's every week. It's like having part of my first wife back. You never married, or did you?"

Müller had never posed personal questions, not once during all the times they drank together. Nor had his letters inquired why Hanbury abandoned Sabine. Was the old man working up to asking for an explanation? Hanbury lamely replied he always doubted he'd be able to make marriage last. "Well, it's none of my business," Müller said.

"I never wanted to cause misery."

"Very noble. Have another brandy." Müller poured one for his visitor and one for himself. "Another question. Why did you upset Sabine the day before yesterday?"

"She told you I called?"

"No. All I saw was a volcano ready to erupt. Her mother got that way sometimes. I learned not to stir when things were that explosive. Something was causing it. I doubted it was her husband. When you announced yourself just now, I knew."

Hanbury was silent. He sat forward on the sofa, studying the carpet, as if seeing the whole Savignyplatz experience with Sabine pass for another review.

"Her face was set in stone," Sabine's father said. "Remember that look? I couldn't help remark someone would soon be mistaking her for a pillar of granite. She turned on me I tell you."

"I shouldn't have called her. I thought she might be over it. How is she?"

"The same as when I last wrote you ten years ago. She bore a son whose second name is after me. Once a week we have an afternoon together. Things are as she likes them, orderly and routine. We always go to museums. A different one every time."

"Museums? Of course. Always the museums." Hanbury couldn't count all the museums Sabine had dragged him to.

"What else? The last one was full of Casper David Friedrich paintings. Typical Sabine scenes. I think she likes the way he does clouds. They're sort of tumultuous. I wanted to cheer her up. I was looking at one and she asked me if I liked it. I told her I liked the frame, delicately carved, lovely, quite wide, big for a small picture. I believed a Rembrandt might have set the frame off a little better – but only marginally. For that frame, on the whole, I thought Casper David had done a good job, and I told her that." Müller spread his hands, as if to ask what else he could have said? "I admit, she laughed. You know how she gets indignant but doesn't really mean it. She was better for a while, but when we parted, I could see she was hardening again. I guess you got to her."

Hanbury nodded. When Sabine stood before a painting, he remembered, she left this world and slipped into another. Going to a museum took her hours. She loved soft, gentle, sentimental pictures, scenes she wanted to live in herself. She was already keen on Caspar David Friedrich then. Explosive sunsets, opalescent dawns, women motionlessly studying maritime horizons, the human species dwarfed by nature, ruins – the works of man decaying – presented as odes. Spirituality on canvas, was how she summed it up. Staring at his brandy glass, Hanbury remembered she would stand transfixed for fifteen minutes before a single painting, by which time he had happily scanned the whole salon. Distantly, mechanically, his inner eye remaining on Sabine, he began to answer Müller's question about what had happened to him in the years since he stopped writing.

"So your father died," was Müller's reaction when Hanbury said the soil scientist passed away while he was on posting in Kuala Lumpur. "That proves it happens. Something to keep in mind." The old man had finished a second brandy and gave his guest the impatient, twisting hand motion of a glass going bottoms up.

"To moderation," Hanbury said, emptying his.

Müller did the refills and explained why he switched from running the marathon to cycling. "Eagles soar." He spread his arms like a giant bird gliding. The roads of Brandenburg were improving, he said, and the annual race for seniors from the Oder River to the Olympic Stadium in Berlin was soon coming up. "It's called *To Olympia*. I plan to win. I'm even training for it."

"I guess you have the time," Hanbury said innocently. This rubbed the old man the wrong way. Provoked, like a startled parrot, he cried, *Time for it? Time for it?* Sorry, but he had *no* time. He had never been busier. For him, German reunification came at a bad time. Just as his practice was drifting to an end and he looked forward to sport full-time, the chaos of East Germany hit his desk. "Why couldn't they have waited ten more years to unify the fatherland? I'd be gone by then. All because East Germans wanted to travel and see Paris, or have afternoon naps on the Costa Brava, or pay a fortune for a cup of coffee with a view of Mont Blanc. Pah!"

It was the East German property mess, the old man explained, that had derailed his retirement plans. "Millions of claims. When you think about it, a country that produces such a mess *deserves* to sink away." He described the problem, which began before the war when the Nazis expropriated the belongings of Jews. After the war the Russians in their zone made things worse, nationalizing industry, rearranging land ownership, throwing the Prussian Junkers out. After that, when East Germany came into being, private property became a truly chaotic notion. Enemies of the state lost it, party comrades acquired it. "And now all those original owners want back what they say is theirs," Müller said with a lawyer's dispassion. "But who is the original owner? It's complicated, a nightmare. Only Germans can create such a mess and then make a maze of rules to disentangle it. It interferes with cycling, I tell you."

Why at his age, Hanbury wanted to know, would he still be taking an interest in other people's property problems?

"It's an addiction," Müller admitted. "A temptation. He began to talk about a case he had been working on, a Jewish businessman who saw the writing on the wall in '34 and sold his business to an Aryan friend before moving to Buenos Aires.

Müller was a different man, Hanbury decided, when he was the lawyer. The tongue-in-cheek undertone to all he said disappeared; his expression lost its irreverence. As a lawyer, even with a few brandies in him, he was serious, incisive. "The Aryan was no friend of the Nazis," Müller continued. "He had nothing but contempt for the SS. So he was detained, tried by a Nazi court, convicted and sent to Buchenwald, his property taken from him. He survived the labour camp. When the war was over he went home. He decided he didn't like the Communists anymore than the Fascists. In the early fifties he quit East Berlin, automatically losing his property again. It's an age-old scam. Create a society people don't want and when they leave, declare what's theirs yours."

Hanbury looked at Müller's legal files, some of them slanting over as if they were tired. *He* was tired. With the brandy in his system, he'd soon be slanting too. His mind was too slow now to consider a society in conflict, sixty years of unstable public order and endless internal conflicts over bits of land. "A German saga," he yawned.

"Exactly," declared the lawyer. "Full of unexpected winners and unexpected losers and it keeps me busy." He pointed the bottle towards Hanbury. "You're falling behind."

Hanbury asked Müller about Sabine's husband. The old man stiffened, saying he had nothing against history, nor the people who study it, but Werner Schwartz dabbled in strange things. Occultism, theosophy, Aryan supremacy, that sort of thing. Müller with a motion of rejection, waved all that garbage away and gave a long explanation why even an objective search for knowledge, historical research, or whatever, could in some areas go too far.

They talked, and the level of the brandy in the bottle continued to go down. They sank deeper into the sofas too, chins boring into chests.

Müller began to reminisce about the *Dorf Krug*, the Village Tankard, where they had often gone, Sabine sometimes joining them. Did Tony remember the time when Uwe, the owner, had dared her to down a schnapps in one gulp and how, maybe to prove something, she'd thrown it back, how swallowing it had hit her hard, her face turning crimson and eyes filling with water? Yes, Hanbury remembered. She had coughed violently and he, feeling somehow guilty, had run to get a glass of water. "Uwe was unperturbed," Müller continued. "I recall he advised she'd made a good start. He urged her to keep it up, that she'd improve with practice."

Hanbury asked, "Is Uwe still around?" "Uwe passed away," sighed Müller. "Kidney failure. We talked shortly before the end. He was a convert then. He tried to convince me of the senselessness of drinking. *One drink after another,* Müller mimicked Uwe's gravelly baritone, *all your life, all to forget the old lady. But when you get home, in that state, you see her double.*" Müller and Hanbury chuckled remembering Uwe. "His son-in-law runs *The Tankard* now. Hey…" Müller studied Hanbury's glass. "…you'll never see double today if you don't get going. What are you waiting for? Evaporation?"

The brandy bottle continued to pass between them, as if they were sailors thirsting after a long voyage. At last Hanbury insisted he ought to get going. In the hallway, by the front door, they stood and swayed. Müller mumbled a complaint about the damage done to next day's training. "Sorry," Hanbury fretted. "Sorry. Very sorry. I stayed too long." This exasperated the old man. "You stayed away too long," he bristled. "And don't come again, not if you insist on snivelling." Hanbury nodded heavily, before Müller, like a nightclub bouncer, shoved him out the door.

The air had cooled and dampness was settling around the street lights, luminescent globes with iridescent fringes. No sign, the consul confirmed blearily, of Sturm's predicted downpour. Once more outdrunk by Sabine's father, walking with exaggeration, he aimed for the Spandau U-bahn station. A small detour took him past *The Tankard*. The pub was brightly lit. The double doors beneath the copper sign of a mug with a foaming head were as inviting as always and, when Hanbury pushed, swung open as easily as they used to.

Inside he paused. His unsteady eye saw Uwe and Albert occupying their corner table near the bar. There was more. He swore he saw himself there, and Sabine too. She was sitting tight against him, his hand under the table massaging her knee, her hand on his upper arm squeezing appreciation. He sat down at that same old corner table and switched off his drunken mind.

A big man in a white apron walked over from the bar. "*Sie wünschen?*" he asked. "You'd like what?"

Hanbury ordered a sausage, dark bread, mustard and a large bottle of pure water. "You're Uwe's son-in-law?" he asked in a thick tongue.

"Sure. Why?"

"I knew Uwe." The son-in-law nodded and went to fill the order.

When the sausage was delivered Hanbury tried again. "See much of Albert Müller?" he asked with a semblance of sobriety. "I used to come here with him quite a bit. We used to sit with Uwe." He took a gulp of cold water.

"Herr Müller was a regular until Uwe's kidneys gave up," Uwe's son-in-law said, viewing his customer skeptically.

"I heard that happened. I hope he didn't suffer. He was always optimistic."

The bartender accepted the inevitable. He grabbed a chair, turned it around and sat with his momentous arms across the backrest. He stared at Hanbury. "When Uwe first learned he had a condition, he came home glum. *Even the best sickness is no good*, he said. He was weak. We were worried. My wife Ilse wanted to cheer him up. She told him not to worry, that we'd help him get through it. Uwe said – I hear him saying it – *I want to do it right, Ilse. If I had to die three or four times, I wouldn't worry about the first time. But I only have one chance. Suppose I do it wrong?*"

There was a cry for beer from another table. Uwe's son-in-law said he'd be back. Hanbury drank more water and devoured the sausage before starting on the bread. Having tapped and delivered a foaming tankard to a customer, the bartender returned. "It took a while before Uwe was dead. He blamed it on his lack of education. *If I knew more about dying, I might have managed it by now*, he said. He had a whole year to think about it. The time passed peacefully and that's how he died."

"I remember Uwe knew something about music," said Hanbury solemnly. "I once told him I liked listening to music. 'Beethoven?' he asked. I said sure. He said he'd heard Beethoven was deaf. He believed that Beethoven, his whole life long, whenever he put a pen on paper to compose, probably thought he was drawing."

"That's right," said Uwe's son-in-law. "Tell me. You've got an accent. Foreigner?" Hanbury nodded. "How about that. It makes our place international. I'll have to tell Ilse." He began to describe Uwe's funeral, saying the preacher had not been an attractive man, but had said nice things. The bartender was lost in thought for a while before rising to attend to new clients.

Hanbury finished the bread and water much relieved that, though Uwe might be gone, *The Tankard* was unchanged. Maybe he and Müller could make it their regular again.

THE RULES OF PROTOCOL

*T*he program of official calls to outfit the new consul with a stable of contacts was in full swing. In those early days Frau Carstens, briskly efficient, targeted Berlin's thoroughbreds.

Sturm, wagon-master, lay awake at night pondering his responsibilities. His was the delivery job: human cargo, an atmosphere of urgency, timely arrivals staged with solemnity. During the day shouts resonated in his mind: *Lights! Camera! Action!* The Opel roared along the avenues. It swerved and swayed, cutting BMWs and Mercedes Benzs recklessly down to size. He raced up to ornate buildings, stopped decisively, jumped out, ran around to open the consul's door, stood at attention, one hand lightly on the handle until the back seat cargo was gone up the steps and swallowed by oak doors. Throughout, his countenance was solemn. Remaining on guard beside the Opel he was fidgety and alert. He felt the pressure of making the logistics work. Herr Gifford demanded military precision.

The Chief of Protocol, at the top of Frau Carstens's list, proved difficult to pin down. First, the President of Poland prevented Hanbury from having a half-hour. Then the Emperor of Japan took precedence. The King of Thailand came. An ayatollah from Iran and the Dalai Lama also bumped the appointment into the future. The consul bided his time. Frau Carstens' list of the city's finest pacers was long enough. It kept him going. Had Krauthilda known what was going on she would have cried: *Wow! Way to go, Tony! Way to hit the movers and the shakers!* Heywood, that self-styled, paternalistic grandee, would have been inspired too. *My boy, you know, I'm proud of you.*

The continuous waiting for an opening in the schedule of the Chief of Protocol was like fishing – patience was needed to land this big one. The staff checked daily with Frau Carstens to see if there had been a nibble.

The picture of the city that emerged from the consul's many conversations was complex. In fact, he was overdosed with information. Frequently a discussion made sense only when he sat down afterwards with Gifford. Gifford knew about the purge of East German communist party hacks. And he made it sound as if he had personally studied the state cancer that was the Stasi. He explained the legal basis for hauling Honecker (and half a dozen other top communists) into court where they stood accused of practising a most exquisite totalitarian sport: randomly shooting defenceless people. Gifford was up on the planned departure of the Russians too: the victor of war retreating as an army in defeat. And he shed light on why it was that a migration was starting up between the two sides of the city: shabby Wessis heading East, newly well-heeled Ossis slinking into comfy Western flats. No doubt about it, when it came to sensing the currents in the diplomatic winds, the consulate administrator was a master.

Gifford didn't talk of this when he went home to Frieda. Whenever Earl referred to his work, Frieda used the opening to make a stinging accusation: they were not rich. She would remind him of his marital vow, the passionate promise to bedeck her with jewels. "Why can't you wheel and deal like...like the businessmen?" she'd ask spitefully. "I love you, Giffy, but I like shopping too." Being called *Giffy* in a Kreuzberg accent drove Earl crazy. It made him bite the folds in her neck. Frieda was big, but when he began his nibblings she discarded her clothes so fast it seemed she was fifty kilos lighter.

One evening, after an afternoon in which the consul had complained to him he was feeling numb because of sitting through a long monologue by the head of a social science research institute on East Germany's post-unification shocks, Gifford inadvertently remarked at home that he was having to fill in a lot of blanks for the new consul. "What a waste," Frieda said. "Giffy, honestly, how can you think about a blank consul? What we need are some blank cheques." Earl grabbed his wife's spreading haunches and whispered hoarsely, "I haven't forgotten the jewels, Frieda. You'll have them. The day is not far off. I promise." Frieda's monumental hips were bare in no time.

Hanbury's call on a newspaper editor was one of the few that went sour. The consul was troubled by it, but Gifford said newspapers were like that. Ignore them, he counselled. Think of the distortions they print. The editor was a certain Dr. Anton Bülow who in the early, friendly moments of the consul's courtesy call made it clear he hankered after the simplicity of bygone days. A red cloth was wrapped around his neck and a pince-nez sat on his nose. Bülow had a habit of holding his head at a downward angle as he looked at his visitor over the lenses. He had a full head of hair and a mossy beard around his mouth, which made him look like Trotsky.

The consul, tutored for the interview by Frau Carstens, asked Bülow about the changing nature of the paper's readership now that the Wall was down.

Bülow was immediately chatty. The phenomenal thing, he said, was that nothing had changed. Wessis read the same papers as before; Ossis were doing likewise. In the newspaper market, he said, the Wall was up, not down. It might even be marginally higher. Bülow digressed on more than forty years of ideological separation. Two German clans had come into existence, he claimed, in a complicated German which kept Hanbury on the edge of his seat trying to decipher it. "They were antagonistic and since we Germans thrive on having a common enemy," he remarked, "we fortuitously supplied each other. It was a convenience we can't now seem to do without."

Bülow liked to think his real strength was international affairs and he asked the consul about Canada, laughingly voicing the cliché about a mouse having to live next to an elephant. The consul replied this was changing. The mouse was learning how to assail the elephant, he said. There were some effective poison darts, for example the export of lumber, wheat and beef.

"It will ruin your environment," prophesied the editor. "I've seen pictures of clear-cutting in British Columbia. It's pretty awful." Hanbury said that cutting trees gave many ordinary people a living.

"But at what price?" asked Bülow thoughtfully, pursing his lips. They exchanged polite views for several more minutes, Bülow becoming excited. An eye behind the pince-nez began to twitch.

As Bülow's moralizing continued, something in the consul snapped. His voice became fractionally more aggressive. "I suspect you don't know our situation," he said curtly. "You have no idea how many trees we have. We've got trees like you've got Deutsch Marks. *All* the trees in Germany wouldn't fill *one* of our national parks. We lose more trees every year through natural forest fires than get cut."

Bülow didn't take this well. His lips now rolled like wringing hands. He talked about the forests of Brazil, Malaysia, and Indonesia and linked them to humanity's increasingly more bankrupt view of itself. In a haranguing voice, he admonished Canada for becoming the Brazil of the north. Pointedly, he asked, since Canada worked so hard at a world-wide image of being a white knight, why didn't it act like one?

A debate on culture, ethics and public morality was on. Hanbury got close to throwing in a few irrational asides on Nazi death camps, but thought the better of it and took another tack. "Not long ago," he said, "I read that a major German bank absorbed a loss of maybe a billion marks as a result of bad decisions by its old-boy supervisory board. When criticized, the President said not to worry. For his bank this amount was *peanuts.*"

Bülow shrugged as if to say, *so what?*

"Take a small country in Africa, like Sierra Leone. A billion marks is maybe eight, nine times its GNP. Would a major German bank take advice on running its affairs from the finance minister of Sierra Leone?" Bülow looked puzzled. "It's the same with trees, Herr Bülow. When it comes to trees, Canada is like your biggest bank and Germany is down there with Sierra Leone."

Bülow's lips stopped quivering, but the tick in his eye was growing worse. "May I quote you on that, Herr Konsul?" he asked in a toxic voice. "If you'll excuse me, I have urgent matters to attend to." He gestured coldly to the door.

When Hanbury described the scene to Gifford, he wondered if he had gone too far. "It's not my role to get people's backs up," he said. They were at the small table in Hanbury's office for the debriefing. Gifford always inquired into the most trivial aspects of the consul's conversations. No detail seemed unimportant. But now he sat there silently. "I guess I blew it," Hanbury added.

"Not at all," Gifford soothed. "Canada as Germany's biggest bank and Germany as Sierra Leone. Splendid analogy. It's time someone took the Bülows of this world on. They do so pontificate. My advice is, think no more about it. Now, if we are finished with that editor, I've been intending to raise another matter. Your house." Hanbury sighed, saying it was an impossible subject.

"Identifying solutions to problems," said the administrator, "is my job." He clasped his hands and rested elbows on the table. "You've been in your house for several weeks. What's your opinion?"

"It's not exactly a residence. I had better accommodation when I was third secretary in San Francisco. I can't invite people there. They'd think I was representing Sierra Leone, maybe worse." He thought about the cramped dining room, the bathroom showing signs of mildew (although the autumn damp had scarcely started) and the kitchen, so small that no self-respecting chef could be coerced to use it, not for five course dinners.

"Consuls from places like Sierra Leone live more luxuriously than you," Gifford said brutally. He made a survey once which showed Third-World diplos lived in sumptuous comfort. The financing, he suspected, came through creative backroom deals, or diplomatic smuggling. Gifford often pondered the opportunities available to foreign representations to generate wealth. "Something ought to be done about your house," he urged.

The consul agreed, but was at a loss.

"First, define the objective," said the administrator. "With your status, your objective, I should think, would be a residence with a spacious entrance hall, a dining room for twenty-four, a drawing room for eighty, an ample kitchen. Upstairs, the private rooms and a wing on the side for guests. Is that a reasonable objective, Tony?" Hanbury agreed it amounted to the standard package. "Objective identified. Now modalities. We need four or five million." The consul laughed, but Gifford was serious. The thumbs of his clasped hands began to twirl. His sweat was running. "It's not as much as it sounds. Real estate turnover in this city amounts to billions every year. A few million is a drop in the bucket. It is a tiny percentage of all those transactions."

"I don't see the connection," Hanbury replied stiffly. "I won't ask

for the money, Earl. I will not let headquarters have that satisfaction."
"I know a few people, Tony. I'll work on it. I'll prepare the ground."
"I doubt we could get a green light." "I think we can."

After numerous debriefings at the small table, Gifford had
concluded the consul seldom spoke the last word, seldom summed up,
or drew conclusions. An advantage of such silence was that it could
be taken as consent. Gifford let the silence deepen. Hanbury studied
the table top. What might he be looking at? Was he immersed in an
immaterial world of abstract concepts? Or was he having a vision – of a
curving driveway, a stately portico, an elegant vestibule, an ornate
winding staircase? When the silence had continued long enough to spell
out unending consent, the administrator got up. From the door he said,
"The computerization project is doing well. I'll soon be asking for
authorization to seek tenders." He sounded harsh.

"Thank you, Earl. Good work. I'm pleased to hear it." The consul
sounded subdued.

⁂

The office of the Chief of Protocol finally called. A strike! Sturm washed
and waxed the Opel. A standard was attached to the right front fender.
He picked out a new stiff flag. This ride would have a higher order of
importance.

He weaved in and out of lanes, hit the brakes at crucial moments,
ignored a stop sign and jumped two red lights. Berliners shook their
heads in consternation. As the car roared up the *Strasse des 17. Juni*, the
Maple Leaf flapped like a banner in a tempest. The consul,
stone-faced, kept his eyes focussed on the distance. Frau Carstens had
done a final inspection, righting his tie, pinning a white carnation to his
lapel. Pedestrians saw the radiating flower, but the passive visage was
hidden in the rear seat's shadows.

Through the Brandenburg Gate, past the Russian Embassy, down Unter den Linden, deeper into the East. A slowdown at Friedrichstrasse caused by clouds of dust from a demolition job forced Sturm to jump the car onto the sidewalk. He honked people to the sides and motioned to a cop to open up a passage. Seeing the fluttering Maple Leaf, the officer hassled people away and saluted the disappearing Opel. Sturm sped on – composed, silent, concentrated – past the statue of Frederick the Great, across the palace bridge with the sculptures of divinely proportioned gods, onto the island in the Spree, past the barren emptiness where the Kaiser's palace once stood. A last right turn, then left.

A uniformed escort stood on the city hall's front steps. As the consul got out, she approached. "*Herr Konsul, ich begrüsse Sie. Herzlich willkommen im Roten Rathaus.*" Welcome to Red City Hall.

Red City Hall, Hanbury thought. Where was that troublemaker Adamanski? "Thank you," he replied. "Such an interesting building." He paused momentarily on the steps to study decorative work done in brick.

They went up a staircase of imperial proportions. The escort said the word 'red' in *Rote Rathaus* had no political significance. It came from the colour of the bricks. The ochre shade was chosen, she said, because at the time of Bismarck and the Kaiser, imperial buildings were sandstone. Berliners, no great fans of the Kaiser, decided that the new city hall should stand out. Red bricks clashed with sandstone. Kaiser Wilhelm reportedly gnashed his teeth when the new civic structure stood in full view from his palace. Naturally, Berliners were delighted when they heard this. Hanbury laughed when she finished. "*Eine schöne Geschichte.*" A fine story. Red as the colour of impertinence. He ought to send Adamanski a postcard.

Much later, when the forces arrayed against him were overwhelming and not even the Chief of Protocol and his great influence could help, Hanbury thought back to the day he first met Gerhard von Helmholtz. He recalled that merely being in the presence of the man made the world seem thoughtfully determined, filled with reason, much less random. The very way the Chief of Protocol moved conveyed a will to lift the world's affairs onto a higher plane. Hanbury never forgot the visit – not his first impression of this imposing man, nor the altercation with the French ambassador at the end.

The office of Berlin's long-serving Chief of Protocol was on the building's south side. Tall window doors accessed a narrow balcony. They would eventually become, in Hanbury's mind, a portal to odd twists of fortune. Who would have predicted during his first visit that a day would come when von Helmholtz would usher him onto the balcony a second time, for a conversation in the rain, claiming that speaking in his office ran a risk of being listened to? Listened to! How? By whom? A sinister notion. And ridiculous too, because already this first time Hanbury noticed that sound dissolved there. The office had infinite room for it to disappear. Upwards, sideways, in all directions. Its sheer size made you feel confidentially alone.

Hanbury's first view of von Helmholtz was of him rising from his desk, removing reading glasses and inquisitively coming forward. Silver hair combed back sharply, a strong nose with a slight beak, and an aristocrat's erectness. "*Konsul Hanbury*," he said in a voice accustomed to command. "I'm pleased to meet you." The consul expressed gratitude that time had been found for him in a most demanding schedule. "I wanted to see you earlier," the Chief of Protocol replied. A slight shake of his head spoke of the inevitability of many things.

"Innumerable visitors. Every one wants to see Berlin. They come and go, but our good fortune is that you will stay."

The phrases born of good breeding stuck in Hanbury's mind. He remembered being flattered. He also remembered making a fatuous reply. He commented on the impressiveness of the building and so much going on outside. "Dust storms in the middle of a city!" he exclaimed. Von Helmholtz nodded politely. "The task of rebuilding the city is enormous." The consul described his own observations and ones he borrowed from Sturm: the stitching together of two public transport systems, bridges being reconstructed, two electricity supply systems being meshed. He made it sound as if technical details fascinated him. This interest delighted von Helmholtz. "For decades Berlin was the centre of German Communism," he said, "but also the focus for the fight against it. Such dichotomy isn't bridged in a few months. It almost seems now that we are back together we have a sense of loss. Berlin as ideological battleground no longer exists. Instead, we are the laboratory for German reunification. Less exciting and more painful." On an impulse, he took Hanbury by the elbow and led him to the balcony doors which stood slightly open. The muffled rattle of traffic drifted up from below. "Let's step out."

Opposite the balcony in the distance were sad grey buildings without architectural coherence. Helmholtz identified each one. Some had dishevelled Roman columns of pompous proportions. Others were in the socialist style of pre-fab concrete cells stacked up. Interspersed were a few ruins dating back to the days of carpet bombing by the Allies. "This was once a fine view," the Chief of Protocol said of the diseased cityscape. "Twelve years of Fascism, a war, forty-five years of Communism. See what it does to physical heritage. East Berlin received a terrible dressing-down. We are determined to make it great again."

Holding the balcony railing, they surveyed the scene. Nearby jackhammers sounded like flat, toneless instruments of percussion. The *Rathaus* trembled. A dust cloud welled up and obscured the view before a gust of air carried it off in the direction of Karl Marx Allee.

"Is the city hall being torn down?" the consul asked with alarm.

"New foundations only. The war weakened them. When the *Rathaus* was rebuilt, like so much else in East Berlin, the footings were left porous. Now we have to retrofit." He nudged Hanbury back inside, closed the doors and led him to two sofas at right angles around a glass-top table. Two cups of coffee had been poured.

Hanbury began the formal part of the call. "You're a Berliner," he said. "I'm interested in your view of what lies in store." A deep and complex question was made to sound as if there was a simple answer.

Von Helmholtz smiled knowingly and ephemerally. He answered slowly to provide context. He started with the Berlin of the twenties, touched on the thirties, forties and fifties, went deeper into the pump-primed West Berlin of the sixties and seventies and the plateau of the eighties. He admitted the gloss was off now. "We hope to regain a spark, a vibrancy," he said, "as in the twenties. We're not planning to be mediocre. But the truth is we don't know what Berlin will be. We need a pioneering outlook, I suppose."

Hanbury nodded. He knew about pioneers. Their will to triumph on the prairies had been special. They wouldn't have survived without it. Dust storms, blizzards, grass fires, cloudbursts, spring floods, locust clouds, mosquitoes in pestilential numbers and the brutal reality of distance. "People usually rise to the challenges they face," he said with optimism. "Our pioneers made it. Why won't you?"

It came out sounding a little absurd, but that's not how the Chief of Protocol took it. He asked some serious questions about the prairie spirit. He wanted to know what so much space does to people; do they feel at nature's mercy, do they sense humility? He became reflective. He explained that when he was young he longed to break away, to be a geographer and cross continents. But the war came along. Afterwards he entered public life. Since then he had managed only pin-point visits to other countries. He had not seen the Prairies, nor for that matter the Steppes, or the Pampas. One day, an optimistic von Helmholtz claimed, he would.

The consul's courtesy call was taking on an unusual tone. A series of signals jumped between the two men and rapport intensified. They told each other more about their pasts. Hanbury described how he had grown up in the vise-grip of his mother's ambition; four hours a day at the piano, at least. The Chief of Protocol said that when he became a teenager he became a soldier.

The story von Helmholtz told was difficult to forget. When the bombing of Berlin began in earnest von Helmholtz was thirteen, old enough for anti-aircraft work, so he was soon manning a searchlight on one of Berlin's flak towers. Thick posses of bombers droned in; the beams on the flak towers searched out and held the intruders. The guns went after them. The sky filled with the spectacle of tracer bullets as bombs rained down. All around, night after night, the city was in flames. For a thirteen year old, not fully understanding, the pyrotechnics were engrossing. The next step was to operate the guns. Leaning back, swivelling, the helmet a little big, Gerhard concentrated on the beams now operated by boys younger than himself. He was good at keeping the sights steady on a bomber and got a few hits. When the bombing stopped, the Red Army was closing in. The boys were next organized into anti-tank commandos. With their grenade launchers – *Panzerfausts* – they were sent into positions on the eastern outskirts of the city. As soviet tanks rumbled in the agile boys sneaked into perfect positions. They couldn't miss. Gerhard knocked out four. It would have been more, but ammunition ran out.

The Soviets were taking Berlin house by house, slowed down by a lonely *Panzerfaust* operator here, some snipers there. In the last days, when German resistance was crumbling, deserters, whether fourteen or sixty, were hanged on the spot. In one of the last nights of the war von Helmholtz also vanished from the scene of battle. The game then was to get from one end of town to the other without getting caught by the SS. Dashing, hiding, zig-zagging, he made his way to Charlottenburg. The family apartment was bombed out, von Helmholtz recalled. His mother, an aunt and two cousins were in the cellar. They quickly burned his uniform. Short pants turned him back into a boy. The family packed some things and left, walking west, picking their way through the lines, arriving three days later at family friends in the country. A Soviet victory orgy was beginning in Berlin; mass rape went on for days, thousands of women being repeatedly violated. Once the Americans had taken control of their sector in the south-west, the family walked back and joined in clearing the rubble. Four years later von Helmholtz became logistics coordinator for the Berlin airlift, which was how his public career began.

Hanbury was slowly digesting all this when a secretary interrupted, saying the French ambassador was waiting. The consul stood up to leave, but the Chief of Protocol gestured that he stay. The French ambassador, his expression said, could wait. Hanbury sat down again. Von Helmholtz didn't dwell long on the '49 airlift, or even the building of the Wall. That was interim history now. It was the current plans for grafting a new city onto the old which excited him. Would the immensity of the destruction be matched by the rebuilding? Friedrichstrasse, Potsdamerplatz, the barren stretches around the *Reichstag* – renewal would have to be massive and historic. "We must find the will. Get out of your office," he counselled. "Walk around. Feel the moment. It's unlike anything that's happened." He made it sound as if Berlin was defying gravity and taking flight.

The secretary reappeared. "*Sie können den Französischen Botschafter doch nicht so lange warten lassen, Herr von Helmholtz.*" No French ambassador has ever lived, she was in effect saying, who could be kept waiting without it turning into an affair of state. The consul checked his watch. "I really ought to go." "Bring the ambassador in," von Helmholtz ordered. Getting up, he said, "The man's mildly pretentious. A little wait will do him good. I enjoyed our chat, Herr Konsul. We must continue it. I talked too much and learned too little." He escorted Hanbury to the door where a glowering ambassador stood waiting.

"*Monsieur l'Ambassadeur*," Hanbury said gracefully.

"*Vous avez parlé beaucoup*," the ambassador said, his voice cutting like a knife. "*Grandes affaires d'état, sans doute.*"

"*Oui, oui. Bien sûr*," the consul confirmed agreeably.

The ambassador cocked a disbelieving eyebrow.

"Think about it," von Helmholtz reminded the consul. "Buy yourself some walking shoes."

The ambassador snorted.

"*Au revoir*," a polite consul said.

The Chief of Protocol turned to the ambassador and, silky smooth, said, "Excellency, I kept you waiting. My apologies." Then the padded door clicked shut.

❧

Outside, because of the long wait, Sturm had lost his concentration. He observed, however, that when the consul finally emerged he was excessively cheerful. Sturm thought he acted like a lottery winner. He shook the hand of the pretty escort and plopped into the back seat with a satisfied bounce. Out of character entirely, as far as Sturm could judge.

Still, a relaxed and happy human cargo relaxed him too. "Went well?" he inquired, driving off. In the rearview mirror he saw that the consul was waving like a lunatic at the girl in the silly uniform.

"Very well," replied the back seat smugly. "*That* man is perfect for *that* job."

"Von Helmholtz? He should be. He's been at it for a century."

"Sturm, do me a favour. Stop at a shoe store."

"A what?"

"I need a pair of walking shoes."

The chauffeur pondered this. "No you don't, Herr Konsul. Forgive me, but getting you around is my job. Leave your feet out of it."

"I'll be doing more walking from now on. Reconnoitering. I think it's time."

Sturm shook his head. A consul in hiking boots? Preposterous. Still, with the back seat seemingly at ease and sounding human, he was inclined to overlook the implications. Slowly he dawdled back to West Berlin. On Unter den Linden a woman in a Porsche flitted by, but he didn't let it bother him. From shoe stores, Sturm's thoughts moved on. He mentioned he'd seen the Chief of Protocol on TV. "Next to foreign visitors he looks good, very good," Sturm observed. "Some of those visiting heads of state look like circus clowns."

"Now, now," the consul tut-tutted.

But Sturm was warming up. "Some have jaws so wide you'd think they were trained to eat spaghetti sideways. One African President we had was so cross-eyed that on Wednesdays he probably saw both Sundays. Then there was an Asian who had a pimple on his neck, except when the camera zoomed in, it turned out to be his head. Beside that crowd, Herr Konsul, our Chief of Protocol is a standout."

"The very word, Randy. *Reconnoitering.* I asked Sturm to repeat it. He also said, *I think it's time.* Something's happening. He's been activated."

Randolph McEwen nodded darkly. He was in a foul mood. The club had been invaded by a horde of Huns – an official dinner hosted by the Brigadier General – and his table had been requisitioned. He and Earl were crammed into a tight corner upstairs with not much of a view. All they had before them was a line of backsides squirming at the bar like horses in a stable. A meta-diplomatic crankiness was taking hold. McEwen snorted at the news that the consul was planning to engage in undisclosed reconnaissance. "It doesn't surprise me," he said. "Not at all. It fits with other things I know."

"He hit it off with the Chief of Protocol," Gifford added brightly. "He came back quite bouncy."

"Von Helmholtz? That *Wehrmacht* type? What did they discuss?"

"Told each other their life stories. Hanbury talked about prairie horizons. Von Helmholtz described shooting down Allied pilots and sending a Soviet tank corps into oblivion. Remarkable, Randy, how friendship develops, but that's what happened. But more difficult to grasp is why he's decided to go walking."

"Friend Tony has decided to go walking?" McEwen took a notebook from his jacket, licked a stubby pencil and began taking notes.

"That's what he said."

"And the reconnoitering part, the *I think it's time* statement?"

"He said that to Sturm."

"Friend Tony told Sturm he was going to reconnoiter, but said nothing about it to you?"

"Perhaps it was an oversight."

"Nothing is an oversight, not with Friend Tony." McEwen's voice was turning soft and malignant. "Something is up. A clever act so far, Earl. Quite difficult to read." He put the notebook away and took a key from a small leather pouch, inserted it methodically into each end of a black case and turned the locks with a calm, deliberate precision. A thick folder emerged.

Earl Gifford sipped his ale. These moments, when all-knowing files emerged from McEwen's briefcase, enticed him. His palms went sweaty. He had the same contracting sensation in his groin as when Frieda stepped onto a coffee table and, hovering over him, disrobed. Gifford licked his lips. He stared at the folder, but he saw Frieda's folds of flesh.

"I'll start out by saying, Earl, that what we have on Friend Tony so far is cause for worry." McEwen surveyed his surroundings slowly, severely, like a hawk on a perch. Ascertaining that no German waiter was observing, he flipped casually through the folder, reviewing the contents in his mind, playing the case through once more, giving his argument a final sharpening. McEwen relished knowing; he loved the power it brought. "Superficially," he said slowly, controlling each syllable, "what is here may seem thin, but my instincts tell me these facts have tentacles. Friend Tony, I suspect, runs silent and he runs deep." Gifford nodded confirmation. Sturm often complained about the consul's deep silence.

"First, the Beavers," the meta-diplomat announced, as if they were a headline. "We know from elsewhere they are eager, hard working and love cooperation. We happily keep an eye on their people abroad. A duty we have, Earl, towards all countries that love the Crown. Likeable chaps, the Beavers. They did their best with Friend Tony. They admitted to some gaps and said they were embarrassed. I admire that. It's not something Uncle Sam would ever do. Still, gaps are gaps. Gaps cause regret. Record-keeping on that side of the pond is not yet an art form. I shall share with you what they had." McEwen flipped to a marker half-way down the folder. "Personal History: Anthony Ernest Hanbury, born 19 March 1943 in Indian Head, Saskatchewan. Father born in Moose Jaw: profession – soil scientist. Mother born in Montreal: née Cadieux, music teacher, housewife. No siblings. The psychological profile concludes his upbringing was sheltered. The father often absent, the mother with the boy full-time. She taught him piano. She believed he would be a world class soloist. Mothers, Earl, love them for being that way, always convinced their children will be the best. Schooling in Indian Head routine. A note from the principal expresses worry the boy sees himself as an outsider. Then off to university in the big city. Saskatoon."

Gifford knew McEwen wasn't solely a schemer. Sometimes, unpredictably, he would relax, which happened now. After pronouncing *Saskatoon*, a impish smile passed over the meta-diplomat's face. "What's the expression used at rodeos, Earl?" he said. "*Whoopee!* I think." They both chuckled for a moment. McEwen resumed his sombreness. "Friend Tony reads political science at the university. He is an average student and goes unnoticed. In the final year he writes an essay with a telling title: *The Evolution of Marxism and Leninism: The Future of East Europe*. The title is extant, but no copy in the archives. The first gap, Earl, a *regrettable* gap. What *would* Friend Tony have been prognosticating thirty years ago? Did he have a political ideal? Does he have one now? It would be nice to know.

"Skip a few years, Earl. Riveting years we'll come back to. When Friend Tony joins the Canadian Service, he is psychologically screened. Fortunately, the Beavers have it on record. Friend Tony is asked, *What caused you most unhappiness when you were young and what is your happiest memory?* The answer to the second question..." McEwen flipped through the folder to a page marked with a blue clip. "...I quote, *Vacations on my uncle's ranch*. We accept that, Earl. I liked the farm, too, when I was young. I look forward to owning one when I retire. But listen to the answer to the first question. Being passed over for the high school basketball team. How revealing. Why didn't he make the team? Can we assume he was too short?"

"He is rather slight, yes, quite slight," replied Gifford. Fresh pints arrived, but McEwen was busy digging deeper in his folder. "Cheers," Gifford said.

McEwen mumbled *Cheers* back and absent-mindedly lifted his glass. "That's exhibit one. Your consul has a complex. Complexes motivate. Napoleon was slight. The Kaiser had a withered hand. Both wanted military domination. Toulouse-Lautrec was a great painter but a dwarf and he spent all his time peeping at women undressing. We could develop a long list. I suspect Friend Tony is as bent as the lot. But he hides his perversions.

"He takes a degree in '65. According to the Beaver records he then disappears from the face of the earth. *International travel*, the file says. No indication where. The Beavers now say they ought to have been more concerned at the time. No attempt was ever made to determine where he went. A *deplorable* lapse. In '67, blithely…yes, *blithely*…he joins the diplomatic service. But where did he spend the years prior to that? What did he do? Was he on the beaches of a Caribbean island performing esoteric exercises to improve his height? After all, his was the LSD generation. Or might he have been in some mecca for the pursuit of his favourite preoccupations, Marxism and Leninism? I'll come back to that too.

"Leave it to the Beavers. Once Friend Tony is in the Service the paper trail is better. His annual performance reports tell us a great deal. If you can stand the lachrymose style and ignore the extraordinary puffery, the reports are quite amusing. Page after page of swollen praise. I ran into that same requirement for volume in India. Funny, how the colonies suffer from linguistic puerility.

"Did he *innovate* that year? Did he *analyze*? Did he *plan*? Did he *organize?* Every year the same answers, *yes, yes, yes, yes.* Why would anyone ask? Of course he did! To do so was his job! Quite incredible annual bombast, the descriptions of the simple fact that someone was working for a living. Where did we go wrong with the colonies, Earl? In my service, we keep an eye on the young ones and a quiet nod decides who moves up. Why were we not able to transplant such simplicity? Nevertheless, here and there in the annals of Friend Tony's performance, one finds a flash of insight, an occasional, entertaining turn of phrase. Listen.

"San Francisco, '68. *Mr. Hanbury admirably came to understand the sociological profundities of this exciting part of California. His providential reporting on the pullulating anti-Vietnam War movement at Berkeley University was accurate, realistic, and powerfully credible. He concluded with very promising reasoning, that the U.S. will not win the war on account of the strong disapprobation amongst America's youth. Accordingly, I have marked him outstanding in the category of political evaluation.*

"Friend Tony is an outstanding political analyst, Earl. It says so black on white.

"Let's skip some years and go to Kuala Lumpur, '83. A gem. The first secretary is completing his second year. The ambassador writes – *Mr. Hanbury's potential is immense. He shows a fine feel for the rules of protocol and could rise to the highest levels in the Service. However, he needs to overcome diffidence. He is superb at developing options for action. Under the category "ability to plan" above, I already set out the example of his judicious determination of which movie houses in Kuala Lumpur would be suitable for showing the new documentary film on the James Bay Hydro Electric Project. However, it should be mentioned here that he was unable to decide which of such options would be best and, as time passed without a decision, only a small theatre was available in the end.*

Unfortunately it was in an outer suburb. The Quebec delegation attending the showing remarked that they expected more from a federal embassy. Training in purposeful decision-making would remedy the defect.

"Hear, hear," said Gifford.

"Most recently, the year's performance harvest came from a certain Irving Heywood. Ottawa, '89. Mr. Heywood writes – *Few directors will have been so blessed with virtually constant and faithful support from their deputies. During my absences, which due to the crushing burden of the international workload were frequent, Mr. Hanbury, a believer in the higher purpose of our mandate, managed Disarmament with a blessedly delicate touch which allowed the full creativity of my staff to be revealed without hindrance.* Do you like that, Earl? Do you appreciate Mr. Heywood's style. Does it remind you of a churchman reporting on the outcome of a Synod?

"A few more random items from the Beavers which have a bearing. It seems Friend Tony was not really qualified for Berlin. He wanted the position, but wasn't sufficiently senior. Since no one with appropriate seniority could be found, his going solved two problems; what to do with him and how to staff Berlin. That too, as we shall see, is of more than passing interest."

McEwen stopped, sipped his bitter and inhaled deeply through his nose. He looked at the ceiling. Earl Gifford knew this was an interlude, a pause. A fresh wave of damning insight was about to be unleashed. But could the Hanbury story get better? When McEwen appeared stuck in thought, Gifford interrupted. "Time-consuming," he said, "going through so much material."

"A responsibility, Earl," sighed the meta-diplomat. "A responsibility. That's the extent of the Beaver files, I'm afraid. Disappointing, frankly. Vital questions left unanswered. But we had that other tantalizing clue, the one you produced – Friend Tony having a previous connection to

Berlin. My presumption was that this might have occurred during the *international travel* period. When that was checked out – here in Berlin – information came in lorry loads. Everyone in Berlin knows Friend Tony: the university, the office for foreign registrations, the police. Even the Stasi had more on him than the Beavers."

Gifford beamed. His info! He nodded with excited jerks; his great jowls quivered.

"He arrives in Berlin in '65 after taking the degree in Saskatoon and enrolls in the Goethe Institute. He has rooms in a building near Savignyplatz. He becomes competent in German and the next year is at the Free University attending political philosophy lectures. Listen to this, in early '67 he is arrested for participating in a left-wing demonstration. Friend Tony claimed he was an innocent bystander, although given his academic interests we can safely assume he was chummy with the lefties. No film footage of him carrying a placard, nor of him turning over cars and setting them on fire. He avoided the cameras. The police let him go. Participating in a demonstration like that without becoming part of the record shows extraordinary cunningness and skill, in my opinion.

"Since we now have access to East German files, I thought, why not peek? And behold, one seeks, one finds. The Stasi files reveal that Friend Tony entered East Berlin on several occasions. Very detailed information. No regrettable gaps; no deplorable lapses. The Stasi did so many things so much better. Our Marxist-Leninist student is followed each time he goes in. There are thorough accounts. Twice he meets a student in the East, a certain Günther Rauch, a true Marxist, a marked man, a thorn in the flesh of the Stalinist elite. Rauch develops a reputation as a trouble-maker. We have not evaluated all the Stasi information. We may not have it all; the files are difficult to penetrate. Might Friend Tony have been employed by the Stasi? A sting operation on Rauch? Or were the two students similarly politically obsessed? If so, has he now returned to re-establish contact with Rauch? Does that explain his eagerness for Berlin? We don't know all the things we should.

"What does it add up to so far, Earl? A man with a debilitating inferiority complex and a record of left-wing activism parachutes himself into a job for which he is unqualified but conveniently in a place where former ideological comrades are enjoying the bounteous ambience of freedom and democracy."

"He went to Spandau!" Gifford contributed heatedly. "No reason given. *I have things to attend to*, that's what he said to Sturm. What on earth could he possibly have wanted in Spandau? Attending to what? My God!"

The meta-diplomat nodded gravely. "It fits," he said. He sank away into dark thoughts, then roused himself. "Friend Tony enjoys the access and influence afforded by diplomatic status – privileges which can be used as a weapon. A secret rendezvous in Spandau? Plans to disappear into the back alleys of Berlin? An uncommunicative bearing? A game has started, Earl. We will have to watch him closely. I shall be informing Uncle Teut." The meta-diplomat stared intensely at his guest. "My preference would be observations day and night. Can that be managed?"

Gifford, motionless, stopped working his pint of beer. He sucked in his breath. "Day and night? That's big time, Randy."

"'Tis. 'Tis. Normally I would contribute a spare spectator or two, but my days are numbered. I lack the means. The world is changing, Earl…" McEwen paused to swallow bitterness. "…My services are being made redundant. Friend Tony may be my final case, my last chance. I should like him to be a big one. Do your best, Earl. It's important. Pull out all the stops."

At this moment, strangely and creatively, Frieda's taunts began exploding in Gifford's head. *Do some wheeling and dealing, Giffy.*

Everybody does. His mind churned. He no longer held the glass. His hands had come together in a prayer-like clasp and his elbows were resting on the table. Sweat formed on his forehead. Might a bargain be carved out of all of this? "I'll speak to Sturm," Gifford said carefully. "He'll have to do it. I'll see how far Sturm can be prevailed upon. We have some control already. Everything Tony does is in the program. We know where he goes."

"Spandau showed the program approach is a little leaky, Earl. He spent time on his own. I should like to catch him red-handed with Günther Rauch. A photo would be helpful."

"The key, Randy, is to win his confidence. Help me with that. His mind would open. If I provide him with things he wants he would see me as an ally. Get my drift? He would open up. We would break the wall of silence. I'm making progress, but if there could be a helpful shove…"

"Girls? Boys?" the meta-diplomat asked harshly.

"Would you believe, a decent place to live?"

⁂

Outside the club, Gifford marched directly to a public telephone. "Get dressed," he ordered Frieda. "We're going out. Champagne dinner."

"Oh Giffy," Frieda moaned. "Since when champagne?"

"Since the day after tomorrow," he said huskily. "After that, you'll bathe in it. Tonight's for openers."

"Oh Gif, how exciting. What's happened?"

"Never mind. Get some clothes on."

"Come watch me," Frieda urged.

"The other way around, afterwards, when the bubbles have taken us to the ceiling."

"*Oh Gif! Ja! Weisst du, ich liebe dich.*"

SPOOKY ALEXANDERPLATZ

hen the consul insisted that time be set aside in his schedule so he could go walking, the office erupted. "Why?" demanded Frau Carstens. Hanbury shrugged, saying he wanted to see up close all the changes sweeping through the city. "*Blödsinn*," she said scathingly. Completely silly. Consuls don't walk. They are driven by chauffeurs. How could he contemplate such a trivialization of his office? Serenely he insisted that a few afternoons each week be kept free.

Gifford was subtler. "No problem, Tony, if you want do some sight-seeing. It's normal." Quickly he added, "Sturm can take you." Hanbury repeated he didn't wish to be driven. That was the point – he'd be doing it on foot. "Yes, I know. Sturm will walk with you. Security. On the streets, you never know."

"It'll be broad daylight. A couple of hours only. Some people walk across Canada and think nothing of it."

"Presumably it's not that dangerous there."

The consul insisted Sturm would not be needed.

An exasperated Frau Carstens, encouraged by Gifford, made one last appeal. "It could be seen as eccentric," she warned.

Hanbury showed her a pair of brand-new walking shoes, suede, in three colours – tan, olive green and maroon – with thick soles. He grinned. "Eccentric? With these I'll be incognito." Resistance withered and Frau Carstens, biting her lip, sprinkled the undiplomatic entry – *aimless wandering* – throughout the consul's agenda.

❊

What went through Hanbury's mind in the early days of his assignment as he criss-crossed Berlin on foot? Would he have reflected on the attributes of great cities: geography and climate, history, architecture, tradition, magnificence blending with intimacy? He'd seen enough of them to make comparisons. As the consul walked he might have thought of Paris. Remove, say, Place Vendôme. What's left? The equivalent of a fine opera, but without its best aria? Or London without Piccadilly Circus? A great symphonic orchestra stripped of the kettle drums? And what is Rome without Piazza di Spagna? Or New York without Times Square? Such glorious gathering places inspire all the generations. They are the mooring places for a city's soul.

But what about cities that had proud squares as testimonials to the human spirit and saw them disappear? What about Potsdamer Platz, a place once filled with throngs of people? Potsdamer Platz: the heart of Berlin before the bombs rained down. After the annihilation it was a collection of ghostly black and burned-out shells. The little that remained after the war was dynamited away, the bricks recovered and recycled into utilitarian structures someplace else. Greatness reprocessed into dullness.

Potsdamer Platz, although quite dead, then got dragged like a corpse over the rocks of post-war politics. The Wall, running through the middle of the city, split it into two expanses of sand and weeds. Potsdamer Platz, now the back end of two cities moving in opposite directions, became forgotten. On the west side, the Wall was covered with graffiti: *Last coke for 10,000 kilometres,* and, *The greatest piece of socialist art the world has seen.* Generations of tourists climbed a wooden platform to peek over the barrier into communism. Before them lay a no man's land dotted with patrol dogs, armoured vehicles, automatic shooting devices, and watchtowers manned by soldiers with binoculars pasted to their faces. The bleak streets in the distance seemed in the grip of evil.

The urban land mines had now disappeared and traffic between East and West was stitched back together (after a fashion). But what next? Von Helmholtz had talked of spectacular plans, a maze of tunnels underground for new roads and fast trains. Above ground: theatres, cinemas, galleries, night clubs, all to be encased in futuristic architecture. Thrusting towers, roofs spanning new piazzas, stirring façades, boulevards and promenades, a calming, artificial lake. Standing on a little rise over the leftovers of Hitler's bunker complex, viewing the vacancy before him, Hanbury dwelled on the Chief of Protocol's excitement. From this vast urban emptiness a new city would take flight.

As he walked, Hanbury thought about the present too, and his position in it. Sabine's angry voice still echoed through his mind, though when he visited their old haunts it felt as if she was symbiotically beside him. But not in the East. She wasn't in his thoughts when he went walking in the East. There was no precedent for that. Back then, during the Savignyplatz days, she refused point blank to come along whenever he crossed over. When he walked in the East, he felt a different presence – of Günther Rauch, an ideologue, a disciple of Marx. For Günther Rauch, too, Hanbury had come carrying an olive branch.

The first time the consul wore his new multi-coloured shoes, he intuitively felt that somewhere in the East, Günther Rauch was waiting for him. He took a train to Friedrichstrasse station. Away from the office, from Frau Carstens's grip on his agenda, he sensed a growing inner animation. Getting out of the train at Friedrichstrasse, Hanbury headed south, his senses keen, his mind ready to receive.

⚜

Günther Rauch had picked Tony Hanbury out easily back then, in the sixties. Everyone wearing fashionable jeans was from the other side. "You're being followed," Günther Rauch advised, with the instant familiarity that is typical of students. "I've been watching them."

Hanbury required a moment to let this sink in. He was staring at a young man on a bench with a large head and a thick wild beard who looked like Karl Marx reincarnated. Hanbury did a slow full circle, as if admiring socialism's architectural efforts around Alexanderplatz. It was true. Two men in cheap, polyester knitted jerseys and baggy trousers stood nearby, looking past each other like bored girls scouring the horizon for action. "Who are you?" he asked.

Günther Rauch had a hoarse voice, like a scraping tool working on something hollow. "They won't do anything. Not to you. It'll be different for me. Since I'm now exchanging words with you someone will be knocking on my door. Want to know what I'll tell them?" Hanbury said sure. "That I offered to open your eyes to the splendours of East Berlin." The student from the West laughed and the one from the East joined in. "I mean it," said young Marx. "Well, maybe not the splendours, but opening your eyes. I'll show you around if you want."

With another shrug, a young man falling in with unscheduled adventure, Tony Hanbury set off with Günther Rauch. Rauch's exaggerated hand movements pointed at streets and places as he explained their historical significance. Generous sweeping circular motions of his arms linked the decrepitude of East Berlin to past political evil. The sight-seeing-cum-lecture continued for two, perhaps three hours, liberally enriched with references to the thoughts of the real Marx. Eventually they were back at Unter den Linden and turned south into a grim Friedrichstrasse, aiming for Checkpoint Charlie and the visitor's freedom. The security detail never left them. Seeing evil in the distance from the safety of the Potsdamer Platz platform was one thing; having it doggedly on your tail, hour after hour, was another. Hanbury wondered whether he'd get out as easily as he came in.

Günther Rauch must have noticed the unease. "Don't worry," he said. "They might detain you for a while to scare you. That's all. As for me. I'm in and out of jail all the time anyway. The Stasi don't know what to do with me." He gave a deep, barrel-chested laugh. "The first time they took me in was after I stood up in a university seminar and said the Politburo was nothing but a bunch of fascists coloured red. The commotion! I was slapped into jail so fast the Gestapo could have learned from it. An interrogation followed. How to describe it? Well, imagine an orchestral suite – a gentle serenade from the strings, some pleasing notes from the harps, then a blast of percussion." Günther Rauch chuckled. "Actually, I liked being the centre of attention. I tried to convert them to my way of thinking. When I was out I told some friends about the treatment, which was enough to put me straight back in." Günther Rauch was suddenly sad. "One day I might find out which of my friends is not a friend."

As Checkpoint Charlie neared, Günther Rauch opened his arms forwards. "As I see it," he said, gesturing towards the barriers, "if I can become troublesome enough they'll jail me permanently until the day when they'll sell me to the West. They do that to my type. They doom us to a capitalist way of life." After more steps he muttered under his breath. "Alright. Let's rehearse our lines. If they press me, I'll tell them you urged me to become a good citizen of the Great Decaying Republic, while you tell them I opened your eyes to the magnificence of Marx."

Hanbury loved it. "Bullshit baffles brains," he cried spontaneously, remembering the expression from Saskatoon where he once heard leftist students in debate.

Günther Rauch ignored this. "If they try to recruit you when they interrogate, you're on your own," he said. "I can't give you any pointers there. The next time you visit, if I think you've started wearing some kind of Stasi medal on the inside of your jacket, I won't ask any questions. I just won't say much anymore. Those invisible decorations are much in fashion around here nowadays. Everybody wants one."

As it was, Hanbury experienced little delay getting out and a few weeks later he was back on Alexanderplatz.

"Get a visit?" he asked Günther Rauch, looking him over for fading bruises.

"Sure. The both of them. They didn't appreciate my tone of voice. Three days and nights in the Stasi lair. I have to say it, the interrogation business was up. I had to wait my turn. Some strays from West Berlin kept whispering all night about their rights. That's the problem with you Westerners, you've got rarified concepts of law. You're out of touch with human nature."

Hanbury suspected this was just a prelude for another afternoon of theories about the human condition, the economic causes of misery, the dialectical process, and the inevitability of proletarian revolutions. But the lecture didn't start just yet.

The bearded iconoclast wanted to air a few practical issues first. "I told the Stasi you're interested in Marx, that I was trying to win you over. I didn't change my tune. It's important in situations like that to think of something simple and keep repeating it, like a nursery rhyme, so that eventually they get it. Well, what about you? Did you get a visit? Did they win you over?"

Hanbury shook his head. "Not even a nibble."

Günther Rauch examined him closely, but if he had suspicions he dismissed them. He switched effortlessly to a treatise on the nature of ownership. "The Stasi think they own me and you and everybody else. But I ask, can anyone own anything, since we don't meet a basic requirement for real ownership, namely, everlasting existence. When you die, what you have goes to someone else. *Nicht wahr?* Isn't that right? That's a telling fact. That's why the Stasi think they can own people. They're convinced they'll be around forever. Interestingly, the Nazis thought that way too."

From here Günther Rauch's line of argument developed randomly as he laid bare once more the underpinning elements of fascism, national socialism, communism, totalitarianism, stalinism, proletarian struggles and the politics of protest. "We've got that here, all rolled up together in a couple of run-down neighbourhoods. I tell you, you're standing in a test tube. This is the spot where theories get proven. It's nice being an actor in one abysmal experiment after another."

Hanbury had a sense of being at a dark play, but for the second time. There was no growth to Günther Rauch's thinking. He said the same thing over and over again. Still, Hanbury liked Rauch's flamboyance, the arms spreading to make a point, the balled hand punching the air to show he meant it. Marching along on drab East Berlin pavement, Hanbury spent more hours listening.

When Hanbury left that second time, once more by way of Checkpoint Charlie, he was detained. The questions came fast. Why did he meet Günther Rauch the first time? Why did he come a second time? What precisely did Günther Rauch have to say? Hanbury had difficulty capturing the essence of all the arguments Günther Rauch poured out, so he lamely repeated they talked first about Marx, then again about Marx, and finally still more about Marx. It was all noted down. After several hours of intimidation the same questions were asked again. Mindful of Günther Rauch's nursery rhyme argument, he repeated the same answers. Eventually they let him go.

"They sure kept you a spell," a crew-cut American checking his passport said. "Saw 'em haul you in. That was 17:49 and now it's 21:11. Do something dumb? Three hours is standard for folks that do stuff out there that ain't smart." Hanbury cheekily replied the time had been used for careful deliberations about whether he deserved the Order of Lenin. The American didn't think that was funny. "Don't fool with them sons of bitches, boy," he quietly advised. Hanbury nodded appreciation. Günther Rauch was entertaining, but of East Berlin he'd had his fill.

❧

And now, sailing along on the thick soles of his new shoes and crossing Unter den Linden, the consul almost imagined the polyester knits were after him again. At one point he even made the same slow turn as years before on Alexanderplatz. He thought he saw Sturm in the distance turning his back. But that was crazy. Times had changed.

Penetrating Friedrichstrasse southwards Hanbury ran into absolute devastation. It forced him to revise all he'd imagined about how new cities arise from where others stood. Poor Friedrichstrasse! It was no longer merely sullen, as when he walked there with Günther Rauch. Friedrichstrasse, Hanbury thought, was a wild science-fiction scene.

In the past, when he'd seen it through Günther Rauch's lens on the human condition, he learned that before the Allied bombing Friedrichstrasse had been a vibrant, restless Berlin street. Up and down its length, life spun around in whirlwinds. Cafés, entertainment houses, pubs. Friedrichstrasse was spicy, parts were scruffy, it never slept. The city lots were small and the owners numerous, which was why, in Günther Rauch's view, it was restless. Hundreds of different decisions on how to eke a living from the street constantly reset the stage. In pre-war days Friedrichstrasse worked, Günther Rauch theorized, because it was a place for people. After the war's carpet bombing, Friedrichstrasse was first a river of rubble, then a place where Soviet and American tanks stood nose to nose at Checkpoint Charlie. As for the future, Günther Rauch had said, look at it, look at the arid, the destitute thinking.

Now, Hanbury decided, the thinking was different again. The street was a self-contained tumultuous world of robots. Machines with jaws at the end of pneumatic necks – mechanized dinosaurs – were perched high on mountains of rubble. The long necks swayed, the jaws sought vulnerable spots in a defenceless socialist architectural quarry and bit away. All along Friedrichstrasse the jaws clacked, probed under roofs, punched through walls, pecked at corners, ripped into the masonry, chewed through cables, nibbled at the edges of exposed floors. Debris plunged down. Below, robotic beetles, bulldozers with reinforced steel roofs, heaved rubble into serpentine lines of waiting trucks. A thunderous scene. Total demolition. A grey-brown mist rose from the steady cataract of bricks. Tiny men with fire-hoses scrambled around, spraying water on the rubble, trying to smother the dust.

Hanbury took in the scene. The spirit of Günther Rauch suddenly sprang up to explain: *Mammon is speaking. His version of the bombs. His legacy of death and disfigurement in Berlin.*

Elsewhere, the rubble had been hauled away and power shovels reached down into soft sand. The roots of Friedrichstrasse's next instalment would be planted deep. Further along, the excavation was finished. The cacophony here was of drills and saws, cement pumps gurgling and rivets being hammered into steel. High above, the cranes drew elegant, slow circles, perilously passing each other, sweeping out great arcs, as if to bless the superstructures rising from the earth.

Günther Rauch crowded in once more and Hanbury began asking questions. What were the chances that these new, colossal constructions would bring exotic acts of self-expression, of spice and life, back into this latest remake of the street? It dawned on Hanbury that for all the swagger of developers and architects, disaster on a grand scale was creeping into Friedrichstrasse. Nearing Checkpoint Charlie's leftovers, he turned for a last view of the ballet of the cranes. What, he wondered, would Günther Rauch have said about all that?

It began to drizzle. Hanbury made his way back to Leipzigerstrasse, then east past the Rote Rathaus to Alexanderplatz. The TV tower stood decapitated by the weather; the whole square was veiled in grey. A bench, like the one from which Günther Rauch first targeted him, offered a view of not much more than just the fog thickening. Hanbury sat down, not noticing the fog, not noticing anything. He was seeing other scenes. His mind focussed on them one after another: Müller pouring brandy in his study; the Chief of Protocol's optimism in a high-ceilinged office; the consulate staff fussing about his comfort. And Sabine appeared too. He couldn't help it. In an imaginary dialogue Hanbury asked her what she thought about Friedrichstrasse. Had she by now seen the famous street?

Back then when they were lovers she hadn't. Domestic bliss was the order of the day on Savignyplatz. Few things marred it except that, always just below the surface, Sabine had a hatred of the Wall and the communist regime behind it. She hated the Saxonian accents at both ends of the transit corridors to the West. She abhorred the way they used machine guns there as instruments of instruction, how a casual gesture of the gun barrel meant the back seat of a car would have to be removed to prove no East German citizens were being smuggled, how a subtle look of complaint from the Westerners in transit – maybe nothing more than a slight hardening of the eyes – would make the machine gun point in the direction of a parking lot full of other defiant West Berliners, and how for four, five, six hours they had the pleasure of being whimsically subjugated to the infinite power of the Great Decaying Republic. By the time Sabine moved into the Savignyplatz apartment, she had enough grievances against the East to last a lifetime. Tony for his part was curious about the feel of things on the other side. He wanted her to come along. *Let's go have a look. For fun.* Sabine looked at him as if he'd lost his marbles. So he went alone.

He didn't really understand Sabine's closed mind towards East Berlin. In other ways she didn't seem shy at all about new experiences. Take those of the bed. She was unburdened there, free and eager for innovation. During the day she was the leader too, trekking off with him to a never-ending feast of museums. The city was even richer when it came to pubs. Hanbury liked visiting them, but little by little Sabine began losing interest in the pubs. More and more she preferred that they spend evenings in the apartment. In between reading novels she began paging through catalogues, always asking Tony whether he liked what she was looking at. But what could he tell her about furniture, crockery and a thousand other household items he'd never thought about?

The East was a taboo subject. But so was the West, the far West, the West as far away as Indian Head. It was not possibly to talk to Sabine about the place he came from. Any existence he might have had before the one with her appeared unimaginable for Sabine. That made it seem as if he didn't come from anywhere. He was ready to admit there wasn't much to say about his background. Growing up in Indian Head, plus a few years of little consequence in Saskatoon, paled in comparison to being raised in West Berlin on the front line of the Cold War. But although his pre-Berlin existence wasn't much, it wasn't nothing either. After all, he survived fifteen years of unrelenting music instruction courtesy of his mother on the only grand piano in Indian Head. As for global politics, true, Indian Head was no spy capital, but you could argue the Cold War was visible there too. American B-52s with bellies full of nuclear bombs lumbered by every day at 40,000 feet, heading north to their patrol routes around the Soviet Union. It didn't seem right that all this pre-Berlin experience should always remain unmentionable. Could anyone blame young Hanbury for asking himself – since sharing on Savignyplatz was simultaneously being embraced *and* rejected – where the housekeeping experiment was heading?

Questions like this accumulated. One day their combined weight was suddenly too heavy. Things tilted. A certainty came to Hanbury the student so quick it shock-froze his insides. His heart ceased beating. He uttered a deep, visceral groan. He knew absolutely he had to leave. Too many unmentionables were being stacked up in a dark corner of the relationship.

Thinking how Sabine would react if he told her made him sick. It would be easier to disappear. He paid three months rent, packed a suitcase, wrote a short note, abandoned his stereo and fled. Years later, he continued to rationalize that the misery he created on Savignyplatz was small compared to what had been prevented. Continuing in this same, self-comforting vein, Hanbury convinced himself that in youth there should be allowance for at least one callous act, especially if lessons are drawn. But deep down he knew this was self-deceit. A coward stays a coward, even if he wants to make amends.

On foggy Alexanderplatz Hanbury's mind, still focussed on the inner stage, saw the coward slink away, only to re-materialize as consul. In the next scene Frau Carstens offered him words of comfort. He'd mentioned to her the cramped, depressing little bungalow located on a narrow wooded lane, squeezed in between the Grunewald and the exhibition grounds. "When you get your things," she had said, "the house will feel better. You'll get used to it." She was right. His things made a difference. The magnificent stereo was set up in the front room. A sofa had been crowded into a corner and an arm chair placed before the speakers. When sound leapt out of the giant speakers, the little room was a balloon filled to the bursting point.

The daily routine contributed to blanking out the bungalow's shabbiness. Arriving back from the social functions where diplomats had stood around like a defeated football team, Hanbury would eat quickly in the kitchen. Then he'd grab a bottle of champagne, stuff a few discs into the changer and sink into the lumpy chair. Rachmaninov, Mahler, Brahms, Schubert, Beethoven. They transported him into a boundless inner sphere.

On the dripping bench between trees rendered indistinct by fog, Frau Carstens faded out. Earl Gifford, crack administrator, now ruled the scene. Waving an arm he swept the concept of bungalow aside and, snapping fingers, made a lovely villa appear out of nothing. Earl Gifford was out to prove the dictum that every top administrator is a world class conjurer in disguise. The consul had studied a piece of paper from headquarters that authorized acquisition of a residence. He noted it had been approved by someone fairly senior. "Incredible," he had said to Gifford. "How did you do it?" Gifford beamed, eyes rising to his halo, but he kept the mechanics of his great act a secret. The consul agreed that the administrator should act on the instructions received. "Let me know when you think you have something I should look at." "I'll need occasional access to the diplomatic seal," Gifford replied quickly. "For legalising documents. To make everything bona fide. To speed things up. Is there a way I can get at it? In case there's something urgent when you're away?" Hanbury thought for a moment; he wavered. "It would be a shame if an opportunity were spoilt merely because we didn't react fast," Gifford added. The consul mulled this over too. "How about this approach, Tony," the administrator offered. "If you're away I check it out with headquarters. If they say – fine, go ahead, use the seal – that would be my authority. I believe that would safeguard all the interests." The consul nodded "I suppose that would work. But inform me." Gifford gave assurances that would naturally be the case. The consul had then taken the seal from a strongbox in his office, put it in a locked cabinet in Frau Carstens's room, and issued Gifford a second key.

The scene with Gifford ended. Hanbury on the wet bench, feeling optimistic, lifted himself out of the long reverie. Once there is a proper residence, he thought, I'll invite the Chief of Protocol for dinner. He planned a party for Müller too, a birthday party for his eighty-fifth. And if Günther Rauch ever surfaced, he would be a regular visitor, maybe stay for weekends. Imagine the creativity of the iconoclast's thinking in the opulence of a diplomatic setting.

Irrespective of that future ambience of comfort and magnificence, his current one, the soggy bench, was becoming uncomfortable. The drizzle hadn't stopped. Hanbury, wringing wet and getting cold, got up and made his way to the S-bahn to take a train back to Charlottenburg.

❧

Sturm, frustrated, missed that train, but the next one came fast enough and he jumped on. As far as he was concerned, the consul could get mugged, abducted, taken hostage or sent out of the country in a chest. He had had enough, not of the weather, but of ghosts. Determined to have it out, the soaked chauffeur made his way back to the office.

It was after hours and quiet. Gifford, in near darkness, was still working. A table lamp lit up his desk. Photos and dossiers of fine houses were piled up in the area of light.

"I'm no good at this," Sturm announced, sitting down opposite Gifford in the shadow. His hair was dripping. "I'm not cut out to play Stasi."

"Did he see you?"

"No."

"Quite sure?"

"He didn't come up to shake my hand if that's what you mean. Sorry, I'm not doing it again."

"Security, Sturm. The Turkish consul has two bodyguards, the Israeli three." Gifford, leaning back, removed his reading glasses and began chewing on the ends.

"Then he should have a real one," Sturm replied. "I'm a driver. I'd break my arms just taking on a karate position. Anyhow, bodyguards don't sneak around."

"I tried to get him to take you along. He refused. We're responsible for his well-being."

Sturm shook his head. He didn't think the consul faced threats. "It was about as eventful out there as watching a pensioner in a park. He walks down Friedrichstrasse gawking at the cranes as if they're pigeons on the fly, trots up Leipziger Strasse infatuated by all those dog-eared socialist flats, then arrives at Alexanderplatz, which has disappeared in the rain and where he looks around as if he's seeing the eighth wonder of the world. I'm behind a tree trying to be inconspicuous. The rain keeps coming down. What does he do? He sits down on a bench, not twitching for an hour. Only his expression changes. First a grin, like he's taking a bath with a girlfriend. A silly look comes next, sort of satisfied, as if someone's massaging his behind. Then he hangs his head as if repenting for a crime. Why all that sitting in the rain? It scared me. It was spooky. It sent shivers up my back." Sturm shook his head gravely. "It's like that all the time. Everyday I think I've got a ghost in the back seat. It's getting to me. It's not my cup of tea. I'm not doing it again. He doesn't need a body guard."

Gifford rocked back and forth behind his desk. In the shadowy light of the desk lamp he lowered his eyelids. McEwen wanted reports, and for that he needed Sturm. "It's true," Gifford said slowly to Sturm. "He changes appearances. Sometimes he looks harmless, then he's distant, then he manages to seem like…well…a simpleton. It doesn't mean he's spooky. Look upon it as a kind of charm."

"Charm?" protested Sturm. "He's got all the charm of a worn-out running shoe."

"It might look like that, but there's more to him than meets the eye. Let's not forget, you don't get to be consul without climbing over the backs of decent people. Do you get the impression he's done that? No. That proves he isn't what he seems."

"Maybe. Maybe not. All I'm saying is, I'll do the driving."

"You have to keep an eye on him, Sturm. We're small. It's family. We're responsible for each other. We have to work together."

Sturm was obstinate. "He's not in danger. I am. I'm getting close to the edge. Also, I don't like walking. If I did, I'd be a postman."

The administrator stopped rocking. "Very well," he said harshly. "It can't be forced. Shouldn't be. But I'll need a log of the places you drive him."

Sturm stiffened with indignation. Not in thirty years of chauffeuring Lord Halcourt had he been confronted with anything so humiliating. "I've got the feeling someone's walking on my tie," he said. "I *already* keep a log. I submit it at the end of every month. What do you want, twice a month?"

"Give it to me weekly for a while."

Sturm stood up, walked out and slammed a door at the far end of the corridor.

Gifford was irritated. Mostly with himself. He shouldn't have made the remark about the car log. It was the pressure. It was coming from all sides. He was having to move fast. The opportunity he had was narrow, but the land beyond vast. He had to give it all his time. Damn unwanted problems on the flanks. Damn Sturm for falling out, just as he was having to focus on the main game. Each day he was out, inspecting villas, making offers, seeking offers on the very properties he just made offers on.

The go-ahead from headquarters got things started. The message, more or less as he had proposed to McEwen, actually made the circuit and wound its way back to Berlin. Handlers somewhere had done a good job of making it sound routine. The order was to the point and the acronym of authorization from someone senior more than convincing. *Acquisition of residence approved. Gifford to explore market and iron out details with headquarters directly.* With this, Gifford plunged in. It took a few weeks to develop momentum, but good villas were in demand. With the Wall down everyone was buying for the future. Soon he was riding the rising market. He bought and sold as fast as he could, with the diplomatic seal providing lubrication. Fifty thousand in profits here, a hundred there. The kitty grew. His share – he deemed a straight one-third was fair – he set aside. As the consul was propelled towards having an official residence, the administrator was amassing modest wealth.

But Sturm wasn't the only problem. There were complaints at home about the time he spent at the office. Frieda needed delicate handling, so Gifford told her it would soon be diamond time. "Oh, Giffy," Frieda sighed. "Can I trust you? You've made so many promises." Earl's close set eyes undressed her with ferocity. "After the diamonds there will be a Mercedes," he said brutally and grabbed his wife.

And there was McEwen who was pressing all the time for information.

Feeding McEwen, satisfying Frieda, deploying Sturm, cultivating the confidence of the consul, acquiring computers for the office, flipping deals on houses – Gifford felt driven. Still, after years of soldiering without profit, it was gratifying that his time was finally worth money. He plunged back into the real estate bulletins piled up on his desk.

Damn Sturm for not playing and damn Frieda, for phoning every night, asking when he would be home. *I love you Frieda. I love each square inch of you. I've always told you: you'll live like a queen. But bear with me. Your Giffy needs a little more time to apply his talent.*

THE WILDERNESS YEARS

*T*ony Hanbury's attempt to erase the Savignyplatz period from existence by filling a suitcase with some clothes, lugging it down four flights of stairs and dashing to the railway station, turned out to be a dismal failure. The experiment in homemaking had branded him, and like all brandings it would be with him forever. As for the impact of his act on Sabine, he never fully realized the extent of the devastation.

She comes home from a university lecture with a shopping bag of things for dinner. Inside the front door she yells, *Hallo, ich bin's! I'm home!* and is surprised there is no answer. The flat is orderly. She notices first that both pairs of his shoes are gone, then that the leather jacket isn't hanging where it ought to. Only in the bedroom, tidy as always, where she discovers the closet is half-empty, does shock begin to hit. She rushes into the living room. Everything normal. Breathing hard she bursts into the kitchen and finds a note: *I have to go back. I have no*

choice. Please, please forgive me. The rent is paid. The stereo is yours. Sabine reads it twice. Her heart ruptures. Whimpering she sinks to the floor.

Throughout the night and into the morning, her face streaked with tears, she feels despair. She searches for reasons, tries to find the grounds that tell her none of this is so. The sun coming up brings hatred. With a hammer she hacks at the stereo. The turntable is quickly smashed; the amplifier and speakers withstand repeated blows, but eventually they break too.

On the train and plane, Hanbury mostly stares out windows. He has difficulty ordering his thoughts. Were he a cynic, he'd be convincing himself Savignyplatz was one of life's pleasant interludes. But he is not a cynic. Were he a romantic, sensitive to others, he'd be detesting himself. But he's not a romantic either. Throughout the trip, he experiences something else – incertitude. Did he do the right thing? Could he have done it better? He isn't sure. He knows if he had stayed to talk it through, Sabine would have convinced him not to leave. That would have caused a huge mistake – of the kind he saw up close when he was being raised. But had he been told as he travelled that his stereo was being savagely dismembered, he wouldn't have known what to say. And if someone had whispered that Sabine was also breaking up into pieces, ones not easily reassembled, an empty look would have settled on his face. He had no inkling then, nor in the years that followed, that the Savignyplatz experiment, even after Werner Schwartz had come onto the scene, would continue to be Sabine's deep abomination.

❧

What did Tony Hanbury do during that time, while Sabine hated?

After scampering back across the Atlantic he spent time looking for a job, wrote an exam, attended an interview and accepted an offer from the Service. The Service, Hanbury considered, had a reassuring feel – of being a permanent hideaway. And it provided insurance against risks such as befell him in Berlin. After all, should things ever get sticky, as on Savignyplatz, an assignment to some distant place would never be far off. His first Service job was in the library – the Abbey – a quiet realm, not greatly different from what he thought such medieval hideaways might have been. In fact, what monks did and what he had to do was roughly comparable. Whereas they spent months hand-copying manuscripts, Hanbury took the overnight cables from the four corners of the world to retool them into a few tight paragraphs. This product served the high priest. Each morning, summaries of the world's great events had to be ready for him on his desk. For almost a year the novitiate laboured from two in the morning until just after the high priest's working day began, with the benefit of going home when everyone else was jostling to get in. His new stereo was a step down from the one in Berlin, the bedsit was less comfortable than the apartment he shared with Sabine, and Bronson Avenue didn't hold a candle to Savignyplatz as a place for observing interesting people, but in his monkish existence Hanbury was not unhappy. He had spare time, which he devoted to listening to music.

⁂

As Anthony Hanbury was being rewarded for his Abbey diligence – by being assigned as vice-consul to San Francisco – Sabine Müller was turning a new page too.

"You're quiet," were the first words Werner directed at Sabine, but she ignored him. They were walking down a hallway after a history seminar. She suddenly took a side door which opened to the street. "Until next week," he called after her. Sabine didn't say much in the seminars, whereas Werner Schwartz spoke up all the time. Outside the classroom she was glacial. He tried various topics, but Sabine would depart quickly, wordlessly. He became an expert at watching her walk away. Delicate hair, fragile shoulders, a hint of a dancing movement in the hips. This didn't change until Schwartz had an off-day, when he didn't dominate the seminar discussion.

"Got the 'flu?" Sabine asked at the end of a session that had dragged.

"I'm not too interested in the 1848 revolution," Schwartz admitted.

"Well, Bismarck's next week. Maybe he'll make you feel better."

"He makes all of us feel better." Schwartz answered, watching Sabine waltz off.

Bismarck promoted the thaw, and by the time the French had been decisively defeated in 1871, when the Prussian King was crowned *Kaiser* and Berlin became *Hauptstadt des Deutschens Reiches*, Sabine had accepted an invitation to have lunch. She next met his friends. Werner Schwartz, she learned, was part of an intricate web of connections. He was planning a university career and, given the people he associated with, plus his intellect, she didn't doubt he'd be successful. The more she saw of him the more she entered into a dialogue – entirely with herself – about points in his favour: a Berliner, smart, decisive, orderly and punctual, an apartment full of antique furniture, many fine old books. Ballast, that's what he had. Everywhere she looked she saw ballast.

Points in favour continued to accumulate, so Sabine moved in with Werner. The apartment she now shared was different from Savignyplatz. It was full of all kinds of things.

❧

In July '69, while moving to San Francisco, the new vice-consul stopped in Indian Head. The soil scientist was away in the fields advising farmers. His mother sat on the front porch talking to herself, mostly in French. She had shrunk since he last saw her. For several days he tried to catch what she was saying, but it was hopeless. To escape, Hanbury spent evenings with Keystone, who showed a lively interest in his plans. After three days Hanbury stole out of Indian Head early in the morning, walking up to the Trans-Canada to catch a Greyhound bus. No one was up except Keystone. "Stay in touch, son," Keystone said across his front gate. "Send us a postcard."

Few places, the consul was sure, could equal San Francisco. Who wouldn't want to serve there? The office closed punctually at five, when he became free to roam. Haight-Ashbury, Chinatown, the Wharf. On the weekends, he went across the Bay to Berkeley. Sitting on sidewalks, lying around in parks, observing the scene unfolding, it was inevitable, given the times, that Hanbury would run into a flower child. Her name was Shirley; she was from Ohio. Shirley's hair went down below her hips. Jeans fitted so tight that everything above the waist seemed voluptuously squeezed out. Her top had fringes on the sleeves and underneath, judging from the trembling, there was nothing but Shirley. She hung out around Berkeley, she explained to Hanbury, because the atmosphere was right. In Berkeley you had to be blind not to see that the establishment was disintegrating. *The revolution is on. It can't be stopped*. She talked to Hanbury about pigs too. *Pigs are everywhere. Half of them wear blue uniforms; the other half dress in blue suits.* Shirley loved going to demonstrations against the Vietnam War and held other views. *I'd burn my bra, but I ain't got one any more.*

The mention of revolution made Hanbury think of Günther Rauch. He borrowed some of his Marx and described certain other of Rauch's theories to Shirley, such as the absurdity of the notion that land (which is permanent) can be owned by people (whose lives are transient). Shirley threw her hair around when she heard this and kept saying, *Wow! Wow! That blows my mind! That's pure truth!* The third time they got together, a Sunday afternoon, reclining on a Berkeley lawn with an acid-rock band splintering the air a stone's throw away, Shirley began asking personal questions. When she learned he was Canadian, she looked bewildered. *Is that some place in Scotland?* She also insisted, with a name like Tony, he must be a hairdresser. When he described his work, Shirley's eyes transformed into empty vessels. The vice-consul reassured her. He said in his job he had to help people. "And it's bread, Shirley," he argued. "Like everybody else, I gotta eat." The confession stirred her. *I like relating to you.* She became personal about herself, saying she spent the days practising a new way of seeing. She explained that the cafeteria in the distance (behind the rock band) wasn't exactly there. Because of Einstein, space was known to be curved, meaning the cafeteria was actually a little over. Everyone, she insisted, should get used to seeing straight lines as curved lines, but the *establishment* and the *pigs* prevented it. Even now, right across America, kids were being screwed up in the schools. *Do you realize eighty-five percent of school kids own a ruler?* She then revealed another intimate thought. *It isn't hormones, it's the stars that make love happen.*

They smoked a joint. That over with, abandoning herself to deep exhilaration, Shirley took control. *Come with me.* Nearby stood a thicket of large rhododendrons. On hands and knees she crawled in like a toddler at play, the vice-consul following. It was peaceful underneath nature's canopy. The acid rock was muted. Diffuse light filtered in. The waxy leaves afforded the privacy of a tent. With one smooth, practised movement, Shirley slipped her top off, mesmerizing Hanbury with the beauty of her breasts. Shirley took his reflection as a faltering, as an expression of male responsibility. *It's OK. I'm on the pill.* Her tight jeans came off quick, panties joining a scanty heap of clothing. The vice-consul now joined in. He was quickly naked too, following which some of the techniques acquired on Savignyplatz came back. He felt he was putting in a credible performance. Afterwards, Shirley wanted to know something. *Where did you learn to fuck like that?* Hanbury didn't want to get into a discussion on Berlin, so he said, "Picked it up on the prairies. You're pretty mobile yourself." Underneath the rhododendrons, this compliment led to a lengthy enumeration of Shirley's lovers.

A few days later, Shirley, her interest piqued in a vice-consul who was both slightly timid and very worldly, knocked on his door. The apartment was spartan and she liked that. She also fell in love with the stereo. The record collection, on the other hand, failed the inspection. *You have weird tastes. You listen to this stuff?* Shirley declared she'd fix the problem. Tony needed exposure to the best music there was. To help the cause, she moved in. Sort of. Her presence in the apartment was off and on. It was determined by galactic signals that only she could read. *We're both free to come and go*, she ruled. *Also, neither asks who else the other's fucking. OK?*

At the office, a new consul general, an intellectual with a close-cropped beard, picked the vice-consul's brain on the local scene and was impressed by what Hanbury knew about the anti-war movement in the universities. He wanted the vice-consul to accompany him on calls to keep notes. He also instructed his young assistant to attend political events. Hanbury was suddenly busy, day and night and often on the weekends. This caused things to switch around in the apartment. Shirley was there more than Hanbury, often waiting for him to come home. *I hung around 'cause I thought you might like a piece of tail*, she'd say, making it sound as if she were offering him some leftovers from dinner. She smoked a lot of hash alone, which made her moody.

One day, a federal cabinet minister came to San Francisco to give a speech. The vice-consul was responsible for logistics, from the VIP arrival at the airport through to a night out on the town. It went well. Cars arrived on time. Doors opened when they should. There was an audience for the speech. A couple of journalists asked a few questions about a crisis in Quebec. What's going on in Canada, they wanted to know, and what the hell is all this about a War Measures Act? The minister loved the attention. He invited the consul general and the vice-consul to join him for dinner in a restaurant of their choice. "Up to you, Tony," the consul general said. "You know Frisco." Hanbury proposed a restaurant in Chinatown.

When Hanbury arrived home to change, Shirley was sulking. *You're always out. Stay home. Smoke some dope. Have a fuck. Listen to the Grateful Dead.* When Hanbury was quietly leaving for dinner, she was sprawled on a large, bean-filled leather bag before the stereo, not a stitch on. It hurt her to see Tony go out dressed in a clean, freshly-pressed blue suit. She shouted after him, *You're a fucking pig.*

The dinner was a great success since the minister had a sharp eye for girls and the restaurant was full of them, mostly office girls on holiday from places like Boise, Idaho, Sioux City, Iowa, and Pierre, South Dakota. The minister winked and nodded and ordered waiters to serve the girls wine. The consul general smiled benevolently. The vice-consul also thought it was fun. After dessert, the minister, beginning to look greedy, said, "Time boys. Time." He shifted a knowing gaze towards the consul general, who redirected it to Hanbury. Both men looked questioningly at him. After a pause, something dawned. Hanbury caught a waiter's eye. "The bill please," he said, "and a taxi."

"You sure?" the minister said incredulously. "No problem with timing?"

"No problem, Sir," the vice-consul replied.

"He knows his way around, Minister," the consul general added.

"Well I'll be dammed. That's incredible," said the minister. "All previously arranged, eh? OK. I get it."

The taxi arrived before the bill. The consul general and the minister went out. Hanbury lingered to arrange payment. Some girls two tables over smiled freely. He sent them a graceful nod, then hurried out. His dinner companions were nowhere to be seen. "Two men leave in a taxi?" he asked the doorman.

"Yassuh. Daddaway."

"They say anything."

"Nope. Wanna taxi?"

"I'm OK," he said to the doorman. There was nothing to do but go home. He thought of Shirley, doped up, spread out on the floor, and took a slow route on foot. Shirley was where he had left her, now snoring. He threw a blanket over her. A few hours later when he left for work, she still hadn't stirred.

"Don't bother with the minister and the airport," the consul general said severely the moment Hanbury got into the office. "He just called. Said he'll find his own way. Sounded angry. Said he'll complain. What happened?"

Without much sleep, a haggard Hanbury needed time to decipher. "What happened?" he said. "What do you mean what happened? Nothing happened. You were with the minister. I paid the bill. When I went outside, you were gone. I went home. Do you know how many bottles of wine he sent into that restaurant? Twelve. Not plonk either. It busted my credit limit. Did he leave some money with you?"

Now the consul general had to let things sink in. When the picture was in focus, he sighed, closed his eyes and shook his head. "Tony," he murmured, "where have you been? Why do you think he was sending wine to all the girls? He wanted them. Some of them. My guess is three or four were game. They were ready to go."

"Where?"

"Where do you think?" the consul general said with exasperation. "I left him waiting for you in the hotel bar. He expected you to bring the girls along. I relied on you to fix it."

"No one said anything about that. I understood he was tired. I wondered why you didn't wait."

The consul general turned and disappeared. Two days later Hanbury was summoned. "He's complained," the consul general said. "Fairly vicious. Claims unacceptable protocol lapses. I explained your side to Investitures. They're inclined to side with you, but they've already assured the minister heads will roll. You can't stay as if nothing happened. You're being reassigned. That's it. Nothing more to say. Life in the Service. Let me have the restaurant bill. I'll launder it through hospitality."

Within days Hanbury learned he was on his way to Washington, demoted to doing passports. No more ministers to be entrusted into his care. Before leaving, he paid three months rent and confronted a sluggish Shirley. "Nothing I can do about it," he said. "Part of the job." Shirley took it fairly well. *I've thought about you a lot. I feel sorry for you. You're not in touch with your feelings. I thought I could change you, get you to relate. But you're sick. You need treatment.* The stereo was bequeathed to Shirley, plus all the home furnishings she ever wanted. Hanbury took with him his clothes and weird records.

⁂

While Hanbury escaped from Shirley, Sabine was cementing things with Werner. During the days they went their different ways, but they connected in the evenings. Sometimes Schwartz came home late. "*Na endlich!*" she would say fretfully. *At last!* She was relieved, yet couldn't hide an undertone of anger. Although Schwartz liked Sabine's fussing if he was late, he didn't understand it and said so once or twice. Sabine wanted to tell him about Savignyplatz, but the right occasion, the right moment never came. The specifics were fading in any case. Lingering were occasional outbreaks of terror which she didn't want to admit having.

Schwartz acquired a teaching position at the University, in History. Sabine took a job at Geissler's. Schwartz used his connections to acquire a bigger apartment on Fasanenstrasse. More of his family furniture came out of storage. Historical portraits of his forbears graced the walls. A large front room became the library. There was a salon, a dining room, spare rooms for guests. They hosted parties. Sabine developed the art of asking his friends interesting questions. That, together with her moody eyes and a habit of not rushing guests, made her an admired hostess. Everyone wanted a few minutes with Sabine.

Everything was beginning to work out. Even marrying Werner Schwartz was working out. In her blissful rush, Sabine paid no attention to remarks by Martina that Schwartz's friends were all of a type – strong-willed, clean-shaven and focussed excessively on success. She once summed them up. "They have a self-confidence that has no basis." Then she became blunt. "Speaking frankly, your husband and his friends strut about like perfect Germans, even though its been proven that we are not an especially remarkable race." Sabine thought Martina was wrong. Her husband didn't strut. He was moving up with a kind of gliding motion, with tranquillity and ease.

Hanbury, after San Francisco, was not moving up. He got shunted sideways. Bunkered down doing passports, he avoided further mishaps. The new stereo he acquired was the finest to date. After Washington came some years in Ottawa, this time living on a quiet street in the Glebe. The landlady insisted on peace and Hanbury used earphones if he wanted volume. Chopin, Liszt, Schumann: fine music for a withdrawn world. At work he dispensed, as Service jargon had it, *beneficences*. He was a member of an underrated sect helping Canadians abroad who have fallen on hard times. Canucks jailed for smuggling alcohol into Saudi Arabia, or smiling at veiled eyes in Tehran, or observing military convoys with too much interest in Ghadafi's Tripoli – the burden of solving all such personal disasters throughout North Africa and the Middle East sat on his shoulders. Problems from all over came his way. A flood of problems. Some days he thought he was getting to know every worried parent between Belle Isle Landing in Newfoundland and Clayoquot Sound in British Columbia.

His mother's funeral in Indian Head was an interlude. At the burial, the soil scientist seemed unmoved, mumbling it was better this way. Hanbury had an evening with Keystone, who told stories about the awesome power of the latest diesel locomotives.

Hanbury's stay in Beneficences was a long one. He was a quiet, credible solver of other people's problems. *Low key*, the Beneficences priest recorded. *Does the job. Could go places if he showed more zip.* Investitures sent him to Cairo, then, as second secretary, consular.

In Cairo he developed a taste for Arabic music. At first he thought it sounded like wailing from a madhouse, but it grew on him. Most evenings in his penthouse flat on an upper middle class street overlooking the Nile, dressed in an Egyptian gown, incense burning, chewing bitter leaves, Hanbury had private concerts which began with a half-hour of Arabian lament, then came back to European music. In those days his taste ran towards Stravinsky, even Schoenberg. *The Rite of Spring*, listened to after a couple of hours of chewing, made him jerk and twitch. He loved his time in Cairo. Only one event interrupted the routine. Eileen from Toronto was spending February there, after January in Istanbul, and prior to March in Greece. Her passport was stolen in the Suk, she said. She swore an oath before the second secretary that she was who she said she was, after which she and Tony compared Egyptian experiences. They went out a couple of times and decided to make a trip together, a few days up to Luxor. She summed up the experience in a postcard from Athens two weeks later. *Thank you for showing me Elysium!*

After Cairo came Caracas and another interruption, this one more serious. Hanbury slid into an affair with Anne-Marie, cultural officer at the French Embassy. At first, innocently, they lunched once a week, then he saw her in the evenings and finally spent the nights in her bed. After a few months, Anne-Marie suggested a vacation on Martinique. Hanbury did a mental calculation (a quarter of a year before his next assignment) and said sure. They passed two weeks on the island as a carefree couple. The holiday was a real success. When Hanbury's time in Caracas was up, the last night with Anne-Marie was subdued. *C'était bien*, she summed up. Hanbury replied, *C'était comme Elysium.* Anne-Marie agreed. *Oui, c'était comme ça. Tu as raison.* Hanbury departed for Kuala Lumpur. A few weeks later Anne-Marie was reassigned to Pretoria. Their correspondence petered out.

❦

In Berlin, Sabine bore a son. His name posed a problem because her husband wanted his mother's family, Prussian nobility, to be reflected in the given names. He proposed *Philip Pöllnitz Schwartz*, arguing that his maternal grandfather, Philip von Pöllnitz, a renowned Junker, deserved to be honoured. For balance, he suggested that Sabine's father could be in there somewhere too. As in *Philip Pöllnitz Albert Schwartz.* Sabine, still in an immediate post-natal state, was horrified. "*Nicholas*," she said. "I've always known if I had a son, he would be *Nicholas.*"

"There's no *Nicholas* in either of our families."

"That doesn't matter. It's a beautiful name."

Schwartz sternly insisted family precedent mattered. When Sabine began to cry, he said they would talk about it further.

Sabine continued to insist on *Nicholas* and opposed using a family name as a given name. First they agreed *Albert* would be the second name. Sabine, holding firmly to *Nicholas*, offered *Nicholas Albert Philip Schwartz*. In her husband's opinion that was putting his grandfather too far back. An understanding was reached that *Philip* would be first choice for an eventual second son. "Or *Phillipa*," said Sabine. "I wouldn't object to *Phillipa* if it's a girl." "We'll see when the time comes," Schwartz said, sounding reasonable, but irked that his son would carry the name of a Russian czar.

❧

In Kuala Lumpur Hanbury became first secretary with new responsibilities, politically and socially. No more doling out beneficences to snotty kids. In Kuala Lumpur he would be doing political work – *administering the sacraments* – full time. He sent off *Notes Verbales*, visited influential Malaysians in their offices where he slipped them delicately phrased *Aides-Mémoires*. He enjoyed going with the high commissioner to *tête-à-têtes* with leading politicians. His status brought with it a house in a large garden full of tropical trees. Birds in the trees squabbled like playground children while insects hummed primordially. Some weekend afternoons Hanbury was so entertained by nature in his garden that he forgot to activate the stereo.

One lazy Sunday afternoon, having been served iced tea by the Malay cook and listening to a delightful interplay of shrill cicadas and shrieking protests from tropical birds, Hanbury had an insight; nothing spectacular, merely a recognition of some existing facts. Passing through his field of vision, in an area roughly midway between the terrace and the luxurious red and purple bougainvillea hedge, was a parade of loving smiles from women he had known. They seemed so real that the bodies to which the smiles belonged could materialize at any moment.

145

Reflecting on this spectacle of love, Hanbury realised how lucky he had been. The smiles could be grouped into two camps: Sabine and Shirley who had moved in, and Eileen and Anne-Marie who had not. It was no coincidence that parting with the latter two had generally been more amiable.

This distillation of experience remained at work far back in his mind, nearly in the region of the subconscious. It was still there when he met Birgit, a descendent of the blondest of all the Vikings.

The high commissioner liked to send his political first secretary to represent him at social events. In a crackling voice he gave the young man wise advice. "Make sure you receive more than you give," he warned. "Listen much, talk little." Hanbury was doing so at a dull drinks party given by the *chargé d'affaires* from Sweden when Birgit breezed in late. Hanbury was fondling a glass of cold aquavit in the presence of his Norwegian opposite and two visiting academics from Stockholm. The Scandinavians believed the world was on the verge of unspeakable horrors, and heatedly discussed which of the many was the worst. Hanbury was about to stroll to another corner of the room when Birgit, who knew the Norwegian, sidled up. She was a conversation stopper. Global horrors were forgotten. Two drooling academics wanted to know what she was doing in Kuala Lumpur. Were it not for the divine blondness of her hair, the playful eyes of fading blue and lovely well-formed lips, Hanbury would have moved along, but he was as hypnotized as the others. Birgit was saying she was in charge of a project, funded by a Scandinavian Trust, to study the role of women in South East Asian society. The Scandinavian men around her replied they found that interesting. They said they were fascinated by the subject.

The background music at the party changed from syrupy Hollywood film scores to something symphonic. Hanbury's ears pricked up. "Sibelius," he said with child-like excitement. "Violin Concerto, third movement."

"Not at all!" objected one of the academics disdainfully. "Tchaikovsky, surely."

"I think it's Grieg," said the Norwegian.

"This is fun," Birgit said, directing her diamond-glittering eyes at Hanbury.

The host was asked to referee. He read off the back of the cassette. Hanbury had it right.

"Are you American?" she asked.

"Saskatchewan," he said.

"Canada," the Norwegian explained.

"Located between the Atlantic and the Pacific," confirmed Hanbury. "Good Sibelius country. We keep hoping one day someone like him will come along."

"Fatuous nonsense," said an academic.

But Birgit enjoyed it. Later in the evening she sought Hanbury out, her smile undiminished. "Are you a music expert?"

"Actually not."

"Where did you pick it up?"

"A place called Indian Head. And you? You're from Stockholm?"

"Further north. Kiruna. Above the Arctic Circle."

"So we're practically neighbours."

Birgit said she loved music and could play the flute. "I *sort of* play the flute," she added carefully. Hanbury let on that he *sort of* knew his way around on the piano. They compared notes on musical training before talking about places they knew in Malaysia. The party was ending. Hanbury, who had the high commissioner's car and driver, offered Birgit a lift, but she had her own car. "I was going to offer you one," she said.

"Perhaps next time," he suggested.

Outside in the tropical night, Hanbury waved to Birgit as the chauffeur opened his door. She waved back, her eyes such perfect reflectors of light that it seemed two space-age beams of blue lit up the driveway.

Some days later she phoned and talked about an institute outside the city which promoted women's cooperatives. An afternoon of international cultural events was being arranged. Birgit had agreed to play something on the flute. She asked if Hanbury could accompany her on the piano. "I haven't played for a long time," he cautioned. "It must be over twenty years. My fingers might creak." Birgit said that generally would be the standard. Hanbury imagined Birgit's lips breathing life into a silver instrument. The vision was compelling. "Don't expect much," he warned. "Not from me either," she laughed.

Birgit did the driving. The piano at the women's institute was an upright, a badly out-of-tune affair. Hanbury had never played on anything like it. Also, time *had* stiffened his fingers. But it came, the old feeling came. The effortlessness returned. Chords came back and he spun them out, hands floating over the keys, steadily more quickly and smoothly, back and forth, hypnotically, like surf breaking on a beach.

"Jesus," Birgit swore.

"It's got a very heavy motion," he complained about the piano, then banged out the first few bars of a Chopin étude. "Dancing with a windmill would be lighter."

"I'm not unpacking my flute," Birgit said. "You do the whole show." But she relented, and they practised a bit. She sent delicate streams of air into a gleaming instrument. The combination of the silver flute, the light blue in two concentrating eyes, the unbelievable blondness of her hair and the rustling of a light silk dress was better, Hanbury thought, than anything chronicled in the Norse myths. She was close too. Had he reached sideways, he could have touched her knee.

The cultural afternoon unfolded with élan. Canada's political first secretary was a hit with the ladies. Twice they insisted that he play something solo. "You were the only one with talent," Birgit said afterwards when they speeded back to Kuala Lumpur. Hanbury noticed she liked driving fast. "Maybe," he replied, "but my talent is lopsided. You're an all-rounder. I don't even know how to drive." A laughing Birgit took the next roundabout even faster. "Dinner?" he inquired, but she had something on. Birgit then suggested he come to her place for dinner next weekend.

It wasn't what he had imagined. Birgit's small flat was full of people. The Norwegian was there. So was the Swedish *chargé* with a wife who wore her hair in braids. Several smiling Indian and Malay women with whom Birgit worked had brought their hungry husbands. All evening long a World Bank economist, a loud man of little humour, declared disgruntlement with Malaysia's oligarchy. Birgit, in a deep-blue, floor-length gown with thin shoulder straps, was a perfect hostess. She kept her guests in drinks and repeatedly led them to the buffet.

"I still owe you a dinner," he said upon leaving.

"Don't worry about it," she said.

"I'll call you."

Hanbury thought of having her for dinner at his villa, on the terrace, surrounded by night sounds. But he decided otherwise. They went to the Hilton. A Filipino band was featured. In between courses they danced. He jerked his arms and, from a kind of crouching position, swayed his upper body. Birgit on the other hand possessed an infinite reservoir of slinky movements. She was as happy and excited as a girl on a first date.

They were seen together regularly the following weeks – all over Kuala Lumpur – in restaurants and discotheques and in the brand new shopping centres. They were also together where they could not be seen, in Birgit's small flat. Birgit was persistently platonic and Hanbury was very patient. Eventually he asked a question he had been formulating for weeks. He managed to deliver it casually, in the same way Anne-Marie had suggested Martinique. "Why don't we fly to Singapore?" he said. "Spend a weekend. Have a look around."

Birgit stopped smiling, saying she couldn't. She should have told him earlier. She had a husband. "And for all I know you've got a wife somewhere," she added.

"I'm married to my career," he quipped, making light of the situation.

More news followed. Birgit's husband, Olaf, was coming for a holiday. Hanbury said that was wonderful. He was sure she was looking forward to it.

In his villa that night, Hanbury's mood was strangely leavened. He attributed this to the music of Bach. Upon departing Birgit's flat, he had decided to listen to Bach.

Two months later Hanbury was spending a Sunday afternoon on his terrace listening to Russian composers. He had placed the speakers outside where they competed with Malaysia's jungle chatter. Unexpectedly, Birgit appeared. "I came by to see how you're doing," she said. The blue of her eyes lacked lustre. Hanbury hurried inside to turn down the volume and arrange tea. She poured her heart out. Olaf's stay had not been a success. He had been pessimistic about their future should Birgit remain abroad. "His mother is behind it," she said. "She's a dominating woman. She demands that he visit her every day." Olaf's mother, it turned out, had criticised Birgit from the beginning and continued to find fault with her after the wedding about such things as the irregularity with which she did the laundry. "It's like a prison in Stockholm. I can't stand the thought of going back. My work here isn't finished either." Hanbury agreed it was a difficult situation. After tea they had a gin and tonic.

"You have a nice house," Birgit said.

"I always thought your place was better. It looks lived in."

Birgit said she was glad he liked it and invited him for dinner the next night.

Dinner for two. Simple. Quiet. As they stood up to clear the table – Hanbury subsequently replayed the scene in his mind a hundred times – Birgit made an elegant half-turn towards him, light blue eyes transfixing his. She took the plates out of his hands. Her lower lip began quivering. They embraced. Birgit nestled against Hanbury's shoulder; he clasped the small of her back. Then began the slow descent of a zipper. In the stillness it sounded like a long subdued note coming off the A string of a violin. Hanbury would never forget the sound of helping Birgit shed her dress.

In the course of the next weeks a love routine became established. One evening on Birgit's bed, both of them wet from exertion in uncooled, moisture-burdened air, she asked why they were always in her flat. His villa was much nicer. It wouldn't bother her to wake up there and have breakfast on his terrace. "The atmosphere is artificial," Hanbury replied. "The furniture is awful. You have so many lovely Asian crafts on the walls. My place is pretty bare." She offered to help him improve the decoration, but he argued it was pointless. "No sooner does the stuff hang than I'm reassigned and it has to come down." A slight movement of air passed over their bodies. Hanbury was on his back; Birgit hovered over him on an elbow, one breast resting against his chest. An edge entered her voice. She said that in some respects he was a cold person. Sometimes she thought he was holding back. It frustrated her.

"It shouldn't," Hanbury soothed. "What we have is fine. It couldn't be better."

"It could."

"Birgit, let's be realistic. In a few months you're going back to Stockholm. I'll be reassigned. Let's enjoy the present."

"I don't want to go back to Stockholm. I think I would be happier living like you – moving around, having new experiences."

"It looks better than it is. Let's enjoy what we have." Birgit thought about this, then rolled onto her back. Later, Hanbury got up, dressed, kissed her and took a taxi home.

The following evening they were invited as a couple to a dinner party. "Sorry about last night," Birgit said casually as she drove. "I didn't mean the things I said. I got my period this morning."

After the party she drove him to his villa, declining the offer of a nightcap. In the weeks that followed, although outwardly the affair continued, they both knew its inner mechanics were deteriorating. Birgit departed before her time in Kuala Lumpur was up. She didn't say whether she planned to re-enter Olaf's prison, or was determined to make a fresh start.

Hanbury missed Birgit. Until Olaf's visit she was a good friend, and afterwards a keen lover. On the other hand, he was convinced someone like Birgit would not be happy living an empty, zig-zag life like his. True, she had expressed anxiety about facing years of tedium with Olaf, but for someone like Birgit a life spent on the move would be at best a temporary solution. Eventually she'd realize she was on the run. She'd want to stop. At the end of the day, for her, someone like Olaf was better. Hanbury was convinced of it. It was a good thing she hadn't moved in with him.

He spent the remaining time in Kuala Lumpur listening to Mozart's music. With a warm glow he marvelled at its regenerative power.

※

As Hanbury retreated extravagantly into fresh self-containment, Sabine was determined to acquire a modest reduction in her working week. She wanted to quit Geissler's bookstore before Nicholas was born, but her husband talked her out of it. Keep your options open, he counselled. So she proposed a one-year arrangement to Geissler, involving the wife of another professor to replace her. He grudgingly agreed.

Schwartz had a reason to urge his wife to stay connected to Geissler's. Rare books fascinated him. Shortly after Sabine went to work at Geissler's, she brought him a copy of an unknown, privately published diary kept by a functionary in Bohemia from 1934 to 1938. It described how the Nazis came in and took over. Schwartz was excited. Where did it come from? Out of the cellar, Sabine replied. Geissler brought it up in a basket with other books. What else was in the cellar? No one knew, she said. The door was permanently locked. Schwartz appeared at the bookstore the next day. His wife showed him around and introduced him to Geissler, whose eyes darted back and forth – from the professor, to the books, to Sabine – before he shuffled off. He assumed his customary observation post by the front door. Schwartz followed. "I'm a professor," he said. "I would like to see your stock. It could be of interest to me."

"Stock?" an alarmed Geissler said.

"Stored books. Books not on display."

"Leave my store," Geissler ordered. "Don't come back." Swaying awkwardly, as if a fugitive, he made his way to the back, hiding in the darkness until the front door jangled shut.

Schwartz gave detailed instructed to his wife on how to spot more volumes like the one from Bohemia. Periodically she came up with one. "What else is in that cellar?" the professor would mutter.

From Malaysia, Hanbury returned to Ottawa. Investitures assured him he had earned respect in Kuala Lumpur. They would respond in kind. "Know Irving Heywood? Ever heard of him?" the clerk asked.

Hanbury raised and lowered his shoulders and shook his head. "Ah. See. You've been in the wilderness too long. Heywood's a rising star. The Disarmament Priory is hot. Your next stop. His understudy."

Disarmament was a bewildering terrain. Hanbury acquired the habit of slouching at his desk, rubbing fatigued eyes with his fingertips, combing hands through his hair while he pondered solutions to bureaucratic battles. The sounds of the daily ordeal were of the telephone ringing non-stop and Heywood's voice trumpeting. Some days it seemed he was standing before the walls of Jericho.

"No corner of the Service is as vital for the future of democracy as the Priory," Heywood confided to Hanbury at the beginning of their five-year partnership. Heywood described the main currents of thinking in disarmament theory since the Korean War. Hanbury listened, but his thoughts wandered back to the sounds and smells of Malaysia.

The Priory drained its members. It sucked them dry. Husbands were too tired for their wives; mothers became estranged from their children. Late at night, in an apartment overlooking the Ottawa canal, Hanbury listened to Gregorian chants. He could cope with nothing else.

PLAYING COWBOY

A few weeks after calling on the Chief of Protocol, the consul's social life went through a subtle transformation, as a prairie wheat field does when the ripening begins – everything was as before, except the hue. For no reason Hanbury could discern, at least not then, the quality of the daily invitations began changing. More and more of them, according to Frau Carstens, were unusual, in a class apart.

In the early days of his assignment Hanbury trooped from one devastating engagement to another. The celebration of diplomatic arrivals and departures were among the deadliest of the forays. "National day" receptions – bloodless, irrelevant events – ran a close second. Art exhibition openings were a dime a dozen. Luncheon invitations piled up, from clubs with lacklustre speakers on parochial topics: *Daimler Benz, New on Potsdamer Platz and on the New York Stock Exchange: German Industrial Might Revitalized.* There were musical events too, in the large eastern European legations located with a kind of we-still-own-Berlin prestige near the Brandenburg Gate.

Routine events attended by listless crowds. Sturm once observed in his inimitable way that the diplomatic corps was about as interesting as a collection of worn out boots.

The Chief of Protocol, playing an artful role, was the agent lifting Hanbury into a different social strata. He told a media friend about the latest diplomatic arrival's new-world freshness, which resulted in a published newspaper interview accompanied by a good sized portrait. To a dowager, a patron of the opera, he whispered the name of the striking new consul in town, a bachelor. The news spread like a prairie fire. Similar remarks were made to financiers and business moguls. No one in Berlin took the Chief of Protocol's observations lightly. And so it was that blue ribbon parties began crowding humdrum events out of Hanbury's program.

One such event he attended was a surprise thirtieth birthday party – drinks with a light dinner following – for Elisabeth, the wealthy great-granddaughter of a minister in the Kaiser's Imperial Cabinet. Von Helmholtz was her godfather. The list of the party's invitees carried his stamp and Hanbury, having met Elisabeth once before, was on it. The guests assembled in a palm-filled conservatory in a Grunewald mansion and waited for her to arrive. In the absence of a host – von Helmholtz had not yet come to weld the party together – a tension mounted. People stiffly held their glasses, tipped them frequently and looked past each other. Hanbury, his interview having just been published in the paper, was feeling buoyant and told someone standing close by a disarming anecdote about a missing diplomatic bag. "Missing? The diplomatic bag?" The astonishment was expressed a little loudly, and the attention of the whole group shifted to the consul.

"That's right. It didn't arrive." He grinned. "It caused so much commotion I thought I was in the middle of a cattle round-up." He shook his head as if it was all quite unbelievable. "Telephones lowed like cows," he added capriciously, "and the fax machine neighed." A titter rose above the rain clattering on the glass roof. Solicitous inquiries were immediately made as to whether the diplomatic bag, that cult object, had in the end been located. "Oh yeah, we lassoed it," a laughing consul reassured the guests.

The metaphor seemed to relax the gathering and a group conversation began. From missing diplomatic instructions the talk turned to the diplomacy of Bismarck. Someone described the chancellor's extensive use of diplomatic couriers and his full control over instructions sent to ambassadors. Bismarck's one-man-in-charge approach had been a good thing, someone said. It brought Germany an extended period of peace. This subject – Bismarck, strong leadership, the start of Empire – really warmed the group up, and when the transition from politics to personalities took place the conservatory filled up with historical anecdotes expressed so loudly they erased the patter of the rain.

The Chief of Protocol arrived just before his goddaughter. The surprise was then sprung on her, and a rich buffet opened with rare wines freely pouring from crystal decanters. Hanbury spent some time next to a woman called Sophia, not a great beauty, but possessing a disarming willingness to talk about herself. She worked for the Treuhand, the agency putting East Germany up for sale. Sipping wine, sampling caviar, and under cover of a polite exchange on the clean-up costs of a socialist economy run into the dirt, she and the consul eyed each other. Eventually they agreed to get together sometime for lunch. The consul next sidled up to a woman who was Elisabeth's doctor. She informed him she was thinking of quitting medicine to seek a seat in Parliament. For a while they discussed how far the right wing could go in Germany before alarm bells would ring.

The party was shifting into high gear. Guests reclined on velvet sofas and dangled glasses from their finger tips. Hanbury continued his professional rounds, searching out people who might be of diplomatic use, acquiring their names to pass to Frau Carstens. In the course of the evening, someone whispered to the Chief of Protocol that the consul, with his charming accent and delightful sense of irony, provided an exotic touch. He helped get the party started. Von Helmholtz listened and said he was not surprised. Later, after the consul had chatted politely with the birthday girl, von Helmholtz pulled him aside. "We're always running into each other," he said, "but we seldom talk. Let's change that." Could Hanbury come for dinner? Could he keep next Friday evening free? The consul said he would be honoured.

When Hanbury left the party and came down the vast front steps, the Opel wheeled up smartly. Driving off, Sturm said, "Had a good chat with the other drivers, Herr Konsul. Quite a house. There's something on there every night. The Chief of Protocol is there often. Makes you wonder how he does it, where he finds the time. His driver and I are starting to get on well since we see each other often now. He's been driving von Helmholtz for a decade. I learned tonight his wife died tragically years ago. Did you know that?"

"No." Hanbury knew little about von Helmholtz's personal life. "How did she die?"

Sturm half turned to the back seat. "A disease. It came on quick. When she was gone he began to work like a demon. There isn't an hour in the week that isn't programmed. Apparently he likes meeting younger people."

Hanbury yawned. "That rules me out."

"Not sure it does, Herr Konsul. It doesn't seem to."

"I've never seen him with young people."

"Not *young* people. *Younger* people. That rules you in."

"It's doubtful. I only meet him at formal functions with invitations that come by mail. And since you open the mail, Sturm, you know about what I'll be doing before I do."

The chauffeur felt accused. "It's my job to open the mail," he said with a prickly undertone. He changed the subject. "I had a glimpse of that Elisabeth *von Sumplace und Sumwhere* when she arrived. She was silhouetted for a moment at the top of the steps, before all the cheering and the singing started. Perhaps it was the light, but she struck me as very thin. If she had stood there naked I think the wind would have whistled through her ribs."

"Sturm!"

The chauffeur waited for more reaction, but there was only silence. He tried again. "All of us saw it. We agreed that's how she looked – ribs like strings on a harp. The drivers are good men, Herr Konsul, professional at passing time. One of them this evening claimed his wife was an angel. You know what another one said? He said, *You're lucky. Mine's still alive.*" Sturm detected a faint chuckle. "The same fellow told us about a friend who said he had just become a father. *The wife doing well?* someone asked the new father. *Sure,* he said. *She doesn't know about it yet.*" The polite rear-seat chuckling was a little louder. "They've got a sense of humour," Sturm said about the drivers. "I hope your talk inside those mansions is as good as it is outside."

Hanbury thought about this. He thought about the doctor, Sophia, and Elisabeth. "It was delightful," he said.

Now Sturm did all the talking, mostly light gossip. Hanbury knew the chauffeurs had few secrets and, as the Opel passed through opulent neighbourhoods in the midnight stillness, he decided to keep von Helmholtz's dinner invitation to himself.

The next day Sturm produced the log for Gifford and was peppered with questions. No, no unexpected stops on the way. Yes, it had been routine at the mansion. No, the consul made no unusual remarks, except – wait a minute – he hinted he suspected someone was tampering with his mail. Yes, he had gone directly home. Yes, he was alone. "And he didn't burp or fart, in case you want to know that too." Sturm was irritated by all the pumping for trivia.

As the chauffeur was being cross-examined, Hanbury received a direct call from von Helmholtz's office with information on the place and time for the dinner. He instructed Frau Carstens to decline a conflicting invitation to a sporting event, claiming he needed an evening at home. Frau Carstens, who loathed all sport, agreed this was wise. The information was passed to Gifford, who instructed Sturm that on Friday night he could stand down.

❧

That Friday the weather was miserable. Gusting winds sent cloud banks scudding by all afternoon. As darkness fell, the city was attacked by sheets of rain. The consul rode in silence in a taxi to the Dahlem address. The street was difficult to find; the driver stopped twice to consult a map.

What did the Chief of Protocol mean when he said an impromptu dinner for some friends? Two hundred guests in black tie? How many more people, Hanbury asked himself, could he meet before they'd blur and become totally interchangeable? Contacts, contacts, contacts. Frau Carstens was insatiable. Every hour of the day seemed devoted to scheming and making more contacts. Some days he felt she whipped him on – as if he were a tired workhorse hauling an impossible burden. Hanbury hoped this dinner would be small. For once it would be nice to remember at the end of the evening the guests he met at the beginning.

The Chief of Protocol's villa was nestled behind tall evergreens. The front door opened as he walked up. Inside, a butler helped him with his coat. Von Helmholtz came into the vestibule. "You found it."

"Sorry I'm late." Hanbury noted the absence of the sound of two hundred babbling voices. The house was dignified and still.

Von Helmholtz took him into a sitting room where his other guests, six of them, nested agreeably around a coffee table. The introduction of the consul over with, they went back to anecdotes about their previous summer's vacations. Hanbury listened to the camaraderie and stole glances at the women. Lovely women, veiled more than dressed, reposed in comfortable chairs, wearing thin silky materials plunging at the front and back. One of them – with her size and shape he was sure she was a fashion model – wore an exquisite lavender minidress. Hanbury's attention shifted to the room. Paintings were crowded together on the walls. It came as no surprise that von Helmholtz was an art lover, but why so many landscapes? Meadows in spring, dramatic forests, lakes between mountains, strong skies. Pretty paintings. Von Helmholtz saw Hanbury studying them. "My wife," he said. "Most of them are hers. I love the countryside and she did too. Shall we go in for dinner?"

The table was round. Hanbury sat directly opposite the host. A chandelier hung low so that the light fused the group into a warm conspiracy. Von Helmholtz rose and began to speak.

"I once heard a story about a caliph who remarked that although he had a thousand friends, he had not one to spare." His voice was introspective. "With the many intrigues in the caliph's court no doubt he needed all of them. I don't have a thousand, but those I have I treasure. I too have none to spare."

Before-dinner speeches are opportunities to express what otherwise is merely thought. The dinner table was still. Where would von Helmholtz's remarks take the guests? They waited, scarcely hearing pots distantly clanging in the kitchen.

"I met all of you professionally, but we soon reached past that. We went through the professional veneer. I value that." Von Helmholtz asked them to listen to a quote from Longfellow.

"Art is long, and Time is fleeting,
And our hearts, though stout and brave,
Still, like muffled drums, are beating
Funeral marches to the grave."

The guests absorbed this. The silence remained immaculate. The host's drift was, if anything, becoming more inscrutable, not less. Von Helmholtz began to talk of art, of Longfellow's view of art, how it reaches into the future. He implied that artists, through their work, acquire immortality. How do we measure up, he seemed to be asking, or rather, how did *he* measure up? Some guests thought he was saying he had lived a life devoid of art, that he was hearing muffled drums, that soon his friends would be all he would have left and without them, without them remembering him, he had no chance of reaching beyond the grave. The guests, trying to fathom if this was his meaning, didn't move a muscle. But if a gate to some secret garden of vulnerability was creaking open, in the next instant it resolutely clicked shut. From one breath to the next, the sentimentality in von Helmholtz's posture disappeared. In the muted chandelier light, he drew himself to his full height. He shifted grounds, beginning to describe the times. He called them alienating. Reason enough, he said, echoing the caliph, for being careful with one's friends.

Von Helmholtz looked them over. His attention lingered on the slender woman wearing the lavender minidress on his immediate right who, Hanbury saw, was the least solemn at the table. Her faint smile at the silver-haired aristocrat had a touch of amusement. It seemed to say he deserved full marks for dramatic effort, but was this the right occasion? She had some influence on him, because von Helmholtz met her eyes and immediately shook off his introspection. He began narrating stories of crossed paths and the web of events which brought them together that evening. Cordula, a theatre director, Viktoria, in charge of Berlin's heritage office, Jürgen, a writer, Anna, a designer, Richard, a lawyer married to Viktoria.

Von Helmholtz went around the table introducing each guest. The name of Hanbury's birth place, Indian Head, was mentioned. "I found it in the atlas," von Helmholtz said. "A dot on North America's Great Plains. I have a passion for studying maps of continents. 'How do people live there?', one asks. What are the customs and traditions? What characterizes the landscape? When Consul Hanbury told me about the prairies, I visualized people spread thinly over a vast area, living without limitations." Hanbury wasn't comfortable with this focus on his home town. He never thought that Indian Head was a place to be idealized, to be seen as some kind of earthly paradise.

The host turned last to the teasingly bemused, black-haired woman on his right, Gundula Jahn. Hanbury was sure one of her forebears millennia ago must have been a model too, sitting for one of those perfect, priceless Greek statues. The expression of irony etched around her eyes said she viewed everything around her as a spectacle to enjoy. She was new in Berlin also and wouldn't be at this dinner were it not for German reunification. Von Helmholtz said she was a journalist and described her talent, the first East German reporter hired by the largest paper in West Berlin. "I can always read what's on Gundula's mind," he added fondly, a hand rested lightly on her shoulder. "The first thing I do every day is turn to her column." The friendly mockery in the journalist's smile intensified.

During dinner Hanbury observed that von Helmholtz's hand occasionally touched Gundula Jahn's, massaging it, letting go. The touching scenes came and went. Young people, Sturm said, that's what he likes. The dinner conversation, as always in Berlin, turned to Berlin. Berlin then, Berlin now, and Berlin to come. Viktoria, sitting beside Hanbury, guardian of the city's heritage, talked of its architecture, what was gone, what remained, what would come. He admired her strong facial features, auburn hair and a bare shoulder so close he could brush it with his own. She talked about the extraordinary decade of transition now in full swing. Living in Berlin was like being in a newsreel, Viktoria declared. Endless, fascinating footage day after day.

Richard, her husband, had a bullying appearance. He attacked East Berlin, which he said was filled with buildings that resembled bunkers. "It's incredible what the East Germans destroyed," he said. "Take one example. They destroyed the Kaiser's Palace because they couldn't separate architecture from politics. The French Revolution didn't blow up Versailles. The Bolsheviks didn't take down the Kremlin. But the East Germans blew up the palace. A country that dynamites its heritage dynamites its people."

"The palace was bombed in the war," Gundula Jahn said. She had been quiet until then.

"But it could have been saved," Richard countered. "It could have been restored. Had Stalin slept there once they would have kept it. They wanted a big square in East Berlin – like Red Square in Moscow – for the May Day parades. That's why they blew it up. I'm for rebuilding a replica. We need our traditions back."

A debate on this and related issues was in full swing. "Why?" Cordula said suddenly, coming out of a slouch. "Why?" she repeated loudly. "Why would we want that palace rebuilt? I don't find that part of the past too edifying. That's the problem here. The past is too recent; it hangs over us. We're dwarfed by it. Ever thought about all the patched bullet holes on the Reichstag? Do we need those kinds of reminders every day on every street? There's only one solution to this problem. Run away. I vote we run to Consul Hanbury's country. Let's be dwarfed by nature for a change."

A silence settled as this perspective was digested. Von Helmholtz, who had been leaning back, came forward. Having seen the fires of war in his youth, night after night, block after block, everything going up in flames, he talked of the fickleness of urban landscapes. Without warning, he turned to Hanbury. "And what about towns on the Canadian prairies? Tell us about Indian Head." Hanbury was taken aback, unsure where to start. "Yes," said Richard sarcastically. "Indian Head. *Indianerkopf.* What happened? Did the cavalry charge and decapitate the savages?"

"Oh no," Hanbury answered pleasantly. "That kind of thing happened further south. No, no. The name is taken from a nearby butte, the forward edge of a small range of hills. When the sun rises above the horizon and the butte lights up, it has the profile of a head. The Indians called it that. They used it to spot buffalo." Viktoria's husband scowled, seemingly disappointed no blood had flowed. Hanbury continued. "The prairies are always changing. One day they're barren and cruel, then they become like the garden of Eden. Strong contradictions. People get addicted to it. No place for Berliners. It's too wide open." He looked at Richard.

"You underestimate Berliners," Richard replied coldly.

Gundula Jahn's gaze had been shifting back and forth between Hanbury and Viktoria's husband, but now came to rest on the consul.

"You must explain, Tony," von Helmholtz interrupted. "Cruel landscapes? Garden of Eden? A touch dramatic?"

"I'll tell you," Hanbury said feeling the journalist's steady, marble-chiselled gaze. "Imagine a place so flat that the horizon circles around, the feeling of being on an ocean where space is difficult to define. And no reference points, apart from a river valley here or there cut out over the millennia. The horizon is the boundary. Where's the horizon in Berlin? The façade across the street?"

"Nothing wrong with a façade across the street," Richard said.

"I'm explaining why some people here wouldn't cope with the openness there."

"But you're the exception," said Cordula lazily from deep back in her chair.

"An exceptional man, no doubt about it," mocked Richard.

"Go on," said Anna, the designer who had said little. "Tell us more."

The consul shrugged. "There's not much more. Well, there's the climate. One year it's paradise, the next, the land shrivels up. Scorching heat in summer. No limits to the cold in winter. The only constant all year round is light. In winter the light is so hard you think the sky will crack. Even at night there's light, the northern light, dancing light. Colours leaping through the sky reflected on the snow. What's light like in Berlin in winter?"

This forced a pause. Wine glasses were refilled. The party sought a new topic. Richard's combativeness had been filed down and he was quieter. It seemed Anna was the only one who didn't want to depart the notion of wide open spaces just yet. "I would like to go to a place with light like that. I've always wanted to go to Russia to absorb its soul. But maybe it's simpler to go to your prairies. Do they have soul?"

"Soul!" said Cordula rising up once more. "That's my favourite subject. Good theatre is pure soul. Good actors need ample soul. And fine directors have magnificent soul." Cordula's energy gathered. "I want to mention another kind of soul – soul as a weapon that goes to battle for others. I know only one person who has that kind of soul. Gerhard, a toast to you." Von Helmholtz protested, but seven glasses pointed in his direction. Following this, they retired to his study where a relieved Hanbury wasn't pressed to answer Anna's question about prairie soul.

The party was ending. Viktoria was the first to say she was tired and departed with her husband. Cordula asked that a taxi be called and shared the ride with Jürgen and Anna. Soon, only von Helmholtz, Gundula Jahn and Hanbury remained. Together they engaged in small talk. Suddenly it dawned on Hanbury that the two would want to be alone. "I had no idea it's become so late. I'm sorry." He wanted to call a taxi too.

Von Helmholtz saw no need for the consul to rush off. "I'm a night owl," he explained.

"I can give you a lift," Gundula Jahn offered. Hanbury, confused by this, didn't immediately respond. He was about to remark it would be a bother when von Helmholtz said, "Accept, Tony. I would." He shrugged and mumbled thanks.

At the door von Helmholtz kissed Gundula on both cheeks and shook the consul's hand. Walking towards Gundula's car, Hanbury said the air had become chilly. She agreed. "At least it's no longer raining," he said, "but it's damp. Look at the halo around the streetlight." She sent him the same, amused, full-marks-for-trying look von Helmholtz had received. Across the street a small square car, a little box on four spindly wheels was waiting. "This is it," she said. "Ever ridden in a Trabi?" She got in, reached over, and undid the other door. Crouching down, squeezing in, Hanbury said, "No, but better late than never. Years ago I visited East Berlin a few times, but had no chance to ride in a Trabi. If I'd got in one, I'm sure the Stasi would have arrested me, plus the person taking me along. Isn't that the way they operated? Were you ever arrested?"

"Not arrested," Gundula said softly. "But they spied on me. I've seen my file. It's thorough."

Hanbury wanted to ask more. But in the night's cold damp the motor wouldn't catch. Gundula turned the ignition key repeatedly. "I actually like this car," she said, "but it's really shitty when it doesn't start." She turned the key a few more times and beat the gas pedal to the floor. The motor turned over pointlessly. As the battery emptied, the sound became a slow sick breathing, and with a last groan the machine was dead. "Shit," Gundula said, hitting the steering wheel with both palms. "Shit, shit."

"I'll give you a push. We used to do that all the time in winter in Indian Head. The winter made people feel they were part of a collective."

"How wonderful," Gundula said sarcastically. "There's only you here. Hardly a collective."

"Two is all we need. I push, you steer. When I yell you let the clutch up. OK?"

The Trabi was light and the road had dried. Even in dress shoes, Hanbury had enough traction. Gundula steered down the middle of the road, the consul yelled, the Trabi bucked and heaved, but the motor caught. Gundula raced off. At the end of the block, she turned around and made her way back in first gear. The Trabi made an uneven, tinny noise, the sound of something sick coughing into an empty drum. As the motor sputtered, clouds of smoke pulsed out the back. "We could have used you in the GDR," said Gundula, all smiles.

The consul felt on top. "Collectivism has its moments."

"That's not funny," laughed Gundula, driving off.

"When I first saw you this evening, I took you for a BMW woman," he said. "All the women in Berlin who look like you drive silent BMWs. I guess they want to feel power, but not hear it."

"I like my Trabi," said Gundula.

"What does that mean? Lots of noise; not much speed?"

"That's mean."

They were soon driving through the blackness of the Grunewald. The Trabi was beginning to produce some warmth and the defrost was making progress. The car's comfort wasn't much, but Gundula's company made up for it. She said, "Good thing you took on that Richard. Why are lawyers like that? It doesn't matter where they get their training: East, West, they all turn into shitheads."

"Some of them are nice enough," Hanbury said, thinking of Müller.

"The ones in the East were bad. They didn't even stick to the law. So you're from some place called Indian Head. It made me think back to my childhood. I liked stories about Indians."

On the city autobahn, Gundula pushed her Trabi to the limits. It clattered like a skeleton. Over the noise, the consul asked if it needed a tune-up, maybe a ring job.

"A what?" asked Gundula just as loudly.

"A ring job," Hanbury called above the noise. "You're burning oil!"

"It's supposed to burn oil. It's a two-stroke engine."

"That's for lawnmowers."

"Lay off," laughed Gundula.

Near the exhibition grounds, Hanbury gave directions for leaving the autobahn. When they turned into his neighbourhood, Gundula said she'd never been to this part of town. She lived on the other side, in East Berlin.

"You're welcome to come this way anytime. That's my place."

"A lovely house."

"A bit small. I'm supposed to entertain. It isn't big enough for that."

"Squeeze them in. It's cosier. Well, good night. Thanks for playing cowboy."

"Next time I'll wear my boots," Hanbury said, getting out.

He wanted to ask her other questions – about a childhood spent reading Indian stories, about her relationship with the Chief of Protocol, about her Stasi file – but he had time for only one. "Tell me," he said leaning down into the car, "talking about being spied on by the Stasi, ever heard of somebody called Günther Rauch?"

"Of course," Gundula said. "Everybody's heard of Günther Rauch. He was famous for a while. Good night. And thanks again for pushing." She revved the engine. Blue smoke spewed out. Hanbury slammed the door. As the Trabi disappeared, the acrid smell of half burned oil lingered in the air.

OLYMPIA

ast of Berlin, sixty kilometres away runs the Oder River, an idyllic waterway which the Allies decided should be Germany's new eastern border in 1945. The land is relatively flat, an exception being a ridge not far from the river. German defenders massed here as the war was ending; thirty thousand Red Army soldiers died getting to the top. From there, their run to the capital of the Third Reich was unhindered.

A different age.

The geography that once allowed the Soviets to shift their tanks into high gear is also good for cycling, and weekend racers attack the landscape like a Tour de France. It isn't only youth that's burning up the roads. The over-sixty crowd is out too, like Albert Müller, except he's over eighty. Shortly after the Wall came down, the Eagles claimed the roads winding from village to village east of Berlin. Since the distance from the Oder to the Olympic Stadium in Berlin is a good day's run, they organized a race. Every autumn now, old men in a thin line streak through the Brandenburg countryside. Fifty years after the Russians, they're the ones encircling Berlin. The event, *To Olympia*, helps them fantasize they're still in their prime.

Albert Müller didn't simply fantasize when on his bicycle. He also had a brutal wish to win, despite most of the competitors being twenty years his junior. He wasn't the oldest Eagle. Scrappy Rudi Metzger, club *doyen*, admittedly in good shape for someone past eighty-four, would take the *Oldest Rider* trophy – from Müller – by eight months. The year before they were both junior to the legendary Ulli Schmieder, eighty-six. But Ulli contracted a cold that spring and passed away. Rudi and Albert joked about their age. "You're too fast for me," Rudi would say to Albert. "But that's fine. What you're really beating me to is the grave." This year Müller felt fit, better than last year when he placed twenty-third. His training was peaking; he wanted victory; he had a chance. Who cared about Rudi's predictions that beyond the finish line a grave lay in wait?

"Come and watch. Take my picture," Müller said to Hanbury. They had resumed their old habit of tipping a few glasses of *Pils* in *The Tankard* once a week. On the Thursday night before the race they sat in the same corner as before, as if there had been no intervening years. "Take my picture when I slip the winner's jersey on."

"You don't have to win," Hanbury said. "At your age finishing is pretty good. I couldn't do ten kilometres, let alone a hundred."

"Not a hundred. A hundred and fifty." Müller sounded irritated. "Your problem is you're not ambitious. It makes you likeable, but you'll never get anywhere. Why set your sights low? Me, I've got a few things to do before my ashes get scattered. *Prost.*"

The starting point for the race was the village of Hohenwutzen near a bridge crossing the Oder to Poland. In the first years after the Wall came down the race was an obstacle course. Brandenburg's roads were disastrous. Bike frames got bent, wheels twisted, limbs bruised. The competition ended in darkness. But once Western money poured in the roads became smooth as laminated tennis courts. This year's race would be hours shorter.

On the morning of the race the Eagles and their equipment arrived in Hohenwutzen in the early hours in trucks and minibuses. It was still dark. A soupy fog hung over the river. Poland on the other shore seemed not to exist. Silently, like a commando group, they checked their bikes. Drinking bottles were fixed; watches set. As the hour neared, they took positions on the edge of a nearby ditch. Old men no longer pee fast and this essential ceremony took some time. Standing there, featherless scalps hunched between shoulders, looking less like eagles and more like buzzards, they pumped themselves up as they emptied their bladders.

"That's morning coffee for you. Drink one cup, piss two."

"You drank coffee this morning? What an adventurer! My old lady serves me warm milk. Coffee's bad for the ticker. It goes crazy."

"So what's wrong with that? Use it as a metronome. Get your legs going. That way you might win!"

"*Win?* What's that? A new drug from America?"

"Hey, Rolli. The last time we stood like this was when we were prisoners of war in Russia!"

"That was different. At that latrine, I remember, we always pissed *into* the wind."

"They wanted us to savour the aroma of defeat."

"Defeat? That's done with. If it weren't for the fog, the Slavs would faint seeing what we've got on show."

"Mine, sure. Not yours."

"I'm talking about my prick. You're talking about your prostate."

Up and down the line, Eagle solidarity bounced around in salvos.

Müller, next to the doyen, heard him grunting. "Easy Rudi," he cautioned. "Push too hard and you'll eject your bladder."

"Rudi needs a catheter."

"Tied to his saddle."

At eighty-four Rudi was good at ignoring things he no longer wished to hear. When he finished, he croaked out a pep talk. "Go Eagles! Let's soar!"

Having shaken themselves dry, the racers did a round of knee-bends, some stretching of stiff joints, and a half-hearted warm-up by running on the spot. Track suits came off. Paunches in tight racing pants bulged out above naked legs. Finally, silhouetted against the light strengthening over Poland, they shook hands. They waited for the shot. Punctually, at eight-thirty they were off. The bunched field quickly thinned into a line taking a south-west course towards Bad Freienwalde. From there the route would be the same sweeping half circle around the north of Berlin that had been taken by a fast advancing battalion of Soviet armour during the final assault in '45. Ulf and Rolli had been taken prisoner at the time.

Through marshland and pine forests, past ancient forts, under gates in medieval walls, skirting the concentration camp at Sachsenhausen, around military camps still full of Russians, the Eagles would eventually come to the city's western approaches. In the late afternoon the fastest riders would be streaking down Heerstrasse, heading towards the stadium. By then Müller, according to his plan, would be in the lead.

The line broke up into packs. A spry sixty-five year old, Horst Baumann, was out front. Müller's strategy was simple. Stay in the first five, resist the temptation to go into a sprint – until Heerstrasse – then pedal like a demon. But that arrogant Baumann was setting a fast pace. The sky was angry and a head wind gusted from the west.

The rhythm of legs pumping creates an hypnotic state. The mind turns from the competition and starts a conversation with itself. For many riders, speeding through a landscape that was forbidden to them after the war, scenes of its final days came back. Actually, bits and pieces of the war were always coming back – every day. Rushing like the Soviets when they powered their way into Berlin, most of the Eagles couldn't help thinking about where they were, and how it was, when the war was ending.

Ulf and Rolli were hustled off to Russia. So were Ludwig, Gottfried and some others. Many more Eagles had been on the western front which had a higher prisoner survival rate. Four hadn't been POWs at all. Their politics had been wrong, so the Soviets threw them into concentration camps recycled from the Nazis.

On straight stretches, the mind turning inward, the Eagles raced against more than each other and the weather. They entered into combat with demons from the past. Müller, doggedly four back from Horst, had his trance too. Born in nineteen-o-nine he had nearly the whole damn twentieth century to remember. Too much for one brain, he often thought. The end of the first war, the abdication of the Kaiser, the socialists seizing power, the conservative backlash, the Weimar Republic launched with fanfare, though it had no staying power. There were the mad days of hyper-inflation during the twenties. The thirties brought the brownshirts and the second war. Then the transition to the Cold War. Four decades of Cold War, the final two providing the best years of the century. In the seventies and eighties, life in West Berlin had been a fairy tale.

A mountain of distracting memories. And, Albert thought, damned unhelpful too. He forced his concentration back on the race. Horst was setting a fast pace and pressing from behind was Gottfried. Who does Gottfried think he is? Does he think he deserves to be near the front because he's only seventy? Work for it Gottfried. No one said it would be easy. Not this race.

※

Hanbury did as Müller had asked. On Friday, he rummaged through unpacked boxes and found a camera. On Saturday, he armed it with film. He also bought champagne, which was cooled all night. On Sunday in the afternoon he started out for the Olympic Stadium wearing his technicolour hiking shoes, which were already showing signs of heavy use.

※

The staff had adopted the habit of looking at the consul's feet. If he wore the suedes they knew he planned to be away. *Reconnaissance*, Hanbury sometimes called it. Sturm referred to it as *Selbstmord*. Suicide. "Herr Konsul, with all respect, in those psychedelic sneakers you're a marked man. If word gets out it's a diplomat wearing them, you'll be crushed to death by the crowds wanting to see for themselves." Gifford was especially solicitous if the suedes were on. "Going any place in particular, Tony? Can we assist?" And the next day. "Saw anything interesting? Met useful people? Don't forget the contact list. Put them on. We'll soon start the Christmas card effort." On a high-tech cushion of air, the consul roamed through fascinating places – Prenzlauerberg, the Scheunenviertel, Pankow – all of them moody, all of them stuck between a desire for transition and a deep reluctance to change.

Hanbury didn't mind Gifford asking about his plans, but seldom replied. They had more important things to talk about. Gifford, that management genius, was fashioning extraordinary change. The office was being redone from one end to the other. And the computers had arrived. Once they were unpacked and wired up, Gifford proposed shutting the consulate for two days. For familiarization and training, he said. The hallway became a classroom and the administrator turned instructor.

"This is how they're turned on," he began. The ladies hesitated, worried the machines would bite, but their courage grew. They began stroking certain seductive keys not found on typewriters – *page up, page down, typeover, delete.* Frau Koehler loved the escape key. Why didn't a key like that exist in real life, she asked. Gifford took them repeatedly through the basics, regularly adding a new twist. "Like ballroom dancing lessons," tittered Frau Carstens, thinking of her girlhood. "Every week we had another step."

More than the others, Sturm grasped the machines' inner logic. As the ladies felt their way forward, he plunged directly into word processing. He pecked away with two fingers. A laser printer whirred. Gifford took the sheet coming out. "What's this?" he asked. "Mine," replied Sturm. The administrator read it.

A leaf falls from a tree,
The wind touches the water,
The lovers sleep.

"Herr Sturm!" cried Frau von Ruppin. "I had no idea!"

"Japanese poetry," he said awkwardly. "I came across some in the paper last weekend. No wonder nobody understands the Japanese."

Frau von Ruppin protested. "It's beautiful. It's sensitive."

"Copy for a deodorant ad, if you ask me," replied Sturm.

By the end of the second day Sturm was experimenting with a spreadsheet for the car log and Frau Carstens was getting the hang of a macro for the preparation of the consul's schedule. Other software was bestowed on Frau von Ruppin and Frau Koehler. With the simplicity that defines great moments, Gifford then declared the electronic office open. The consul was applauded: it would have been unthinkable, they told him, without his impetus to modernize.

"Well done, Earl," he said to Gifford later. "Two days well spent." They were in Hanbury's office. Gifford was on the floor connecting wires that linked the consul's computer to the telephone system for access to databanks, stock exchanges and other real-time information. "No problems paying for all this?" the consul asked. "All tidy, Tony. Ample spending authority. Computers don't cost much nowadays." Gifford got up, his face red from the exertion. He pressed a few keys. The screen woke up. Graphs, tables, information bulletins – the whole universe it seemed – flashed by. "The world is at your fingertips," he said. Trying the buttons himself, Hanbury asked about progress with the new residence. "Going well," Gifford assured him. "A week or two and we'll do some viewing."

"No problems with the money aspects?"

"None. Headquarters understands you're not well-housed. They know it's a good time to invest. They recognize where the future lies."

"High time they did that. I appreciate what you're doing, Earl."

Gifford left the consul, returned to his desk and initiated a series of tests. No one knew the computers were linked into a network which he controlled. He searched out Frau Carstens's macro; instantly it appeared. Tests with the other work stations were equally successful. Spectating made easy, grinned Gifford.

At home too, the atmosphere couldn't be better. Frieda had been ecstatic over a new diamond necklace. All evening, wearing nothing but the diamonds, she ran around the apartment. It was, she said, to concentrate Giffy's attention on the light the gems threw out. Her nudity was infectious, so he joined in. Frieda hung the necklace over his erect penis. "Now *all* the family jewels are together," she cried. They became wild with desire. Afterwards, Frieda admitted she understood now why Gif was having to spend so much time at work.

Frieda had her diamonds and he had a Mercedes. Not an every man's Mercedes, but a big 600 model. Outside the city on the ring road – that masterpiece of engineering by Germany's finest autobahn *artistes*, that space devoid of limits – he'd take the car to 250 KPH. For years he'd wanted to own the autobahn's left lane, streaking up on cars incapable of doing more than 190, flashing headlights, scaring drivers out of their wits, sending them swerving to the far right. Stay there forever, Gifford's grin commanded as he accelerated past.

Diamonds for a woman and a fast car for her man. The computers were in. Soon the consul would have a mansion. Life was unfolding as it should. Gifford estimated a few more weeks of working the market would do it, a few more deals, a few hundred thousand more skimmed off the margins. When the proceeds amounted to five million it would be time to quit. Keeping the long string of buy and sell transactions hanging together – the diplomatic seal preventing the precarious edifice from tumbling – required nerves of steel. A couple of times he resorted to tough language. *I represent a sovereign state. It's assets are thirty million taxpayers and a chunk of real estate that's the second biggest in the world. And you doubt this statement of intent?* The pressure was without precedent. No one should want to do this for a living all the time, he had concluded.

Satisfied with the computer tests, he departed for the club. The military guard saluted when the big Mercedes drew up.

"Hello Earl," Randolph McEwen sang through lips that scarcely moved. "How are you? Trust the family is well?" Gifford said things had never been better. Over their first pint, McEwen gossiped about developments in the Allied Powers Coordinating Committee, now enlarged by an outwardly friendly Russia. "It's agreed the occupying powers will leave Berlin, but who goes first? We think it should be the losers of the

Cold War." McEwen peered at Gifford over the rims of half-glasses. "Funny, isn't it, Earl?" he mused. "The Russians knew more about us than we about them. They should have won. But they lost. That's why we think they should get out of Berlin first. Not co-temporally. Not jointly. But *first*."

Gifford nodded.

"There was some soggy mumbling by the Hun," McEwen said darkly. "Shouldn't there be just *one* goodbye party, he said. As if we – us and the Russians – are family. But that won't be. All the same, it's creating a spot of work. The Hun has a rather ponderous mentality. He likes things written down." McEwen shook his head in disgust. "Well, over to you, Earl," he said, brightening once more. "What's the latest with Friend Tony?"

Gifford took a long, thoughtful sip. "Some things are going well, very well indeed, Randy. Others, to be frank, continue murky."

"Who has he been seeing? Anyone of specific interest?"

"I think so." Gifford pulled a paper from his pocket. "Fascinating pattern. He meets people. The names go on the contacts list. He invites them for lunch. All quite proper. But look who, Randy. It's of absorbing interest I'd say, for him to have so many friends so suddenly in high places."

Gifford read through the list, the functions of the people on it, the locations where the consul met them. Top bankers, prominent jurists, illustrious politicians, well-known artists, big name impresarios, influential industrialists. Reviewing it took Earl and Randy into a second pint.

"I'll take that." McEwen stretched out a proprietorial hand. "I doubt it contains much of *real* interest, but we shall check. Anything on the unofficial side, Earl? Visits to cosy out-of-the-way flats? Long walks in the Grunewald with individuals unknown? Anything of that sort?"

"A little short of help on that side, Randy. As I said. It's murky. Sturm keeps the car log, but there are holes. I have asked the consul about his free time, but he is reserved. How did the weekend go, I ask. Listened to music, he says. Farfetched, I think. Don't you? Listening to music. The whole weekend."

"Your driver Storm…"

"Sturm."

"Quite. Sturm. Has he reported anything?"

"I mentioned last time. Sturm won't play. No change in that. He did say the consul voiced suspicion his mail is being monitored. But overall, not much comes out. Sturm complains about his silence."

"And is it? Is Friend Tony's mail monitored?"

"Not really. Not yet. Not unless you want it."

"We're not quite ready for that yet. Still, he suspects it's happening. Proves he has something on his conscience. Most regrettable – the chauffeur not helping."

McEwen sank into thought. He closed his eyes. His head fell to his chest. It shook slightly, almost a shivering, as he created and rejected the options he knew from a lifetime of weeding out duplicity. McEwen's instincts told him something was waiting to be discovered, but identifying it required resources and his were disappearing fast. He came to a reluctant conclusion. He would have to approach Pullach, obtain the support of Graf Bornhof. So deep in thought that he looked asleep, McEwen's face turned hard.

When he stirred, Gifford spoke. "Three areas stand out where we need more information. Speaking frankly, I don't know how to get it. I'm reluctant to hire an agency to monitor. Some things a diplomatic mission shouldn't be seen to do."

"Of course. Of course," murmured McEwen. "Three things, Earl?"

"First, Thursday evenings stand out. He seldom accepts engagements then. Sturm takes him home and stands down. Fridays he looks the worse for wear, as if he's been out late, possibly carousing."

"Every Thursday evening. How remarkable. A secret society?"

"Second, he continues to go walking, always in East Berlin. He makes no secret of it. Once he let the word *reconnaissance* slip. But reconnoitering what? Why solely in East Berlin? It nags, Randy, it nags. And third, weekends. Who knows what he's up to on weekends? It's difficult to accept he listens to music two days straight."

McEwen lifted his pint slowly to his lips. "I shall have to think Friend Tony through more thoroughly," he finally said. "He's more complex than I suspected. Anything else?"

"Yes. Proceeding nicely on the other fronts. The computer network is in. Tests were good. I can access his work now. Might stumble on something."

"Helpful," nodded McEwen. "Very helpful."

"And arrangements for a residence are nearly final. The effect is as predicted. His confidence is increasing. Only this evening he expressed gratitude. Intimate chats are just around the corner, I think."

"Good. Do keep up with the house. We shan't cut corners."

"Indeed, Randy. Imagined that would be your view."

"Some news from my side. The Beavers are on side, eager to assist. They are worried about their man here. As I would be. I shall be in Pullach next week to work on other matters with Uncle Teut and I will raise these vexing indicators surrounding Friend Tony. We may need a little of his help. The tedious fact is, Uncle Teut tends to question everything, always wants more information. Extraordinary how the Hun's mind works, Earl, wanting to see the ultimate result of an operation before he can bring himself to launch it. Of course, he has had his setbacks, throughout the whole century really..." McEwen emptied his glass in a joyless way, as if mourning someone's passing.

The next day, Gifford sat down with Hanbury to practice the telephone dialling software. "A marvellous time-saver, Tony," the administrator said enthusiastically. "Click here and an index pops up. Click a name and you see everything you need to know about that person. Click here if you want to call. The rest is automatic. Your phone buzzes when the connection is complete." The consul, Gifford sensed, was impressed. "This chap here, incidentally, has been helpful finding you a new house. Reliable. Eager to assist. We shall have a short list soon. Then comes the viewing."

"Do what you think best, Earl."

"See the beauty of the system? Try it. Makes you feel on top of things."

"I will. Incidentally, I'll be out this afternoon. Scheunenviertel."

"Shouldn't Sturm accompany? Rough part of the city."

"I'll manage, thank you."

Back at his desk, Gifford punched a code into his computer, entered the network, clicked a few commands and accessed the consul's C drive. He scrolled through and experienced a rush when he saw the consul had created his first file.

❧

The Scheunenviertel was a suggestion from Viktoria. She mentioned this quaint neighbourhood to Hanbury at von Helmholtz's dinner and afterwards sent him a pamphlet with a map showing the places of interest. The afternoon was marked by sporadic, slashing downpours; the consul's suedes turned into sponges and water crept through to the inside of his coat. But he scarcely noticed. Trekking through cemeteries he studied names on Jewish gravestones in one, and of Huguenots in another. He discovered the places of eternal rest of famous personalities: Hegel, Fichte, Schinkel, Heinrich Mann, Bertolt Brecht. Nearby in Oranienburgerstrasse the New Synagogue with its restored gold dome stood resplendent, as if the rain had cleansed it. Under an overhang, he read in the pamphlet that the Scheunenviertel, the barn quarter, when it lay outside the city walls, sheltered vagrants, beggars, swindlers, forgers and whores. Jews thrown out of principalities further east came along, so that centuries later it was a location where the Nazis did some concentrated killing. After the war, communism's disinterest brought on a slow decay. Roofs collapsed, stucco peeled, mortar leaked from between the bricks. And now, the smashed windows, like diseased eyes, seemed to look onto a world whose future had resided deep in the past.

The consul also saw that despite socialism's wreckage the pride of former builders still clung to the raw masonry, as Viktoria had said. Cornices from Rome, columns from Corinth, cherubs from the baroque. No wonder she had ruled that every brick would be protected. She was also right about a phalanx of artists now moving in, supported on the flanks by second hand bookstores and utilitarian drinking halls.

That same afternoon, it dawned on Hanbury that the Scheunenviertel could be a neighbourhood for Günther Rauch. Gundula said he had been famous. What did that mean? Was he dead, maybe buried five graves over from Bertolt Brecht? Or was he hiding out, living in a cellar hovel, behind a door miserably slung forward from one hinge? Hanbury also concluded that a house to house search for him in the Scheunenviertel was not really practicable. In contrast, locating Gundula after the dinner party had been easy. One ring of her extension and he was through. "Cowboy!" she exclaimed, surprised. It seemed she expected him to have disappeared into the sunset forever. He asked if they could get together. Lunch? "Why not," she replied. "I'll invite you. The paper has a club, or is that too ordinary for you?"

Hanbury had begun reading Gundula's columns. In the Trabi she had been vivacious and on the phone she was breezy, but her columns were otherwise. Her descriptions of social problems were thoughtful, sensitive and moving. They read like a struggle to define compassion in a post-socialist world.

Sopping wet, his head full of both Günther Rauch and Gundula Jahn, Hanbury entered a dive on Auguststrasse to warm up. Stools stood around on a wood floor; dripping candles furnished light. Near the bar some locals sat around in sleeveless T-shirts, tight pants and jackboots laced up. Some had shaved scalps, others were decorated with tangles of hair in the Iroquois style and streaked green, or purple or pink. Hanbury went to an empty corner. Busying himself with mopping up his dripping head, he was a pathetic figure, a sort of shrunken postman. They took no notice of him. A girl came sauntering over from behind the bar. Her eyes were set so far back in their sockets that she resembled a survivor of the Black Death. He asked for a double espresso and a brandy. When she returned, she pointed out he was a little wet. Not smart to be out today without an umbrella, he admitted. She heard an accent and a conversation began. Where was he from? What was his business in Auguststrasse? Hanbury made up answers as they went along. He claimed he got lost walking in the direction of the University.

"You're a professor?"

"Indeed."

"A lost professor?"

"Yes, quite lost."

"Absent minded too?" Her laugh was hollow.

"Occasionally, yes."

"The burden of knowing too much?"

He said he hoped that one day that might indeed be a problem. Speaking of knowing things, given this interesting neighbourhood, could she tell him something?

"What?"

"Do you happen to know a Günther Rauch?"

"*Natürlich.* But of course." He was well-known. A legend. A fighter for freedom.

"Does he come in here to drink?"

She didn't know, since he'd never been pointed out to her, but if he did it would not be surprising. Men of greatness, huge legends in their time had lived all around Auguststrasse. Unlike some clients nowadays, she said, motioning to the jackbooted conspiracy behind her. Actually she heard Günther Rauch's name mentioned as recently as last week. There was an anniversary. Something he did, a storming of some citadel of evil.

Hanbury asked more questions, but she had no answers. He ordered more brandy. In such weather, apart from an umbrella, the next best thing is an overdose of spirits, he told her. The girl repeated the word overdose, gave a shrill laugh and went to get the bottle. Once he felt warmer in his gut, Hanbury got up to leave. At the door, he heard the girl shout from behind the bar. "Hey, professor, you writing a book on Günther Rauch?" "No," Hanbury shot back. "I want to ask him about another legend. He used to tell me about a friend of his – Karl, Karl Marx." "Ah, that one. He turned out to be a disappointment." The locals looked up, sensing an alien presence, but the foreigner had gone.

Günther Rauch lives, Hanbury thought triumphantly, and this could be his habitat. But how to penetrate it? Gundula Jahn? Her columns explored life in environments similar to this one. Could she help?

❧

Hanbury wanted to mention the Scheunenviertel to Müller, who knew such places from his youth, but it was pointless. That night in *The Tankard* the old man had been fixated on the race. Even when Hanbury promised he would take pictures at the finish, Müller had nodded gratitude, but hadn't shaken his tightness. He kept drumming the table with his fingers. And now, camera ready and the chilled champagne wrapped in a towel in a bag slung from his shoulder, Hanbury arrived to record the moment.

The finish line on the mall before the Olympic Stadium consisted of two poles with a banner strung between showing two fierce eagles and the title of the race printed in bold letters. When Hanbury walked up, friends and families of the racers were already waiting. He had time to kill and strolled into the stadium built for the '36 Olympics. Two-thirds of it is dug into the ground. From a distance it's a low oval of repeating square columns that gives an impression of power. Inside, ground level turns into a bird-like perch high up. Rows of seats funnel far down to the track. Walking around the oval, Hanbury retraced steps he once took with Sabine. She had told him about the Games, pointed out the box where Hitler sat, and stopped before the mural with the names of the gold medal winners chiselled into stone. "Count the number of times you see Jesse Owens' name," she had ordered.

In the distance hands began clapping. Hanbury hurried back to the mall. The crowd had grown. The first finishers were in. A wreath had been hung around the neck of the victor. A TV camera followed him. Hanbury worked his way through to the banner where ancient racers were being mobbed. He looked for Müller. Grandchildren were being hoisted onto tired shoulders, cameras clicked, home videos whirred. Admired by the young, the geezers strutted like young cocks. This was how they wanted to be remembered.

Hanbury counted the Eagles that had landed, but lost track at twenty. He proceeded to the forward fringe to watch the ones still coming in. Figures continued appearing in the distance, legs pumping, heads low, leaning into a final sprint. Some riders, nearing the finish, reared up and raised their arms in triumph. The crowd clapped; families cheered; grandchildren waved flags. In this scene of general happiness Müller stepped off his bike. He hadn't raised his arms or punched the air with a balled fist. He came in unobtrusively, looking passive, as if he'd just completed a boring errand. Hanbury worked his camera. He took a picture from thirty meters, another underneath the banner, one or two as Müller got off his bike. Müller was out of breath and unsteady on his feet. Hanbury kept snapping. A woman and a man began congratulating the old Eagle, patting him on the back. Holding the champagne bottle ready for uncorking, Hanbury moved up to join this little circle.

"Albert. Well done. You did it," he said. The woman holding Müller affectionately by the arm turned.

During the days and weeks that followed, this moment played itself out in Hanbury's mind so often that it broke up into a series of still shots.

Hanbury froze, as Sabine did. He recalled afterwards that his immediate thought was that she looked the same. The eyes were moody; the face had its sensuous, smouldering passivity; she seemed preoccupied with the gravity of everything. Sabine said nothing. She looked at Hanbury; she looked at her father; she let his arm go. Without a word she turned and disappeared into the crowd. The three men watched her go. Müller, still out of breath, took a moment, then made a spiralling upward motion with his finger accompanied by a swooshing sound. A rocket going up. At the apogee his hand opened and descended in an arch. Fireworks exploding. He shook his head, as if disgusted. Afterwards he said that, yes, he had been that, but it was disgust at his pathetic performance in the race, not his daughter's behaviour.

"You two haven't met," he said at last. He introduced Consul Hanbury to Professor Schwartz. "You two should have a lot to talk about, seeing you have Sabine in common. Excuse me while I change my shirt." Each viewed the other. Hanbury sheepishly held up the bottle of champagne. "A glass?" He worked the cork in silence until it popped, filled a plastic beaker, passed it to Sabine's husband, then did the same with another. "To Albert," he said. They drank with civility.

"Excuse me," Schwartz finally said. "Who are you?"

"Not what you think."

"What am I thinking? I'm not thinking anything. How do you know my wife? Are you a client in the bookstore?"

Hanbury said he knew Sabine a long time ago when they were students.

"She didn't seem happy to see you."

"I imagine she wasn't expecting me. A shock."

"A shock? I see. And why are you here?"

"To take photos."

Schwartz ignored this. "Albert said you are a consul. British?"

Hanbury described his position.

Müller returned in a training jacket and with a towel thrown around his neck. "I see you've become friends," he said. Schwartz excused himself. Hanbury passed Müller a beaker of champagne, which the old man downed in a gulp. "Hold the bottle high," Hanbury said, steadying his camera. The ancient Eagle looked into the camera, but without much triumph. An element of gloom clung to the crevices of his face.

ANARCHISTS

*O*nce the Iron Curtain was gone tens of thousands of people from Eastern Europe began filtering into Germany each month to claim asylum. But, in truth, it was the prospect of welfare which drew them, more than political freedom. Spending a few weeks on the run, sleeping a night or two in a forest, crossing a river in a leaky rowboat before arriving in Germany – minor inconveniences on the way to a social stipend ten times the average wage in Romania.

The reaction of Germany's far right was a brutal whipping-up of fears that the foreigners grabbed jobs, took away good apartments and, worst of all, would eventually dilute German blood. The backlash took the form of Molotov cocktails lobbed into asylum seekers' shelters. Accompanying all this was an increase in the desecration of Jewish graves and the defilement of monuments that serve as reminders of the Holocaust. Deep inside the German forests, neo-Nazis practised occult rites. Journals around the world ran stories that questioned whether Germany reunified was slipping back into nationalism, political violence, xenophobia and all the other things that had happened in the thirties.

Von Helmholtz, grim-faced, was alone. It was late. An official dinner for the Danish foreign minister had been marred. The man made an off-the-cuff remark in his dinner speech, reminding everyone that Hitler wormed his way into power while the German elite watched from the sidelines. Hitler's treacherous invasion of Denmark was not forgotten, the minister said. He asked uncomfortable questions about the current situation. Guests shifted in their seats. Later, the Chief of Protocol took the Danish ambassador by the arm, saying the remarks were unhelpful. The ambassador nodded gravely. A digression, he explained. Not part of the prepared text. He would ask Copenhagen for clarification.

The appearance of deterioration – fire-bombings, right-wing thugs assaulting foreigners, a pattern of light sentences for convicted neo-Nazis – had to stop, von Helmholtz decided. He also knew the real right wing danger was subtler. It lay with ordinary people incapable of changing from the old way of being German. A symbol was needed, something effective, to influence German attitudes and turn the tide of world opinion. After dinner, having seen the foreign minister to his hotel, von Helmholtz went to his office to conceive a plan. Towards midnight he dictated a three-page memorandum onto a tape. One page, for the police, outlined the need to get tough; another, to the courts, urged sentences that would deter; the third was for the media. He wanted one hundred thousand demonstrators in Berlin marching for tolerance and against xenophobia.

According to the plan they would converge from East and West on the Lustgarten, which with its military-parade-square emptiness would be ideal. Nothing there for a huge crowd to destroy. The event would be light on speeches, just enough to make the purpose clear, maybe just one – by the German President – and then rock bands to get the crowd to sway and cheer.

The idea took root. Political parties, community groups, clubs, schools, radio stations, multipliers everywhere got into the act. Special fares were offered by the railway; public transport in Berlin would be free. Diplomats were invited too, so that foreigner ministers around the world would get the message. Hanbury received a note from Protocol. Attached was a map showing the VIP area that would be roped-off.

❦

The Sunday began with the city hunkered down in a cold, clinging fog – the type that causes water to drip from trees and attacks the membranes of the nose. The consul faced a choice that morning: stay home and listen to Tchaikovsky, or go out into the graveyard weather to watch Germans declare multicultural love. Some days before, when he had lunched with Gundula in her paper's club, she became enthusiastic about the rally. Was he going? The consul said he wasn't sure. She teased his indecision and her laugh echoed (and beckoned) for days. In the end, he decided against Tchaikovsky and for the demo. When he set out, the fog was lifting, but he took no chances, not after the Scheunenviertel. He put on his new jacket, Gore-Tex, *wasserdicht*.

When the consul emerged from the underground near the Brandenburg Gate onto Unter den Linden he was overwhelmed by a flood of humanity. They made a fluttering sound, like a flock of birds in flight. It was the noise of thousands of soft soles beating the pavement, everyone going in the same direction. Families, old couples, people dressed formally in scarves and hats, and youths in scruffy jeans. All of Berlin, from Kreuzberg to Dahlem and Wedding to Wannsee seemed on the march. These were the masses streaming in from the West. The swell arriving at the Lustgarten from the East – Prenzlauerberg, Marzahn, Pankow – was no different. In his new relaxed, outback-type jacket and faded shoes, Hanbury melded in and became one of them.

Which was how he felt. The feeling had been growing. An oddly different experience from the other assignments – Kuala Lumpur, Caracas, Cairo, the places in the States. Was it Müller, who made the difference? Or von Helmholtz? Or Gundula Jahn? Or even the nearness of Sabine, and now her husband with whom he'd spoken a few times? Maybe it was all of them together.

Müller. Hanbury thought back to their last *Tankard* session. In between complaints about losing the race, the old man coughed repeatedly. He wasn't in top form: his glass of *Pils* scarcely left the table. The beer sitting there, losing its fizz – it bothered Uwe's son-in-law. He inquired why Herr Müller was resting his elbow. No reply from Müller, not even a scowl. To avoid upsetting him further, Hanbury didn't mention that Sabine's husband had called him several times.

Hanbury's first impression of Schwartz at the stadium was that he resembled a financier more than an academic. He had a formal bearing. And a sneer. But on the phone a few days later, he was friendly, almost familiar. He apologized for being curt when Sabine ran off. He had been taken by surprise, he explained.

"That's all right."

"You see, I had difficulty understanding what was happening. Sabine tends to daydream and I thought she might have forgotten to tell me something."

"No problem."

"We talked about you," Schwartz continued. "She told me the story and, of course, that's fine. It happened long ago. Still, she wishes… she would have preferred it if you hadn't come back. By the way, she doesn't know I'm calling you."

Hanbury thought this over. Sabine's husband talking about his wife brought her strangely near. For a few seconds he relived the intensity of the moment at the stadium.

"No need to talk about all that's happened," Schwartz suggested, waving the Savignyplatz period aside like crumbs off a table. "I'm a historian. I try to see the past objectively." He said he was engaged in a study of diplomacy; he believed he and the consul would have much to talk about. Could they get together?

"No problem."

They decided when and where and Schwartz hung up. He had been so charming, so easy-going that Hanbury wondered why Müller had such a low opinion of his daughter's husband.

An hour later, still intrigued by Schwartz's call, Hanbury left for lunch with Gundula. On the way Sturm talked of bread. He had come around to the view, he informed the back seat, that bread in the East was better than in the West. The consul doubted this, but Sturm was insistent. "Think about it, Herr Konsul. It makes sense. Everything in the West is done by machines to maximize profits. So breakfast rolls come out of the oven full of air. You think you're getting bread, but mostly you're buying holes. In the East, the baking is done by hand. The bread has substance."

"Do they skimp on yeast?" the back seat skeptically replied.

"I don't think so," countered the chauffeur. "They just don't overdo it." From bread, he moved to *Wurst*, which Sturm argued was also better in the East. And then to fish, freshly caught in the numerous lakes around Berlin. "Our diet has improved since the Wall came down," he pointed out. "We're living off the land again."

In the entrance hall of the publishing house, waiting for Gundula to come down, Hanbury viewed a display. Copies of original front pages headlining Berlin's historic moments were on show: the day the Communists began building the Wall; soldiers shooting people racing to get out and leaving them to bleed to death where they dropped; a picture of a border guard chucking his weapon and leaping through a gap in the barbed wire (and making it!); JFK's visit in '63; twenty-odd years on, Reagan making a speech before the Brandenburg Gate in '85, daring Gorbachev to open it; Gorbachev visiting Honecker in '89 saying *History punishes those who act too late*. Well, Hanbury thought, history did its job. Two months later the totalitarian regime was gone. Still more pictures showed tearful East Berliners in their Trabis surging through the opened Wall.

Hanbury, absorbed in old news and young history, didn't notice Gundula coming. "Cowboy!" she said. "Entertaining yourself?" She was dressed in jeans and boots and a sweatshirt with the paper's logo. She looked different than in the minidress at the Helmholtz dinner, but there was the same bite in her voice.

"Look," he said. "I've discovered an age when Trabis didn't need pushing."

Gundula began laughing. "There was no alternative then," she said. "No cowboys. Cars had to start."

The newspaper's club was on an upper floor. In the elevator Hanbury inquired how her car was doing. Gundula said she had taken his advice: Trabi had been serviced. He still made noise, but it was a healthy sound, like the purr of an animal mating. "Seen the latest Trabi bumper sticker?" she asked. Hanbury shook his head. "*When God created other cars, he was just practising*." He laughed and was about to quip that Trabis mating Trabis should be a good thing, since the species seemed destined for extinction, but the elevator stopped.

The club was imitation-British: leather sofa ensembles for private conversations; wood-panelled walls covered with prints of pre imperial Berlin; a photo collection of famous international visitors. The building had been constructed next to the Wall as a beacon to press freedom and the club had provided good views of the mined no-man's-land in the city streets just below. The inevitable effect of this reality on visitors, this direct confrontation with Communism, was a fuller appreciation for the need of policies that matched the other side – tank for tank, missile for missile. The same view now led to a different amazement. Land mines (and thoughts of missiles) had been replaced by a giant aerial web of entrepreneuriallyminded building cranes.

The paper's old hands, sipping lunchtime drinks, broke off their gossip when Gundula walked by. She flashed them her smile. They studied her guest. Not someone they knew. Gundula didn't often bring outsiders to the club. Usually she sat with the pros, the cynics, the instant analysts who entertained her with tales of journalistic prowess during the golden age – when the enemy lurked across the street. She led the consul to a table away from the others. A steward took their orders. When he left Hanbury said, "I've been reading your columns."

"That sounds serious."

"I enjoy them."

"If that's true, they're a failure," Gundula said.

"I mean the style. The issues you write about are something else again. I don't know enough about them."

"That I accept," she said.

"I take it people in the East aren't happy. They see that freedom has a downside."

"They've got no problem with freedom," Gundula snapped. "That's what they wanted for forty years. The problem is the West's dog-eat-dog version. Making the transition takes time. The society is in shock." She looked out the window.

"Your piece on skinheads in Schwedt was riveting," he said. "Are they really terrorizing the place? It sounds like Dodge City."

"You know Schwedt?" a surprised Gundula asked. Hanbury shook his head – what he knew came from her column. "A typical post-socialist town," she said. "People living mono-cultured lives in repetitious blocks of flats. The jobs are gone. Families are breaking down. The kids see nothing functions, not even the police. So they vandalize and terrorize. They shave their heads. They look for scapegoats. What's to stop them?"

"Last week I was this close to a bunch of skinheads," the consul said nonchalantly, showing Gundula a narrow gap between his thumb and forefinger. "I went into a pub. There they were." He chuckled. "I don't know how I survived."

"I guess you're talented."

"It's something I learned in Indian Head...I mean, ducking out of beer hall brawls."

"I can see you doing that," she said. "I can see you using table legs as camouflage."

The steward brought the food. Hanbury delved deeper into the problems of East German towns like Schwedt. Gundula, low-key, as in her columns, described the causes of neo-Nazi attitudes. She mentioned the demonstration against hatred towards foreigners. The paper was supporting it. "A hundred thousand people are expected," she said. "You should go. Diplomats should see it."

Hanbury said he hadn't decided yet. "Protocol is making arrangements. Maybe there'll be a diplomatic bus."

Gundula looked at him with disbelief. For her, the rally was something that should be felt, something that provided impulse. Dainty diplomatic dances – one hesitant step forward, two firm ones back – were new for her. "Join the marchers," she urged. "You don't want to be part of a flock of penguins stepping off a bus. You'd look ridiculous."

Hanbury hadn't come to spar with Gundula over diplomatic niceties. He wanted to hear her laugh again, as she had in the middle of the night in front of his house. He wanted to listen to her impertinence. He wanted to see the sarcasm in her eyes that said she didn't believe a thing he said. Intriguing him most was her Stasi file. As they ate, he waited for an opening to ask about it. But it was Gundula who questioned him, as if she was after material for the next day's column. She wanted to know all about hooligans in the drinking halls of Indian Head.

"Not really hooligans," Hanbury said, back-pedalling. "I shouldn't have labelled them that. Just strong boys. After a dozen beer they like doing some light sparring. It's best then to keep your head down because they might try an experiment: what breaks faster, their knuckles or your jaw."

"I see," Gundula said. "Civilization's veneer disappears that fast?"

"Sure. But it comes back. When a woman gets hold of them they turn into hard-working farmers and join curling clubs in the winter."

"And what happened to you? Did you have cracked knuckles or a broken jaw?"

"Neither. I told you. I watched. From underneath the table."

"And the women there aren't interested in men that hide?"

"That's it," Hanbury said with twisted triumph. "And what about you? The other night you started telling me about your Stasi file." Gundula shrugged as if there wasn't much to say. "I'll make you a deal," he said conspiratorially. "I'll lift the curtain on secret prairie drinking rites if you tell me where you come from."

"But I don't mind talking about that. I lived near the Baltic. Ever been there?"

"No, but I guess the Stasi were."

"They were everywhere. They even worried people would swim to freedom across the Baltic Sea. A swim to Sweden – it would only take five days. They were so stupid."

"How did you end up in Berlin? How did you get to know Gerhard? I have to admit something. At his house…I thought there was something between you two."

Gundula pealed with laughter. The veteran journalists lunching two tables over stopped spooning their soup. "Thank you for thinking that!" she said. "My turn. I'll try one on you. Have you slept with Viktoria?"

Hanbury dropped his fork. "What makes you ask that?"

"You looked down into her bust all evening."

He remembered Viktoria next to him, her skin in touching distance, the thin halter holding up her dress. "I was looking at her shoulder," Hanbury said meekly.

Another burst of merriment from Gundula. "Wonderful. A cowboy who saves Trabis, has never bruised a fist and admits to a fetish for bare shoulders. Is every cowboy in Indian Head like that?"

Hanbury became still and Gundula realized she might have gone too far. Dropping the irony from her voice, she described how she went from doing nothing special in East Germany's north to being a widely-read columnist in Berlin. After the Wall was down travel agencies sprung up everywhere. She first worked for one in Schwerin, then in Berlin. One day she read about a competition run by the paper. Participants were required to write a 300-word portrait of a prominent Berlin personality. The best one would make it into print. Gundula decided to enter, but write about whom? She went for the best known man in the city. Von Helmholtz agreed to an interview. The Chief of Protocol, the multi-layered man with a centre somewhere inside all that perfect breeding, opened up to Gundula, his past, the pitfalls of his work, his views on political and social issues. The material was original and Gundula wrote a piece that was both humorous and serious. She caught von Helmholtz's character perfectly. The chief editor told her it demolished the competition. "They offered me a job doing stories on East Berlin. One day they gave me my own column. Maybe Gerhard is behind it. The editor is one of his protégés. He helps people along, although I don't know why he'd do that for me."

I do, Hanbury thought, keeping his insight to himself. Instead he joked, "Maybe von Helmholtz has a fetish too. Maybe he likes journalists with class."

"I see. Well, I understand your fetish better."

Dessert came and Hanbury changed the subject. "Can I ask you something. Would you help me find Günther Rauch? You said you know him."

"I know of him. I've never met him. Why don't you try the phone book?"

"He's not in it."

"And why do you want to see him?"

"He's an old acquaintance." Hanbury described his student visits to East Berlin. "I want to see how he is. I should have tried to contact him after I saw him the last time, but I didn't. I want to apologize for that. Everybody seems to know him, but nobody knows where to find him. I don't even know why he's so well-known."

"He was briefly famous because of what he did after the regime fell. He organized a group to stop the Stasi destroying their files. For a few weeks he was a hero, then he faded from the scene. I suppose his politics weren't right."

"He'll never have the right politics. Could you locate him? If questions come from me, you know, being a diplomat, people wonder." Gundula said she'd think about it.

As Hanbury was leaving, at the entrance to the building, her face again took on an impish smile. "So don't forget the rally. And don't forget your cowboy boots. Otherwise I might not spot you."

❧

Fat chance of spotting anybody, the consul now thought. How many hundred thousand were there? He was locked into a human tide slowly moving past the Opera, past the imperial armoury, across the bridge onto the island in the river. Locating Gundula would be impossible, so he decided to aim for the VIP area next to a stage put up at the far end of the Lustgarten. People were coming to a halt, the continuous arrivals on the periphery were causing compression at the centre. Hanbury squeezed through an increasingly denser crowd. At a security cordon he showed identification and slipped into the area reserved for VIPs. Gundula had been right. In their dark coats the motionless, hunched diplomats stood around like penguins in slumber.

One of them woke up. "Canada!" he sang in welcome. He fingered Hanbury's waterproof jacket. "You dressed for the occasion. Such courage." Another said, "I considered it. I almost decided to dress casual." This started an animated discussion on the staggeringly high price of clothing in Berlin, which converted slowly into muted criticism of the distance they were forced to walk in formal attire through the security cordon. A Scandinavian complained police patrols had not been provided to ensure safe passage of official cars through Berlin and a Latin American observed no escorts were available with free umbrellas should it start to rain. The group then compared their getaway plans once Germany's President had spoken, how best to race back to the sanctuary called Dahlem.

Von Helmholtz appeared. He shook hands, thanking the diplomats for coming. They congratulated him that such a huge crowd had been assembled. "It will send a message to the world," prophesied the representative of France. Hanbury moved towards von Helmholtz and asked if everything was as expected. "Yesterday's prediction was three hundred thousand, but the estimate keeps rising. It could be four. But, the police have picked up a rumour. We're worried about trouble." Von Helmholtz surveyed the front ranks of the crowd.

Hanbury had never seen four hundred thousand people together in one place. Most remarkable was the stillness, the queer silence. An air of duty had settled over the Lustgarten and its neighbouring boulevards and squares. It seemed almost half a million people in an immense, open-air temple were waiting for a religious act to start. Von Helmholtz excused himself. Shortly after, the stillness was broken by a scattering of applause. Von Helmholtz was now on the stage in the company of the President of the Federal Republic of Germany. Everyone sensed the aura of noble purpose with which they walked to the front. The Chief of Protocol spoke into the microphone. His voice jumped out of a hundred speakers. The sound echoed lightly off the wall of the Berlin Cathedral and further back, more faintly, off the glass face of the Palast der Republik. He thanked the people for coming, described their common aim and the symbolic nature of their act. *Meine Damen und Herren*, he announced, *der Bundespräsident.*

The President spoke without a prepared text. Words from the loudspeakers filled the Lustgarten and reached towards the far corners of Marx Engels Platz. It crossed the river, echoing down Unter den Linden. The people were attentive. In understatement he addressed the past, its horrors, and the fear ordinary people feel when faced with tyranny. Every society has a potential for tyrants, he said. Every society is obligated to find ways to keep them down. He described the power a society acquires when toleration and vigilance are in balance.

Hanbury, looking at von Helmholtz, saw him suddenly stiffen. He made a series of rapid, scarcely noticeable signals. At the same moment there was a rustle in the crowd. Hanbury turned. Objects were flying through the air. One hit him on the shoulder and clung. An egg, wet and sticky, dripped down his jacket. Another, better-aimed egg got the President on the side of the head. Still more landed on the stage with no effect. It was over in seconds. Von Helmholtz stepped to the President to rub the worst away with a wipe or two of a handkerchief. Hanbury perceived vaguely that the rustle in the crowd was now moving to the sidelines. Undercover agents had jumped on a half dozen assailants and were hustling them away. No one had said anything. No shouting. No commotion. In those few seconds the same queer silence reigned. The President and the Chief of Protocol, close to the microphone, were heard whispering, their indistinct exchange sounding like a wind moving through a stand of trees. The President shook his head. He would not back away. Unfazed, he intended to continue. His voice betrayed no change in emotion. Reason and persistence were his weapons for this fight.

Two hundred metres deep in the crowd it would have been difficult to notice something had happened. People saw the Chief of Protocol go towards the President and move away to the side, no more. But TV cameras saw it differently. The image speeding around the world was of a President assailed and of a demonstration that had failed.

When the President finished and a rock band began setting up, the diplomats departed. Several commiserated with Hanbury over his soiled jacket. The Scandinavian made a little joke about bird droppings; the Latin American concluded the mishap proved that people in public life should wear washable garments. Von Helmholtz came along, saw what had occurred and asked Hanbury to walk with him to his office. The official part of the event was over; the rock concert would be routine.

As they walked the Chief of Protocol vented his anger. "They weren't neo-Nazis," he said grimly. "Merely anarchists. Ineffective, pathetic creatures who lack purpose. Still, we know what the headlines will say. I'm sorry you were hit."

"No harm done." Hanbury replied, keeping up with the Chief of Protocol's fierce pace. "It was the President who got it on the head. Otherwise everything went fine. Everyone was calm. The mood was serene."

Von Helmholtz slowed. The sun was setting behind them through banks of clouds; one strip was nearly black, another lit up red and beneath it a luminous ribbon of yellow. "We knew something was planned," he said. "Dozens were intercepted. Seven or eight got through. It shouldn't have happened. We gambled. We didn't succeed. I must say, the President took it well. He asked if others were hit. When an opportunity arises I'll introduce you to him. You're his only co-victim."

"Maybe Gundula Jahn will do a column on it," Hanbury said. She was still in his thoughts. Where had she been at the rally? Had she seen what happened? "Maybe she can recover some ground with a good piece."

Von Helmholtz doubted it, but the mention of Gundula changed his mood. Some of his tension drained off. He praised her talent as a journalist, but said he worried she was becoming too identified with the problems of the East. "You could help. You should try to interest her in international affairs. She needs to widen her scope before she hits a dead end."

In the Rote Rathaus courtyard, von Helmholtz commanded a car and driver to take the consul home. Hanbury argued he could find his way, but the Chief of Protocol insisted. "You're one of us now, Tony," he murmured, opening the door of a limousine. "You too have been embarrassed by the Fatherland."

❧

The Monday papers gave the incident in Berlin front page treatment. Randolph McEwen sitting in the breakfast pavilion of a Munich hotel was deciphering the story. The indoor garden with banana plants and palms might be fine in summer, but on this frosty Bavarian morning it was filled with cold convection. On the other hand, the article he was translating – word by word – provided unexpected inner warmth.

Eggs on their faces, he thought. A rally against xenophobia! A batty idea. In the old Berlin, the one administered by the Allies, the right wing would have gotten short shrift: infiltration of the neo-Nazis, hooligans rounded up as they slept, quick judicial arrangements. But now... well...deep down the Hun's brain was soft. The demonstration proved it.

Delightful though the headlines were, they didn't alter McEwen's mood. Guidelines for the transfer of operational control of security and intelligence gathering in the Berlin arena to the Germans were part of the agreement on the withdrawal of foreign troops. In accordance with this unknown blip on Germany's reunification map, McEwen was in Munich to bare his networks to new German counterparts. Who would have predicted a day would come when he would be forced to swallow a pill this bitter?

Transfer an intelligence-gathering function! An absurd notion. Yet, it was all spelled out in detail in an outrageous, secret annex to the Two Plus Four Agreement which charted the reunification course. Not only that, but the fine print said the handover of Berlin Station operations would be in Munich, in the suburb of Pullach, in Uncle Teut's own complex. An insult in itself. *We won the wars*, McEwen kept thinking. *I shouldn't have to go to Uncle Teut.*

There was worse. New operations during the changeover period were to be double key. McEwen needed Uncle Teut's approval for every initiative as his own resources disappeared. Could there be a greater ignominy than a career ending in dependency on the Hun? McEwen's frustration was so great he felt his spleen was on the verge of rupturing. Berlin was so delightful before Europe changed. Tussling with the Soviets had been amusing. Uncle Sam had been supportive. Double keys with Uncle Sam meant operations moved like lightning. But Uncle Teut was different. Uncle Teut was grave. He was ponderous. He needed time to think things through. He only acted once the highest court in the land granted clearance. By the time an operation began, the Libyans, Iranians, or Iraqis, not to mention the Russian Mafia, had had their day. Half a nuclear arsenal might have been smuggled in and out. Uncle Teut lacked two ingredients for success: flexibility and instinct. His complicated rules rendered a distressing certainty: operations that were permanently jammed.

The egg-splashing yesterday showed the rot. In a sardonic corner of his mind, as he methodically deciphered the front page story, McEwen composed a few remarks he would soon make. *Sorry to hear about Berlin, Alex. Frightfully embarrassing. I heard the anarchists had intentions. How did they get through? Dressed as police agents?* Nothing wrong with goading Uncle Teut. Uncle Teut wasn't above delivering insults himself. Why else had an Oxford man been named for this partnership undertaking. Partnership undertaking! That's what the fine print said.

Alexander Graf Bornhof spoke English with such nearly perfect Oxford diction that whenever McEwen heard the accent he felt robbed blind.

No Hun should be allowed to steal the British soul by speaking like a don.

Graf Bornhof *pretended* to be friendly; he liked to *show* himself cooperative; he *made out* he was self-effacing. The Oxford veneer made him difficult to deal with. But today, at least, McEwen had the unexpected gift of a smelly egg laid in the Hun's own tidy nest. It mitigated the humiliation – a little.

The humiliation deepened after breakfast. Transportation to Pullach was in a Mercedes 600, V12, bullet-proof, with a communication system and voice scrambler in the trunk. *Somewhat* more comfortable than McEwen's own imported compact. A *little* faster. *Slightly* better equipped. *Real* leather seats. And so deeply, deeply silent.

He loves to rub it in, the Hun. We won both World Wars. We won the Cold War. We win all the wars, but it's the Hun that profits.

The gate to the Pullach complex slid aside. Papers were checked. *Für Graf Bornhof*, the driver snapped. *Warten Sie!* Wait, ordered the guard. He telephoned, then returned. *In Ordnung.* That's fine. McEwen heard the exchange as a series of short verbal explosions. McEwen knew Pullach by now, but he didn't like the place. He didn't like the sound of it. He didn't like the sound of the orders.

He was escorted to the conference room. As always, fruit juices, soft drinks and a thermos with good coffee were on offer on the table. Christmas was not far off and there was decoration too: holly twigs, red candles and trays of Christmas cookies. Interspersing the colour were small poinsettias alternately red and white. Into this festive atmosphere Graf Bornhof and two subordinates arrived.

"Randolph!" Graf Bornhof exclaimed with delight.

"Terribly pleased to see you, Alexander," came the flat reply. "Starting the annual celebration, I see. Very pretty." He nodded to the decorated table.

"I shall pass your compliment to the ladies. They are quite excited at this time of year. And why not? Intelligence work can have a human face. Allow me to introduce my colleagues." Graf Bornhof presented Herr Seidel and Herr Heine. "Howwayuh," said Seidel. "Hi," Heine added. American accents. Uncle Sam trained. Seidel was bald. Even his eyebrows were thinning into nothing. He wore rimless glasses which heightened the effect of the naked head. A Himmler clone, thought McEwen. But Heine was an imitation Ivy Leaguer: well-trimmed hair, a Harris Tweed jacket, and thick-soled brocade shoes.

They settled around the table. "Good to have you here again, Randolph," Graf Bornhof said. "Trip went well?"

"Got out just in time, I'd say, Alex. It turned jolly nasty yesterday in Berlin. The President pummelled with eggs. What went wrong?"

Graf Bornhof's smile dried up. "We had an emergency post-mortem last night," he said. "The enforcers flew in and when we sat down, that was indeed the question. Where was the mistake? Was it the information, the manpower, the control system? Once we pieced things together, we decided the question should be otherwise. What went right? Almost everything went right, Randolph. The event was high risk – there were enough arguments against it – but overall it worked. Four hundred thousand people, orderly and peaceful. About fifty anarchists were intercepted on the way, sifted out from four hundred thousand participants. Seven got through, but they were dragged off the moment they cocked their arms to throw. I believe only one egg landed." Graf Bornhof relaxed. How close to perfection can one get, his posture asked.

"Excellent work, Alex. Suspected as much. I know from experience how challenging such events can be. The line between what goes right and what goes wrong can be faint, difficult to define. Too bad about that one egg…and on the President too."

"Indeed," said Graf Bornhof.

As Graf Bornhof spoke, Seidel, the Himmler clone, had been fingering a stack of newspaper clippings. "Correction," he drawled in a gutturally modulated southern states' accent. "See here. A diplo was in the line of fire too." He pulled out a story with a paragraph circled in red and placed it in front of his boss who pushed it impatiently to the side.

"A diplomatic incident as well? Oh dear, worse than I imagined," McEwen said.

Graf Bornhof didn't bite. "Shall we commence?" he said.

The agenda had two items: Phase Three of the handover and, at McEwen's request, the need for an urgent twenty-four-seven, double-key operation.

No aspect of the partnership undertaking caused McEwen more pain than Phase Three. Phase One catalogued Berlin Station operations. Phase Two passed electronic listening facilities, targeted mostly at Russian military camps around Berlin, plus surveillance responsibilities of *German* threats in Berlin, over to Uncle Teut. But *Phase Three* hurt. McEwen was to bare his covert networks and transfer control.

With two half-round slotted keys, McEwen opened a case. He removed a dozen thin files marked *Top Secret*. He grabbed the top file, his least complicated operation, a pipeline into Berlin's Lebanese underworld. Three Arab-Israelis with Beirut credentials had infiltrated the Lebanese community. The information haul – details on arms deals, timetables for shipments of chemical weapon ingredients, circumventions of export controls on inertial guidance systems – was significant. The meta-diplomat, master of Berlin Station, described the network, the procedures for information downloading, the intercepts of shipments destined for Libya, Iraq, Iran. When McEwen finished, Graf Bornhof took the file, studied it, asked questions and passed it to his subordinates who also looked it over.

They worked their way meticulously through all the files. Information on the breakaway republics of the former Soviet Union had been obtained from a group of social workers looking after refugees. There was a nearly completed organization chart of the Berlin branch of the Russian mafia put together by a diverse group – office cleaners, taxi drivers and some long haired youths running a bogus parcel delivery service. Reports had been assembled on an international armaments dealers' association that met in a picturesque villa on the Tegeler See, using as cover an annual conference there on improving aid flows to poor countries. McEwen also had a handle on an international biological warfare cartel run from the laboratories of the Free University under the code name *Sherry Trifle*. And an army of paid informers in the Russian Army in East Germany had been productive over the years, but this group was beginning to disperse. Clerks in three banks in Berlin reported on the laundering of profits from European sales of pirated video and audio tapes from China. The fake patents business, the heroin trade, shady forms of counter-trade, Russian girls sent into prostitution around the world: the files were portraits of the black side of humanity. They symbolized McEwen's view of the world, and his stand against it.

As Phase Three proceeded and McEwen's world passed into the responsibility of Uncle Teut, the ticking of a wall clock sounded like a dirge. Regularly a cuckoo defiantly stepped out, but its voice had been suppressed, so there was only the sound of a mechanism whirring. Which was how McEwen felt. He darkly believed that the clock, so sadly emasculated, had been hung there for a purpose.

Seidel, eyes full of admiration, was the most vocal of the three. "Hey!" he would say. "This is neat. Real good. Full marks. Congrats." Graf Bornhof was fascinated too, but more subdued. "Ingenious," he occasionally allowed. "Clever. Innovative, Randolph. A master's touch."

McEwen didn't need to be told that. Innovation was his hallmark. He'd always been months ahead of global developments: Rhodesia when it became a break-away republic; Uganda at the time of Idi Amin; Jo'burg when apartheid was at its ugliest. He had had a stint in Cairo where he predicted the assassination of Sadat. In New Delhi he knew Indira Gandhi would not live much longer. Some of his networks still functioned, still churned out information, just kept ticking over – as regular as the bloody cuckoo clock. Berlin Station was the culmination. A lifetime of experience had come together. It had a master's touch. He had predicted three anti-communist revolutions in eastern Europe. But the Wall was a very special chapter. *Twelve hours. London knew twelve hours in advance that the Wall would open. Uncle Sam was informed by London thirty minutes later. We knew every peep made in the East German Central Committee. Had for years. And what did Uncle Teut know? Nothing beyond what he watched on television. The Chancellor was out of the country when it happened. He had to hurry back the next day!* Resentment welled up in McEwen. Look at them. Three excited children eager for the goodies which Master Randolph was hanging on their Christmas tree.

As Graf Bornhof and his men looked through the files, McEwen thought about the next agenda item. He rehearsed what he had on the consul. The case was not yet well-enough defined, but an instinct told him it was big, a major post-Cold War operation. If handled with discernment, Friend Tony would be his valedictory address. He had worked on the twenty-four-seven proposal for hours. Sipping port, puffing Havanas, he had read through his material, sifted, re-read, thought. His chin had dropped to his chest and he had closed his eyes. Who owned Friend Tony? What was the game? He had contemplated the quarry to try to gain entry to its soul. A patient, cunning man, the consul, a type that's the most dangerous of all.

The handover, coupled with explanations, questions and further elucidations, neared completion. McEwen indicated casually that a few, rich items were not yet ready for Stage Three. "The diplomatic scene, for one," he said. "Subversion arriving via the diplomatic bag, that sort of thing. Insight about that channel has consistently been put to good use elsewhere: Mozambique, the Kurds, the Tamils. Next time, Alex? Is that alright? Move along to agenda item two?" McEwen was fiercely calm.

"Of course," said Graf Bornhof. "A snack, Randolph? Are you familiar with *Nürnberger Lebkuchen*? A local delicacy. It competes with shortcake I'd say, and Christmas pudding."

"Better than both, I'm sure," Randolph McEwen said politely, taking two.

"Agenda item two then," Graf Bornhof said brightly.

"We have a little problem in Berlin at the moment," the master of Berlin Station began thoughtfully. "Actually, it could be a big problem if something isn't done. If things get out of hand you might have to do the clean up, Alex."

McEwen returned Graf Bornhof's pleasant gaze. He described the proven value over the years of a reliable source in one of the diplomatic missions, the initial suspicions the consul had triggered, the Spandau mystery, the solitary walks in East Berlin. He laid emphasis on Hanbury's diffidence, the best ever seen, an extraordinary manipulation of an image. Expertly, always in a low, sometimes mournful voice, eyelids drooping, McEwen wove the facts into a story. A troubled upbringing, a two year gap in the official biography, the evidence in the Stasi archives. "Those files are useful, Alex. I've looked at them. They record secret meetings Hanbury had in the late sixties in East Berlin." McEwen's voice dropped further still. "At the same time he was arrested at a disturbance instigated by the Red Army Faction in West Berlin, but immediately released. Lack of evidence. Next, he's home. He joins the Canadian foreign service." McEwen's tranquil hands momentarily unclasped with disbelief, as if the lunacy of it was too great to comprehend. He remained lost in dismal thoughts, shaking his head, until Graf Bornhof asked him to continue. With a tremor the master of Berlin Station restarted.

"He throws a blanket over the Berlin period. No one knows about it. He embarks on a dull career. More than twenty years of foreign service humdrum. A feint, Alex. A marvellous example of taking time to acquire perfect cover…" McEwen's voice trailed off. "I don't have all the answers, but I know this: he's been a sleeper all these years and now he's becoming active. Something big is happening. We must step in. Twenty-four-seven. I don't see an alternative. We ought to set it up, double quick." The master stopped; his eyes narrowed to slits.

Graf Bornhof cleared his throat. "Well," he said, "food for thought, if not quite sustenance for action." "And this guy is Canadian?" said Heine in his Ivy League accent. McEwen nodded wearily. "I'll be damned." Heine continued. "Then he's the one that got it at the rally. Look, he's the other guy that got an egg." He pushed the press clipping back under Graf Bornhof's nose who, with scarcely a glance, shoved it towards McEwen. "Jumpin' Jesus," Seidel said. "We're letting him get that close to the President?" McEwen nodded. He appreciated the alarm. "Let's not rush," cautioned Graf Bornhof. He pointed out that twenty-four-seven operations were difficult to set up, and expensive; there were legal implications deriving from the constitution; it had to withstand the scrutiny of the courts. "I know," the master said wearily. "I know all that."

Heine, taking a cue from his boss, became skeptical. "Let's falsify for a second," he said. Falsification, the art of accomplished second-guessing, was an analytical tool he acquired at Harvard. "Flip it around. Put an opposite interpretation on the facts. The facts are good, very good. No quarrel there. Just falsify them. Interpret them a hundred and eighty degrees different. What's left? What's the haul then? What's the minimalist, not maximalist, view."

"Quite a considerable bit, I'd say," McEwen said icily.

"Let's have it, Randolph," declared Graf Bornhof.

McEwen methodically opened a folder and removed a ribbon-wrapped sheaf. "We were able to keep an eye on him for a few days. We assembled a few shreds of information – that's all – shreds – not a full picture, not yet a vast panorama. Not long after he arrives in Berlin, he drops his guard. He tells a member of his office staff he plans to move about incognito. Why *incognito*, we ask. Another time he lets the word *reconnaissance* slip. Then he worries someone is monitoring his mail. We follow him. He heads for East Berlin, *twice* changing trains en route. He goes to Alexanderplatz in strikingly awful weather. He *pretends* he's a tourist. There's a downpour, but he persists. He sits down on a bench, the same one where twenty-five years earlier he met up with a member of East Germany's left wing. Do you know how far left the East German left was, Alex? It was so far left even Marx would have seemed far right. He sits in the rain and waits. For whom? I'll tell you. We know from the Stasi files he was waiting to take up contact with Günther Rauch. Do you know who Günther Rauch is, Alex?"

Graf Bornhof, half skeptical, half intrigued, shook his head.

"Günther Rauch is an extremist committed to unending revolution. When a revolution has been completed, people like him switch sides, so they can start a new revolution. They revolt against the revolters. *Permanent revolution*. As in *Mao*, Alex. I was *in* Peking. I *saw* the Cultural Revolution. Not pretty. Yesterday anarchists threw eggs at the President. Tomorrow Günther Rauch may chuck a bomb." The master paused.

"Why that conclusion?" Heine asked.

"His background," McEwen argued. "He was an arch-dissenter in the GDR. Committed to its overthrow. When it fell he led a collection of vigilantes to the Stasi complex and drove them out like Christ flailing the moneylenders from the temple. Did he consolidate then what he gained? Did he fall in love with democracy? Did he take a seat in Parliament like the other dissenters? No! He switched to the side that used to jail him! Günther Rauch, Alex, is back to agitating for a proletarian revolution."

All three men looked at McEwen. "I'm told, he's bitter," mused McEwen. "Lifelong revolutionaries who are bitter do strange things." He became confiding. "At a minimum he might be giving orders to knock off presidents of banks. At a maximum, who knows? Hijacking nuclear bombs? And now his old friend with diplomatic immunity has returned. Diplomatic immunity, Alex, can be handy if you plan to deal in dangerous materials."

"It *still* doesn't add up to much if you change the perspective," Heine objected once more.

"And I haven't bloody finished," McEwen said testily. "Here's a list of people the consul is cultivating. A distillation of a distillation of who's who in Berlin. Why is he spending time with *all* the VIPs?"

"Oh shit. All diplomats do that," snapped Heine.

"Possibly, in ideal circumstances. But ninety-nine times out of a hundred a diplomat wouldn't stand a chance cracking into society at this level. Somebody is catapulting him along. Question one – who? Question two – why? Think of the consequences of so much influence in high places."

Graf Bornhof was shaking his head. "Randolph. Randolph."

"I still haven't bloody finished," McEwen said, eyes blazing. "A couple of days ago he contacted a female journalist. Not any journalist, but the one stirring up trouble in the East with her weepy columns on new social evils."

"Her name?" asked Heine.

"Gundula Jahn. Heard of her?"

Graf Bornhof again shook his head. "We're only now gearing up in the East."

"A file on her is being assembled as we speak. It comes as no surprise that the Stasi had plenty on her too."

"The Stasi had plenty on everyone, including themselves," said Graf Bornhof.

"I doubt..." said McEwen menacingly, "...I doubt I could keep my diplomatic spectators together if this piece of work is not performed. I fear things would fall apart. You would have to start from scratch when you take over in Berlin." In the ensuing silence, McEwen began collecting his papers.

※

The Mercedes was taking McEwen away from Pullach. Senior executive class to the airport courtesy of Graf Bornhof, a cheap tourist seat from there to Berlin. The master had enjoyed the final scene. Seidel with his drawl regrouped the quickest, arguing the loss of a window on the diplomatic scene could be significant. He became impatient with Heine's ongoing second guessing. But Graf Bornhof was conciliatory.

"It would be expensive for us, Randolph," he said at last.

"Don't use Mercedes 600s then. Cut costs."

"We might find a way to do it for six weeks."

"Two months."

"It will take a month to set it up. We need authorizations."

"Get them in two weeks."

"Impossible. We have never obtained an approval in less than four."

"I get mine in twelve hours."

"You don't have a constitution."

Saying goodbye, Graf Bornhof had pressed a box of Christmas cookies into McEwen's palm and closed the Mercedes door. The Pullach gate slid open. The car surged noiselessly ahead.

CHAOS

The egg incident – *droppings from a little bird* – was forgotten quickly in diplomatic circles. The reference to the consul was deeply buried in the papers and scarcely noticed, Gundula excepted. She clipped the article and sent it to Hanbury in an envelope marked *personal.* A photo was enclosed, grainy, taken from far away and blown up. He was clearly recognizable in the VIP area – mouth open, eyes aghast – watching the dripping mess. *The Cowboy strikes again!* her impertinent caption read.

"That Gundula," he thought. He regretted not having run into her at the demo. He believed that in two sentences or less she would have distilled the motivations of four hundred thousand people into something he would understand. That ability – reducing complexity into simpler components, fashioning order out of chaos – always eluded him. A reason to admire her, to look forward to her columns.

❧

Chaos was something he wanted to avoid, though it confronted him daily. It arrived courtesy of his countrymen. Quite a few had a habit of parking themselves in the consulate reception area, where they put on dramatic shows of lives they had managed to gum up. Innocents robbed of passports, welshers claiming destitution, deviants insisting on cost-free lawyers, the sick insisting on help to get home to be healed. Effective exporters of personal problems. The consul instinctively shied away from them. He'd seen enough of that business in Cairo. What would he do without Gifford, he often thought, that tireless solver of all problems, that efficient dispatcher of the consular freight.

Consular duties were not the only tiresome things. Viewing houses, Hanbury believed, was little better, but this was an obligation he couldn't shirk. Gifford said money was available and a quick decision was essential. Real estate prices were about to go out of sight. "A green light from headquarters?" a disbelieving consul had asked, studying the administrator across the small table. "That's remarkable." Gifford, with a slight bow, confirmed a wonder had indeed occurred and proceeded with a briefing. Elbows on the table, hands clasped in a pose of prayer, beads of sweat breaking out on his forehead, the administrator revealed that options for a residence had been narrowed down to fifteen. "Some are beauties." "Fifteen?" an alarmed Hanbury had said.

❧

It took several weeks to view them all. Gifford, affably seated beside the consul in the back seat of the Opel, provided details as they went: price, location, condition, floor space, size of dining room, size of drawing room, suitability for live-in servants, garden, overall appropriateness as a diplomatic residence, and so on and so forth. He had written a computer program, he said, to ensure accurate analysis and an objective ranking. Wandering through villas together, some empty and sounding hollow, others packed with garish furniture accumulated over the generations, Gifford took photographs – to aid recall. "You could entertain a hundred in here easy," he told the consul as they sauntered through an imitation Greco-Roman palace built in the ostentatious eighteen-nineties.

Throughout the confusion, half-deaf to complex considerations of layout or modernisations done or pending, Hanbury remained aloof. In fact, he became steadily more non-committal. After days of tramping through innumerable rooms, he complained that his mind and vision were blurring.

"The decision is yours," Gifford said crisply when they were driving back from the last candidate, a massive, neo-Gothic mansion in a tangled forest on a rise overlooking a lake between Potsdam and Berlin. It had been built close to the Babelsberg studios by a German film magnate in the twenties, but was requisitioned at war's end by the Russians. During the next forty years Red Army officers trod the mansion, so to speak, into the dust. A battalion of vagrants would have had difficulty achieving their level of destruction. The place was stripped bare: faucets and light fixtures were gone; hardwood floors had been ripped out; doors were missing, hinges included; gaping holes in the walls showed where electric switches used to be. In Russia, it was rumoured, such objects had more value than military pensions. "Not this last one," replied Hanbury. "It would take years to get it back in shape." "I've read the Russians plundered all the houses," Sturm interjected from behind the wheel. "Scorched earth. Like with Napoleon. Must be something in their genes."

"The house is sound structurally," Gifford pointed out. "The large hall at the side has potential, a ballroom possibly, with a view towards the lake. Imagine the woods on the opposite shore lit up at night. That would stir the Germans. Soften their edges. A not-unimportant representational objective." Gifford, composing this scene, sounded as if the house would be his ticket to a career in films. "Balls are popular in Berlin," he added. "A consul throwing a ball? People would notice that." "I don't know how to dance," said Hanbury. Sturm interrupted them once more. "The house poses problems for drivers." "How so?" the administrator asked sharply.

Sturm, a world authority, explained. The best places have a circling drive in front, sufficient room for parking on the side, and a separate entrance for the drivers. This one had no drivers' quarters and there was practically no room for parking. Messy. A foreign government shouldn't cause a parking problem. In that house, from a driver's point of view, a ball would be disastrous. Sturm recalled, for the benefit of Gifford, that next to Lord Halcourt's manor there had been a huge car park and spacious chauffeurs' quarters in an adjoining barn. "Could the side hall be turned into a drivers' room?" he speculated. "It does have that lake view. Drivers would appreciate it. A ballroom could be added on the forest side. People don't study the natural landscape when they dance." "Drivers should spend their time studying the depth of the shine they put on cars," said Gifford coldly. "It's important to get it right," Sturm persisted. "If drivers are unhappy, things break down. Appointments are missed. Things aren't delivered properly. It's chaos. If drivers are treated well, there's less scandal, more order." "Is that in your computer program, Earl?" the consul wanted to know. "Do you have a category for ease of parking and drivers' quarters?" "Of course," said Gifford.

Even with the neo-Gothic mansion off the list, the choice was huge and Hanbury was unable to make up his mind. Neither the computer analyses, three dozen pages of dense facts, nor the objective ranking swung him one way or another. Gifford pressed for a decision. The consul again went through the hundreds of photos and reread the stats, but did not advance. On some days, Gifford suspected, he actually receded. "It's difficult," Hanbury sighed. "It's impossible to make the *right* decision. All of them are fine, really."

He even tried a mind game. He imagined Gundula as hostess receiving guests at the front door. Which of the many available front doors suited her? The black one? Her hair was black. The white one? Her skin was very pale. A double front door? She was quite slight. Should there be many steps, as in a ducal palace? But Gundula was not pretentious; she would scoff at too many steps. Actually, Gundula looked superb opening the doors of all the houses. But then, she would be elegant slipping aside a grass curtain serving as entrance to a hut.

"It's not as if you have to choose a wife," Gifford said when he observed the consul repeatedly going through the pictures. "It's only a house. It isn't forever."

In the end, when purchase options threatened to run out, Gifford made the decision. "If we don't strike now, we'll have to start again. We might even have to settle for that place in Babelsberg. The computer says the Greco-Roman mansion. That's the one we go for." Hanbury, relieved the crisis had broken, agreed it was the best.

The mansion, a dream turned into reality by a wealthy archeologist a century before, had an excellent Dahlem address. Even in that exclusive neighbourhood it was considered special. A row of Doric columns along the front imitated a Greek temple. Inside and out, it possessed lovely symmetry. Delightful classical elements decorated the windows. Splendid double doors – copies of a Roman centurion's palace in Sardinia – opened to a superb, round vestibule. The dining room's ceiling imitated one in a bishop's opulent summer residence in the high country near Rome. The salon was large enough to double as a ballroom. A music room had a wide view of the grounds. Private quarters on the second floor were tasteful, intimate and quiet. The driveway and in-ground parking passed the standards set by Sturm. A side entrance led down into a bright room in the cellar which was connected to the vestibule by an intercom. Sturm, speechless, went into his new emporium. A large smooth table stood in the centre – a great platform for future chauffeurial debates – surrounded by numerous upholstered chairs. He slumped down on one and closed his eyes. Still dizzy, he visualized elegant *soirées* in the magnificent garden hosted by the consul and imagined the drivers taking their chairs outside, positioning them under an ancient beech to enjoy evening birdsong. Sturm loved the sound of nightingales. He remembered them behind Lord Halcourt's manor in the days he courted Betsy. As for Hanbury, he saw himself on his prospective steps – not so many that they were pretentious – gazing down on the driveway curving past the portico and wondering whether one day he would admire Trabi bedding down there for the night.

"Well done Earl," he said, when the ink was drying on the contract. Gifford beamed. On his way home, overwhelmed by raw success, he bought Frieda a gift, yet another ring, this one a ruby, to symbolize joy. The gesture brought a rich reward. That evening Frieda insisted that nothing she might otherwise be wearing should take attention from the blood-red stone. A little later, dangling from a little thong, the ruby decorated Gifford too. The consul's residence put the Giffords into seventh heaven as much as it had Sturm.

Minor renovations were required; interior decoration would take a little time; a delay of several months was expected before the consul could move in.

Although outwardly indifferent to the news of delay, Hanbury felt a twinge of regret over it all the same. There was a letter from Zella in which she announced she was being assigned to Ankara and asked if she could take him up on his offer to visit Berlin. Did he have plans for Christmas? He recalled her high expectations that he would be housed in luxury in Berlin. Would the bungalow spoil a visit? But Zella's uncomplicated charm jumped at him from the note and in his reply – *Yes, do come!* – he hinted only that Berlin might not be all she was expecting. He also asked her to pass on his regards to everyone he knew still left in the Priory, adding tongue in cheek: *Tell Heywood I now appreciate what it's like to have to carry the whole show.*

With the dates of Zella's visit stamped firmly in his mind, Hanbury turned to a mountain of pre-Christmas invitations. Most would have to be rejected. "Let's be careful which ones we accept," he cautioned Frau Carstens. She stiffened, scarcely believing her ears. "As always," she replied with disdain. For her, if there was a problem with the daily haul of invitations, it was the consul not making commitments. He put decisions off. To keep things moving she was acquiring a dictatorial touch. "You must accept the Wintergarten gala," she ordered. "It would be impossible not to. And the next evening is the première of a documentary film on the bison. You have been asked to speak; you have little choice. By the way, are those beasts still around? I thought they were extinct."

The consul informed her a few herds survived in parks. "I guess I could give a talk," he mused, "although I've never seen a buffalo."

"Maybe there's one in the zoo."

Frau Carstens processed the invitations. All the evenings filled, except a few before Christmas that he insisted be kept open. "And the Press Ball in January?" she demanded sharply. "Are you interested?"

"I don't know how to dance."

"It's televised. People go there to be seen. No one dances. It's too crowded."

Hanbury's interest perked up. The Lustgarten rally had been crowded; no one could move there either. "I'll think about it," he said.

Frau Carstens reminded him it was a ball. "You'll need an escort," she said severely.

When he was alone, Hanbury fingered the Press Ball invitation and on impulse called Gundula.

"Cowboy!" she exclaimed. "Congratulations on your act of bravery. Throwing yourself in front of an egg aimed at the President. Is that taught in diplomatic school?"

"Thank you for the picture. Where did you get it?"

"The photo department. By the way, your western outfit added character. Have you started keeping horses?"

Hanbury chuckled. "The only ones I've been near recently were under the hood of a Trabi and they sounded sick."

"Trabi has never felt better. He's been serviced. I told you that when I invited you up here for lunch."

"Speaking of invitations, ever been to the Press Ball?"

Gundula had not.

"Would you like to go?"

A silence hung between them, then she said, "I don't think it's my *milieu*."

"There would be advantages," Hanbury said playfully.

"Such as?"

"You could introduce me to your press friends."

"That's true. Some of them still talk about you in the club."

"And I hear you don't actually have to dance there."

"But I love dancing," protested Gundula. "I'm good at the quick-step."

Hanbury did some quick thinking, but decided to plunge on. "I'm not," he admitted. I'm better at slow steps, the slower the better. But if you show me how to quickstep, I could show you how to waltz without moving."

"Waltz without moving," she asked with deepening interest, "a diplomatic step?"

"It demands skill," Hanbury confirmed. He wished he could see Gundula through the phone. Did she have her head thrown back in noiseless merriment? No one he knew had a sharper sense of humour. "Now take journalists," he continued. "Quickstepping is all they ever do. They probably don't even need music."

"You're perceptive, cowboy."

There was another moment where neither said a word, when the conversation could have gone in one of several directions, but Hanbury brought it down to earth. "Even if we do different steps, it doesn't mean we shouldn't go to the same ball," he said quietly. "It might be fun." That settled it.

He asked about her work. Some days had passed since her last column. Gundula replied she was working on something new and it hadn't jelled yet. "I'm exploring a new perspective. By the way, progress on your friend Günther Rauch. He's around – that's confirmed – but he's not in politics. Still interested?"

"I don't care about politics. I only want to see how he is."

"It might take a while to pin down his whereabouts. The route is not direct." As Gundula was hanging up, she thanked him for the invitation; she looked forward to it, she said.

When Tony was in grade six, the square dance teacher in Indian Head emphasized that *compatibility* was essential for couples if they wanted to be good dancers. Tony wondered what she meant, because he and the girls from the outlying farms lived in divergent worlds. He went to square dancing only because his father insisted, arguing it was part of an all-round, prairie education. Tony's mother disagreed. She wanted him to use lunch breaks for complicated finger exercises to keep his piano technique nimble. Tony himself would have preferred to be outside, studying rabbit tracks in the snow. The father prevailed and that winter Tony practised compatibility twice a week with a beefy daughter of the land called Bonnie. Forty years later, Bonnie, ironically, was the reason Hanbury considered the Press Ball might work. If he had survived being trampled by that determined little girl, dancing with Gundula, he was sure, would be like levitating.

Faint recalls of square dancing had faded when shortly afterwards he prepared to go out. "Where are you off to?" Frau Carstens demanded. "The zoo," he said, passing her desk and pulling on a coat. "Buffalo viewing." "Sturm will drive!" she called, but saw he wore his walking shoes. "No need!" he yelled back, surging out the door. It wasn't a complete fabrication. He took the direction of the zoo, but went past it, up Budapesterstrasse, to the park for the appointment with Schwartz.

Hanbury knew the Tiergarten from years before, an island of tranquillity in a sea of turbulence, but he had obtained a new perspective from Sturm. On the way to a meeting with the minister for city planning Sturm informed him it hadn't always been so peaceful. When the Allied bombers swooped in for their runs, the statues of great Germans in the clearings trembled under the explosions of a city going up in flames. Uncannily, high over the park golden-winged Victoria on her column, affectionately referred to as Golden Ilse by Sturm, remained untouched. Sturm went on to claim it was because the Tiergarten wasn't really a park. Manoeuvring slowly in dense traffic around the Victory Column, he explained it was a location for certain supernatural events. "It may look like a park, but it's really a camp for ghosts. See the statues? Ghosts in them come out when the sun is down. The park is full of statues, so it gets busy. On the night of the first of May the ghosts of the Soviet soldiers who died in the fighting for the Reichstag come out too. They're in a big grave, up ahead, by the memorial. That's two thousand more ghosts! Things are really hopping then. There's hardly any room left for the living. Myself, I don't go near this place at night."

Sturm made a nifty move into an opening in the traffic, cutting off a woman in a Porsche. She lowered her window. "Are you blind?" she yelled. Sturm, gloomily preoccupied with the proximity of ghosts, was not about to take this. "No," he shouted back, "but some people have a mouth so big I can see through them." "If you can see so good, I guess you can see why I think you're a dink." Hanbury followed the exchange with interest. The woman was pretty. She had lovely red hair and a well-formed mouth tastefully highlighted with dark lipstick. "I can see so well through your big mouth that I have a good view of the inside of your asshole!" cried Sturm. "Sturm," cautioned the consul. "Easy." "*Dann sind Sie wohl ein Arschficker!*" the redhead screamed, accusing him of sodomy. "Ah," Sturm said with practised denigration, waving her away, "*Sie Arsch mit Ohren.*" Having reduced the beauty to no more than a fat ass with a pair of ears, he rolled his window up. She beat the dashboard of her Porsche, but the traffic began moving. "Phew," said Hanbury. "Good thing we don't come by here often." "It doesn't mean much," a relaxed Sturm said. "It's the ghosts. People shout to keep them distant. Deep down they don't mean it."

Ten minutes later Hanbury mentioned the traffic snarl around the Victory Column to the city planning minister, who felt confronted. He stared at the consul with eyes set deep in an emaciated face. "We have to condense fifty years of development into five," the tired man lamented. "But we have a solution for the traffic." He pointed at a wall map and for half an hour reviewed the advantages of tunnelling beneath the park.

The traffic tunnel was controversial, but Schwartz supported it. He believed it might help a city which was spiralling out of control. Almost overnight, too much of everything had come into Berlin – from countries to the east. Refugees, beggars, gangs of thieves, foreign workers. Traffic was endlessly choked. Chaos. As far as he was concerned, the new excesses should be removed – at a stroke. Bold decisions were needed to re-establish order. But what was there instead? To drive home what he meant he liked to point at Berlin's *Flächennutzungsplan*, a land-use blue print. It was a perfect piece of fudge, a sad escape act for politicians. Schwartz ridiculed it, likening the thousands of dabs of colour to a bad impressionistic painting. What did it do? What were its result? Streets dug up, filled in, dug up again; scaffolding permanently confiscating sidewalks; cobblestones piled up on intersections; bridges pulled apart; one-way-street signs appearing randomly, then overnight being pointlessly reversed. The plan symbolized democracy running rampant, so everything ceased to work.

❧

At least the Tiergarten remained exempt, a sanctuary for contemplation, a preserve for the bundling of thoughts. Which was why Schwartz had suggested it to the consul. In the Tiergarten they could have an undisturbed talk. Making his way to the entry gate, Schwartz thought back to the stadium scene. It had unfolded fast, too fast to think. Sabine's flight had been unsettling enough. But then came Müller's claim that he and the intruder had his wife in common! Schwartz prided himself on not being easily shocked, but at the stadium – as the figure before him calmly poured champagne – he had come close.

Sabine, when he caught up with her, was livid. "Who was that?" he demanded. She trembled, not saying a word. "Let's go for a walk," he said. They entered a cemetery near the stadium. Proceeding along the rows of graves, he waited. "I knew him long ago," she finally said, partly defiant, partly apologetic. "He called a few months ago. I told him to go away." The late afternoon light was disappearing. The graves were as graves should be – silent and in full repose. Schwartz asked what *long ago* meant. "Before I met you." After more questions a story came out which was not especially unusual. Schwartz wasn't surprised. He wasn't even surprised his wife never told him. Everyone has secrets. He had his. When she came to the day when the Savignyplatz affair ended, she began to cry. "This is ridiculous," she said, pulling out a handkerchief. Schwartz suggested looking on the consul's return as a gain. "He might be interesting to get to know. Think of his experiences around the world." But Sabine was resolute. "He humiliated me. I want nothing to do with him."

In itself, the Savignyplatz affair was uninteresting for Schwartz, but a functioning diplomat was different. What of the world's affairs had he seen up close? More intriguingly, what local entrées did he enjoy? In the cemetery, Schwartz decided to cast a net, if only to see what it might bring.

For the rendezvous he chose the gate into the Tiergarten opposite the former diplomatic quarter. The consul might be interested to see the area where decades earlier his trade was plied. A gas lamp cast a faint illumination around the entrance. The air was chilly and Schwartz's breath lit up before drifting away beyond the range of light. Dampness was on the attack. The lamp post was drenched with evening dew and a frost, creeping out of the ground, was hardening the wet into a wispy white. In his flaring loden cape he was a pyramidal silhouette rocking patiently back and forth.

The consul came up with shoulders hunched. When he was a few steps away, Schwartz extended a hand from inside the cape. "You found it."

"No problems."

"I'm glad we have a chance to talk. It was awkward at the stadium."

The consul agreed. He hadn't expected Müller's family would be present at the race.

"We were all surprised. No doubt Sabine's father was playing a trick." A silent understanding went between them that no more need be said about the scene. "By the way, embassies stood here once." Schwartz gestured to the street behind the consul. "Diplomacy was an expanding industry in Berlin a hundred years ago. I admit I once considered the profession, but one has to believe in the national positions. Shall we go this way? I know a café."

Proceeding into the park, he inquired into the consul's work. Conversing quietly they passed a lake in amongst the trees; it was a black mirror holding up the forming fog. When Schwartz heard Hanbury had worked on disarmament questions, he became excited. A subject involving the great powers, he said. He began to set forth his view of Russians. "They treat the world as if they're in a bazaar. They posture, they threaten, they haggle. International agreements mean little to them. You must have noticed that."

The consul recalled the proof he assembled on the illegally deployed radar in Siberia, the Salt II violation. "We were planning to stand up to them," he added. "We had the evidence, but the Cold War ended."

"It would have been the right thing to do." Schwartz took the consul's arm and slowed him down. "Now take us," he said ominously. "We Germans. We have acquired the habit of making no decisions unless it's by consensus. As a nation we've become addicted to self-appeasement."

Within the intimacy of the thickening mist, Schwartz's low voice was compelling. "That may be happening everywhere internationally," Hanbury said evasively.

"You see!" Schwartz declared. "You know what I mean. Appeasement signals the death of an important political art, I mean the art of manipulating fear." He came to a halt and prevented Hanbury from going forward. "Fear," he emphasized. "Not terror. Terror is effective in the short term only. People react unpredictably to terror. But they respond rationally to fear. A distinction Hitler didn't make. One can speculate on what might have happened if he had. He might have coasted on forever.

Another lesson he didn't heed was never push the Anglo-Saxon world beyond a certain limit." Hanbury listened quietly. "East Germany made the same mistake. They adopted some of Hitler's formulas. You must have seen how clumsy they were. Sabine told me you used to go there."

The reference to Sabine stirred Hanbury and he laughed self-consciously. Something in Schwartz's voice made him open up. "I could never get her to come along," he said. "I was going to lectures on socialism. Where I come from we don't have a feel for that sort of thinking. I was curious about a functioning communist state and went to have a look." He chuckled when he told Schwartz about trying to share impressions of Stalinism with Sabine. "She wouldn't talk about it. Absolutely not."

"Is that why you didn't marry her," Schwartz asked casually, "because she didn't share your curiosity for political ideas?" He made it sound as if he wasn't married to Sabine, as if she were a distant relative, as if for purposes of this conversation she belonged to Hanbury more than him.

"I didn't believe she would leave Berlin," Hanbury replied simply. The fatalism he had back then was creeping back. "No matter how I looked at it, it was going to be painful – me not able to stay, her unable to leave."

"I'm sorry she remains set against you," Schwartz said. "I tried to convince her to let bygones be bygones, but some things can't be forced." They continued talking about Sabine, dissecting her character, treating her like an epic *femme fatale* and thus, in a way, confirming what Müller had claimed – that she was a woman they shared.

Over a beer in the café, Schwartz became interested in Hanbury's background. "Don't mind my questions," he said disarmingly. "The pursuit of a historian. We love biography. What did your father do?" The consul spread his hands. There wasn't much to say. He talked about the prairies and the role of a soil scientist whose life was spent in a contest with nature. "I think he won. He certainly received enough awards." Hanbury then turned Schwartz's question around. What was the professor's family like?

"No award winners on my side," Schwartz said distantly. "Not in the last few generations. No medals either. Losses only. My father died in Stalingrad when I was in the womb." The forebears on his mother's side, he claimed, had been more interesting. She had been a *von Pöllnitz*, a family with roots going back to the time when an Elector in the Hohenzollern family declared himself King in Prussia. A certain Oscar Pöllnitz, owner of a brewery at the time, was far-sighted. He gave the young royal house good discounts and in return his name acquired the prefix *von*. This started a dynasty which acquired and developed huge land and industrial holdings all over Prussia. "But it was nationalized by the Russians. All my mother had left at the end of the war was some property in West Berlin, a few paintings and my father's books." Schwartz's voice had darkened, but he seemed then to dismiss the losing hand which history had dealt his family.

The story caused Hanbury to think of Müller, hard at work, poring over files, untangling the German property mess. He asked if some of the family assets might come back. Schwartz replied there wasn't a chance. "It's because of the spirit of compromise." Appeasers were in power now, he argued, and sympathy for the fate of the great families such as his mother's had ebbed away long ago. "Today's politics have no backbone. Deterioration is everywhere, from the handling of the great issues of state all the way to the breakdown you see in the streets." He described Berlin's graffiti plague, the unchecked vandalism and rampant mugging and the daily wave of break-ins, including in his own neighbourhood. "Chaos is everywhere. It's time someone did something about it." Had such concerns come up in the consul's many meetings?

"It has," Hanbury confirmed, "one way or another."

"Tell me about it," the professor urged. "Tell me with whom you talk about such things. Whom have you got to know?"

Hanbury laughed, as if to say, *whom don't I know?* He rattled off a list. Schwartz listened, both nodding yes and shaking no. He might have been reviewing a stack of doctoral applicants. "An interesting start," he said.

"The Chief of Protocol was helpful."

"Von Helmholtz? You've fallen in with him?"

"Does he get a nod or a shake?" the consul playfully inquired.

"He could have been a great man."

"But...?"

"He's too liberal for most peoples' tastes."

⁂

Hanbury had occasion to think back to this first meeting with Schwartz and how they bantered about Berlin's elites. Schwartz was a rich source of information. Anecdotes on public figures emerged by the bucketfull. Hanbury recalled, when they got up to leave, that Schwartz suggested they had barely scratched the surface of innumerable subjects. Why not get together again? Hanbury had agreed. Already then he reflected on the situation's irony – that the irreparable situation with Sabine was being overtaken by an acquaintanceship with her husband. As for Schwartz's strong opinions on public issues – his flashes of political contempt – the consul saw these as a spillover from too intense an academic life, a mild and not-uninteresting eccentricity. He did not realize – how could he have? – that in consenting to see more of the professor he was reordering his future and tampering with fate.

ON EARTH AND IN HEAVEN

lbert Müller – provider, competitor, practised non-conformist and sometime father-figure to a member of the Berlin diplomatic corps – died suddenly in his sleep. The direct cause of death, pneumonia, he once vaguely predicted. But it really began with a fall from his bike when he broke three ribs.

Word flashed through the Eagle community and the collective foreboding was immediate. Not a few of them had that late-life habit of calculating when they went to bed what the chances were of getting through the night and seeing the next day. When a comrade doesn't make it, the calculation seems to worsen. The Eagles' mood at that evening's crisis meeting in a Charlottenburger pub was sombre. No wisecracks rippled back and forth across the table. They stared into their glasses. At last, Rudi Metzger, the oldest living Eagle, spoke.

Mensch! he croaked into the morose stillness. *Was seid Ihr alle für Angsthasen!* He accused them of shivering like scared rabbits in a burrow. "Where's the Eagle spirit?" he demanded. "Do we crash when it's time to soar? Don't forget, Albert's looking down. I'd say right now he's disgusted, seeing us crying in our beer. I'll tell you what he'd say if he were here." Rudi's voice changed, suddenly sounding like Albert. Mouths around the table fell open. Had Rudi transcended, had he become a pipeline linking heaven with earth?

Eagles! I always wanted to win. I've done it. I got here first. And I've an early observation: up here all the roads slant down and the wind blows only from the rear. I've got to say it, heaven beats Brandenburg hands down.

As Rudi spoke, his eyes lifted to the dark beams of the ceiling, but now he lowered them and glowered. "That's what he'd say. I'm sure of it. Let's drink to Albert." His voice was back to being old and raspy. Mugs were raised, but eyes remained trained on the table top. They saw Albert leaning into a curve, full tilt, afterwards berating younger legs for being timid. But, little by little, a murmur started and finally Horst Baumann asked for attention. He believed a delegation should be named to liaise with the next of kin on funeral arrangements. This launched a practical debate which dispersed the sombreness.

※

Hanbury learned of Müller's death through the weekend paper.

The last time they were in *The Tankard* the old man had been bothered by a rumbling cough that came from deep inside. Since then, shackled to his schedule, Hanbury twice missed the weekly trek to Spandau. He made a mental note to contact Müller, but kept postponing it. On Sunday morning – the stereo was playing – Hanbury paged idly through the paper. His eye passed over the obituary page. He almost didn't notice the announcement: *Albert Müller, Rechtsanwalt*. In fact, he finished turning the page and flipped back only because he thought he had seen something familiar.

Curiosity was his first reaction. Someone with the same name and profession as Müller? Then came alarm. He worried, yet did not fully believe, this was *his* Müller. Then the full truth settled like a huge weight on his chest. He couldn't breathe. He felt hot. He felt cold. His hands rose to his mouth and stuck there. *His* drinking companion, *his* instructor in the finer points of life was *dead*? Hanbury's eyes bulged with horror.

He crumpled the paper, got up, slammed a button to silence the stereo and walked in silent circles. He went to the window to look at the empty street. Finally, no longer able to bear it, Hanbury broke down and sobbed like a child. He had not experienced this depth of feeling any of the other times he encountered death.

Pulling himself together, he returned to the paper. He smoothed it against the floor and read three *In Memoriam* announcements for Müller. The first, an elegantly sized notice, was from the family and carried the names of Sabine, Werner and Nicholas. It said: *He was suddenly taken from us, but in our memory he lives.* A second came from the Legal Association which recalled his high standards as a lawyer. The third was from his club.

ALBERT MÜLLER
Leader Amongst Eagles.
His friendship warmed us.
He soared to heights which others shunned.

Hanbury was looking at the words but was seeing Müller: Müller cussing him for living on the sidelines; Müller at the Olympic Stadium, beet red with effort and in love with physical exhaustion; Müller judging his fellow man, with mischief oozing from every wrinkle on his face; Müller seeing absurdity everywhere he looked and loving absurdity everywhere he saw it. The difference between Müller and most everybody else, Hanbury realized, was the difference between gazing down from the heights and gaping up from the trenches. Müller took life both seriously and as nonsense. He harboured no ill will; he had no hard feelings; he was never sentimental. He let people be and he – semi-detached, quietly, in his own way – carried on.

Still on the floor, Hanbury had an urge to go to the place where Müller always glittered: *The Tankard*. Make a pilgrimage, sit there, mimic Müller's art of living.

Outside, the day hung in suspense. Light filtered down through pinholes in a celestial pewter sheet. As Hanbury began the march to Spandau, a wind picked up and the pewter fractured into dark inky patches edged with violet. For a while, in the west, as on the day when Müller claimed his thirty-third spot, the light was dramatic, but the sky closed up once more. An intermittent rain began and when Hanbury finally stood on Müller's street a storm was flailing about in earnest. He looked at the dark windows of the house and observed a minute of silence, then doubled back to *The Tankard*. Uwe's son-in-law behind the bar was busy wiping glasses.

Hanbury took off his jacket and with a flapping motion scattered water in a wide perimeter. "Herr Konsul," Uwe's son-in-law said. "You're the last I expected. The usual?" Hanbury nodded. "I got the news." Uwe's son-in-law, working the tap, skimming off excess foam, was silent until he had created a tankard with a perfect head which he placed before his customer. "I didn't expect to see you again," he said once more. "I only ever saw you with Herr Müller. You're welcome anytime naturally. Alone or otherwise."

"How did you learn he died?"

"Ilse told me. She heard about it at the baker."

"Do you know how it happened?"

"At first there was an accident, but it couldn't have been too bad. He was alive when he went into the hospital. The hospital did the rest. Hospitals!" Uwe's son-in-law shook his head in disgust. "Ilse and I kept Uwe out of the hospital. He lived another year because of that. It wasn't much, but it gave him time to think about the end."

"What kind of accident?"

"Riding in the forest. A blackout. Crashed into a tree. Broke some ribs. You know, you can live with broken ribs. But what do doctors do? They operate!" Uwe's son-in-law made signs of a deeply felt abomination.

"Is that when he died?"

"Not right away, but it was the operation all the same. Those doctors, they work fast. They were cutting into poor Herr Müller before anyone could stop them." He shook his head thinking how his best customer had fallen into the devil's clutches. "The reason I know this is because his daughter came in, Frau Schwartz. Nice looking lady. No resemblance to her father. Know her?"

Hanbury's heart skipped a beat. He sipped through the foam and with the back of his hand wiped his upper lip. "She was here?" he asked casually. "I used to know her. We sat over there back then, Uwe, Müller, his daughter, myself. Those were good times."

"Is that how it was? Well, as I was saying, Frau Schwartz came in. She said he'd been well enough to talk about his accident. He told her he was convinced he should have had more speed. The tree he hit wasn't all that big, he said. If he'd gone faster he would have felled the thing, like those karate artists, you know, the ones that smash through bricks. The trick is to have momentum."

"What did he die of if it wasn't the tree?"

"His lungs filled with water. As if the doctors didn't know that would happen if they operated." Uwe's son-in-law closed his eyes once more at the satanic goings-on in hospitals, then rustled in a drawer behind the bar. "Frau Schwartz gave me a photo to remember Herr Müller. I appreciated that." He took out a frame and studied the picture. Suddenly he peered at Hanbury, then back at the picture and shook his head. "I'm damned," he said. He beamed and handed Hanbury the photo. "Here. That's you. You're in it." The bartender looked happy as a cherub that a younger version of his client was now residing in his drawer.

"This can't be. I didn't know this picture existed," Hanbury said. It was the four of them twenty-five years before. Uwe was pulling a mock angry face; Müller, hair sticking out like Einstein, had puffed up his chest like a prize fighter; Hanbury, half-turned, held up a glass and smirked as if he had a deep love for the camera; and Sabine – how old was she? twenty-one, maybe twenty-two – she looked so fine it took his breath away. "She takes after her mother," he said, studying the moody veil that hung around her eyes. "In looks, she wasn't like her father."

"That's what I just said too."

"Why did she bring it in?"

"She was sorting his things. She said the picture belongs here, that the people in it belonged together when it was taken and they deserve to be together, here in *The Tankard*. Maybe you can hang it on the wall, she said. That got me thinking about history. So we're going to create a picture gallery of our customers on the stairway down to the toilets. I asked Frau Schwartz about the third guy – you. I didn't realize it was you. Who's the clown with the grin? I asked. Anyone that grins like that should wear a headband to prevent his face from cracking open. Sorry, Herr Konsul. It's the truth. Here look at you. You're nearly unrecognizable. Herr Müller would've called you a *Knautschkommode*."

"*Knautschkommode?*"

"Sort of an accordion. With that grin someone should have taken you by the ears and pushed and pulled to get a squeak out. I said that to Frau Schwartz."

Hanbury had a strange sensation. Sabine talking with Uwe's son-in-law about him? "And she said?"

"She laughed. She said I was close. She complimented me on my understanding of human nature. Well..." Thick lips pursed in modesty. "...why else am I a bartender? She really is a great lady. She said back then, if you were anything, you were a *Flitzpieper*, a little bird that flits around. I had to laugh. Ilse was like that when I met her. She wasn't reliable either. Maybe he's grown out of it, Frau Schwartz then said, referring to the figure in the photo. I didn't know it was you, but if I had I would have told her you are now a VIP. I liked Frau Schwartz. She made me promise to look after the picture. It was a day or two ago."

Rain driven by wind assailed the windows. Hanbury on the bar stool was motionless. Only a fraction of his mind was listening to the bartender's descriptions of other candidates for the new picture gallery next to the toilets. Mostly he was sifting through what he'd heard. Suppose the account of Sabine's visit to *The Tankard* was only partly accurate; even with that limitation her attitude was light years different from at the stadium. There, she would have trampled on the photo. Here she wanted the bartender to put it on display. He continued the rhythm of lifting and lowering his *Pils*, but his innards churned. What belonged together has to stay together. Why would she say that? Hanbury's sadness about Albert's death was acquiring an overlay of hope.

He paid for the *Pils*, zipped his jacket high and eased into the rain. A dash to the U-bahn was followed by the steady rocking of the train. The hypnotic effect helped with the mental composition of a note. In the bungalow he put it down on paper, sealed it in an envelope and, resolve undiminished, walked it to a mailbox before retiring for the night.

Dear Sabine: I saw the notice in the paper. I am deeply sorry your father passed away. No one was like him. Parts of him belonged to many people, but no one has lost as much as you. I feel your sorrow.

The only person I know who came close to having your father's pleasure in living was Uwe. I remember the two of them sharing stories. If only those moments could have been recorded. Was it Uwe who once called me a Flitzpieper? Whoever it was, no doubt he was right, but of course it was long ago.

With the support of your family and friends I hope you will get through this and find the strength to carry on. – Tony.

❧

Rudi Metzger and Horst Baumann were calling on Frau Schwartz in her apartment. Horst was doing the talking. Rudi confirmed all he said by whispering, *Jenau, so isses. That's it, that's right.* Sabine was composed as she poured tea. She said she knew the Eagles meant a great deal to her father.

Sabine had discovered there was no choice but to maintain composure. Many people needed to express their sadness; she was the only one they could do it to. The trauma of the accident, the roller-coaster days in the intensive care unit, the few last precious conversations she and her father had – he partly flippant, partly earnest, she hanging on every word – the phone call from the doctor that it was all over. Then came the burden of funeral arrangements, notices to be sent out, innumerable decisions to be made. And everyone who had a claim on her father's time now wanted to claim some of hers. Where in all this was there time for grief?

Tony's note arrived an hour before Herr Metzger and Herr Baumann came. She read it twice and put it with the others. What the two Eagles were saying reminded her of Tony's note. They too claimed her father had meant a great deal and had belonged to them, although they knew her loss was greater. She thought back to the note.

It had a feel of wanting to communicate something subtly, but what? *Flitzpieper*. The word struck her. Words like that popped out of her like they did out of her father. She remembered using it recently at *The Tankard*. But back then, had Uwe really called Tony a *Flitzpieper*? She didn't recall.

She listened to Horst who was describing the meeting of the Eagles and slowly coming to the point: the Eagles hoped to play a small role in the funeral ceremony. "In what way?" she inquired kindly. "We had hoped," Horst said solemnly, "that Rudi – Herr Metzger – might speak." "*So isses*," confirmed Rudi. Sabine nodded, but it demonstrated a thinking process, not that she had decided. "The day of the funeral hasn't been settled. It's difficult to get a slot," she said. "*Jenau!*" agreed Rudi, adding he knew it was a busy burying period. Old people at this time of year, with the flu making the rounds, were dropping like flies. "In my apartment building there's been three gone down these past two months. There's fewer old folks all the time. My friends are getting to be young. It's fine to have young friends when you're young, but when you get old you need some your own age. Like Albert. His spirit inspired us. It's still with us." Afterwards, on the street, Rudi and Horst agreed the daughter possessed all the finest qualities Albert used to deploy sparingly: cordiality, politeness, graciousness, restraint.

When a funeral time was fixed, Frau Schwartz called Herr Metzger to confirm he could speak for the Eagles. Rudi immersed himself in preparing an oration. He was on the phone to Horst. Ulf and Dieter called with ideas. A session in the pub was devoted to reviewing the text, but everyone had a different opinion. Some wanted the suffering of the war years emphasized; others that Albert had been an outstanding lawyer; one Eagle insisted there should be a reference to the fact that he had two wives. Rudi protested too much was being added. He was scratching the margins full, his handwriting getting worse as his impatience grew. The sheets were beginning to look like something out of an asylum. Finally he thanked them. "It's coming together now," he said. "I know how it should be."

❧

Several days before the funeral, a printed black-edged card in an envelope was delivered through the bungalow mail slot. On it stood Müller's name in capitals, the commencement and completion dates of his long life, plus information on the time and location of the memorial service. Hanbury turned the card over. No other signs. He thought about its meaning – a reply to his own note? – and of the process that brought it to him. He checked his schedule to see if he was free.

Frau Carstens desired to see the consul urgently on the morning of the funeral, but he kept his door shut, wanting no distraction. Even at that late hour he struggled with a question. Was the card an invitation, or would his participation in the service trigger a reaction like at the stadium? A now-or-never moment was chiselled on his watch. When the time came, he yanked the door open with angry determination. Frau Carstens, jarred by the violence, grabbed her reading glasses which threatened to slip off her nose. "An appointment," he snapped, throwing his coat on, striding past her desk. She pointed at her scheduling book, her mouth frozen into speechlessness. She recovered enough to demand to know where he was going. "A funeral," he said harshly. Frau Carstens cried that Sturm should drive – *especially to a funeral!* – but he was gone. She frantically checked her files for a protocol notice about a death, but drew a blank.

The sidewalk in front of the chapel was full of life. A previous funeral was ending. Its mourners were spilling out as the Müller party was waiting to go in. Into these two flocks mixing awkwardly in one spot, Hanbury made a quiet entrance, joining the back of the Müller party filing in. The chapel, a circular pantheon-like construction with a dome, had sitting room for perhaps eighty, but Müller was drawing a good crowd. At least forty mourners were forced to stand. Hanbury sought a spot on the periphery, relieved that the structure with shadows behind a semicircle of interior columns provided anonymity. From there he viewed the coffin. It was embellished by a bouquet of small red roses. Around it lay expansive floral wreaths and around the wreaths stood a colonnade of vases full of flowers.

Hanbury recognized several Eagles from the stadium. Uwe's son-in-law was there too, shoulder to shoulder with Ilse. The family slipped in through a side door and took seats close to the coffin. Hanbury froze. He studied Sabine. Shuddering with guilt he slunk deeper into the shadows. He saw her son – he had his mother's anxious eyes – clinging to her arm. Her husband held the other. Hanbury, looking at Sabine and at the coffin, became miserably preoccupied with things living and things dying.

The ceremony began with music, a piece from Telemann. It seemed to postulate that the human spirit is irrepressible, that it has no choice except to move forward. The bold, carefree, triumphant cadences might be a portrayal, Hanbury thought, of nature. He couldn't help seeing wheat fields dancing to the prairie wind. The imagery transported him to another funeral he had attended, staged not in a chapel, but under a much larger dome.

❧

The June weather for that other funeral had been perfect. A westerly breeze puffed white clouds forward under a deep blue heaven. Not a speck of dust was in the air that day, nowhere over a million square miles of prairie. The soil scientist had achieved much, and everyone who had profited from his work was in attendance. Universities and governments, co-ops and seed companies, sun-bitten farmers. The many admirers hung around on the edges of the main event in separate clusters. Because the little prairie chapel couldn't hold a tenth of them, the pasture next to the cemetery became a makeshift holy ground. The breeze, bearing smells of black earth and a promising crop, blew playfully into the microphone, as if God Himself had come to play a role. The pastor said a prayer and read from the Bible; the eulogy repeated what everybody knew. Dr. Hanbury, researcher emeritus, following a stroke, departed the world at sixty-seven. In his life he had arranged, amongst other things, for the important switch from ploughs to discs to work the land, for shelter belts of trees to be planted to break the wind, for the introduction of a Russian strain of crested wheat grass which holds soil in place at times of drought, and, as his time on earth was ending, for the acceptance of zero-tillage-cultivation, a technique that stops the wind from sucking moisture from the ground. The list was long. Without his drive and determination, who knows, half the prairies might have become desert. The eulogy scarcely mentioned the family, except that a wife, an accomplished piano teacher born in Montreal who tried to bring culture to the area, preceded him in death by many years. The son, it was admitted, continued the tradition of serving, although he went abroad to do so. Afterwards, in the cemetery, on a rise surrounded by rich fields that stretched as far as the eye could see, prairie soil clattered down on the casket. The son was no more than a minor spectator at that event because from start to finish, really, it belonged to science.

In the round chapel it was Telemann's music rather than the voice of God that whispered into a microphone, followed by a pastor making a short reading. Then came the eulogy. An old man, older than Müller, Hanbury estimated, came forward. There was a touch of the performer in him, for he looked at the mourners with a steady eye and gazed meaningfully for a moment in the direction of the family. In a creaky voice, difficult to hear in the spaces between the columns, he began to talk about an eagle and the nobleness of a life lived high above the fray. He described the deft use of up-currents on good days and of powerful wing strokes necessary to fight down drafts during inauspicious weather.

Hanbury moved forward to hear better. Caught by the dignity of the metaphor presented in a nearly breaking voice, he came into the light. As he listened intently his attention once more moved from Müller's coffin to Sabine. With a start he realized she had seen him, but her eyes betrayed no feeling, neither anger nor surprise. It was as if he was supposed to stand there, that he was meant to fill that spot. She studied him steadily. Or was she looking through him and so dismissing him? He shuddered, deflecting his eyes to the flowers on the chapel floor and back to the coffin, before easing back into the shadows. The doyen now placed a hand on the casket. *You're our advocate up there, Albert, and we know your spirit will be with us when we Eagles soar.*

It was the way Rudi Metzger spoke, more than what he said, which touched the listeners. Some dabbed their eyes, others cleared their noses. Amongst the Eagles, here and there, tears flowed without restraint. But Sabine was composed and dignified, her head high, one hand rubbing the cheek of her child. Another piece of recorded music played before the Müller party filed out. Caught on the side, Hanbury was amongst the last to leave. Outside, the mood was now busy, relieved, nearly buoyant. Hanbury picked his way through, not seeing

Sabine coming until she stood before him, viewing him with the same passive patience as in the chapel.

Masking a fresh burst of inner turmoil, he blurted out two words. "My condolences." Even as he said them he knew he had seldom sounded so stiff.

Sabine nodded. "Thank you. Also for your note. I appreciated it."

"Your father meant a great deal to you." But this too came out without much feeling. They stood in silence.

"Thank you again." Sabine turned away. Hanbury had an urge to take her shoulder, to ask her to wait, to talk everything through, starting at the beginning, but she was slipping off, back into the pack, towards her family. In the distance, he saw Schwartz was engaged in holding the hand of a bored and jumping Nicholas. As Sabine went, everyone was saying something to her. All received a graceful answer. A large woman in a white fur coat breezed towards her. Hanbury saw their short embrace. The platinum blond asked Sabine questions and looked in his direction. Rudi Metzger infringed and Sabine must have congratulated him for he looked pleased. Sabine began attending to her father's other friends. All the Eagles wanted a moment with her.

The next day Frau Carstens, not having found a reference in any of her sources, queried him on the name of the deceased VIP.

"It was a bird," a muted Hanbury replied, "which became a spirit and flew off."

This ticked Frau Carstens off quite thoroughly. The consul's tendency to acquire a look of religious serenity when she asked direct questions drove her to distraction anyway, and now this: a bird turning into a spirit! What next? Visions of a white dove carrying an olive branch? Fiery chariots racing to heaven? "Shall we review your social obligations?" she said.

She began with the Wintergarten opening. The old variety theatre had been bombed and after more than forty years its revival would be a big event. "Sturm *must* drive. If you arrive by taxi you won't be photographed." Hanbury, his mind still full of the funeral, still calculating what to read into Sabine's sparse words, nodded absentmindedly to Frau Carstens. She moved to a luncheon event the next day where politicians and diplomats were to discuss ways of bringing foreign culture into Berlin's desolate eastern neighbourhoods. There was more – dinners, concerts, receptions, parties – all of it tying him down until he felt as immovable as Gulliver. Frau Carstens, having arrived at the bottom of his social balance sheet, eventually ran out of steam.

Suppose she knew about the hidden ledger, Hanbury asked himself. Would she explode? Müller's funeral, drinks with Schwartz, Zella's upcoming visit, Gundula escorting him to the Press Ball: strange, unreal, illegal entries, thin slivers of privacy in the vast wasteland of his public life.

❧

On the way to the Wintergarten, the consul reflected on human nature and its capacity for transition. Solemn funerals one day; frivolous night life the next. Would Sabine allow herself a night out? He doubted it. She would be home writing thank-you notes for the wreaths and the flowers. He had thought it over and, in retrospect, he recognized that a stark finality marked her voice when she thanked him for writing her a note. It was best to assume that what she'd really said was that she didn't want a scene and would he now please leave. Yes, the funeral was the absolute end of the line. Hanbury resolved he would not talk to Schwartz about being at Müller's service.

Instead, he listened to Sturm. The day had been damp and sombre once more, but inevitably sometime during the Berlin winter an immunity sets in. No doubt that was the reason why Sturm talked with the happy release of someone who knows he's recently received an effective vaccine. His mind as always was on the East. "Know where Cottbus is?" he asked, knowing the answer would be no. "Near Saxony. Nice place. Enriches Brandenburg in my opinion. I wasn't sure I should go. I worried my car would be newer than my cousin's and it might look like I was showing off. Turns out he ditched his Wartburg long ago. He's got a Passat now – new – makes my Fiat look dated. Wonderful to see him in his first real car. My cousin used to be a truck driver, except he didn't drive much. The truck was always breaking down and spare parts took weeks. His happiest dreams before the Wall came down were of a world in which spare parts were always instantly available. Imagine his joy, landing the job of parts manager at a new Volkswagen dealer. He's in heaven. He's won all the company prizes for dedication. He's worried about his neighbours though. He said they aren't doing so well. All the neighbours think their neighbours are worse off. That's what's nice about the Ossis, Herr Konsul. They care about their fellow man." Sturm rambled on: new TVs, modern washing machines, microwaves, stereo systems, state-of-the-art video recorders – all now available in Cottbus, all being stacked up everywhere in tight, socialist-built flats. He continued rattling off the long list of new Eastern modernity even as the Opel swung into Potsdamerstrasse.

In the street ahead were a thousand lights attached to a façade. Powerful, rotating beacons on a flatbed truck in front played hide-and-seek with the clouds. Under a canopy over the sidewalk, red-suited doormen stood at the ready. "Nuvoh Riesch," said Sturm in an imitation Oxfordshire accent. "That's what Lord Halcourt would call it. He didn't like to be seen in company like that. Keep one hand on your wallet in there, Herr Konsul. With the other cover your face. Lord Halcourt would have."

Frau Carstens's prediction notwithstanding, no photographer took a blind bit of notice of the black Opel when it drove up. Two enormous Mercedes limousines held greater promise. One of the red-coats did open the Opel door, but mainly to plead with Sturm to move along quickly. Hanbury, looking elegant enough in his evening suit, stepped out and proceeded up the thick red carpet. But all eyes were on a couple behind him, a tennis player maybe, or an Olympic runner, accompanied by a leggy fashion model. In the foyer he took up a position in a corner. TV cameras on pedestals swept over the party. Celebrities were being interviewed. A matron with long, fluttering eyelashes leaned into a microphone. How heady, she was chiming, to see the Wintergarten get a second wind. To loud cheering and much clapping she predicted the city would soon regain the giddy mood of the twenties when it had been chock-a-block with the avant-garde. *It's intoxicating*, she sang. It rang out like a bell in a magnificent carillon.

Hanbury, tirelessly nodding to acquaintances, drifted into the performing hall. Memorabilia on the walls – costumes, posters, blown-up photographs – portrayed the great days of Berlin cabaret. Under a ceiling twinkling like the Milky Way, the champagne flowed, the women looked ravishing and friends embraced. A giant victory party, sure, but for what?

Having shaken hands with others at his table, the consul sat down to gape about at the rest of them. Who was accompanying whom? Which tables had the heavy hitters? Hanbury noticed the Chief of Protocol at the front, reviewing arrangements. He disappeared, coming back moments later with the President of the Republic amidst a scattering of applause.

The lights dimmed. A medley of Berlin tunes came from the musicians' gallery. Waves of colour, clever stage sets, blasts of music, a chorus line of four obscenely fat but funny energetic ladies, sad clowns, amazing magicians. The audience, happy that a sugary fairy tale had been reborn, even if it lacked real spice, loved the show.

During the intermission an attendant asked the consul to follow her to the front where von Helmholtz waited. "I want to introduce you to the President," he said. The Chief of Protocol took three steps, whispered to the head of state and gestured to the consul to approach.

"I understand you're a fellow casualty," Germany's President said.

"I'm not good at ducking flying eggs," the consul laughed.

"I'm not either. I'm sorry you were hit. It does not reflect well on us."

"It can happen anywhere. In my country people in one province have been known to walk over the flag of another. A couple of flying eggs isn't much compared to that."

"Perhaps. Perhaps not. It depends on the depth of the motivation." Hanbury was about to make a positive remark on the conduct of the crowd at the demo, but others pressed in. His audience was over.

"I hope you aren't disappointed with the show," von Helmholtz remarked, accompanying him back to his table. Hanbury replied neutrally that some of the acts were good, but von Helmholtz's opinion was firmer. He believed something was missing. "The Wintergarten is *in* Berlin again, but it's not yet *of* Berlin. Am I too severe? By the way, Gundula tells me you two are going to the Press Ball. We should discuss her some time. She may need your help." Hanbury was about to say that was most unlikely, that it was the other way around in every conceivable way, but the Chief of Protocol had spun off.

Glasses at the table stood refilled. *Prost,* he said to the other guests. They studied him closely. "You know the President?" The man who asked had bushy eyebrows, a gleaming scalp and strands of hair that hung from the sides over his neck like a silky curtain. "We saw you talking to him."

"We only met just then," Hanbury explained. "We had a misfortune in common." He described the ruckus at the rally.

"I saw that on TV," said an ample woman in a gaudy floral dress. "I saw the eggs fly. You were hit?"

"Right here." Hanbury pointed at his shoulder near his chin. "A bad aim. Five centimetres this way and I would have had it in the face."

"Scandalous, what happened," she said. She believed the authorities should come down hard on hooligans. "It didn't used to be that way."

The man with the devil's eyebrows slipped Hanbury his calling card. The consul dutifully replied in kind. Each studied the other's, as if the bits of paper contained secrets. Hanbury read the name: Dr. Kurt Stobbe, the chief archivist for the Stasi files. But Stobbe vocalized his discovery. "A consul!" Immediately he came around the table to a vacant chair beside the diplomat. "Would you object if we talk?"

"You have a fascinating position," Hanbury countered gracefully. "The Stasi files?"

Stobbe regarded the consul intently from under his great eyebrows. "We're just beginning to scratch the surface. When the state plays peeping Tom and writes down what it sees, the archive becomes gargantuan. We're finding interesting things: Olympic doping, terrorist support, money laundering, arms smuggling, cover-ups for war criminals. The entrails of a nasty regime. We want to share what we have with foreign governments. Come see me sometime. I'll explain what I mean and give you a tour."

"Well thank you. Maybe there's a file on me," the consul joked. "I went into East Berlin as a student. I was usually followed."

"Sure. We'll do a search. I'll show you how they organized their information. My door is open." Hanbury was about to ask Stobbe whether he'd ever heard of Günther Rauch, the reported saviour of the files, but the theatre was dimming for the second half and Stobbe circled back to his side of the table. A spotlight caught his smooth scalp, making it look like a chunk of gold. It added to his air of drama. In the semi-darkness Hanbury gave him a thumbs up.

The second part of the gala was imported too. Top acts from around the world. The highlight was an American who grunted, smoked cigarettes and set his insides on fire. Smoke puffed out from everywhere – nostrils, ears, his shirt collar. The audience laughed until tears flowed.

Once the curtain was down, guests lingered. Stobbe and his frumpy wife left first. He waved to the consul to reconfirm the offer. Hanbury answered with another upward jab of his thumb. That same moment he felt a touch on his shoulder. A corpulent woman had come up. "We know each other," she said. Hanbury studied her a moment, nodding to win time. He was acquiring a habit of forgetting people faster than he was meeting them, but blonde hair streaked with platinum and heavy lipstick belongs to a type not easily overlooked. Even so, nothing was connecting. His mental search must have been written on his face. She said, "Yesterday. At the funeral. You were talking to Sabine Schwartz."

"Yes. Of course," Hanbury replied, still racking his brain out and alarmed at the reference to Sabine.

"My name is Martina Ravensberg, and you?"

He said his name.

"An English name."

"Yes."

"And a friend of Sabine. I am a friend of Sabine."

"Not a friend. I knew her father."

"But she went to you. I've known Sabine since we were children and I could tell there is something between you. She's never mentioned an Englishman. How strange." The voice's accusatory undercurrent made Hanbury shrug, as if to say, Am I responsible? His mind was skipping back to Savignyplatz. Had Sabine ever mentioned someone called Martina? "Are you in business? Real estate? I love London," he heard the woman say.

"An English name, but not an Englishman," he corrected. More pushy questions assailed him. Despite a growing irritation, Hanbury identified himself more fully.

Sabine's friend was instantly rapturous. "A consul! Delightful! What a discovery. Could we have lunch? Tomorrow? The next day?"

"My secretary keeps my schedule."

"Of course. A busy man." Hanbury spread his hands and brought them together as if to apologize for the tyranny of his diary. "Here is my card," she said. "Call me."

Hanbury gave a quick nod and moved to the exit.

Where was the evening's magician, he asked himself. Where are the sorcerers when they're needed? He could use one now. Get him to deploy occult power. Ask him to erase the last two minutes out of the continuum of time. Hanbury felt his inner space had been defiled, that the purity of the previous day's moment with Sabine had been stained. Outside, he scowled, crumpled the platinum blonde's calling card and chucked it to the side.

TWENTY-FOUR/SEVEN

At ease behind the wheel of his Mercedes, inspired by twelve cylinders of power, Gifford was weaving his way aggressively up a busy Kaiserdamm. Other motorists, respectful of the outward urgency of his mission, made room. Beating others to the lights, getting there first – like winning a medal at the Olympics, thought Gifford.

Lunch with McEwen at the club.

"Earl?" McEwen had exclaimed on the telephone. "I say. Come down for a nibble. Been reading reports. Rivetting. Want to tell you about them."

More than some pre-Christmas socializing, Gifford speculated. New information? Must be good to justify a lunch. He took a peek at the consul's C-drive before he left. A command copied the contents silently to his own computer. A second later, a laser printer ejected sheet after sheet. Love this modern technology, Gifford said to himself.

The guard touched his cap as the big car passed the barrier. Arrive in a Mercedes, Gifford thought, then they salute. His response, a slight nod from deep inside the chamber of luxury, confirmed he always knew a day would come when it would be like this. But not even the makers of the Mercedes can do much about the sudden drop in dignity an owner suffers when he vacates the immaculate interior. A quick attack of cold rain mixed with sleet made Gifford lumber, inelegantly, as fast as his great weight allowed, from the car park to the club entrance. With his squirrel's head stuck to a fat bear's body, he resembled a figure carved onto a totem pole.

At the corner table McEwen was fiddling with a black case. "Delighted you could make it at short notice, Earl. How's Frieda? Looking after you?"

"Couldn't be better, Randy."

"Splendid. I'm a great admirer of marital bliss, Earl. Don't laugh. I am." From the case McEwen extracted a file kept together with a ribbon and placed it on the table with a pat – to attest to its value. "I do hope your marriage is in good shape," he said. "It will need to be to survive what I have to show you. Might cause thoughts of hanky-panky, moral crisis, that sort of thing. Shall we order?"

McEwen kept Gifford in anticipation. As lunch was served, the administrator was invited to report on progress, so he presented the C-drive printout plus recent versions of the consul's program. The meta-diplomat studied them with care. "Friend Tony is still walking I see. Whereto, we ask. A continuing conundrum. To be resolved soon. Twenty-four-seven is not far off, Earl. Bornhof rang this morning. He had a spot of trouble with Cologne. Cologne has the home mandate and wanted proof the catch would be worth the fishing. Don't know why he bothered with them. Could have set up his own operation. Ninnies they are, the world over really, the chaps with the home mandate, always having to see the shark inside the lagoon before hanging out some netting to prevent the beast from entering." McEwen sighed. "But eventually they see the light. Friend Tony will be watched around the clock. A few weeks of that and I expect they'll realize the waters are infested. Anything else Earl, anything not on paper?"

"A few items. Some days ago, quite unannounced, he ran off to a funeral. We checked who might have died. Nobody we could find; not a single flag at half-mast in Berlin. It struck us as odd."

"That was when?" McEwen brought out a stubby pencil, licked it and began to write.

"Tuesday."

"Ah. The day before the Wintergarten. He was seen there. Did you know that?"

Gifford nodded. "*That* was in his schedule."

"Got chummy with the President, I'm told. Doesn't fit, does it? How does a diplomat get to be chummy with a head of state? Two personalities, Earl. One for you and me; one for another, hidden set of friends. In my view, what we see is cover."

"Damn fine cover," agreed Gifford.

"He's a clever man, but I dare say he'll tumble. We merely have to discover the connections between things that are made to seem unconnected. A funeral last Tuesday? What's the death rate in Berlin? Two hundred a day? Dead easy to find the names." McEwen put aside his notebook and picked morosely at his food.

Gifford, chomping energetically on some uncooked greens, thought McEwen looked tired, a man feeling the weight of age. "Ever had one like him, Randy?" he asked to fill the silence. "I imagine you've seen a few bent ones in your day."

McEwen stopped eating. He seemed to tap into the past, opening up inner filing cabinets of memories. "Nothing *quite* like him," he finally said. "That's the charm, Earl. Each wandering child has its own reasons, its own way of wandering. I helped the Aussies with a girl in Peking. Poor creature had decided to give China a helping hand. And of course the Oxbridge boys can be frightfully deceptive. Brought a few of them back from the brink, I dare say. But similarities with Friend Tony are remote. It's the gap, the twenty-five years between the young man in Berlin and today's accomplished older version. Only a man of remarkable patience will hibernate that long. Admirable patience, Earl. Dangerous patience. I'm finished when Berlin Station shuts. Gone next summer. Out to pasture. I want him, Earl. Badly. My last hurrah." His eyelids drooped until they nearly closed.

"You'll get him," Gifford said, munching with dedication.

"That's all on your side? House hunting going well? He loves you more everyday? Opening up his soul nicely. That was the plan, I believe, you playing father confessor."

"He's out choosing draperies this very moment. He's been chirpy as a parakeet the last few days. We're starting to have some very decent chats."

"Lovely. Keep stroking. Every slip is helpful. Well, my side then." McEwen again patted the ribboned file. "*Gundula Jahn.* You don't know her? Never heard of her? Nowhere to be found on the C-drive? Correct?" The administrator thought, then shrugged. "Part of your catch nevertheless, Earl. Recall you mentioned his visit to the local paper? Useful information that. We followed through. He had a jolly lunch with her. Just the two of them, he and Jahn in a corner, very cosy, very jolly. He hasn't mentioned her to you?"

"Sorry," said Gifford.

"A columnist. Writes about how bad the Ossis have it. Weepy stuff. But she's more than that. The Stasi file on her runs to six volumes."

"Isn't that good?" Gifford wondered. "Nowadays, I mean."

"Earl! You're jumping to conclusions. Let's first ask ourselves what is in the Jahn file. It tells us that Gundula is a delightful little devil, a regular temptress, a siren, the kind of woman one should *never* want on the other side." McEwen undid the ribbon. With elaborate ceremony – as if pouring tea or taking snuff – he took out some sheets. In a monotone, he commenced a life story which started in the north, in Schwerin, where Gundula's father had been a renowned swimming coach.

"Important point, Earl. A successful chap. Produced those flawless machines that won Olympic gold. In the vanguard of the doping movement. May well have applied the fifth or sixth generation steroid developed before anybody else learned how to spell the word. With each Olympic success he rises in the state's esteem. Boys come from all over to be trained. Russian ones too. A truly happy socialist family, the Jahns. But then dishonour strikes. Gundula's older brother defects to the West at a swim meet in Vienna."

Flipping through the file, the meta-diplomat described how, after the disgrace in Vienna the Stasi listeners gave the family the full treatment. "Day and night, Earl. The result? There's nothing about our little siren from age seventeen to twenty-seven that we don't know, her deepest thoughts being a possible exception.

"Although under surveillance, trainer Jahn was not easily dispensed with, so the spectacular bodies kept coming to Schwerin. Then something happened. Seeing the tide of world opinion was moving against steroids, Jahn stopped administering them. This paved the way for accusations of not demonstrating socialist behaviour. Belatedly he was blamed for his son's defection. The accusation is based on a recording of a soulful discussion Jahn had with his wife, from 2:59 am to 3:47 am on September 8, 1979. In the darkness – the trainer and his wife were lying awake in bed – he reproached himself for their son seeking Austrian asylum. *It was my doing. I was the one that wanted him to compete in Vienna.* Half a dozen years had gone by since the defection, but this self-reproach was conveniently interpreted as an admission he had planned it. It constituted proof he'd been anti-socialist all along."

McEwen took a deep breath. "What about our siren, Earl? Let's backtrack. Naturally she admires the big, strapping boys that parade through the Jahn household. They love her too: big brothers, little sister. A certain Vladimir arrives from Leningrad for a year of training – a special arrangement agreed to at high levels. Olympic gold is written all over Vladimir. Trainer Jahn's job is to administer the magic substances that will get him there. The files record that Vladimir and Gundula become affectionate while walking along Lake Schwerin at 10:52 on the evening of June 11, 1981. Some embraces are observed in the twilight, a bit of fondling takes place. They leave the path and move into dense vegetation, emerging 41 minutes later when it is nearly dark. The file surmises sexual intercourse took place. No photos. If sex did not occur in the bushes, then it definitely did at 00:33 that same night – on some mats in the weight training room next to the Jahn residence. The room is permanently wired for sound and the files are precise. Our little siren's effect on men is ample. It takes Vladimir a mere 18 seconds to reach orgasm, though it is assumed it is his second of the night. At 01:29 am he starts again and performs well for 1 minute 57 seconds. Remarkable, Earl, the Stasi precision when it came to chronicling acts that undermine the security of the state.

"Six months later Vladimir is back in Leningrad and Gundula now fixes on Georgi from Murmansk. Then comes Valentine from Minsk, Ivan out of Moscow and Vassiliev from Kiev. She reportedly ignored Karl from Leipzig, Horst from Dresden and Frank from Rostock. No value judgements were made by the Stasi about this soft spot for Soviet boys.

"Pictures, Earl. We have them too. Don't tell Frieda I showed them. Keep our reputation intact. Which ones are suitable for you? Here. Have a peek. Don't drool. Superb photographers, the Stasi. In case you're having difficulty recognizing the bodies, that's our siren, in the middle. The others – count them, six – are men. Notice they're unclothed, Earl? Stark naked little heathens. Ever seen so many stunning bodies in one picture? Look at Gundula. Small, but perfect, quite perfect. Taken on the beach at Usedom. The object they are chasing is, I believe, a volleyball. A few more, Earl? I'll choose them randomly. What is changing and what remains the same? Everything is changing, only Gundula is constant. She's progressing from her eighteenth to twenty-first year. Yes, Earl, you're right. She's changing too. She's getting better. Oh, here's a rare snap. Gundula inside some clothes. Another walk along Lake Schwerin. That spectacular male rear end she is palming belongs to Vassiliev. Ah, thank you. I shall put these works of art back.

"What happened to the boy lovers? She maintained contact only with Vassiliev. She travelled to Russia, spent a summer there. Vassiliev stopped swimming to become an engineer. Naturally their letters were intercepted, copies made and put on file. Gundula becomes an opponent to the regime once her father is shunted aside. She had nothing to lose. Her brother's defection denied her opportunities. She was expected to take a job sewing buttons on shirts, but she refused. Instead, she joined groups that discuss redefining socialism, how to transform it into something with a human face. She writes about this to Vassiliev, who writes back counseling her to be careful. Too late. The Stasi now have real material on her. Conform, they threaten, or see your family pay.

"And then, Earl, European communism crumbles. The Stasi are stopped in mid-flight. The last thing on the siren's file is a letter from Vassiliev in which he says he is now a nuclear engineer at a reprocessing plant in the Ukraine. We don't know if she answered. Moscow Station is checking into it." The meta-diplomat retied the ribbon. "And now Friend Tony is seeing her. I assume you see the connections."

"Indeed," Gifford replied gloomily, not seeing a single one. All he saw was photos disappearing into a folder.

"They're working on a project. Someone is directing them. I feel it."

Over dessert they lapsed into gossip. "The Hun is eager to see us disappear," McEwen said with bitterness. "It won't be long and this club will be his. Rather humiliating, really."

"Entirely outrageous," Gifford agreed.

On the way out, Gifford still wasn't seeing connections, at least not between the consul, the journalist and a Russian nuclear engineer. All he saw were lingering images of photos, of the siren's smile and the wavy outline of her body. Suddenly he clenched his teeth. She's too small, he told himself, feeling the onslaught of a brutal desire for Frieda, *his* Frieda, from Kreuzberg. A new image came on strong, of Frieda on her back and she was moaning. *Oh, Gif. Yes, yes. Oh, Gif.* Let the consul have that skimpy bird, he thought. I've got two of her with Frieda.

❧

At the same moment those images were torturing the administrator, Hanbury faced a torment of his own: buying draperies. Gloomy, feeling oppressed, he was in Charlottenburg, ringing a bell on a well-manicured building. He was there to make decisions, not just on draperies, but eventually on dozens, maybe on hundreds more household items. The residence required carpets, kitchen tiles, bathroom fixtures, chandeliers, wallpaper, and the like. He had tried delegating, but the staff told him this was his piece of the action. The way he now stood at the Charlottenburg door – shoulders stooped, looking burdened – a random passer-by would have concluded he was there to confront doom.

Letters cut into solid brass above the bell said *Das Meisterwerk. By appointment only.* After nearly a full minute – the consul beginning to hope a reprieve was in the offing – Herr Neumeister, the agency's proprietor, opened the door. He popped his head into the street. He was short with a blond moustache and thin hair, and wore an oversized jacket in brilliant crimson. The way he moved and looked with wonder at the world made Hanbury think of a chick hatching. Herr Neumeister bade the consul to enter.

Das Meisterwerk consisted of cavernous consultation spaces arranged in a figure eight around two internal courtyards. The lighting was subdued. In all directions cave-like hollows contained marvellous items: Persian carpets, marble sculptures, rows of vellum books by French enlightenment writers, Gobelins furniture, oriental textiles, boudoir ornaments, antique paintings. Neumeister whisked the consul through the salons and, arriving in an open area decorated as an imperial council chamber, motioned him to a vast chair which resembled a throne. Hanbury sat down. Neumeister, with short quick motions also like a chick's, poured champagne, said *zum Wohl*, sipped, and reclined in the Roman style on a dark blue divan where his fiery jacket showed still brighter. Propped up on an elbow, he brought his fingertips together.

"Herr Konsul." The voice was high pitched and extravagant, as if he was some emperor's secret consort. "I was informed you have numerous decisions to make." Hanbury nodded. Neumeister described the philosophy of his service: to enact a harmonious meshing of the human personality with the physical environment in which it resides. "As I sit here," he crooned, "as we enjoy champagne together, I am psychoanalysing you, Herr Konsul. Don't be offended. It is part of my approach. I am trying to determine what you were, who you are and what you may become. It will be my task to guide your inner essentiality into effective decisions. My assistance to clients is based on *character effusions* and I have to say that at this moment *character effusions* are leaping out of you – powerfully, like solar flares. Very, very explosive." Neumeister studied the consul. Suddenly he snapped, "Why did you decide this morning to wear *that* tie?"

Hanbury handled his tie and allowed it to flop back down. It was in grey monotone with a faint blue stripe. "My ties are all the same," he explained. "This one, another one. There's scarcely a difference. It makes the mornings easier, not having to decide."

"Fascinating. Unbridled utilitarianism. Very, very effective."

"I was informed today would be draperies," Hanbury said, making it sound like a lament. "Perhaps some plain ones would be best."

"Even the material of *plain* curtains, Herr Konsul, upon close examination shows intricate work. I would not put draperies into categories such as *plain* or *patterned* any more than I would people. If I may say, my reading of you is that you wish to proceed quickly, too quickly perhaps. That may be dangerous. Decisions on the *kinds* of material to look at is often put off until a second appointment."

"I had hoped it wouldn't be necessary to look at too many samples."

"Is that a valid perspective?" Neumeister asked, narrowing his eyes.

"I like to avoid clutter. Clutter makes me uneasy."

"I'm beginning to understand," murmured Neumeister. "Normally we would first engage in an examination of the psycho-dramatic atmosphere you wish your residence to acquire. But why not? Why don't we sample first, then analyse your needs afterwards. And I do concede your point – clutter-avoidance is eminently valid. Follow me." With the champagne bottle and glasses in hand the two men circled the second courtyard towards the very back.

They entered a room full of veils suspended from the ceiling. "It looks like a steam bath, but it's pleasantly cool," Hanbury observed, extracting a strange comfort from the thin materials pressing in on him.

"Some say they have a feeling of protection here, like a returning to the womb." Neumeister disappeared into the textiles, but soon returned. One by one, from somewhere, he hauled out catalogue upon catalogue of samples.

The options being put before the consul made his head spin. "I don't know," he said repeatedly. "I just don't know."

"You find them all equally striking?"

"Perhaps." Hanbury estimated the accumulated books of samples before him contained several hundred possibilities. "If you were in my position," he said to Neumeister. "What would *your* choice be?"

"I normally hesitate to take that step on behalf of clients until the *third* session. Personalities are complex structures of ambitions, hopes, fears, anxieties. I do not move to active counselling until I have a complete understanding of the nuanced desires of my client. But, although it is early, my feeling with you, Herr Konsul – a prominent and successful diplomat – is that something in the direction of the pastel world would be appropriate. Your tie supports that. Subtle greys against a backdrop of pastels. It is a most provocative thought." Neumeister cleft numerous layers of veils violently apart and revealed an immense set of shelves. From a lower compartment, he pulled a binder with a velvet cover. "Last week I was asked the same question by the Foreign Ministry. You are aware the foreign minister has acquired an official residence in Berlin? Here – this is the material for the sheers in his salon. And this – feel it – so divine – curtain material for the dining room. You see the unifying logic in the samples? As guests move from room to room, differences in patterns become decipherable while thematic colourations act as constants and connect. Such harmony is essential for successful entertaining. Tests show that guests are uncomfortable if the decor in one room clashes with another. These are unusually elegant materials."

"They are," the consul said. He asked what else had been proposed for the residence of the German foreign minister. Neumeister, with a fresh flailing of his arms, elaborated on key elements of the German Rococo, gained momentum and went forwards to Neo-classicism, then came back to the weighty excellence of the Baroque. The foreign minister had instructed that all movements in German art were to be represented in his residence. *Jugendstil*, Neumeister informed the consul, would dominate the patio. In one villa a unity would arise from all the great epochal tastes – from the first Hohenzollern king to the last

German kaiser. It required a most careful selection of accessories. Colour schemes, lighting concepts, wallpapering, tapestries, drapery railings – the entire plan for the foreign minister was described to the consul. Neumeister's pace picked up and his queenly voice developed a scratchy twang, like an old gramophone played at too high a speed. Not only that, but Hanbury's steady nodding of approval was taken by Neumeister as an impulse to go faster and faster so that at last, swamped by a wave of his own excitement, he halted in mid-sentence, half way through announcing that the manufacturer of the bidets would be the fabled KPM porcelain factory in Berlin.

The consul shrewdly saw an opportunity. "I'll have all of that," he said with perfect calm. "What's good for the German foreign minister can't be bad for me."

"Everything?" Neumeister asked incredulously.

"The works. Don't substitute a screw, not even for the curtain brackets."

"Normally all this takes six, sometimes seven sessions. Such unusual decisiveness. You are a man of truly powerful impulse." He regarded the consul with eyes that had begun to worship. "Shall I arrange details with Herr Gifford?"

"Yes. No need to mention the foreign minister. Tell him *we* worked it out."

"I understand, Herr Konsul."

❧

Outside, Sturm had been patiently parked down the street in front of a neighbourhood transvestite club. When the consul had regained the back seat of the Opel, the chauffeur shared his observations. "I've been watching the boys arrive," he said. "Legs like pencils. One Juliette looked at me so hard I thought he'd ask me to play Romeo. Back to the office?"

Hanbury replied he wasn't in the mood. He felt tired. "Go for a drive," he instructed. "Have a look around."

Sturm put the Opel into motion. "Lord Halcourt would sometimes say that." Sturm widened his mouth, stiffened his upper lip and mimed an English accent. "*Tour time Sturm. Down to the river. Look for a trout. See how the hay is in the hollow.*" He paused. "Except this isn't Oxfordshire in summer, Herr Konsul. It's Berlin in winter in case you hadn't noticed. There's nothing to see. In the office at least there's bright pictures on the walls."

"I've had my fill of brightness. That was a close call in there. I want to forget Neumeister. Drive Sturm, go anywhere."

Sturm obliged by making a lengthy circle through the inner city. He used the time to describe in detail the daily rhythm of life on Lord Halcourt's Oxfordshire estate.

Hanbury for his part concentrated on the beams of light of oncoming traffic defined by damp-choked winter air. He began to see them as rapiers held by invisible fencers – attacking, fading, pouncing. An internecine war. His attention shifted to unmoving, passive bystanders – the buildings along the streets. Block after block, they squatted in silence. Hanbury studied a structure, released it, took in the next. Stony faces, deeply weathered, skin peeling off. Glowering old hags. Sturm's bearing was for East Berlin. When they crossed where the Wall once stood, the mood changed. Streets became populated by structures resembling dead torsos. Dark ruins and near ruins. Everywhere, roads were ripped open, bridges were out of action, broken tram lines disappeared into mounds of sand. Trucks transporting rubble crawled around. And as they went, Sturm presented evidence that Lord Halcourt, in his English way, had been something of a Nazi.

Hanbury wasn't listening. The hypnotic effect of the skirmishing lights provided blissful release. Quietly he took the pulse of his current situation: Müller dead, Sabine talking to him at the funeral, her friend wanting him to go for lunch, her husband interested in having a drink. There was Gundula too. She would soon have to teach him how to dance. But most immediate of all was Zella. She would be stepping off a plane in days. Hanbury admitted it. None of his previous assignments had provided a mosaic as rich and varied as this.

Sturm completed the Halcourt dynasty saga. His own role in it came next. At the age of twenty he went to explore England on a bicycle. In Oxfordshire he chanced upon a hapless British nobleman on the side of a country road studying a flat tire. Sturm took over. Soon the clipped voice sang, *I say! Well done. I've always wanted a German chauffeur! Stay on a bit.* Sturm did, married Betsy, who worked in the next village, and remained chauffeur until Lord Halcourt died. Then he brought Betsy to Berlin.

The vast circular route through the city continued. In the darkness, Sturm pointed out some sights. Back once more in the west, as they passed Tempelhof airport, scene of the airlift in '49, Hanbury perked up. He thought of von Helmholtz, the start of the great man's career, and asked if the place was still being used. Sturm, pleased there was a sound from the rear seat, said, yes, definitely yes.

The next day Gifford reached a quick understanding with *Das Meisterwerk* on the residence's interior work and furnishings. He made a show of informing the consul. Resting his thick elbows on the small table, he lingered to talk.

"Sturm tells me you saw Tempelhof," he said pleasantly.

"Yes. Time I saw it. Apparently it still functions."

"Allows you to fly into the heart of the city and back out."

"Useful for some people I guess."

"For who? What's your view?"

Hanbury shrugged and switched subjects. He was distantly interested to know where the administrator had found the money to pay for so much interior decoration. "It's a game," Gifford replied. "One learns to play it as one goes along."

⁂

In the run-up to Christmas the office mood was light. The consul gave each lady flowers and invited the staff out for lunch.

"And how will you celebrate, Herr Konsul?" Frau von Ruppin asked at the lunch, sufficiently inflamed by a second glass of wine to dare ask a personal question.

"Church on Christmas eve," he replied. "The *Missa Solemnis* on Christmas day."

"We were thinking we might go to church this year," a mellow Frau Carstens said. She was moved – by the wine, by the season, by the piety of the consul.

When the meal was over, they trooped off in different directions to spend Christmas with their kin. Except the consul. The staff lunch had delayed him and he hurried to the airport in a taxi. He nearly missed Zella's arrival. Running through the terminal, he saw her dragging a suitcase on rollers to the exit. Breathing hard he caught up. "Hi, Zella!" He took her by the shoulders and apologized. "I wanted to meet you at the gate."

"Hi, Tony." She kissed him on both cheeks. For a moment they were silent, gauging how they should behave towards each other – and how much they could assume – then Zella pushed on. "I've arrived in dinkier places than this and managed," she said cheerfully. "I've been shouted at three times so far. Are people around here always so friendly?"

"It's good to see you. You must be tired."

In the taxi, once or twice looking out the back, Zella talked about her flight and the passengers she met. Hanbury used the time to prepare her for the bungalow, making a small joke about not living in a palace. But when Zella saw his place, if she had expected a mansion, she didn't show it. She called it snug. Hanbury lugged her suitcase to a spare room where he had tacked some posters on the walls the night before. Afterwards in the living room, seeing the armchair squatted before a stereo system flanked by two huge speakers, Zella asked if he always sat there by himself. Hanbury, seeing the room from her perspective, quickly pushed the armchair to the side and pulled the sofa out of a corner into the middle. "More livable already," he puffed, switching on the stereo and putting in a disc.

They gossiped on the sofa for a bit. Zella bubbled with news of people Hanbury had forgotten. She was excited about being in Berlin and wanted to know the main attractions. What would they do? He proposed a Christmas concert, dinner at Kempinski, a visit to a Christmas market the next day followed by searching out some remnants of the Wall. Decisions on museums and nightlife could be made as they went along. "Three days is too short," he said. Zella yawned and laughed at once. "Jet lag," she explained. He urged her to get some rest.

In the early evening, Zella's batteries recharged, they left for the Berlin Cathedral, that cavernous temple, testimony to a hubristic concept of the Christian deity. Still, for a well-staged Christmas concert it was splendid. They stood amongst two thousand believers. *Oratorios* and *Glorias* rose into the apex of the great dome and echoed down. Zella sang the carols in English while Hanbury, never a singer, croaked out a toneless second voice. Over dinner at Kempinski, Zella passed along the latest news of Irving Heywood.

"He's no longer in the Priory," she said. "A promotion. Investitures Priest. He's a real fan of yours. Did you know that?"

"I never much liked how he sermonized."

"But he thinks the world of you. I showed him your note. He loved it. He asked me to tell you he misses the Priory. He said when you were in Disarmament the place was full of zip. He remembers how you stirred up the Russians."

"Stirred up the Russians?" Hanbury exclaimed in a voice rising with disbelief. "That's what he said? He was joking."

"Well sure," Zella laughed. "It was just his way of reminiscing."

Changing the subject, Hanbury asked Zella about herself. She told him stories of her upbringing in Yellowknife. "Did you know I'm half Cree?" she asked. "My mother's a full blood. She's still there. I don't know who my father was."

Hanbury realized that behind the veneer of happy enthusiasm existed a woman who had managed to triumph over her past. "I'm sorry. I didn't want to bring up bad memories."

Zella smiled. "No complaints. I had friends there. Real ones. It's been more difficult since. Deep down I still live in Yellowknife."

Afterwards they walked along the Ku'damm where decorated trees twinkled. The temperature had dropped below freezing and Hanbury wrapped a protective arm around Zella. Occasionally, as in the taxi where she sat half-turned to glance backwards through the window, she looked behind. "Looking for Santa?" he joked.

Back in the bungalow, Hanbury placed a disc in the stereo and joined Zella on the sofa where they sipped champagne. At a certain moment their communication became wordless and a gentle kissing began. Immodest chuckling initiated a game of I-dare-you-to-go-further. A shirt and a blouse became unbuttoned. After more unspoken signalling they left a trail of clothing on the floor and made their way to Tony's bed.

The whole next day spent roaming through Berlin, Zella was excited as a schoolgirl. She loved Schloss Charlottenburg, was overwhelmed by the bust of Queen Nefertiti on show across the street, trilled out sounds of joy on the Christmas market next to the ruin of the Memorial Church and spent so much buying trinkets that she joked she could soon open a stand in a Turkish bazaar. The cold, dry weather was holding. Happily swinging their plastic shopping bags, in step and arm in arm, they retraced their Ku'damm walk of the night before.

"Are there security problems here?" Zella asked casually. Hanbury said there were instances of coloured people being assaulted by skinheads.

"I mean, for you. Diplomats. Do you have security escorts?"

"Only the Israeli and the Turk, I think."

"I have the feeling someone is keeping an eye on us."

"Nonsense. That used to happen on the other side of the Wall. Those days are gone."

"Maybe. Maybe not. I worked in the Crypt once. We were trained to be aware of our surroundings. Yesterday I thought the same car was behind us the whole way in from the airport. Last night, when we walked, I wasn't sure, but the same figure seemed never far away. Today there's someone fiddling with a map always in the middle distance."

Hanbury made light of it. Investitures was following her, he joked. Someone dispatched by Irving Heywood was making sure she would take up the Ankara assignment. He was about to begin a slow turn, as in the old days on Alexanderplatz, but Zella, laughing aloud with a sudden show of mirth, stopped him. The grip she put on him was fierce. Rising on her toes to kiss his cheek she gave a cold order. "Don't let them know we know they're there. Keep walking. Tell me your life story. Make it silly." Her fingers sunk into his arm like talons.

Once more they walked. When Hanbury had collected himself, he said, "My life story? If written down it would be the thinnest book on earth. This is crazy, Zella." She giggled at what he said, gripping his arm once more. "If you don't believe me, at least pretend. Let me feel better. Let's play we're going to give them the slip." Hanbury was ready to do that much for Zella. "Of course!" he roared with side-splitting laughter. He swung the shopping bag – heavy with ceramic Christmas ornaments, wood carved candlesticks and pewter angels – exuberantly at his side. "Know the subway system?" Zella grinned. "Is there a station where lines cross?" She threw her arm around him and snuggled her head against his shoulder. "Lots do," he said, hugging Zella with his free arm. "OK," she smiled. "Time for the rails. Do as I say."

Filled with the spirit of the season, they went into the underground and studied the transport map. Even Hanbury noticed someone dressed in grey with a street map arriving on the platform. Zella wanted to be shown the connections. They made a show of tracing a journey. Zella liked the confluence of lines at Wittenbergplatz. The train came. The platform cleared. At the next stop they stepped off and followed a passage over and around to a connecting line to Wittenbergplatz. The figure appeared too, and took his turn studying a schema on the wall of train lines. On a new train as it rumbled off, Zella explained what would happen next. "We'll get onto a connecting train at the next station and when the doors close we jump. You double over with laughter and point in the opposite direction. We'll see if he gets off. Even if he doesn't make it, stay in character. It doesn't mean we're out of the woods. There's such a thing as double-teaming." It sounded like she was quoting a paragraph in a manual that exists in numbered copies only in the Crypt.

"Zella," Hanbury argued, "it may not even be single teaming. Why would we be followed? Those days are over, here. That stint in the Crypt has done things to your imagination. In a big city there's always somebody behind you."

"Keep laughing," Zella warned with a sweet look. "No one should go through life without one assignment in the Crypt. You get a clearer view of human nature."

At Wittenbergplatz they did it like professionals. They got on a train to Ruhleben. When a mechanism hissed Zella yanked Hanbury out as the doors were slamming shut. On cue he burst into laughter and pointed at the opposite rails. A platform attendant harangued them. *Mensch! Sie sollten zurückbleiben!* Idiots! You're supposed to stay back! The attendant looked up and down the train. All the doors were sealed. He signalled the all clear and the train rolled off. "Sorry," Hanbury shouted. "Wrong direction." The attendant, resigned to having witnessed yet another near death on his platform, dismissed them with a wave.

Zella and Tony took a train east. At the next underground hub they made yet another connection, this one north. Numerous people were changing trains and Zella was uncertain whether double-teaming was taking place. But once off at Friedrichstrasse and going up to ground level, she had no more doubts. There they stood entirely alone. "Did a plague pass through?" Zella asked in the middle of the deserted street. Cranes were motionless and bulldozers in the pits stood around like toys forgotten in a sand box. "You'd notice if someone was on your tail around here." The solitude relaxed her.

The afternoon brought more exclamations of childlike joy from Zella, first as she stood before the trays of pastries in the Opera Café, then, half an hour later, on the steps of the ancient altar of Pergamon in the museum. She showed a proprietary interest there in a relief map of Asia Minor which portrayed important Turkish archaeological sites. "All waiting for me," she said. In the afternoon's descending darkness, after a beer in the Nikolaiviertel and a bus up the Prenzlauer Allee – Zella casually confirming no one was behind them – they walked a short distance to the Gethsemane Church. Inside, with a few other early arrivals for the service, Hanbury explained that East Berliners had marched from here to topple a communist regime. Zella, impressed, studied the ceiling.

The church filled to standing room only. Between Christmas carols belted into the holy night, the preacher spoke about freedom, their gratitude for the gift of German reunification, the need for patience to make it work, and the necessity for vigilance against too much power ever again being held by the state. Afterwards, in a boisterous Prenzlauerberg pub populated by other refugees from Christmas Eve, Zella asked about the preacher's sermon. The stillness as he spoke had impressed her. "Even Christmas around here is political," she concluded when Hanbury finished explaining.

Later, in the bungalow, Zella motioned to keep the front room dark while she studied the street and the parked cars. "Phantom viewing?" Hanbury asked with a hand on the light switch. Zella concentrated like an animal sensing danger. With a shrug she turned and flicked a finger, a sign for Hanbury to flip the switch. "All the world's a stage and I'm in charge of lighting," he said. A disc went into the stereo. "Theme music for the play you're producing," he joked. "What is our play, Zella? A spy thriller? A light comedy?"

Hanbury's lack of alarm threw a switch in Zella too. She approached, intertwining her fingers with his. "How about something adult?" she said. But on the sofa she talked about the church service again. It had moved her. She wondered how the people there had survived Communism. She had met several Russian ambassadors in her day who always had an air of distance. She said she often thought of Russia, especially its lack of stability. It worried her.

"I was pretty close to what was going on in Russia in the Priory," Hanbury replied. "Some of the information in classified reports I read was frightening." The disc had run its course. He stood up to replace it with something lighter. "Take all that uranium and plutonium that's sitting around," he said. "Weapons-grade nuclear material like that has value." Zella, shaking her head at absurd, yet real and frightening possibilities, agreed. "I know it's possible to buy it," she said. "There's dealers around. There's a market for it." Music once more came out of the speakers. "We'll leave that problem to the CIA," Hanbury declared. "Do we really want to talk about that? I have a Christmas present for you." He produced a small hand-painted porcelain bowl from Meissen. Zella was deeply touched.

The next day, before she did anything, before even putting on a robe, Zella got up, went to the front room and studied the cars on the street. Afterwards she crawled back into bed. "What was that about?" he asked, reaching for her. "A weather check." "It must be freezing out there. It's cooled you right off. Come here."

After breakfast, they went walking in the Grunewald. "I took a look at the parked cars this morning," Zella said. "About thirty metres down the street one of them had someone inside studying your house. The same car was there last night, but I couldn't see if it was occupied. When we left just now, the car was gone, but another one, same model, was parked in the other direction, also someone in it."

"Someone waiting for his girlfriend," Hanbury said.

"Would you mind stopping to retie your shoe?"

"Sure, Zella. Want me to switch socks while I'm at it?" He bent down. Zella took a few more steps, then turned to watch him. "Well," he asked. "More phantoms?"

"Somebody back there just stopped."

They continued their walk, taking side trails deep into the forest. Eventually, if there had been a phantom, he was gone. As they came out the forest Zella, masking premonitions about distant apparitions, asked breezily, "What's on tonight?"

"How about a transvestite show?"

"Perfect!" she cried, clapping her hands.

"I know one in a nice neighbourhood."

Later in the day on the way there, they repeated the routine of jumping from a train as doors were closing. "Just in case," she said grimly.

That evening the transvestites – one of them, Hanbury supposed, was Sturm's Juliette – were in top form. Lithe, slender-limbed men. They had the neighbourhood audience in stitches. Hanbury was a failure at translating their repartee, but Zella, drinking glass after glass, rose above the limitations of language and developed transexual empathy. The Juliettes made her fight tears. "If I could live in a neighbourhood like this I'd stop travelling," she said during a break. "I'd settle down and get to know my neighbours. They're wonderful."

In the early hours they crawled first into a taxi and then directly into bed.

"No checking of parked cars?" Hanbury asked in the darkness.

"It's over tomorrow," Zella murmured. "I'm going to miss this."

"The phantoms too?"

"I guess we'll find out if it's you or me they're after."

"I'm sure it's me," he said pensively. "No one would tangle with you."

"No more talking," Zella whispered. "Let's get close. I want to feel you."

The next morning, Zella instructed the taxi driver to head for Bahnhof Zoo. "But you're flying."

"The railway station," she said firmly. They entered Bahnhof Zoo quickly. At the last moment, Zella turned from the stairs going up to the railway lines and dragged him down into the underground. They took the first train that came along, went one stop and got off. "I think you're taking this a little far," he complained.

"No. We were being followed again. I don't want them to know I'm flying. A computer could figure out in seconds which passengers today arrived three days ago. My name would jump out in neon lights. I don't know if it's you or me, but something's going on. We're supposed to report stuff like this."

"It's the Russians wanting to recruit you because of your experience in the Crypt."

"Don't make jokes like that, not about the Crypt."

"No? They must die laughing reading reports on people like us."

In the next taxi, this time to the airport, Zella became more relaxed after a few checks through the back window turned up nothing. At the terminal she kissed him lightly on the cheek. "I had a lovely time."

Hanbury kissed her back. "Christmas would have been dreary without you. You made the days come alive. I got used to you being there day and night. I'll remember it."

"My turn next to show you an exciting place," she said warmly.

"Yellowknife?"

"You're on."

"I guess that's it then."

"I hoped it would be like it was. You've got your career, Tony. I have mine. We intersected for three days. You made me feel good about myself. Thank you."

Hanbury kissed her other cheek.

"One last thing. Stop trusting. Look over your shoulder. Think about what's coming at you from behind."

At the gate she blew him a final kiss and disappeared. Hanbury felt empty. Performing a slow turn, he scanned the area, but no one in a grey coat and fiddling with a map was anywhere in sight.

THE WELL-TEMPERED DIPLOMAT

All through January Berlin slumbered in a cold fog which, as days turned into weeks, began to squeeze the city like a fist. People lost their bounce. Laughter became rare. If someone tried, it came out sounding hollow and forlorn, as if the Cold War at its most virulent was back.

The weather began its change on New Year's Eve. As the freezing Christmas wind played itself out, the air became motionless and dampness seeped in. Guests at von Helmholtz's party, staged in an old pump house transformed into a restaurant near the canal, clinked glasses – *Prost Neujahr!* – and went outside to hear fireworks cannonading in the streets. That's when they first noticed the stealthy wet-cold reaching in, not stopping until it chilled their bones. Worried about the feast losing its exultant mood if they stayed out too long, they hurried back into the pump house. Hanbury reclaimed his dinner jacket from the shoulders of a spirited elderly lady of Czech descent who had been telling him all evening about the joy of owning a casino in Baden Baden.

The little daylight that penetrated the fog that January had an exhausted quality. It was how people felt. Unable to see further than half a block, everyone started living at the centre of a fatigued, collapsed existence. Some were frightened by the shrinking, as if the fog was a perverse preview of old age, a foretaste of their own senescence. The city's institutions lost definition too. Golden Ilse with her fiery wings of triumph on the Victory Column was swallowed up; the Tiergarten became haunted enough to house every ghost spawned since creation; and Frederick the Great, on his horse on Unter den Linden, while his outline did not entirely disappear, had never been more muted. As the fog hung without moving, the air lost potency. The city, that normally lusty organism, seemed at the mercy of a sapping disease. Like a patient it lay still and brooded.

Such was the weather when the consul and the journalist went to the ball. It was unchanged a few days later when they drove to Prenzlauerberg to search out a drinking hall called *Friedensdorf*. According to Gundula's information it was in this pub that they stood a chance of catching up with Günther Rauch.

Because the January sombreness is predictable, Berliners arrange for gaiety by having balls. Every strata of society has one: the police, the fire fighters, freemasons, taxi drivers, sport clubs, socialists, capitalists, everybody. But the Press Ball towers over all. For half a dozen hours in the middle of the winter it is the centre of the universe. That winter, for Hanbury, the Press Ball became a seminal event. Long afterwards, when his Berlin assignment was history and when he worked at unravelling the complex tangle of causes and effects that led to his demise, he concluded important seeds were planted there. He just didn't recognize them at the time.

The evening began routinely. In a timely fashion he set out for Gundula's flat. He had studied the route to Marzahn and took the S-Bahn line that cuts through the heart of the city from west to east. Curiously, whenever he now took a train, Zella's mind corrupted his. She had been much in his thoughts after she left and he was keeping an eye on things. But he was never really sure whether figures were reproducing themselves in the middle distance. And so, on the evening of the ball, partially to be prudent and partially to have fun, he acted as Zella would have. Because of its honeycombed structure, he used Friedrichstrasse station for a complex act. Trains arrive and depart there on several levels, and stairs and passages go in every direction. The happy flip side of Friedrichstrasse station's confused layout, Hanbury reasoned in accordance with Zella's teachings, was that tails can be shaken there without much effort.

Hanbury got off the train, left the upper S-bahn level by going down three flights of stairs to the lowest level, walked the full length of another subterranean S-bahn train platform, and took a second set of stairs back up to ground level before exiting the station into Friedrichstrasse. Having crossed the street he next descended into the U-bahn system and paced-off the full length of yet another platform. Up to street level again where he doubled back to the main station, re-entering it by a different door and climbing more stairs back to the S-bahn tracks where he had started ten minutes before. The next train heading east soon came clanging in. If someone had been following, the consul thought sardonically, he'd be vertiginous by now after all those twists and turns.

Hanbury's caution would still be holding a few days later when Gundula drove him to Prenzlauerberg and he looked back several times through Trabi's small rear window. But in a fog one pair of weakly glimmering headlamps is like all the others. "Lost something?" Gundula would ask. "Just wondering if anyone is behind us. A habit I have." "Tell me about it," Gundula would say. She could tell stories stretching back years about Stasi Peeping-Toms. During the drive Gundula would be strangely distant – the opposite of what she had been at the ball.

After the Friedrichstrasse antics, Hanbury sat in the train in a state of happy anticipation. A dozen stops along, in the city's far east, he got off and found a taxi. Minutes later, after zipping up the Allee der Kosmonauten, the driver wheeled into a vast expanse of sterile blocks of flats, an ant-heap, a slice of heaven to a doctrinaire socialist. The driver manoeuvred through narrow lanes between the featureless urban towers. No wrong turns, no hitting of dead ends. He had a nose for the one-way alleys. He pointed at a graffiti-decorated entrance. The consul told him to wait. He pressed a buzzer. Gundula was down in seconds. She informed the cab driver where to find room to turn around, but he knew. He lived in the ant heap too. The two of them were bantering immediately, exchanging one litany after another about the shortcomings of the local administration. In his Berlin dialect the taxi driver claimed that only rich Wessis went to the Press Ball. "You'll be lonely," he cautioned Gundula. "You'll be the only one there from Marzahn."

"I'm only going for a look," Gundula reassured him, as if Wessi viewing was a lower category of betrayal than dancing with them. Hanbury was stealing glances at Gundula, his eyes lingering on the long dark coat buttoned to the neck. Her dark hair was brushed back exposing small, unostentatious earrings. As she and the driver conversed in a tribal language, Gundula's face lit up. Put her on the Victory Column, Hanbury thought. Have Gundula replace the golden winged angel. With her power to radiate, from up there, she would disperse the fog in no time.

Gundula, Hanbury had observed, was not given to much personal decoration. She scarcely wore jewellery and for the ball had few signs of make-up. She probably knew that tiny earrings on her had more impact than strings of diamonds dangling from the earlobes of other women. Only later, when they were checking their coats, did the full impact of Gundula's preparations for the evening unfold. As the overcoat came off, a dark-red minidress came into view. "You look lovely," Hanbury observed with conviction.

"I didn't know what to wear," was the cheerful reply, "but, I knew it had to be red."

"It suits you. First things first. Let's find champagne."

Hanbury led Gundula upstairs to the bars where drinks were being poured as if the world was ending. Arm in arm, stopping every few minutes to sip, they explored. On the outside, the Berlin Congress Centre is an emulation of a fat, futuristic spaceship. Inside, the intergalactic vessel, a complex of halls and lounges, had plenty of passengers on board. The journey promised to be fascinating. The men, naturally, were all one anothers' clones. But the women! Each one aspired to be a work of cosmic art. Parisian see-through blouses, Latin American dresses cut provocatively up the sides, ballooning oriental trousers, low-cut frilly Viennese waltzing gowns with busts promising to burst out of confinement. The concubines to the super rich were recognizable by their cleavages – all of them lovingly prepared for public viewing in West End tanning studios. In one hallway Hanbury and Gundula saw well-known TV personalities behaving with an energy that seemed to say they would all soon be each other's next lover. In other side rooms, women snappily done up in men's suits leaned on yet more bars and, judging from the wobbly ankles in high heels, a few slinky men had come dressed the other way around. But by the time the thousands were congregated in the enormous inner hold, when the great ship was casting off, Hanbury knew that few in the sealed structure held a candle to Gundula. It wasn't a conclusion arising from bias; he saw it on numerous faces. Everybody stared at Gundula, up and down, and up again.

"Why red?" he asked when they were seated in the ballroom.

"To set off your penguin outfit. Make you look important. Enhance your social standing." Gundula smiled the smile of reason.

"It's not like that," Hanbury protested. "People are probably wondering how someone nondescript like me is out with someone glamorous like you."

"That's not what they're thinking," Gundula teased. "They're thinking, why does a prominent diplomat bother with an Ossi, and a gaudy one at that." The distance between sarcasm and truth can be vanishingly small and only Gundula's little smirk, the upturned corners of her mouth, betrayed her real meaning.

"You're the famous columnist read by thousands."

"And hated by a good two-thirds of them. By chance, they're all Wessis."

Hanbury said he refused to believe it. "I think you're a star. Anyway, Ossi, Wessi – it's got nothing to do with me. Let's drink to the opening of the Wall. Without it neither of us would be here."

Their eyes met and from somewhere deep in space an interstellar burst of energy zapped the consul, hitting him in the spot that triggers uniquely Earthian sensations, in this case a stirring in his groin.

The magic hour came. The band began a Viennese waltz. Anxiety appeared on the consul's face. "I did tell you I don't know how to dance."

"Yes, but I don't believe it. You have natural grace. You'll pick it up."

"I never even properly learned the square dance," he warned. He explained the dancing he had done with little Bonnie and how he once saw a neighbour – Keystone – get his wife into motion at a community centre in Indian Head. Keystone hopped twice on one foot, before shifting to two hops on the other and back again, bringing his steel-capped boots down hard onto the linoleum floor. As he hopped, he turned his wife's arm like the crank on an ancient tractor. Tony, in a corner of the centre, had mimicked this and thus learned the *Keystone Hop*. But the distance between it and higher forms of dancing, Hanbury was sure, was too great to be bridged.

"I'm sure it's much the same," Gundula reasoned. "Cowboys jumping, Viennese aristocrats gliding – the difference is only of degree. What they have in common is feet moving to music. Do you have a feel for music?"

"I sometimes listen to it," he answered evasively.

"Get the rhythm inside your head and let it sink to your feet."

Gundula got up and led him to a corner of the dance floor. Outside the paths of the free-wheeling enthusiasts she coaxed him. He began by moving stiffly on the spot. *Pinocchio*, she teased. But it changed. After looking down a while with an awkward angle of the head, eyes fixed on Gundula's dainty feet, the wooden puppet sprang to life. Without warning his feel for music did sink to his feet, which began to tap out the equivalent of a keyboard rhythm. And once he owned the rhythm with his feet, it spread back up so his whole body moved with harmony. Gundula led him into ever faster turns. Eyes closed but keeping up, the consul felt cold sweat being replaced by hot perspiration. Having travelled light years beyond Keystone's wife-cranking hop, he was suddenly out amidst the distant constellations, travelling at their speed. "I didn't know dancing could be like that," he said when the band stopped.

Gundula laughed. "A little overdone. We'll work on economy of movement next."

They went back at it. The slow waltz was mastered, no problem, but the quickstep was a disaster. "It's not natural," he complained. On the other hand, he truly came into his own with the samba beat, which lent itself to primitive leaps. Gundula spurred him on with unrestrained, head-thrown-back laughter. Their tiny sphere on the edge of the great dance floor in the ship heading out towards the stars filled up with immense vitality. In the Indian Head community centre, had there been a competition between the consul and the railway engineer, deciding the winner would have required a toss up.

Vitality was missing in Prenzlauerberg where the street lights in the fog produced a sallow, yellow hue, making the façades look undernourished. Gundula knew where to go. "Around the corner, second door on the left," she said with indifference. "What are you going to say to him?"

"Ask him how he is. It's been twenty-five years."

"And if he doesn't remember you?"

"I'll just leave."

Which is what Gundula did after the exertion of the samba. She excused herself during the band change. Hanbury watched her go, seeing the hint of rebellion in the way she put down her heels. He drifted over to the ballroom doors. Couples by the hundreds criss-crossed. He nodded hellos. Richard von Ringsdorf saw him from a distance and waved. Hanbury thought he might glimpse Viktoria's bare shoulder, but no luck. Sophia came by, hanging on the arm of a blond boy with slicked-down hair, saying it was ages since they saw each other. The consul pleasantly agreed. Cordula was there too, done up in feathers inside which she seemingly hid a thin man half her age. She whispered to the consul that his name was Otto and that politically he leaned towards the Greens. Then, unexpectedly, Martina Ravensberg stood next to him, as at the Wintergarten. Hanbury, not having seen her coming, could not escape.

"I knew you would be here," she said. She leaned towards him with a slightly stooped and threatening posture. The level of her voice dropped nearly to a whisper. "You have been on my mind. Once or twice I thought of calling you, but I put it off. That isn't like me." It sounded like a warning. Hanbury looked at her, past her, and back at her again. She leaned so close he observed the powdered downy hair on her upper lip. He also noticed that Martina's eyes were not quite synchronized. At this close range she seemed to be looking at him twice. Unsure which of the two eyes he should look into, he said, "I don't understand."

"I was balancing my interests against Sabine's and I'm afraid she kept winning."

Hanbury took a moment to digest this. "I still don't know what you mean."

"We talked about you," she said with unconcealed triumph. "I told her you and I were getting to know each other. She didn't take that well. Then she told me all about Savignyplatz." Hanbury didn't move. "I think you should call her," Martina advised. Her countenance was as inscrutable as a poker player's.

It seemed the January fog was reaching in to affect his vision. He looked backwards into time, then forward, and saw nothing in the mist in either direction that provided grounds for listening to this woman. "I don't think it would be wise," he said flatly.

"We'll discuss it next week," Martina declared. "Tuesday, one o'clock. You know *Rheinhardt's* in the Nikolai Viertel?" He nodded. The idea that he might see Sabine again was hypnotizing. A rotund man walked up. She introduced Professor Kraft. Hanbury learned he was a linguist. He listened patiently to the professor's perfectly acquired English. Martina, not understanding a word, expressed delight that the two men shared a medium from which she was excluded. When Kraft paused for air, the consul fled.

At the table, in a slouch, hands wrapped around an empty glass, Hanbury's inner eye went through one involuntary vision after another: Sabine walking next to him along the riverbank in Spandau; Sabine preoccupied with nest building on Savignyplatz; Sabine in a white hot rage at the Olympic Stadium; Sabine dignified at her father's funeral. The visions blurred. Sabine in the inner world was fading because in the outer one Gundula, with a jaunty step, was coming back. "Are you sad because your glass is empty?" she asked.

"Why is the quickstep so impossible?" he countered, lifting himself out of his slouch. "Let's get some more champagne."

It was then that Gundula, sipping from a fresh glass, delivered the news. "Progress on Günther Rauch," she announced. "Are you free Tuesday evening? I know where to meet him." It took Hanbury's mind off Martina's disturbing interruption. "They say he's not polite to strangers," she warned. "Half the western hemisphere has sent journalists his way and he hates story seekers."

"What is it about him, Gundula?"

"He took on the Stasi. Pierced the dragon. He's a folk hero, a saint. St. Günther." Hanbury wanted to know more, but she said Günther Rauch could tell his own story. What she knew of it was second hand.

A band flown in from Harlem began to play Soul and Gundula became excited. Soul was her favourite. Hanbury learned he could dance to Soul, especially the slow numbers. The band's rhythms captured them both and made them one. Between numbers they held hands. Jamaican Reggae was next so they took another walk, arms around each other.

Hours later, the space vessel, completing its long cruise, berthed back in the real world where the fog hit the disembarking passengers with the ferocity of an ice cold shower. "I'll take you home," Hanbury said.

"You don't have to. I can get there by myself." But he insisted. "Cowboy manners?" Gundula asked, eyes glinting. "Are they written down somewhere?"

"In a thick book."

They scarcely spoke during the early morning cab ride back to Marzahn. Gundula was alert enough, but she and the driver lacked a common wavelength. Hanbury's mind was shutting down; he fought to keep his eyes open. Off the Allee der Kosmonauten, Gundula directed the taxi into the melancholy ant heap. When it stopped, Hanbury told the driver to wait. He took Gundula by the arm as they walked to her door. "I heard right?" she said. "You asked him to wait?" Hanbury mumbled yes and on autopilot, thanked her for a lovely evening. "Think nothing of it," she replied. "You better run. Your taxi's waiting."

Hanbury squeezed her hand. "See you Tuesday. *Sankt Günther.* Right?"

"Bring your book of manners," she advised. She turned a key and was gone.

Walking back to the cab, Hanbury noticed the hoarfrost. The air's damp was settling out in coral-like formations, fairy tale beauty, even in Marzahn. "Grunewald," he instructed the driver. The driver was surprised. "We've just come from there." "My turn to go home." "A circle," observed the driver. "My wife believes in circles. I don't. I believe in sine waves." "At this time of night," the consul yawned, "I believe in everything."

❦

Monday morning in the office, the consul could have sworn the weekend frost had found its way inside. The air was warm enough, but the atmosphere was frigid. Frau Carstens's face was carved with deep lines of bitterness. When he asked what was wrong, resentment burst forth.

She had seen him at the ball. On her TV. Twice. First in a moving camera shot. He looked nice enough in his evening dress, but ridiculous too, since he was leaning idly against a pillar, hanging out alone, when everybody else was there in couples. The commentator had suggested in that posture he looked like a *ballroom cowboy*. The pain! And later the camera focussed on him on the dance floor. Why hadn't he told her he wanted to go? She would have fixed him up with a companion. "Also," she continued icily, "why would you dance with a total stranger like that columnist!"

"*That* columnist?" he asked.

"The one in the flimsy dress. Gundula Jahn is her name, if you want to know."

"How did that come out?"

"Society spotters identified you both."

"I didn't know…"

"Her name? You didn't introduce yourself when you asked her to dance?"

"I didn't need to do that…"

"You didn't ask her escort whether you might dance with her?"

"How utterly ridiculous…"

Under the relentless attack the consul had no chance to explain. Frau Carstens, eyes blazing as if conducting a blitzkrieg, pushed on. "I'm informed she is not held in high regard." She got up and disappeared in the direction of the washroom. Hanbury, shaken by the depth of her feeling and the enormity of the misunderstanding, thought of waiting at her desk to explain, then changed his mind. It was all too preposterous for words.

The next day communication continued to be sparse, so Frau Carstens was not informed of his lunch at Rheinhardt's. Late in the morning he simply took his coat and quietly walked out.

Hanbury took the S-Bahn to Alexanderplatz, then came back to the Nikolai Viertel, crossing the space where he and Günther Rauch used to meet. The Stasi's playground had disappeared into the impenetrable brew. The weather had been explained in a front page article quoting a professor at the university. The cause was an inversion, warm air up high trapping cold air below. There being no mixing, oxygen was being used up, the professor estimated, at a rate of a half-percent a day, adding that in ten more days it would get serious. He used a stoppered bottle with a burning candle to demonstrate the smothering. The story went on to describe how in the city's pubs customers were belting out the famous ode to Berlin's clean air – *Berliner Luft* – with special verve, and prayers of thanksgiving were reportedly being given in cabarets that the factories in the East which once belched like volcanoes had closed. All the same, crossing Alexanderplatz, the consul smelled the unmistakable, acidic pungency of burnt brown coal.

Martina arrived at *Rheinhardt's* shortly after he did. She was out of breath. "A big day. Closed a deal. I'm glad you're here. Someone to celebrate with." Hanbury politely asked what the deal was about. "Firewalls in Mitte." A beautification project. "Have you counted the firewalls in Mitte, Herr Konsul?" He answered he had not, but he'd seen a few. Gaping cavities in the urban landscape where buildings once stood were now defined by austere walls of solid brick. Ravensberg Creations, Martina claimed, had landed a contract to turn 300 of them into works of art. "If only my papa were alive." They ordered drinks.

"Has your papa been dead long?" he inquired solicitously.

"Quite long. He did not experience the Wall coming down. Too bad. We escaped before it went up. We used to live in Pankow. I've moved back there now into our old house. You need to feel the eastern pulse if you want to profit from it."

Hanbury had heard dozens of escape stories. Every third person in West Berlin has one. Tunnels, balloons, snorkelling, scuba diving, fake hulls in boats, concealed compartments in meat transport trucks, false fuel tanks in small aircraft – the ingenuity of people in the people smuggling business has no limits.

So, how did Papa Ravensberg get out?

"You're interested?" Martina said. "We had a routine escape. We left what we had behind and walked out. Mama with my brother into the French Sector. Papa took me into the American Sector. We met up at Rathaus Schöneberg where we all wept." Martina laughed quietly remembering how nervous her papa had been. "Shall we look at the menu?"

The lunch had the makings of an endurance test the way Martina was talking. She looked disinterestedly at her food and indifferently past Hanbury while her mind wandered. Finding cheap artists for *Creations* (luckily there were plenty in the East); living in Pankow (friendlier than Dahlem); advertising in the East (it had to be done differently from the West). She became personal too. Her mother throughout the years complaining about poverty; her father reacting defiantly. *What do you want me to do*, Martina mimicked him, *ask the Almighty to take out a rib and turn it into something better?* Martina as a young girl: withdrawn in a world of fantasies. Sabine as a young girl: acting hers out. The monologue had no direction. Or did it? When she got to Müller's funeral, most of her life's terrain had haphazardly been sketched in.

What struck her at the funeral when everyone was standing around outside, Martina said, was the way Sabine walked up to Hanbury. "She was determined. I was keeping an eye on her and saw that when she noticed you nothing else mattered. Who is that man, I asked. Who has Sabine been keeping from me?"

"She didn't say much," Hanbury said, putting up a defence.

"True, and you said less. When a man and a woman say that little to each other, something is going on. And then the Wintergarten, Herr Konsul. When I recognized you and you told me who you were, the mystery became oh-so-delightful."

Martina described how she confronted Sabine. "At first she didn't want to talk about it, so I threatened, a little." Martina giggled. "I said

I had started seeing you, that you had a nice feel about you. Was I going too far?" She described how Sabine became livid. Why the anger? Martina asked. What's so special about the consul? To her he seemed like just another interesting man. The consul was none of Martina's business, was Sabine's answer. Martina said she didn't understand. Anyway she was planning to make him her business. Another prize exhibit for her den of tomcats? Sabine asked acidly. Why didn't Martina hang out on the Strasse des 17. Juni after sundown with all the other public women if she couldn't keep her nymphomania under control. Martina was grateful for the suggestion. And, since Sabine wasn't pulling punches, she wouldn't either. She accused Sabine of leading an overly orderly existence, an act normal people can't follow. Normal people can't be that perfect, Martina said. That's why she had her tomcats. She *needed* them and wasn't afraid to admit it.

Sabine broke down. *That isn't true*, she said, *I know disorder. I've had as much as anyone.* She claimed that Tony Hanbury, a stray student, caused more disorder in her life than anyone should ever wish to have. Haltingly, then torrentially, and in much more detail than with her husband, the Savignyplatz story once more came out. The waiter in *Café Einstein* avoided their table. Only when a soggy handkerchief was returned to Sabine's purse did he approach to tell them that the dessert special of the day was built up around the passion fruit.

And now, in *Rheinhardt's,* the consul focussed on one word. "Disorder?"

"That's what Sabine said. Other than the problems with her step-mother, I think you are the only disorder she ever had. You're special."

"Did she mention the Olympic Stadium?"

"Oh yes. And then, after her father died, she found your letters to him. As far as I could make out, they came from everywhere. You *have* travelled. That's clear. She's angry with you for creating disorder. She's angry you wrote her father, but not her. She's angry with her father for not saying he was in touch with you all those years. All in all, she is, well, angry. But I think she wants to see you."

"I doubt it would be wise," said Hanbury. "Her husband would wonder."

"Her husband? He plays no role. Husbands, wives, pah, of no consequence. People like you and me, we ignore them. You don't look convinced. I'll be indiscreet. Her husband is the cause of Sabine's need for order. She has a natural weakness for it, true, but he has turned her into an addict. Someone should help her kick the habit. Why not you?"

"You don't understand. I don't want to pick up with Sabine where we left off. I only want to get re-acquainted, maybe become friends."

"Friends? Nonsense! It would do Sabine a world of good to have a side interest, a dependable lover. Take my advice, Herr Hanbury, go to *Bücher Geissler* where she works. Stir things up." Martina patted his hand with a wise affection. "And I want to be kept informed how you make out."

Hanbury looked at the expensive platinum-blond coiffure, the steady eyes that seemed to come at him from two directions, the determination that hung around Martina's glistening red mouth, and understood why Ravensberg Creations was winning contracts.

⁂

For the remainder of the afternoon, a distracted consul immersed himself in other people's lives. Strangers marched into his office. Passports, oaths, authentications of wills, certificates stating that marriages could proceed: his stamping hand dealt with all such needs. But another part of him was not there. That part of his mind hung motionless at the centre of several competing and perfectly balanced forces – Sabine and Gundula. He was silent when Sturm drove him home. Only later, when the sputtering of Trabi's engine and a tinny horn sounded outside, did he come out of suspension.

"I don't know why I'm doing this," Gundula said, turning onto the city autobahn. "I almost decided not to come." Her voice was cold.

"How so?" he inquired. The change in Gundula's mood puzzled him.

"Günther Rauch has his circle of friends. I don't think you're their type."

"Are you?"

"Barely."

"If we feel we don't fit, we won't stay. I only want to say hello. Thanks for this, Gundula. I tried to call you Sunday. I wanted to ask how you survived the ball."

"I was out all day," she said grimly, putting her boot down and pushing Trabi to the limit. The plume of smoke behind was a permanent black tunnel in the fog.

"I would like to ask him about his fight with the Stasi." Hanbury shouted to be heard above the noise.

"Ask him what you like. I might not stay," she yelled back.

"The Stasi got to you too, didn't they?"

"Why do you ask?"

"Don't you remember? After Gerhard's dinner you said all your boyfriends were on file."

"What the Stasi did to me was disgusting."

"Maybe they had a file on me – from the Günther Rauch days." He hoped to provoke flippancy in Gundula, to bring her out of her distant mood, but she didn't budge. Where was the Gundula with whom he danced to Harlem Soul?

"You're better off not knowing," was all she cried back.

The noise level dropped when Gundula left the autobahn and made her way through Wedding towards Prenzlauerberg. "If I had a file I might understand how you feel," he said.

"Why?"

Hanbury glanced sideways. She wore a black suede jacket with the collar turned up and tight white jeans. Someone should be painting her, he thought. "Ever heard of a Dr. Stobbe?" he asked casually, still trying to conquer her distance.

"Why?"

"Maybe you met him researching your columns. He's in charge of the Stasi files."

"I'm sure he leaves a trail of breadcrumbs whenever he goes in to find the way back out. Those files reach to the moon and back."

Once Trabi was parked amongst his peers, she took him to a building with a double wooden door which creaked. Behind was a cobble-stoned passage leading to a courtyard where socialist cars of various types, all of them beat up and stripped, lay about in a composition of anarchistic art. A hand painted sign read *Friedensdorf.* There was a distant rumble of many voices.

"Something left over from the old days?" Hanbury asked.

"A hot bed of dissent."

"Against what?"

Gundula didn't answer. She continued down some steps and went in. *Peace Village* might be its name, but there was no restraint in its assault on the senses. The noise level was higher than Trabi's engine at top speed. Beer glasses were in heavy motion, and with the crowd sucking neurotically on cigarettes the smoke hung thick. Tattooed arms were standard and every nose seemed pierced with metal rings. Artists? Intellectuals? Skinheads? A new political elite? Gundula and Hanbury moved through. *Entschuldigung,* the consul kept saying, excusing himself with every squeeze.

How do you find someone you knew twenty-five years earlier when you're searching in a place so full the view is limited to six inches? Gundula pushed on. They were coming to the back where there were side rooms, leftover bomb shelters from the war, also full of smoking and drinking figures.

As things turned out, it was Günther Rauch who did the discovering. "*Das ist nicht wahr!*" It's not true! The booming voice was like a detonation. Günther Rauch was coming forward fast with outspread arms. "*Ich glaube es nicht!*" I don't believe it! he thundered. Hanbury only had time for a glimpse and saw that Günther Rauch was almost twice as wide as he once was, with a paunch big enough to hide a football; red hair turning grey stuck out in all directions making the head enormous; the face was wider with eye sockets deeper and the beard longer. But that's all Hanbury saw because a bear hug smothered him. When he emerged, he tried to regain composure. "Günther," he said calmly. "How are you? I've been hoping to run into you." "*Mein Kamerad!*" Günther Rauch replied, laughing, but on the verge of tears. He kissed Hanbury on both cheeks. "My best traitor. Twice you came to see me. Then nothing. I was ten weeks in solitary on account of you. Did anyone tell you?"

"I hear you gave it back to them with interest not long ago," the consul said.

"You heard that? How far did the news travel? Across the ocean?"

"Gundula here told me."

No one after a lifetime in a police state shakes the habit of suspicion. Günther Rauch looked Gundula over. He asked some questions. She stood her ground, asking the same questions back.

"She's fine," Hanbury said. "She's got a Stasi file too."

"Everybody has one," grumbled the world authority on Stasi files. "The Stasi were so addicted to shit they ate from their own asshole." But suspicion drained away. "The Stasi may be history," he said to explain, "but they left a space behind and we all know nature abhors a vacuum. Today's version, thank God, is hopeless." He addressed Gundula. "Thanks for bringing this traitor around."

"Anything to please a consul," Gundula shot back.

"Cowboy," said Hanbury quickly. "My best friends call me cowboy."

"Consul!" Günther Rauch exclaimed with loud delight. Some villagers looked up. "Here? In Berlin? Fantastic! A great career!"

The consul shrugged. "It's a job."

"Ah! We must celebrate. Sit down. You too," he ordered Gundula. "Heinz!" Günther Rauch roared. "*Pils!* For everybody."

An elated Günther Rauch squeezed Hanbury's cheek, touched his hand, put an arm around his shoulders. "We could have been friends," he kept saying. "But you didn't come. I thought you were dead." Hanbury, needing to atone for twenty-five years of silence began to fill them in. He described his travels. Günther Rauch listened. No one can do that much travelling, his shaking head seemed to be saying, and manage to come through alive.

"What I have to tell you is meagre," Günther Rauch admitted when Hanbury insisted it was his turn. "I tried, as you know, but did not succeed in becoming a public nuisance. I wanted to be subversive; they told me I was a joke. I always hoped they would sell me to the West. "Now if I'd had some help...if my views had been smuggled out by a friend and published in Western papers, I might have seen more of the world too." He took Hanbury by the ears and playfully shook his head. Gundula watched a one-way love affair between two grown men.

"Eventually they said I would be a street cleaner," Günther Rauch continued. "So I swept East Berlin for more than twenty years. The same round, over and over again, an endless repetition. I had a good look at the proletariat at ground level, I can tell you, and I learned they were confused. No wonder. The Communist party was Fascist more than Marxist. So when the chance came to throw it out..." Günther Rauch faltered, dropped his great head onto his chest. He closed his eyes. "I lived and breathed the revolution," he murmured. "Those months in eighty-nine were the finest."

Hanbury raised his glass. "To revolution," he said cheerfully. Beer mugs clashed. Günther Rauch again told Gundula she had done well to bring the traitor by. "Everybody says you're a hero," Hanbury claimed. "How did you do that?"

"By chance. Pure luck. How else? For years, I cleaned the streets near Stasi headquarters. I knew their habits. After the Wall opened I could tell something was going on." Günther Rauch, thoughtful beer-hall commentator, described the day when he was sweeping as usual and keeping a close watch on the Stasi complex.

First, he noticed signs of torn paper blowing about in little eddies underneath a delivery ramp. A strange event for a bureaucracy which treated every scrap of paper like gold. And smoke was rising from a chimney which had not smoked before, not even in the dead of winter. It didn't smell of brown coal either. Bits of matter in the smoke glowed. Paper being burned! Günther Rauch quickly knocked on a few reliable doors behind which the regime's overthrow was always the first prayer in the morning and the last incantation at night. His citizen's committee assembled before the Normannenstrasse complex.

At the gate, Günther Rauch in a reverberating voice demanded to see a ranking officer, but none was left. As the smoke continued to rise, so did the indignation of the citizen's committee. The Stasi had been stealing pieces of their lives for as long as they remembered and, watching the chimney emissions, they knew it was their files, their lives going up in smoke. With resounding authority Günther Rauch announced he had been invested with the Will of the People and had come to take control. Five minutes remained before the People would act.

The gate slid open and confusion set in. The news had spread that the Stasi were being overthrown. Citizens arrived from all over. No one in the complex knew who might be Stasi, who was citizen's committee and who was there to hunt for souvenirs.

Günther Rauch's first act was to stop the burning. Workers in coveralls were told to support his cause. They said, as always, they would follow orders. File destruction was stopped. Incinerators were shut off. Bags of torn-up files were counted, recorded and sealed. Doors were locked, keys signed for. All in all, an exemplary neo-Prussian changing of the guard. Looting had started, but was stopped. Time to clear the building. Souvenir hunters were seen running off with life-sized portraits of Honecker. *Better to have my picture stolen, than to have my corpse strung up*, cried someone, mimicking the high pitched, scratchy voice of the former dictator.

"Us Ossis can't stop reading them," Günther Rauch said with bitterness, referring to the files. He asked Gundula if that wasn't true and yelled at Heinz to bring another round. "They called it a socialist paradise, but all the regime was really good at was snooping."

Günther Rauch and Gundula began to compare notes on how their files became so thick. Who generated the information? For Günther Rauch the relevant people included a student friend with whom he spent three summer vacations and whose wedding he attended. Also there was Franz, a placid, middle-aged man whom he often met for a chat on a bench in the neighbourhood park and, later, a street cleaner like himself. For Gundula they included an aunt, a school teacher and a neighbour across the street, a nice lady who kept a garden and regularly invited Gundula for tea.

When Gundula described the people who informed on her, Günther Rauch nodded and looked burdened. They described the other disappointments, other sequences in their life stories – thoughts, attitudes, feelings – things that can't be put into a file. Günther Rauch sat back in his chair, a beer mug in one fist, the other knocking the wooden table in harmony with the cadence of his voice. He was treating Gundula like a pupil. He encouraged her, corrected her, agreed and disagreed with her.

But Hanbury saw she was quicker and cleverer. She left him behind in exposing the underlying weaknesses of a society of double standards, duplicity and lies. Only bombast made the difference. Bombast, Hanbury saw, kept Günther Rauch in charge.

As for the final outcome of the revolution, Günther Rauch admitted he and the citizen's committee soon lost control. It didn't work out as they wanted. The proletariat is always unpredictable, he confided. You could hardly say, once the regime had been kicked out, that a new and improved solidarity set in. Everything was suddenly ruled by markets – labour markets, financial markets, global markets. To get something, to go anywhere, to achieve, you had to wheel and deal and race around and compete.

Gundula was saying less and less and Hanbury wondered whether *Friedensdorf* was opening up old wounds. But Günther Rauch, he could see, was gathering momentum for a monologue. Villagers sensed it too. They leaned forwards on their chairs, straining to catch his words.

The West set about colonizing the East, Günther Rauch postulated with a firm knock on the table. A whole society – factories, farms, parks, clubs, kindergartens – was decreed to have had no value. Now only money talked. And labour, the highest good in the world after only the human reproductive act itself, had been reduced to nothing more than a cost input, an entry on a ledger. *Imagine being told you can no longer make love because economists say it's too expensive,* said Günther Rauch to disciples roaring with laughter. *Even I have been affected,* thundered Günther Rauch. *Hand-pushed eastern brooms are out. Too slow. Too costly. Imagine me! Günther Rauch. A luxury item!* A roll of palms drumming on the tables reached down *Friedensdorf.* Hanbury saw Gundula was becoming pensive.

"What we need," Günther Rauch declared, "is a new party. An Ossi party. To fight colonization." Villagers cheered. "Marx-based. Pure

Marx. Stalin's corruptions not allowed. And we'll achieve power through the ballot box." Some cheers, some whistles. Günther Rauch turned to Hanbury. "What do you say old friend? Will you visit me once I'm respectable. Or do you take as dim a view of parliamentarians as you do of Marx?"

"From broompusher to lawmaker," someone yelled.

"From *Friedensdorf* into the *Bundestag*!"

"I propose a toast to Karl," roared Günther Rauch. More and more villagers were leaning around the corner of the alcove.

"We'll need money," a realist proclaimed.

"Can you make a contribution, Herr Konsul?" Günther Rauch demanded loudly. "My friends. This man is a diplomat. He'll help us." Günther Rauch clamped a fist on Hanbury's shoulder. "You have international connections. We need their support."

"No problem," the consul smiled wryly. "A few phone calls and you'll all be in power."

Günther Rauch started laughing. He laughed so hard he nearly wept.

❧

Hanbury and Gundula walked back to Trabi in silence.

"I can take a taxi," Hanbury said. "It's out of your way."

"No," Gundula said coldly.

She drove a few blocks. Without warning, on Kollwitzplatz, she pulled over and cut the engine. "There's something I have to say."

Hanbury glanced at Gundula. She was nearly hidden inside her jacket collar.

"Tonight was good," she said. She had her hands on the steering wheel and looked through the windscreen at the square's feeble lights. "You handled him well. From what I've heard, Günther Rauch doesn't warm up to people. But you told him things and asked him questions and got him going. Well done."

"Not me. It was you. You two did all the talking."

"He wouldn't have tolerated me for thirty seconds if it hadn't been for you. He toyed with me, but he wanted to impress you."

"I don't think so, Gundula."

"But now what? Will you see him again?"

"Well, yes. Occasionally. Of course the air in *Friedensdorf* is bad. And, well, you noticed too. He does go on."

"Occasionally, you say. You'll go see him occasionally. Not too often. When you consider it suitable, then you'll go see Günther Rauch?"

"I imagine so. Gundula, what is this?"

"I ask because it seems to be your general approach."

Hanbury said nothing. He also fixed his eyes on the emptiness of Kollwitzplatz. In the little park, he knew, stood a statue of Käthe Kollwitz. He had seen it on his walks. She sat on a pedestal, calm, stripped of illusions. Some minutes passed in silence. He tried to come to grips with an inner agitation. Finally he asked, "What are you driving at?"

"Look at you. You make an attempt to find Günther Rauch. You let him know you've gone to some trouble. You get him going. He falls in love with you all over again. I imagine that's what happened twenty-five years ago. What will happen next? Because the air in *Friedensdorf* is irritating, you may not bother to see him again until you're both seventy. I want to know if that, generally, is how you treat people."

"Günther Rauch in love with me? That's absurd."

"I don't think it's far off. He called you his best traitor. It sounded like he was joking, but he wasn't. He missed you all those years."

Hanbury thought about this. "I don't think that's fair. And it has nothing to do with you."

"No? Another question then. Why did you take me to the ball?"

Hanbury's confusion deepened. "I thought it would be fun. I don't know many women."

"But you know some."

"I suppose, yes."

"Then why me?"

"Gundula. This is odd." He felt as if she was forcing him to cross a river covered with broken ice: one misstep would send him under.

She pressed on. "You could have taken others, but decided on me. Why?"

Hanbury shifted his weight in the narrow confines of the Trabi. "I invited you because I like you," he admitted glumly.

"You like me?"

"Yes."

"But you want to keep it a secret." Hanbury sighed, but held his tongue. "Well then, what do you like about me?"

"Gundula, for heaven's sake!"

"Tell me. We need to get to the bottom of something."

"Bottom of what?"

"First tell me why you like me." She still gripped the steering wheel, but was turning slowly towards him as if she was giving in to a terrible anger.

Trabi, in the cold fog on Kollwitzplatz, was not a warm place. Yet Hanbury was sweating. He took a deep breath to keep his voice from trembling. "I like your eyes when they flash."

"That's all?"

In the middle of the perilous river Hanbury had no choice but to go forward. "I like it when you tease...I like it when you teach me how to dance..." He was close to faltering. "I don't understand. What does this have to do with Günther Rauch?"

"Nothing. It has to do with me. When you asked me to the ball, it meant something. It was a lovely evening. But how did it end? First, you insist on going back to Marzahn. *I want to take you home*, you said.

I hear you saying it. When we got there, you instruct the taxi to wait. You shake my hand. Very professional. Why? A sign that the consul's duties are done? Proof of a well-tempered diplomat?"

"No!" he cried. "The ball had nothing to do with my duties. You're wrong about that. We could have gone to a pub to drink beer. I would have enjoyed it more. I'm not much of a dancer."

"A cosy beer? Like tonight? You put on a professional performance? Think of how you treated Günther Rauch. Asking, probing, smiling, nodding. Your interest *appeared* genuine. Perfect diplomacy. Well done, Herr Konsul!"

"You're reading too much into nothing," Hanbury protested blandly. "I was tired after the ball. I scarcely recall what happened. I fell asleep in the taxi on the way home." The view into Kollwitzplatz was disappearing because the windscreen was fogging up. "What should I have done?" he asked, resigned.

"You could have sent the taxi away. You could have *tried* to stay the night." Gundula's voice was subtly changing, away from the volleys of accusation. "I don't know whether I would have asked you up. Probably not. But there would have been no harm in trying. What I want to say is, don't treat me like a professional contact."

Gundula started Trabi's motor. They drove off in silence.

"I'm really sorry about the ball." Hanbury said. "I felt great on Sunday. I tried to call you to say that. I would like to try some of those dance steps again."

"The music was good," Gundula agreed.

"Those guys from Harlem were terrific. They opened my eyes. They really did."

On the city autobahn Trabi went calmly. Gundula explained why the Harlem band impressed her. She hummed a few notes to demonstrate her point. At the bungalow, Hanbury asked, "A drink?"

Gundula looked him over, head shaking, eyes back to teasing. "No thanks. You need time alone to study that book of cowboy manners."

"It's thick. Suppose I never finish it?"

"Let's put it this way – once you have, let me know."

Hanbury stood on the sidewalk thinking this over. Trabi's engine roared. Gundula popped the clutch, but the engine died on the spot. Hanbury opened the door. "If you're gonna hang out with cowboys, get yourself a decent horse."

"Get away!" she laughed and tried again. With some coaxing Trabi, that dapper creature, disappeared into the fog.

Inside, he put a new disc into the stereo, a compilation, *The Best of Soul*. He set the volume loud and listened critically for a while. His thoughts wandered – to Gundula, furious with him for reasons he found deeply fascinating – to Günther Rauch, to whom an olive branch had been delivered – and to *Bücher Geissler*, an unknown place he felt compelled to explore.

CELLAR VISITS

*W*rapping up her father's affairs, Sabine found, was a full-time job which lasted weeks. Inheritance formalities, an apartment to be cleared out, organizing donations of his things: a bleak converse, she thought, to preparing the Fasanenstrasse apartment for Nicholas's arrival. Settling the estate was not merely a disentangling and redirection of objects. It was also a separating out of the physical from the spiritual. In the end little of her father remained, except what she carried of him in her head.

Everyone was supportive. Werner drove back and forth to Spandau for the things the family would keep. Lisa, who knew charities that supplied Russia, helped with the clothes. Martina arranged for a second-hand furniture dealer, who warned on the phone he paid only for antiques. Herr Geissler, throughout, was strangely understanding. "It needs to be done," he whispered, staring into the distance. "It needs to be done well." Sabine had never seen him look more disturbed. Had his tunnel vision become fixed on a looming question with no answer: who one day would settle *his* estate?

The weather didn't help. Every day Sabine recalled an opinion of her father's. No one should be allowed to die in winter, he once said. Winter deaths are too tough on the ones left behind.

When sleepless nights are spent staring at the darkness, and when the day ends in the middle of the afternoon and the mornings are so dull you can't make out the street from a second-storey window, some moodiness can be excused. For weeks on end, Sabine and Herr Geissler were in this respect peculiarly synchronised. The melancholy Geissler had taken to standing more motionless than usual near the front of his store to stare at the January fog. One day he saw it end. The agent – a cold wind – began pushing a few snowflakes around, and hour upon hour he was mesmerized by the white flecks that died upon impact with the sidewalk.

Geissler was so transfixed by the snow that he almost missed the arrival of an unimposing customer. The man halted in front of the store and paused to read the name in metal letters glued in a semi-circle on the window. The door was opened diffidently and closed gently. The string to the bell scarcely moved, so the jangle was subdued. Geissler felt less animosity towards customers who entered without arrogance.

"Good day," the customer said softly. Geissler indicated he was welcome with a severe nod. He observed the customer unzip a waterproof jacket, shaking off the wetness. Underneath, he wore a pin-striped suit. The shoes didn't match either. The colours clashed and they were badly faded, as if the wearer had trekked through acidic swamps. "May I have a look around?" the customer asked politely. "*Bitte*," Geissler said brusquely. *Please*. He waved his left arm towards the shelves rising to the ceiling. The customer handled the books with respect. He surveyed a row, title by title, occasionally pulled one out, holding it like a treasure before slipping it back. Different, Geissler thought. Most customers came in with questions barked out as orders. He adjusted his view away from the snowflakes. The customer's slow progress from aisle to aisle was inspiring. Why couldn't everyone browse like that?

Frau Schwartz was re-arranging titles in a far aisle. Geissler watched the customer turn into that aisle. He saw him address Frau Schwartz and how she dropped a book which hit the floor with a loud clap. The customer knelt down to pick it up. Geissler had never seen Frau Schwartz so agitated. She had been withdrawn these last weeks, mourning her loss, although she still dealt with customers well enough, correctly if impassively. But this one, dressed formally and informally at once, polite, educated, he changed all that. She became flushed, looking around as if she wanted to escape. The customer, as he talked, paged through the fallen book. They talked in hushed voices for five minutes. On the way out, the customer gave Geissler a genteel nod.

Geissler took a few hobbled steps into the aisle. "Who was that?" Frau Schwartz's countenance was once more morose. "An old acquaintance." She went back to ordering books.

"He is a foreigner."

"Yes."

"English. Only an Englishman would wear a banker's suit with shoes like that." Geissler was excited. His eyes behind the thick lenses flicked wildly.

"Not English," Frau Schwartz replied.

"He's not German," Geissler insisted.

"No. He's a consul. From Canada."

"*Der Konsul von Kanada!*" Geissler said with soft wonder, returning to the window.

The next day the customer was back, just before midday. He entered with less hesitancy. This time he wore a dark top coat and dress shoes, disappointing Geissler. The previous day's version, more eccentrically clothed, had better fitted his concept of the fearless adventurers who once upon a time explored a frozen north. When the customer greeted him, Geissler blurted, "I have a cousin in Canada. In Whitehorse. Have you heard of Whitehorse? A wonderful name. Who wouldn't like to live there?" The consul slipped into a professional demeanour. "Whitehorse? Surrounded by the mountains of the Yukon. A lovely part of the country. What does your cousin do?" Geissler fixed his stare at the consul. "He wrote he panned for gold." "Ah, yes, flakes in mountain streams. I hope he found some. But I'm sure you're more successful. This is a wonderful store."

Geissler gave a pained smile. Eyes full of pride flitted back and forth between the customer and the dusty books. "Your shoes are different today," he said awkwardly.

"I was out walking yesterday and happened to be in the area. Today I have invited Frau Schwartz for coffee."

Geissler jerked his head back to the street, sinking into himself, thinking of a Yukon river gravel bed glistening with a million specks of gold. Hanbury randomly took a book off a shelf. Paging through it, he waited for Sabine. When she appeared she asked if he had met Herr Geissler. Hanbury said they had chatted. Nonetheless she introduced him. The consul took a step forward to Geissler who half-turned. Hanbury saw the right arm was missing and without hesitation extended his own left hand. "I'm honoured to meet you," he said. "The same," Geissler muttered. Few people intuitively acknowledged his war wound.

A week later, the customer showed up again. He took time to talk to Geissler, asking questions: about the difficulties of maintaining a specialty book store and about the books – where did he get them? Geissler gruffly replied he had thousands of them stockpiled in the cellar. "It sounds like you have a treasure," said the consul.

Once the consul and Frau Schwartz had left, Geissler thought about the gold in the consul's country's rivers being taken out by his cousin, and about his hoard of books one floor below. A treasure? He decided next time he would invite the consul down.

Despite the many years with Geissler, Sabine was unaware her father's death had shaken the bookstore owner profoundly. She had no reason to think Geissler had deep anxieties about death. He never mentioned it. Her father, on the other hand, guided as he had been by a happy unconcern, was always glib about it. Even on his deathbed he had been convinced it would be a matter of days only before his strength would rush back. Reclined deep in the hospital pillows, he had important things on his mind. He was breathing hard, with more difficulty all the time, but he claimed that's what it was like in the *Tour de France*, especially in the gruelling uphill heats in the Pyrenees that test endurance. Sabine was next to the bed. Whatever her father was thinking, she could see he wouldn't win. Pneumonia was doing the winning. Yesterday he spoke in sentences. Today he gasped between each phrase. It broke her heart, being helpless as he struggled.

He was preoccupied with more than going uphill in the Pyrenees. He also lectured her. On the notion of reconciliation. *Suppose no one ever forgave…How many million people died in the last war?…And for what?…We started it…Somebody forgave us…Imagine where we'd be if they hadn't…*After all the many years he wanted to say something about Tony too. *You don't need to forget what he did. Just forgive.*

The last things Sabine wanted to talk about was war and death, or forgiving a former lover. She wanted her father, as he neared his end, to say things about her mother. And she wanted to tell him about Nicholas who was like him. In a weak whisper, Müller continued. Sabine had to strain to catch the words. *Anyway…what did he do?…panicked…ran off…avoided a decision…Once or twice I've done that too…*Limply he squeezed Sabine's hand. *Listen, next year…I'm going to clock more kilometres than the others…There's a neat trophy for that…You and Tony, I want you at the banquet…So you two can talk.*

That night Müller died.

These were not his last thoughts. He became materially minded enough for a few minutes to tell her where his will was kept. He recommended a lawyer to take over the legal cases he was working on. He wrote his bank account number on a piece of paper. He dictated the telephone number of the Polish cleaning woman who wouldn't need to come for a week or two. But reconciliation with Tony was his last request, and few things have the power of the deathbed.

Sabine considered she honoured his wish at the funeral. She accepted Tony's condolences. She appreciated them. She *showed* she forgave. That done, she planned to forget. But then Martina asked about him, boring into the subject, insistently, painfully, like a hammer drill. When Martina didn't stop, she lost composure. Once the story was out though, Martina agreed not to meddle. The Savignyplatz affair thus once more exhumed, was buried again.

Then Tony walked into the store. Sabine knew it was Martina's doing. She tried to maintain her poise but dropped a book, which made the confusion worse. Tony confirmed he wouldn't have come had Martina not pressed him. He was abjectly apologetic. "I don't want anything," he said. "I don't wish to bother you. I have some pictures of your father. Would you like them?"

"Pictures?" Sabine asked.

"I took them at the Stadium. I'll send them to you."

"Bring them."

"When?"

"When you like."

That evening Sabine made a point of informing her husband that the consul had visited the store. "Him?" Schwartz replied. "The one who upset you? He struck me as a decent man. Invite him for dinner some time." Werner, Sabine thought, could be casual to the point of being callous.

The photos broke Sabine's heart all over again. From Geissler's they had gone to a coffee shop, a stand-up place, and leaning on a table with Hanbury beside her, she studied them. She saw her father surrounded by other exhausted cyclists. There was a close-up of him glowering at his defeat, but holding a champagne bottle like a Grand Prix racer; in another, closer shot he gazed into the camera with a look that was part triumph, part pathos and part cheek.

"He knew it was his last race," Sabine said. "You can see that." Hanbury asked about the cycling accident. She described the operation, her father pulling through, until the pneumonia set in. "His mind was fine, but his voice wasn't working," Sabine said. "He was fighting for air." All around them lunch-time noise was growing, but Tony and Sabine didn't hear the clatter. They were concentrating on picking their way forward in a conversation that covered difficult terrain.

Hanbury described how, having read the obituary in the paper, he went to *The Tankard* where Uwe's son-in-law showed him an old photo. "He said you brought it in. When was that picture taken, Sabine? We were so young then. Those evenings with Müller and Uwe, the four of us. I'll never forget them." Sabine admitted she found Tony's letters in a box amongst her father's papers. At first she intended to throw them out, but then she read them. "You wrote my father, but you never wrote me. Not one try. Why?"

Hanbury attempted to explain, but the words came out mechanical, bloodless. Gripping his empty coffee cup, staring into its interior, he searched there for adequate descriptions of his failings, how they demonized him on Savignyplatz, how one day they hit him like a freight train, stunning him, making him stagger off. Incapacity for commitment, inability to make decisions, irrational fear of intercultural mingling, a tendency to cowardice. Did she want a longer list? Cowardice feeds on itself, he explained, meaning he could write Müller, but never found the courage to write Sabine. But no matter how hard he tried, the apology that was twenty-five years in the making was halting, even confused. Sabine could see he was struggling, that he was sweating out contrition.

"What does all that have to do with you coming to the store?" she asked. "Was there a special reason?" Yesterday in the store *he* had been composed. Now it was the other way around.

Hanbury faltered even more. He said something about becoming older. Nothing since Savignyplatz had added up. The way things were then counted for more than he could ever have predicted. "The sessions in *The Tankard* were like being in a family. I haven't experienced anything like it since. I'm glad I had a chance to see your father during his last months."

Sabine believed he was trying to say that he had come to Berlin hoping to lever part of his youth into his middle age. She accepted it. With her father gone, she was beginning to feel the same way. She too needed a new thread to run through and connect experiences. "Do you still listen to music?" she asked, her tone gentler.

"Oh yes," said Hanbury, brightening.

"You were beyond reach when you were inside your music."

"Do you still read as much?"

"When I have a spare five minutes." The conversation halted for a moment, then Sabine continued. "Your letters to my father said nothing about other people. You wrote about countries, or politics. The only personal news in all those letters was that your mother died. You never married?"

Hanbury shook his head. "No, no. Oh no. It wouldn't have worked."

"But no shortage of girlfriends. You must run into Martina's type everywhere."

Hanbury explained Martina's type didn't appeal to him. "You never mentioned her back then," he said. "She never joined us at *The Tankard*."

"We went our separate ways for a few years. Martina had a good figure in those days. She gave me a complex."

Hanbury glanced at Sabine and saw a slight pout. No different, he thought, than what used to slay him on Savignyplatz. "You shouldn't have had a complex, not because of Martina," he blurted. "No one was more beautiful than you. Martina's type can't hold a candle to you." This conclusion came out spontaneously and embarrassed both of them. They were silent for a while.

A woman came along to clear away empty cups and plates and muttered accusations about them standing there so long. "Can we do this again?" Hanbury asked outside. Sabine hesitated before nodding yes. That evening she showed her husband the photos of her father. "It's how I remember him." Schwartz again asked if she had invited the consul for dinner. Sabine replied she doubted he'd have the time, given his many social obligations. A week later, Sabine casually informed her husband she and Tony had met for lunch. They were in the sitting room that was lined on one side with books and on the other with austere portraits of Schwartz's Prussian forbears. A clock ticked. Schwartz continued reading. "Good," he said slowly. Some minutes later he added, "And you talked about what?"

"His work. My work. We had another talk about what happened between us. I understand better now why he ran away. Perhaps we *should* invite him for dinner."

"Why not? He must have interesting experiences to talk about."

"He had one today. Herr Geissler took him into the cellar. They spent half an hour there. I asked Tony afterwards what they did. He said they looked at books. Books as far as the eye can see. There's twice as many books downstairs as upstairs."

"Does he know anything about books?" Schwartz said, looking up.

"I don't think so. Piles of old books that are new is how he described it."

"I thought Geissler only went there by himself."

"As far as I know Tony's the only one he's ever taken down."

"Well, Geissler has a new friend, and so do you," Schwartz said nonchalantly. "Maybe we should all have dinner."

Schwartz went back to his reading. But Sabine saw her husband's concentration was broken. He ceased turning pages. A frown came on his face, as it did when he was preparing for difficult university debates.

⁂

Sturm was in form, on account of being in the East, driving down Karl Marx Allee, heading for Normannenstrasse. Hand it to the backseat, he thought. Not many other drivers were asked to navigate their diplomatic cargo to ports of call as exotic as this. "One of the great streets in the city," Sturm said admiringly of the wide avenue.

"Looks copied from Moscow," the consul replied. "Stalin's taste, if you ask me."

"I like the room here, Herr Konsul. Four lanes each way. Nothing wrong with that even if it's on account of Stalin. People treat each other better when there's room for traffic. Have you noticed? In the West we're always shouting at each other. A woman in a Ferrari called me a navel-fucker the other day."

"And you, what did you call her?"

"A blown-up paper bag. What else? Women in cars like that are pumped up with smelly hot air that arrives courtesy of rich old farts."

"Maybe it isn't the streets, Sturm. Maybe Ossis *learned* not to shout. Suppose the Stasi heard you shouting? They would have picked you up, right? And given you a dose of psycho-torture." This idea forced Sturm to reflect.

The Stasi were preoccupying Hanbury. He was thinking of Günther Rauch. Kurt Stobbe had invited him to the Normannenstrasse, but Günther Rauch was the motivation. Günther Rauch *and* Gundula. Both of them. He wanted to see the files. He didn't want to see *their* files.

He just generally wanted to see how lives like theirs were sitting on a shelf. In *Friedensdorf*, when they shared the dark side of their backgrounds, he had been a bystander. Seeing the files, Hanbury reasoned, might change that. It might allow him to contribute next time to their rapid fire dialogue.

He also believed, having heard Günther Rauch on the subject, that he could now speak with some modest authority on the methods of the East German secret police. His ideas about Stasi psycho-torture, for starters. Now he went further. "To keep you in line," the consul enlightened Sturm, "the Stasi might have blackmailed you into signing a phony letter, maybe to someone outside the country, in which you would hint you worked for the CIA. Once you'd done that they'd have you by the throat. Forever. They could use it to charge you with treason anytime. Then they'd deepen their relationship with you, force you to inform on your friends, your in-laws, your family. Maybe that's why people here don't shout. They learned it was better to get by unnoticed." To tease his chauffeur further, he added, "Perhaps it got in their genes."

Sturm thought this over too. The consul was being fairly talkative. Again. A change had come over him in the last weeks. He was often away for mysterious lunches, but came back talkative. He talked to everybody, not just to Herr Gifford. He even made jokes to Frau Carstens. It was inexplicable, but Sturm wasn't complaining. A talking consul was better than one entombed. But that wasn't all. When the consul talked, like now, he was also making sense. The conclusion – the existence of an Ossi gene that made them quieter than Wessis – was sound. Sturm wished he'd made that observation. On the other hand, on matters like genetics, or Stasi practices, he couldn't take a back seat to the consul. Sturm owned this territory. He felt compelled to stake it out. "My brother-in-law knows someone who had that happen," he said matter-of-factly, "you know, getting framed, accused of links to the CIA. From what he told me – and I know this for a fact – I believe it was worse even than you think." That silenced the consul. At the Normannenstrasse complex, the gate swung open and the Opel rolled in. Hanbury got out and looked around.

So this was the scene of Günther Rauch's finest hour? Hanbury wished Gundula were along to share the moment. He hadn't seen her for weeks. Getting through to her had become impossible, although the reason for it could be seen in each edition of the paper. A breathless rush of columns was appearing. Gundula seemed to be writing as if her time was running out. Hanbury suspected the contents were inspired by their evening in *Friedensdorf*. Everyone was talking about her. Half the city was in an uproar. If she could get so much inspiration out of a few hours in a smoky pub, Hanbury thought, imagine what she would do if she spent time roaming around the Stasi complex. In the macabre stillness he drew himself up and entered the building with defiance. *OK Stasi*, his body language seemed to say, *he who laughs last laughs best.*

A guard, detached from the world with his feet up and a nose stuck in a tabloid, took scant notice. He must have thrown an electric switch, however, maybe with a wriggle of his foot, because a security door opened. A rheumatic woman with a bent back and stiff hips soon shuffled up. *"Für Herrn Stobbe, nicht?"* Hanbury nodded. They plunged into a dark hallway that smelled of cheap disinfectants. And every four paces, a door. Endless halls and endless doors, all sealed, the remnants of absolute bureaucracy having gone down to absolute defeat. *St. Günther drove the vermin out and preserved the catacomb for future generations*, the consul proudly thought.

The woman knocked on a door with Stobbe's title marked on it in black felt pen. Hanbury found himself in a small ante-room with straight-backed chairs and a surplus interrogation table. Another woman, more mobile than the first, came in. Dr. Stobbe would be there shortly, she announced. Did Herr Konsul want coffee? "Please," he replied pleasantly.

Hanbury could feel Stobbe arriving. A shock wave preceded him which progressively transformed into noise. A determined step, a loud voice issuing orders, a door handle snapping. The consul rose and when they shook hands he thanked the archivist for seeing him. "No problem," Stobbe said in English. "By the way, it's Kurt." He seemed a different man from the Wintergarten, less reserved, a German imitation of an American. "I studied in the States," he said. "So with you, here, I'm Kurt. And you?" His secretary arrived with a tray. "We can speak free," he assured Hanbury. "She doesn't understand. How're things state-side?"

"Canada," the consul reminded Stobbe.

"Canada? Right. Canada. We're honoured by your visit." When the archivist said *Canada*, the spheres of his head – the gleaming scalp, bulging cheeks, round nose, large eyes and second chin that dropped down like a halo – connected up in merriment. He waved the secretary out. "Sit. Sit," he said. "So, you've come to see the files. Good, good. Cream in your coffee? We need your interest. I want you to know that. Sugar? No? I knew it. You look it. You know…" He bent forward towards Hanbury over the once-serviceable interrogation table. "…the documentation the Stasi put together has no parallel. Some goes back to the Nazis. Many wrongs need to be put right and the information for it is here." Stobbe jabbed a finger towards the floor. "Beneath us," he whispered. He leaned back, plunked multiple sugar cubes into his coffee and grinned. "By the time we finish some wicked folks will have stood up to admit guilt."

"Sounds like you need a body guard," the consul said.

"I've got two." Stobbe said with pride.

"No bodyguards before?"

Stobbe chuckled. "Before Berlin I was curator of the Gutenberg Museum. Mainz. Know it? The first printing press in the world. I looked after early printed books, mostly bibles. Not a bad transition, leaving the Bible for the Devil." Hanbury had not counted on meeting up with a wobbly sense of humour. Getting insight into the Stasi files could be an uphill fight. But Stobbe switched his mood. The spheres on his face stopped playing. He turned grim. "My job is to put the files in order so we can get at what's in them. What we've seen so far isn't pretty. Ever heard how you make rats paranoid? Give 'em unexpected electric shocks. That was the Stasi approach. Keep everybody off balance. People usually knew they were being listened to, but no one knew who did the listening. That does funny things. Have you been reading that woman, Gundula Jahn, in the paper?"

"I read all her columns," said the consul.

"She's an Ossi you know. And she's got her spot here." Stobbe's finger pointed down again. "Not a small one either. Big." He spread his hands about a metre wide. "The Ossis love her for what she writes. The Wessis hate her. I'm a Wessi. But knowing what I know about the files, I think Jahn is right. I've become a fan of hers."

"So am I," Hanbury affirmed.

"Extortionists, thieves, blackmailers, informers. They were every-where. The Stasi probably screwed around in your country too." Stobbe's mirth was coming back. Hanbury could tell by the way he puckered his mouth. "Buggering Canuckland!" He laughed. "Spies, Nazi war criminals, folks like that. If you've got suspicions, we can help you pursue them. I guarantee cooperation."

"Thank you."

"OK. A tour." Stobbe gulped the last of his coffee, spooned out the remains of the sugar cubes and stood up. They proceeded along empty hallways, down some stairs, through thick prison-like doors and down more stairs. Hanbury lost his orientation. How had St. Günther mastered this maze?

"When the Stasi were here, this place hummed like a central railway station," Stobbe said. "Twenty thousand of 'e m in this complex alone. Organized like the military. Generals, colonels, captains, that kind of thing. There's about a hundred of us now. So it seems a little empty. A little haunted." He punctuated this with a fiendish laugh.

"Is it true the Stasi began to burn the files?" the consul asked.

"Sure," the archivist said with a dismissive wave, "but they didn't get far. They tried a little shredding too, but their shredders weren't too good. So they started tearing the files up by hand. There's a few thousand bags of torn up papers. We'll get all that glued back together. But mostly everything is in top shape. We've got a hundred and eighty kilometres of material to go through. That's a hundred and fifteen US miles, Canuck. Not far in your country, but a damn good distance for us."

In a public area in another wing, Stobbe took Hanbury to an old woman sitting behind a large desk. She was knitting. The weathered granny resembled a maligned little doll. "*Frau Rommelsberger*," Stobbe said, "*dieser Herr ist Kanadier.*" Frau Rommelsberger, hard of hearing, looked up, smiled sweetly, but kept on knitting. She didn't miss a stitch. The remorseless needles continued clicking. "He is a consul," Stobbe said more loudly. "He needs a badge."

"Yellow, green or blue?" Frau Rommelsberger asked with instant accommodation. She turned her perky eyes on Hanbury who asked about the difference. "Yellow for day visitors, restricted to the reading room. Green is general access for one day. Blue means you're one of us." She made it sound like a colour code for tickets to a circus.

"Green for now," said Stobbe. "If the Consul ever comes around and needs a blue, give it to him, Frau Rommelsberger. He's here to help."

"There's a new procedure for blue. Herr Schmidt decided last Friday. There's a form. Two photos are needed." She pulled an application from a drawer.

"New head of security," Stobbe explained. "The staff is growing. Last month ten. Today a hundred. Next year a thousand. Then we won't know who's who."

Frau Rommelsberger heard this. "I was the first one," she said triumphantly. "When they stormed the complex, my daughter went to see. She took me along. The place was messy. I stayed to clean-up. Then they asked me to sit at the door to check who's coming. Then they said I was hired. Imagine. Part of the revolution. In charge of passes! Never had better work." She giggled, still not believing her good luck. "We had a revolution in '53 too. My brother threw a bottle at a Russian tank. They shot him. In this one no one got shot."

"If the consul comes in for a blue, don't bother Herr Schmidt," Stobbe ordered. He handed Hanbury the application. "Fill it out and bring two pictures." To the granny he said, "The consul's good as gold."

"Well, I know that. Got identification?" Hanbury gave the reliable Frau Rommelsberger a calling card. She used it to write out a green pass, made a note on the back and filed it. She pinned a piece of green cardboard on the consul's lapel. "Have a nice time," she said, dotingly brushing some lint off his shoulder.

Stobbe led the way back down into the cellar and explained that the Stasi had a devious way of keeping track of information. It was done by a system of cross-referenced indices. The Stasi trusted nothing, not even themselves. Each index was managed by a different group. Several indices were required to locate a file. Names led to numbers, numbers led to codes, codes led to file slots. Agents and agents' contacts – the informants, *die Spitzel*, ordinary people ratting on their neighbours – were registered under cover names: Vulcan, Fox, Racer, Moonlight, Perfume, Rocket. Other cards linked cover names with themes – Olympic doping or terrorist support – and with periods, like the Munich Olympics or the rule of Willy Brandt. The process that yielded information was tangled. "Over a hundred thousand worked in the Stasi organization, all told," Stobbe claimed, "and the brass didn't want any one of them to know too much. F16 is a general name index where the process starts. Everyone is in it. Over six million entries. Most of 'em are victims, but a couple of hundred thousand were rats. Ratting was an industry in East Germany, except you couldn't tell who did it. Even now it's tough to distinguish them. Well, here's the starting point. F16. Everybody's here, the good, the bad and the ugly."

Stobbe threw open a door. Rows of filing cabinets under banks of weak lights reached towards the far corners of a cavern. A solitary researcher was fingering through a cabinet. After making a notation he left. "This is the heart of a security machine characterized by Prussian thoroughness, Bolshevik zeal and Fascist ruthlessness."

"Are you in here?" the consul asked.

"No," Stobbe declared. "I've looked. They left me out. I never visited the GDR."

"I did," Hanbury said.

"I remember you saying that. Let's have some fun. Let's look."

Stobbe walked down an aisle with half a million H's. "OK," he said. "H, A, N." He flipped through a drawer. "Not here," he said. "But that doesn't mean we're finished. Sometimes they ordered phonetically. How would your name sound in the Saxonian dialect? HON? HIN?" "Maybe HUN," Hanbury joked. "Or *Huhn*," said Stobbe, laughing as he used the German word for a chicken. For a while he clucked like one. A few yards along, HIN drew a blank, as did other phonetic variations. Stobbe worked his way back, now checking out possibilities with the umlaut. Hanbury believed they were on a fruitless expedition, but why not see it through, he thought. "Well, well." Stobbe grinned. "Here you are. Under HAEHNBURY between *Haehn* and *Haehne*." He eased a card out. "Anthony Ernst."

The consul looked over Stobbe's shoulder. "A mistake. Not Ernst. Ernest. After my mother's father. Ernest Cadieux."

"Too late to fix it. Can you live with Ernst?"

"It's been that way since '67. I guess, a few more years won't matter."

"You shouldn't have said that, Canuck," the archivist said with disappointment, "I hoped to figure out when you visited." He looked at the back of the card. Something held his attention. "Someone looked for you in F16 not that long ago," he said. "When there's a *modern* search, a notation gets put on the back. Look, last October."

"October?" Hanbury thought back. "That wasn't long after I arrived. Something to do with my accreditation?"

"Sure. I guess. That must be it. OK. Well, we know you're one of the six million. Bet you didn't expect it. Stage two. See that notation in the corner. That's the F22 number. We'll write it down."

Departing the index room, the consul was intrigued. The bizarre kinship between Gundula and Günther Rauch was no longer beyond his reach. He was part of it too. He could mix in next time. The idea buoyed him, as if he now had membership in an exclusive club. But as they moved deeper into the underground labyrinth along ominous shafts, a disorientation set in. Was it the poor ventilation, or the confusing hallways? Or was he beginning to sense that, like all memberships, there would be a price? As they walked he developed a faint anxiety which did not mix with fascination. A nagging feeling developed that, as happened to Gundula and Günther Rauch, an unseen corruption had been festering for years inside his private life.

Around a corner the passage widened. A light bulb hung from a wire over a wooden partition. A gate stood open. "This was as far as the F16 crowd could go," the archivist explained. "They brought the F16 numbers here and the F22 battalion took over. F22 wasn't allowed to know the names in F16, while F16 didn't know what the F22 numbers implied. Only someone higher up could put the two together." Beyond the gate, they entered into the F22 hall, which was smaller than F16. Stobbe quickly found the next card. "As I suspected. You were an F17 case," he said critically.

"And what did F17 do?"

"F17 is the foreign enemies index. There are a couple of dozen subject indexes. F47 is control officers. F77 is cover names for the Stasi collaborators, the spies, the rats, you know, your friends and neighbours. F80 kept track of the places they bugged and the places used to debrief the rats. Others dealt with artists, scientists, athletes, terrorists. Quite a bit is cross-referenced. But F17 is foreign enemies and that's you. Had enough? Sometimes at this point, people get queasy. They get worried about the truth."

"I want to see my file."

"You want to see it through. I understand that. Let's see where to look. CZ70654, WPG66, GINHD, BSAV. Looks like gobbledygook, but it isn't. Let's note that down. We could find you in any one of several spots in F17. Which one makes most sense?" Stobbe pursed his lips and pondered.

Hanbury studied the notations too. "That first number – CZ70654 – could have been my passport. I look at numbers like that everyday. WPG66 is Winnipeg 1966, where that passport was issued. GINHD… I don't know."

"G is often *Geburtsort*, place of birth."

"Of course. Indian Head. And BSAV…. Maybe Berlin, Savignyplatz. Why…it's information straight off my visitor's visa!" exclaimed Hanbury.

"We're gonna hire you tomorrow to run our foreign inquiries section," beamed Stobbe. "Off to F17. We'll look under BSAV. *Indian Head* would have given the Stasi archivist a cramp of the tongue. *Berlin Savignyplatz* would have made him salivate. Nice place to live as a student. Non-stop drinking. Easy West Berlin girls. Am I right?"

"I was busy with other things," said Hanbury. He thought of Sabine – as she was then and how she was now. At their last lunch she was as talkative as in the old days. *A museum next week?* she had suggested. He immediately agreed, as he had back then. Strange, how some things were forever changed, but old patterns were starting to return.

F17 was a small room. There had only been some 50,000 foreigners deemed to be state enemies and by looking under BSAV Stobbe fished Hanbury out right away. It listed the dates and time he spent in East Berlin, the checkpoint he used, plus a registration of some kind – AFO (HAII) / HAIX-ABTXIV – and yet another number, C9LK8347. "I can't help you there," Hanbury said.

"No need to, Canuck,"chuckled Stobbe. "This one I can figure out. "AFO means your file is in the category of foreign enemies, *Aktenfeindobjekt.* Cases like yours were the responsibility of *Hauptabteilung II*, or *HAII.* That's Main Branch II where your file material was processed. The slash before *HAIX* means a cross reference to *Hauptabteilung IX* – Main Branch IX, where they dealt with investigations into domestic criminal activity. *ABTXIV* is Division XIV, a part of Branch IX, which was responsible for interrogations of domestic prisoners. But why would you be linked to that? What did you do in East Berlin, Canuck? Initiate subversion? Were you detained?"

"I just went for a few walks," he said. "No different than nowadays."

"Well, they suspected you of something. AFO C9LK8347. That's your file identification number."

They went back into the subterranean corridors. Stobbe opened a few doors to show the files, neatly kept in slots, from floor to ceiling, shelves and shelves, as far as the eye could see. Room AFO was inconspicuous. "East Germany's foreign enemies," Stobbe said, generously stretching out his hand as if he had successfully pulled 50,000 rabbits out of one hat. "I often ask myself how many enemies were real and how many were imagined." Hanbury's file, four or five centimetres thick, was located quickly.

"Well," said Stobbe, handling the weighty paper, "That's more than a few tourist visits worth." They went to a moulded plastic table and matching chairs in a corner. The file was tidy, the contents registered on the front cover. Stobbe, sitting at the table, began to recite. His voice echoed through the foreign enemies chamber. "A description of your first visit – nine pages; a description of your second visit – seventeen pages; the transcript of an interrogation – later that same day. Observations made during lectures you attended at the Free University. A report on a search in your apartment near Savignyplatz. Reports obtained under a cooperation agreement with the KGB: San Francisco, Washington, Caracas, Kuala Lumpur. GDR Embassy reports: Ottawa and Cairo." Hanbury sat stone faced. "Sound like you?" Stobbe asked with a vicious look.

"Christ yes," Hanbury said. He was chilled. The early fascination had dried up. He wasn't even disoriented any more. Stobbe's recitation had put him into a free fall, a nightmare, where a pounding heart wakes the victim just before impact.

"Now you know what Ossis feel," Stobbe said brutally.

"It's as if I'm looking at my own embalmed corpse."

"We talked about Gundula Jahn. Well, she's got a hundred times the file you've got. If you got embalmed, she got mutilated." The archivist began to flip through the consul's life. "I'm curious why they had that cross-reference to the interrogation section. Let's look at document seventeen." Stobbe went through the papers with the practised fingers of a teller counting banknotes, in a blur. "My turn to be surprised! You're cross-referenced to Günther Rauch. That's good company you kept. No wonder they kept a watch on you through the ages." Hanbury grabbed his file to see. "You want some time?" Stobbe asked. "I hope you don't find any letters from your mother which you never saw before. That's happened too. I'll be back in half an hour."

"Thanks," mumbled Hanbury.

Once alone, Hanbury experienced the sickening feeling people have after engaging in something deeply private and finding out they were observed. Petty details and innocent acts were treated as grotesquely important. A lip reader must have been around during his walks with Günther Rauch, because he was liberally quoted. The note on an intrusion into the Savignyplatz apartment was surgically neat. The layout of the apartment, the furniture, the records, the posters on the walls, the clothes in the closet, the double bed. It read like a lab report. A tentative conclusion was formulated that he shared the space with a woman. *Unknown, pending more investigation.* An addendum described a second search of the apartment. In cruelly objective words it described that the stereo lay on the floor, smashed, with the many records also broken into pieces. No sign of the man; still no information on the woman. Then came a Russian component to the file, partially translated into German. In cities Hanbury lived without an East German diplomatic presence, the Soviets acted as their proxy. But when the GDR had an embassy, Cairo for example, and later Ottawa, the reports piled up. His job descriptions. His vacations. Names of people he had long forgotten.

Everything had been sucked into the voracious file. Too much to read. Hanbury flipped through the material; it was accurate, but irrelevant too. The file slowly began to affect him on a different level. It seemed to say that he was something sadly shallow. So, the stereo got smashed, he thought.

Kurt Stobbe returned. "I'll come again if you want more time," he said gruffly.

"No thanks. I've seen enough. Nothing to learn here. It's insignificant but accurate. What throws me is the detail, year after year, meticulously kept."

"A Stasi specialty. They lacked feed-back loops telling them they were on a wild goose chase. Once started, they couldn't stop."

Hanbury's file was returned to its slot. Stobbe closed the door behind them; it sounded like an undertaker closing a coffin. Making their way out, Hanbury struggled with the idea that his mediocrity would be eternally on a shelf, that future generations viewing him through the warped lens of the Stasi would have masses of material to mock him. The thought was so disturbing that he planned to talk to Gundula about it. It was a quandary she ought to write a columnabout, if not to make it more palatable, then at least more comprehensible. At the exit, Stobbe reminded him to come back any time. "Let your people know we can help them unmask surviving Nazis."

"I'll make a point of it," the consul said.

❧

Sturm was walking purposefully around the courtyard. "Scientific investigation," he explained. "I wanted to find out why prison exercise breaks only last 30 minutes. Now I know: if you walk in a circle any longer you get dizzy. I went around so often I thought my eyes were catching up to the back of my head."

"I wonder if that happened to your Ossis," the consul replied glumly, taking a seat in the Opel. "They must have had eyes front *and* back. And even with that they might not have known how much they were being spied on."

This puzzled Sturm. Behind the steering wheel he thought it through. "Maybe they did know," he said. "Let's take genes. Maybe they knew it was happening, but didn't let it bother them. Maybe they developed a Stasi-resistant gene." He brought the Opel into motion.

Departing the complex, Hanbury thought about Gundula's recent columns. They were on the same subject. Stobbe understood what she was saying, but many others were outraged. Nobody was neutral. The paper was printing letters, strongly held opinions both ways, every day. Warfare on the editorial page. Hanbury had talked to von Helmholtz about it; he had shaken his wise head. "She's running down her journalistic capital too fast," he warned. "I'm worried she's writing herself out of subject matter. Have you tried to interest her in international relations? One day she may need it as an out." I will, Hanbury had concluded then, but now he thought, not yet. First he wanted her to write a column expressing how *he* felt about having a file.

Hanbury admitted he was obsessed with Gundula's columns. He clipped them, slipped them into transparent sheaths, organized them in a binder, and generally treated them like valuable works. There were two Gundulas, he thought, and both enticed him. There was the irreverent, energy-packed dynamo that zapped him every time they were together. And there was the Gundula that came through in print – intelligent, thoughtful, absorbed. The second Gundula, the one he studied in the clippings, the unapproachable Gundula, had certain qualities – a moodiness and a world-weariness – which reminded him of the Sabine he once knew. It was too soon to generalize about today's Sabine, but he believed she might have changed. She seemed less dreamy, more realistic and adaptable. Two Gundulas to think about, but two Sabines also.

The columns causing the uproar were based on the contents of a journal, a diary Gundula claimed to have found. It spanned forty years and had been kept by someone called Gregor Donner Reich. Hanbury had suspicions about its authenticity. Gregor Reich's debut in her columns came soon after the evening in *Friedensdorf.* Was the journal's arrival on the scene linked to Günther Rauch? Gregor Reich's diary was complex, full of controversial musings, too many to absorb quickly. In the back seat, Hanbury had a sudden need to gather his thoughts, both about the Normannenstrasse complex he'd just seen, and the fascinating diary Gundula had found. He wanted to get away from Sturm's chattiness, to travel more slowly, to shut out the world.

"Let me out," he instructed the chauffeur. Sturm stopped talking, but kept driving. "Stop please. Right here." The consul's words were pronounced calmly but precisely.

"Here?" Sturm protested. "What for?" They were on Warschauerstrasse, not far from the river, and it was nearly dark.

"I'll walk," the consul said. "Fresh air. Clean out the lungs. It was stuffy there."

Sturm was indignant. "Walk? It's fifteen kilometres to your place. It'll take three hours and the scenery is awful. Clapped-out warehouses along the river. Anyway, you don't have your walking shoes on, Herr Konsul." The last objection was expressed as a logical *coup de grâce*.

"Doesn't bother me. The next corner. Stop."

When the consul stood on the curb, Sturm gunned the engine and spun the wheels. The Opel swayed dangerously on some gravel, but he mastered the moment and was gone. Continuing on foot, Hanbury believed three hours would be too short. He needed more time than that – a week, a month – to digest the many pieces that constituted his Berlin assignment. They seemed somehow connected, but he couldn't see them ever adding up.

The Warschauerstrasse led to an amusing bridge with funny towers, perhaps inspired by the tales of *A Thousand and One Nights*. It had been entirely destroyed by the bombing and hadn't existed for fifty years, but it was being rebuilt. He admired it for a while before turning north. He walked past the East Side Gallery, a stretch of the Wall still up along the river now covered with pop art. One scene showed Brezhnev and Honecker in a tight embrace, passionately kissing on the mouth.

Holzmarktstrasse, Karl Liebknechtstrasse, Unter den Linden, Strasse des 17 Juni. Moving from East to West wasn't physically complicated, even if all else about it was. As Hanbury entered his bungalow and before he had decided whether to listen to music for the remainder of the evening, or reread Gundula's columns, the phone rang. It was Schwartz. "Am I disturbing you?" he asked calmly. Schwartz had an ability to send quiet reason down a wire, not by what he said, but by the inflection of his voice.

"Oh, hello. No. I was about to catch up on some reading."

"I wanted to say how pleased I am that you and Sabine are becoming friends. It's doing her a world of good. After her father's funeral she was down for some time. Understandable, of course. But she's much improved."

Hanbury replied he wasn't sure it had to do with him. "But I admit I feel better too. I owed her an explanation. It was time."

"She told me that. I'm sure it's made the difference. We plan to have you over for dinner soon. We know your schedule is demanding." Hanbury said he would cancel every conceivable official function to have dinner with them. "We can check dates out later," Schwartz said. His voice developed an edge. "I also wanted to see if we could get together in the next days. There's something I want to ask you. You may be able to help with my research. I'm looking for a book."

The consul's visits had become routine. On the day he was scheduled to appear the atmosphere in *Bücher Geissler* brightened. The store seemed to shrug off its air of sluggishness. There was anticipation, a sense that excitement would be coming in through the front door. It caused Geissler to be restless. He would pace between the back and the front all morning. As the hour loomed, he would take up a permanent position near the door. "*Sind Sie sicher?*" You are sure, Frau Schwartz? he would call, if he began to fear the consul might not show. It was no different today. All morning he hovered expectantly around Sabine.

The day was special for Geissler because he had found an old letter from his cousin, mailed from the Yukon, containing a description of a remote, grizzly-populated mountain range. The mountains, the cousin had written, would yield gold. The letter was written thirty-five years before, but in such remote regions, Geissler assumed, time stood still. No one person could prospect such immense territories in a short time. The cousin would be at it still. To be sure, Geissler wanted the consul to confirm that nothing in the passing decades would have changed. He had the letter in his pocket.

The consul arrived early. A pleased Geissler grunted a greeting before the door bell stopped jangling and immediately thrust the letter at him. His eyes enlarging, he told the consul it was from his cousin. "Read it," he commanded. Hanbury calmly accepted the letter and attempted to decipher the scrawl. He studied the paragraphs one after the other, first the front, then the back. He made out a few words – *Yukon, Gold, Grizzlies* – and also the signature, *Ferdinand Geissler.* "Fascinating," the consul said. "Your cousin was quite a writer."

Geissler took the letter back. "Mountains," he said. "Forests. No people. A cabin in the wild." He shook his head with wonder.

"It's like that there. No doubt of it," the consul confirmed amiably. Geissler stared with deep abstraction at a button on the consul's coat. Hanbury began to describe his own part of the country: the prairies. No mountains, no forests, no grizzlies there, he admitted, but you could go for a whole day on a dirt road without seeing a soul. Peace to observe hawks soar and swoop in their hunt for gophers. Geissler looked as if he was hallucinating.

The consul gently changed the subject. He said he needed Geissler's professional advice. A friend of the consul, a professor, had asked him to locate a book that was needed to fill a gap in a university collection. "University?" asked Geissler suspiciously. The consul's country with its vitality, wide open spaces, wild mountains, secret rivers and animals that hunted other animals, could not possibly possess anything as anaemic as a university. "That was my question too," the consul said smoothly. "Why would a university look for a book? They're supposed to have *all* the books. Of course, even a good university collection might have difficulty competing with your store." Hanbury watched Geissler think about this. He heard steps. Sabine was coming to the front. "*Guten Tag, Frau Schwartz,*" he said, breaking the silence. "*Guten Tag, Herr Hanbury,*" Frau Schwartz said back. "You're early."

Geissler wished to hear more about hawks, and eagles too, and bisons and big mountain cats and he didn't wish Frau Schwartz to take the consul off for lunch. He placed his left hand firmly on Hanbury's forearm. "What century?" he asked urgently. "This one. The modern history department," the consul said. "A special project." He turned to Sabine. "I'm looking for a book. Perhaps Herr Geissler has it in his cellar." "Then you two should look for it," she said. "I can't leave for half an hour."

Geissler watched Frau Schwartz return to the store's recesses. His grasp of the consul's arm loosened with relief. "Come," he ordered. Descending the protesting stairs, he muttered the word *evil* several times. It was his designation for the current century. When they stood in the cellar, Geissler gestured towards the thousands of books piled up.

Hanbury assumed he was being invited to make his interest more precise. The project in the university, he said, was about totalitarianism. Why does it get started? How does it sink roots? What carries it forward? How is it made appealing to the masses? There's lots of material on the Bolsheviks, Stalin, Ulbricht, Honecker, Franco, Mussolini. And Hitler, of course. But parts of the Nazi record are thin. The most powerful Nazi rites and insignia were kept secret. The consul said he had been told that only a select group of Nazis had access to the most powerful party symbols. It was widely known that these symbols – hieroglyphic pictures, sigils with religious meaning, runes with mystic significance – existed, but what they were and how they exerted power was known only to a very few. Apart from the swastika itself, a few of the symbols were on the *Totenkopfring* – the Death Head Ring – worn by members of the SS. But there were many more. The book he had been asked to find, the consul added, described all the secret Nazi symbols and associated rites. The little volume had apparently had a printing run of a few hundred copies only, exclusively for the leading Nazis, so even in its day it was rare. No copy was known to have survived the war. Despite that, the consul wondered, might *Bücher Geissler* be a place worth looking?

Hanbury and Schwartz had rehearsed the details of this potent Nazi publication during a lengthy session over beer. Yet, much of what the consul said to Geissler was improvised, especially when he described the morbid impact of secret Nazi rites. Even as he was speaking, Hanbury wondered where the things he was saying came from. He knew little about bigots, zealots, anti-Semites, political maniacs, or other cults. Sardonically he thought, I've learned to imitate Irving Heywood – make things up as you go along.

"No," Geissler said brusquely. It wasn't clear whether he knew he didn't have the book, or whether he refused to look. "Books like that should be burned."

"That's the purpose of the study," the consul continued soothingly, "to get rid of what books like that stand for. The right wing isn't dead. Fascists could come out of hiding. To fight them we need to know their language, understand their religion. We've got problems with the right wing in my country too. War criminals in hiding, neo-nazi cells, anti-Semitism, denials of the Holocaust. Things like that. It's important to recognize the right wing early on, before they've done their damage. How do you counteract the spell they put on ordinary people? Understanding their symbols, their secret language, it's vital. That's what the study is about. The book, if it exists, could be important."

Geissler was staring at the consul's jacket button again. He seemed far away, on a distant continent perhaps. In the half light, slightly stooped, wearing a khaki shirt, the bookseller almost looked like an explorer. Hanbury knew Geissler had longed to be one in his youth. Von Helmholtz told him that. Hanbury once casually mentioned to the Chief of Protocol that he had been in the cellar of *Bücher Geissler* and was fascinated. Von Helmholtz replied he knew the Geissler family before the war.

☙

"Not many people find their way to *that* store," the Chief of Protocol had added. "Even fewer get to know poor Ludwig. If you are going to visit places like *Bücher Geissler*, you'll soon know us better than we know ourselves. And when that happens we'll be forced to keep you." The Chief of Protocol had sent the consul a fleeting smile.

"It was mostly a social call," Hanbury had said. "I know someone who works there. Herr Geissler then showed me his old books."

"I haven't seen Ludwig for years. I thought the business was wound up." Von Helmholtz told Hanbury that before the war, because their families had close contact, he had been invited to the great Geissler villa several times. Ludwig was the youngest of three brothers.

"Were they Nazis?" Hanbury had asked, having seen dusty cabinets in the *Bücher Geissler* cellar full of Nazi publications.

"Winfried, the father, was. Of course, in those days many people were. The two older sons were enthusiastic about Germany's world domination prospects. Both were killed at Stalingrad. But Ludwig didn't want to fight. He didn't want to sell books either. The black sheep in the family. He wanted to explore. At one of the family parties he took me into a wild part of the garden which he pretended was a jungle." Von Helmholtz smiled as he recollected the thicket of Forsythia and Lilac bushes. "Ludwig had clipped the shrubs in one spot and created a little clearing. He told me he was going to retrace the journeys of Livingstone and Stanley. He was five or six years older and I was impressed. It started my own interest in geography. Later, when Ludwig was old enough to travel he asked his father for permission, but Winfried would have none of it. He wanted

Ludwig to join the army and accused him of lacking patriotism. It was difficult for Ludwig. In the end he had no choice. He was drafted. By then the two older brothers were already dead. Ludwig was assigned to the African Corps. I wondered at the time whether Winfried intervened. Maybe having lost two sons, he wanted to make a gesture to the one he had left – a nod in the direction of Ludwig's dream. Ludwig came back from Africa with one arm gone. A story made the rounds in Wannsee that Winfried cried, not out of grief that Ludwig was an invalid, but out of joy. He had proof that all three sons achieved military honour."

The consul and the Chief of Protocol were on the fringes of a huge reception and were making their way slowly to the exit.

"Did Winfried have a *special* link to the Nazis?" Hanbury had asked.

"Oh, I think so. The tradition of the family had always been to sell enlightened literature, but Winfried turned the store into an outlet for Nazi propaganda. I don't know what happened to all that material."

"It's in the cellar. I suppose they put all the Nazi stuff there when the war ended. I've seen it."

"Poor Ludwig. An eccentric child in a Nazi family, denied his African dream, sent there to fight, returns handicapped, has to live off a family business he hated as a child and now owns the literary remnants of the Nazis who destroyed his boyhood aspirations. Enough to turn him into a troubled man."

"He seems wretched."

"What did you do to get him to take you into the cellar?"

"Nothing. We talked about his cousin who panned for gold in the Yukon. It excited him."

The Chief of Protocol was running out of time. A prime minister's motorcade was waiting. "Likely you rekindled a dream," von Helmholtz had said. "You must tell me about the Yukon one day. Most of us dream about such places."

And now, in the cellar, Geissler looked as von Helmholtz said he did in the days when he could still hope to become an explorer. The distant, glassy stare seemed focussed on what might have been – a life dedicated to crossing continents. Hanbury waited patiently for the reverie to end. He looked around at the books piled up and under tables in dangerously leaning towers and strewn haphazardly on metal shelves. The cellar was a turbulent sea of books, too wild to cross in places. A hundred years of German literary output. Prominent in one corner were the cases of Nazi publications. Hanbury had noticed them the first time, but Geissler had directed him away.

"The other details?" Geissler said, suddenly back from an imaginary safari. He jerked his head savagely towards the consul.

"A reference was found by the police in a handwritten bibliography when they moved in on a war criminal," Hanbury said pleasantly, drawing on the script Schwartz had reviewed with him. "A major find. The items – numerous Nazi books and pamphlets – were being photo-reprinted in Taipei, from where they flooded back to neo-Nazi cells in the Americas, Western Europe and more recently Poland, Hungary and Russia. But the book on Nazi rites and decorations – the *Orden* book – though listed, wasn't in the Taipei reproductions. *Blutkreis – Totenkopf – Ehrenkreuz* was the title. Circle of Blood – Death Head – Cross of Honour. The printer was in Nuremberg – Weitling, is that possible? – the publisher was in Munich."

"Adolf and Hartwig Weitling. Brothers. Nazi printers. Lehrman in Munich did the publishing." Geissler turned and hobbled off. He had a painful way of walking, a shifting of weight from side to side, as if one leg was too short and had to be dragged up from behind. After some metres he stopped. "Come," he ordered the consul, gesturing with his one arm to the far part of the cellar.

Because he went so awkwardly, Geissler sent several of the leaning towers tumbling. He stopped each time to stack them with his one hand into higher, still more precarious monuments. Hanbury tried to help, but couldn't get past the bent body. Geissler muttered darkly about disorder. Approaching the far end of the cellar, Geissler became more hectic. A panic seemed to seize him, as if the century's evil miasma was reaching out.

"It really is a treasure you have," Hanbury said soothingly "Better than your cousin's in the Yukon."

Geissler was breathing hard. The struggle was wearing him out. "No," he said. "No."   His elbow went up high, as a shield, as he stumbled past the Nazi cabinets. A door at the far end opened inwards. The bookseller went through, waving his arm before him like a blind man. He grabbed a string, yanked it, lighting a bulb swinging from the ceiling. The room they entered was once used for storing coal. Wooden shelves, hastily knocked together from planks of different sizes, seemingly rummaged from rubble, lined the sooty walls. On these planks were still more books, two, sometimes three rows deep. Many of them had jackets decorated with swastikas, or eagles, or rifles with bayonets. Some of them sported the SS death head, the *Totenkopf.* "A bad room. *Verbotene Bücher*," said Geissler, with apprehension about all his banned books. His forehead was lined with sweat.

"I'm causing you a lot of trouble," Hanbury apologized. "Maybe I can look for the volume. You can go back up. I'll be very careful."

"No," Geissler resolutely said. "I know where." In the scarce light, he inspected the titles. He swept a whole row violently onto the floor to get at the second row. A heap of books formed on the floor. The rampage continued. "*Lehrman Verlag*," Geissler kept muttering. "*Lehrman Verlag.* The *Orden* book."

Geissler intensified his destructive search and in the faint light Hanbury perused a few of the volumes. *Neuadel aus Blut und Boden*

(Blood and Soil: The New Elite). *Rassenkunde des deutschen Volkes* (The Science of the Race of the German people). *Der Führer schützt das Reich* (The Führer Protects the Reich). *Geburt des Dritten Reiches* (The Birth of the Third Reich). *Heilige Runenmacht* (The Holy Power of the Runes). *Wir und die Juden im Lichte der Astrologie* (The Jews and Us: What Astrology Tells Us). *Luzifers Hofgesindel* (Lucifer's Court Servants). The intellectual underpinnings of the Third Reich were accumulating on the floor as if being prepared for the torch. From time to time the consul nudged a book aside with his shoe, or let the volume he was looking at drop, where it disappeared amongst the others.

Geissler suddenly cried with horror. *Das einzige Exemplar!* The only copy! He turned wildly towards the consul, shoved the thin volume at him as if he couldn't handle such corrosive poison and stumbled away bent over like a hunchback. Hanbury watched him scurry off. Before the stairs, with his one arm Geissler sent more towers flying, as if even with only half Samson's divine strength the whole temple of Godless evil could be sent tumbling.

The consul methodically picked his way through the mess. The outwardly innocent little volume had disappeared into his suit pocket. Upstairs he wanted to have five more minutes with Geissler to settle him down. He thought of describing the tundra, but the owner of the books had fled.

Over lunch Sabine asked, "What happened down there? Herr Geissler came up as if he saw the devil. He ran into his office and slammed the door. Did you find what you were looking for?" Hanbury was evasive. "It was a small book and difficult to locate in the bad light. He seemed tired. Maybe he was annoyed his time was wasted."

Sabine didn't probe. She wanted to know whether he had been to the Brücke Museum in Dahlem. She reminded him they were there once before. Hanbury remembered it. He then casually asked whether she had smashed his stereo back then. Sabine admitted it. How did he know? "I half suspected it," he said.

A few days later when Hanbury handed Schwartz the book, the professor had difficulty hiding his excitement. "I can't tell you what it means for me to have this. It's an unusual find. I'll do a paper on it in a bibliographical journal. Of course, I'll express my thanks to you in a footnote."

"No need for that," said the consul. "It was nothing. Geissler found it, not me."

"I know," replied Schwartz. "But you got him to do it. No one else could have."

"It was his cousin in the Yukon. Geissler did it for his cousin, not for me."

Schwartz laughed. "The one that searched for gold?" He rubbed the cover of his new book. "This is my gold."

The little volume, Hanbury saw, gave Schwartz the same inner pleasure as Geissler showed the first time they went into the cellar to view his treasure. And Stobbe had that air when he showed off the Stasi files. All three of them – the historian, the bookseller, the archivist – in their different ways they were custodians of what once was. The consul believed he was acquiring an understanding of what the professor meant when he referred to the thin book as gold. "I can see why it's valuable for you." he said. "Some days ago I was in a historian's bonanza." Schwartz stopped playing with the *Orden* book. "I mean the Stasi files."

"Normannenstrasse?" Schwartz asked, his forehead wrinkling into a frown.

Hanbury told him about the tour he had. "Kurt Stobbe. Know him?"

"By reputation only. Why did he show you around?"

"He thinks I could find evidence there on Nazi war criminals who have gone underground in Canada." Hanbury shrugged. "Anyway, war criminals aren't my responsibility."

The professor studied the consul. "Even if you tried, you likely wouldn't get far. Not with the Stasi files. We historians run into this when we stand before an archive. A starting point is required. You need a way in."

"I didn't like the place," Hanbury said. "Geissler thinks there's evil down there in his cellar, in his books. But those files are worse."

Schwartz laughed. "We historians don't distinguish. If you do want to round up some old Nazis and need a starting point, let me know. I can help. After all, I'm now firmly in your debt."

SHERWOOD FOREST

*R*andolph McEwen on the train to Munich was using the time to read. His resources had been savaged and Berlin Station had ceased to fly. Even cheap train tickets now provoked stinging questions from sullen clerks in accounting. The wheel of fortune creaked and McEwen was no longer moving upward. A sordid deterioration. Something to keep from Graf Bornhof.

Life in a slower lane. It took a little getting used to, facing days of tedium. On the other hand, time had opened up for newspapers, time for reading instead of scanning. Which was what the meta-diplomat was doing on the train. A thick stack of clippings on the seat opposite waited for him, like a terrier expecting attention from the master. An abused pocket dictionary, finger-stained and pages rumpled, was going through another workout. A light workout. Because Gundula Jahn's style was penetrable. McEwen found she didn't invent words that went on for a full line. Nor did she fashion sentences that continued for a dozen column inches. He didn't like the normal, local journalistic style.

Sometimes you'd have to wade for five minutes through a newspaper sentence, not knowing until the end whether Honecker should or should not be released from jail, if an accused East German border guard had denied or confessed to murder, or whether a stalwart bishop accepted or rejected accusations of having been a Stasi spy. Always the same thing – tortuously intricate considerations poured into each and every sentence before the main thought was completed. As far as McEwen was concerned, it showed a neurotic way of thinking.

But Gundula Jahn was different. She had a sprightly way of putting things. Compared to the others, reading her was like a levitation, an airy flight over the swamps of German prose. And the views she expressed – through her friend Gregor the mouthpiece – were lucid. McEwen had become a fan of Gundula. He had never met her, but he had begun to like her. Too bad she got herself involved with Friend Tony now that his end was near.

An excellent report out of East Berlin from a lingering spectator provided the breakthrough. Plutonium smuggling, clear and simple. The consul's jig was up. And so, regrettably, was Gundula Jahn's. And, for good measure, Günther Rauch's too. The whole nest would soon be cleared away. Graf Bornhof must have the same proof. Why else a summons to Pullach for an urgent off-the-record chat? The graf had been guarded on the phone. As he ought to be, sitting on a mountain of new, explosive information.

His instincts, McEwen congratulated himself, had once more proved reliable. As predicted, retirement would come after a final, dazzling display of intuition and a deft assembling of known facts. A multi-national ring had crept into the post-Cold War security vacuum and he, Randolph McEwen, had smelled it. Within the year he might expect a presidential citation from Uncle Sam, a medal from Uncle Teut and, who knows, an enamelled maple leaf tie-clip from the Beavers. Could a knighthood then be far behind?

Immersed in a syrupy glow, Randolph McEwen found the journey pleasant. A good occasion to reread Gundula's columns. He enjoyed contemplating her character as it jumped off the pages. A piercing writer. Full of subtle mischief and vitriolic wit. The columns, McEwen considered, were a feat. For weeks, every day, Gundula built a story. *The Life and Times of Gregor Donner Reich.* Gregor was described as having been a slight and wistful man with a precise moustache and thinning hair. Before the Wall came down, for decades, he ran a modest but useful business in a remote corner of East Berlin: a repair shop for all kinds of broken things. In the soothing atmosphere of the shop, no damage was as bad as first appeared. Gregor was dedicated and industrious, unassuming and friendly. An example, Gundula claimed, for the whole Neighbourhood.

Yet, Gregor Donner Reich was different from his neighbours. Not in any outward way; outwardly he lived like them. What distinguished Gregor was his *seeing* eye. Not that he wished to be observant – it happened against his will. He couldn't help it. He was always observing and registering things happening around him.

Randolph McEwen almost clapped his hands upon deciphering this passage. He identified with Gregor. It could be a burden, he agreed, to have insight into all the sub-surface goings-on.

Gregor was special in another way as well, because he wrote down what he saw. In fact, Gundula drew on Gregor's writings in telling his life story. Actually, she claimed in her column, Gregor had two seeing eyes. The *outer* eye observed people and events in the Neighbourhood which he described in letters to his mother. He ended all his letters to his mother with an endearment and his initials: *Your ever-loving GDR.* But Gundula also had access to Gregor's secret diary in which he chronicled what he saw with a kind of *inner* eye. The diary had to be kept secret because certain individuals in Gregor's Neighbourhood – he affectionately called them *Bozos* – had they learned of it, would have thrown him into jail. Even if he had been *suspected* of keeping a diary, it would have gone badly for Gregor; in the Neighbourhood inner eyes were *verboten*. Therefore, Gregor kept the diary hidden in a plastic bag, inside some greasy rags, behind black oil tins, under several bent bicycle wheels, in a far corner of the shop. Gregor wrote in his diary only in the depth of night in his room at the back of the shop with the shutters shut. But the letters to his mother he wrote during the day, in between repair jobs. By the time his mother got them, he knew, half the Bozos in the Neighbourhood had read them first. To her he always wrote nicely about the Neighbourhood. He made it sound like paradise.

McEwen was entertained by Gregor's situation. He intuitively understood it. The need to keep a secret fix on things went deep in many people. He had recruited many spectators around the globe in his decades of success. He knew what made them tick.

Gundula began to describe Gregor's daily life, quoting frequently from the letters to his mother. Gregor is happy in the letters because by definition the Neighbourhood is that way. Everybody has a job and no one ever loses it. They live in good apartments; the rents are cheap. Crime doesn't exist. Mothers are satisfied. They have careers. Their infants are looked after cost-free. Children lack behavioural problems. With permanent smiles they join choirs, gymnastic clubs, or symphony orchestras. Quite a few go on to win Olympic gold medals. *All* is free; *everything* is provided. Gregor is successful too. He becomes the secretary of the local angling club, a responsible position for which he is rewarded. He and two neighbours are encouraged to apply for – and they receive! – permission for a permanent spot to pitch tents in a communal camp ground beside a big lake not too far from where they live. Gregor writes he feels even closer to his neighbours now because they can plan their vacations together. Their tents are pitched a half-metre apart. They find joy in practising equality and in sharing.

But the story in the secret diary is different. Gregor's inner eye formulates questions. Everyone has a cheap apartment alright, but why does it take eight years to get one? Why in a land of plenty is it a problem to get a couple of new spokes for a bike? And, if life is so perfect, why do people want to leave? Or, why are children ill after swimming in the lake? Gregor would like to know the reason for people waiting twelve years to get a Trabi, yet Bozos seem to get them on demand. Gregor has a thousand questions.

Gregor writes a lengthy digression in his diary on the charms of being a Bozo. *Bozodom* is what he calls the dauntless apparatus running the Neighbourhood's affairs. The interplay between Bozodom and the Neighbourhood is an enduring subject for Gregor. His inner eye focuses on curiosities. Gundula quotes a telling passage from the diary in her column to help her readers get the flavour.

> *Although no one is without a job, only half the people work. Although only half the people work, Bozodom's targets are easily exceeded. Although the targets are exceeded, there is nothing in the stores to buy. Although the stores are empty, Bozodom claims everyone has much more than needed. But although everyone's needs are surpassed, most people hate the Bozos. And although Bozodom is universally despised, it claims that more than 99.9 percent of the people vote for it.*

McEwen guffawed with delight when he unscrambled this. He lifted out a notebook, licked a pencil and copied the passage. Such insight should be kept handy. Gregor's secret questions never stop. There is much for the inner eye to see. What is it about the world outside the Neighbourhood that is so dangerous? he asks. Why is no one allowed to see it? Or, why do Bozodom statistics show great wealth when everywhere he looks – bridges, roads, buildings – are crumbling?

And why *The Firm*? Why does The Firm snoop into ordinary people's lives, forcing neighbours to live in suspicion of each other? Gregor confesses to his diary that even during the jolliest moments in the campground, neighbours don't talk openly. Not even husbands and wives, he states, dare discuss Bozodom frankly, unless they're in a boat far out in the middle of the lake.

One day Gregor writes excitedly to his mother. He has learned Gorby will be visiting. He tells her he aims to go and see him. Gregor hopes he can touch Gorby's coat. A diary entry of the same date explains this. Gorby is rumoured to have a cure for certain congenital diseases which derive from Bozodom.

The letter he sends her afterwards is even more enthusiastic. Many people touched Gorby. Gorby said great things. Everyone was inspired. This inspiration builds into fervour. Gregor is writing like crazy trying to record the changes. Gorby, it turns out, was quite the healer, because one day the Neighbourhood wakes up and finds *The Cure* has taken. Not only are Bozodom's cancers eliminated, Bozodom itself is gone for good. Gregor is free to bring his diary into the open. He fills pages with spontaneously-felt, euphoric observations. Neighbours can finally talk. And they travel! All in separate directions. They travel until they drop. They know of the fabulous wealth amassed by the Relatives on the other side of the Wall and they go wild with anticipation. Nor do the Relatives skimp. They promise that a huge train full of goodies is being loaded. But more! Soon on its way will be the *Miracle Machine*. For forty long years the Neighbourhood awaited this.

Gregor's *Life and Times*, thus far, were spread by Gundula over about three weeks of columns. Then she informed the Gregor fans, that he was going through a major adjustment, a personal crisis of some kind. For example, he stopped writing to his mother. Perhaps he could no longer keep her happy with good news. In any event, only the diary record remains to trace the rest of the story. Yet, even Gregor's diary is no longer crisp. Frequently the entries are a confused jumble of observations with the inner and the outer eyes mixed up. It seems the euphoria in Gregor's Neighbourhood over the Cure began ebbing.

Gregor claims in his diary that many in the Neighbourhood are beginning to experience terror. Before, under Bozo rule, the rules were clear. There was fear, sure, but all the same a peculiar form of security reigned. That's gone. Some people in the Neighbourhood now actually think life is getting worse. Gregor attributes this to the Miracle Machine. Gundula speculated to her readers about this contraption. Gregor saw it, she explained, as something intangible: a phenomenon, possibly metaphysical, arising from the non-sense of being. McEwen put the paper and the dog-eared dictionary down and clapped. He loved this part. The non-sense of being! A concept typical of the Hun.

Gundula quoted Gregor's diary again:

> *We asked our Relatives to send it in, their Miracle Machine. How badly we wanted it even though we didn't know how it worked. They said it would set itself in motion. Up front is a hopper for raw materials. Inside, unknown miraculous processes are at work: design, competition, productivity, financing, marketing. What notions! As in alchemy! And with a pinch of labour, nifty products come out the other end.*

Gundula wrote that Gregor recorded his neighbours' expectations. They thought they would soon be surrounded by splendour; life would be like the pictures in glossy magazines. But what really happened? The Machine arrived, as the Relatives promised, and they laid down rules for it to work. Step one was that everything in Gregor's Neighbourhood had to be *privatized*. The Machine couldn't work unless all the factories were *owned* by somebody – it didn't matter whom. Then the Neighbourhood was informed certain laws and regulations were required. Without that, the Relatives argued, the Miracle Machine would not start up. Ever seen them Wessi laws? My God! They require more shelf space than the files assembled by the Firm. What next? As the Machine creaked into motion, nearly everybody lost their job. And all the things that *had* been free were, so to speak, thrown out the window. Clubs, sports facilities, theatres, symphony orchestras, day-care – everything disappeared. Something-for-nothing was not possible in the environment that the Miracle Machine required.

Now, if you look objectively at what is going on, Gregor said with a touch of his old sharp perception, what arrived wasn't a Miracle Machine at all. It was more like a Flattening Machine, a Steamroller. Many in the Neighbourhood, according to Gregor, felt fooled. The Relatives, according to a whispered Neighbourhood complaint making the rounds, kept the *real* Miracle Machine for themselves, while the Steamroller they sent in was designed to *never* stop flattening.

Randolph McEwen loved the columns dealing with the Steamroller. He re-read them several times. Overweening pride, gaudy wealth, the *what-I've-got-you-can't-have attitude*. A perceptive description of the Hun. Give Gundula credit. Over the top of his reading glasses McEwen looked out the window of the train. He pondered needling Graf Bornhof. Fingers drummed the pocket dictionary as he weighed options. Quite delightful, really, how Gregor heaped disdain on the Wessi's love of rules.

McEwen suspected that the Steamroller notion provided enjoyment to other readers too, judging from the flood of letters to the editor. True, some of them showed faint signs of hostility. Some Wessi readers, for example, argued they had worked long and hard to improve their situation. Ossis shouldn't think they got to where they were without sacrifice. Gregor didn't seem to appreciate this, they pointed out. Such views, however, were a mere trickle and the editor must have been undeterred, because Gundula stayed on the editorial page. Through Gregor, Gundula next explored a subject called *Morbidity.*

Soon after The Cure had taken, after Gregor stopped writing bouncy letters to his mother, many of the questions he once committed to his diary were being answered. The whole Neighbourhood had answers. Actually there were now *too many* answers. People were overwhelmed; they had never wanted to know *that* much.

An entry from the diary held McEwen's attention.

> *The Neighbourhood is beginning to realize it underestimated the corruption by the Bozos. Corruption was of various kinds. The Bozos were expert at supplying themselves with material comforts. That was known. And the Neighbourhood is now becoming aware how the attitudes of children were manipulated by the Bozos. But even this is nothing compared to learning about the pervasiveness of The Firm. The Firm's informers were everywhere. Model citizens, highly regarded authors, respected bishops, athletes, actresses, professors, stalwart members of the Neighbourhood. They all snooped for the Firm.*

It is morbid to know, Gregor wrote introspectively in his diary, that Bozodom was so corrupting, and more morbid still that no one did anything about it. He next claimed that the Neighbourhood, even the members who kept their distance from the Bozos, were now subjected to an all-inclusive suspicion from the Relatives. The Relatives were developing a habit of looking at everyone in the Neighbourhood as having fed at Bozodom's trough. This, Gregor claimed, was the most morbid of the post-Cure let-downs.

At this stage in the publication of Gregor's *Life and Times,* unhappiness on the part of readers really began growing. The editor began to receive more and more unflattering letters. Wessi readers didn't like being accused of harbouring anything so superficial as an *all-inclusive* suspicion. They had suspicions, they admitted, but they were nuanced. Anyway, they were paying taxes to get the Neighbourhood back on its feet and they should be allowed some indulgence. Ossi readers on the other hand repudiated letters written by the Wessis. A literary war broke out. McEwen tried to follow it, but he didn't grasp all the deeper meanings.

Gundula became still more controversial with an episode she called *The Devil and the House of God*. Gregor had done some scribbling in his diary about disturbing things he heard about the Church. He made the observation that Bozodom liked to pin medals on the chests of churchmen. Some of them were receiving so many they looked like soldiers returning from the front. Of course, the medals were not for bravery, but for *cooperation*. Was it administrative cooperation? Gregor speculated. Were the medals for devising a socially acceptable way of believing in God? Or was it for helping out with snooping? Did Bozodom convince churchmen to help spot troubled people? And what role did they play in the mystifying disappearance of money which members of the Neighbourhood occasionally inherited from relatives on the other side? The Church was helpful funnelling funds through the bureaucratic complications of Bozodom, yet most of it never arrived.

We trusted in the House of God, not knowing it too was in a pact with the Devil.

Once this section of the diary was paraphrased in Gundula's column, the mailbag to the editor was stuffed fuller than a Christmas turkey. This time Wessis rubbed their hands with glee and certain Ossis howled. Wrong! Wrong! Wrong! they shouted in their letters. The Church had been the catalyst, they said. The Church prevented the Cure from turning bloody. But others argued this missed the point. In the days of Bozodom, it would have been normal for the Church, like all the other institutions, to have developed a split personality. Why not come clean, they asked. It's a good question; why did churchmen accept Bozodom medals?

The editor's phone rang off the hook. *The Life and Times of Gregor* was threatening to get out of hand. Letters, the editor believed, are an important part of democracy, but they shouldn't trigger intra-tribal warfare. Time for a talk with Gundula. Was there not some way for Gregor to stop writing his diary? he asked. Couldn't Gregor go back to writing letters to his mother? Impossible, Gundula replied. Gregor could never go back to looking at the world as in the pre-Cure days. In any event, Gundula told the editor, Gregor's mother had passed away; his repair shop had folded. All he had left in life was scribbling in his diary, a habit he would keep until he died. This gave the editor an idea. He wished to know about Gregor's health? Was he suffering from too much good food and drink, or from a broken heart, or something? Gundula got the point. She asked the editor to give Gregor a period of decline, a chance to look back at his not especially long life. That was possible, the editor said. In fact, it made sense.

The days that remained for Gregor were the ones which Randolph McEwen loved best. How marvellous it would be to shove each of the final columns right under Graf Bornhof's nose.

After the strategy session with the editor, Gundula informed her readers that Gregor had confided to his diary that he was not well and was becoming philosophical in the way people do when they know they're fading. Gundula wrote that Gregor wanted to get at the origins of certain things that shaped his life. He was formulating a new question. Was Bozodom something that arose from within the Neighbourhood, or was it forced on them from outside? After a struggle, Gregor concluded the answer was both yes *and* no.

The Bozos, Gregor recalled, wore red socks. There seemed to be a competition for whose socks were the reddest. Bozos whose socks were more than red, whose socks were *one hundred and ten percent red,* acquired the finest privileges. But let's not forget, Gregor reminded, that before the red-socked Bozos came along, when the Tribe was whole, before it broke up into the Neighbourhood and the Relatives, there had been other Bozos, brown-shirted ones. Many members of the Tribe were happy with the Bozos in brown. They loved and admired the Greatest-Bozo-Ever. Does this imply there was – or is – a certain predilection in the Tribe for rule by Bozos?

McEwen licked his pencil nervously. His eyes took on a look of greed, like a fortune seeker at the entrance of a cave containing fabled riches. Feverishly he made more notes. What really happened after the Greatest-Bozo-Ever lost the war and the Tribe was split? This was the question Gregor addressed, as he neared the end. The Relatives, he observed, were given a few quick lessons in how to run a pluralist democracy by their opponent who thrashed them in the war. The former enemy behaved honourably, like a Teacher. The Relatives, devastated and hungry for a better life, learned their democracy lessons quickly. Furthermore, the Teacher spent money to help democracy sprout roots. The Relatives and the Teacher, suddenly like-minded, became close friends.

But in the Neighbourhood, the victor was a Bully who had been wearing red socks for years. The Bully insisted that the Neighbourhood become his spitting image. A few people were tasked to make the likeness complete. It's interesting to note, Gregor said in parenthesis, that the red-socked Bozos aped the methods not only of the Bully, but also of the brown-shirts. Both Bozodoms relied on a Firm to keep a close eye on the people. Their soldiers marched in the same odd way, legs flung high up in the air before the boots were smashed down on the pavement. Both systems insisted that photographs of children should always show them smiling in a hearty, wholesome way. And, in both cases, people with normal aspirations, such as wanting to get out of the country, were shot.

What does this add up to? It is arguable, Gregor explained humbly, that many members of the Tribe wanted the brown shirts. But the red-socks were imposed and almost no one in the Neighbourhood wanted them.

> *Freedom was a gift to the Relatives, but the Neighbourhood had to free itself from the red socks. Freedom fought for – and gained – is of a rarer type, more precious, less likely to be squandered, than when brought in on a platter.*

These, Gundula informed her readers, were Gregor's last written words.

The end, she wrote, came quickly. Gregor asked to be buried in Potsdam, on a hill overlooking a fine old palace. For centuries this hilltop has been dotted by a collection of fake ruins. Gregor's gravestone, Gundula wrote, is camouflaged amongst the ruins. But it's there. Momentarily confusing for visitors is the fact that the name *Gregor Donner Reich* is not chiselled into the granite. He had thought about it, he said just before he died, and he didn't believe his name was too important. The forty years or so he had been around had been melancholy and sometimes down-right ridiculous. These were the qualities he wanted expressed on his gravestone. And that's how the inscription came to read: *Gloomy Daft Remains.*

McEwen put the clippings carefully back into his briefcase and stared at the passing Bavarian countryside. He had experienced a sense of loss when Gregor died. During the weeks that Gregor ruled his corner of the opinion page, McEwen had eagerly opened the paper every day to begin translating Gundula's latest instalment. Even though Gregor's *Life and Times* were over, force of habit still made McEwen turn the pages – to see what Gundula would be turning her attention to next. But Gundula was no more, at least not on the political pages. It was as if she too had died.

McEwen stiffened. What was he doing? Getting sentimental over Gundula? No matter how good a journalist she was, she was still in collusion with the consul. No matter where and how well she might be hiding, a knock on her front door would have to come. McEwen sighed. He hoped she would cooperate. How splendid it would be if she agreed to round out the evidence against Friend Tony. Once he was out of the picture, repatriated by the Beavers, she could be reprieved. With her wit and spirit and ability to sting, she should be left free to roam.

⁂

The Munich hotel, with the indoor tropical garden as breakfast nook, was no longer affordable for Berlin Station, so McEwen spent the night in a rooming house not far away. Early next morning he walked to the hotel and loitered in reception. On time, a silent predator, the Mercedes 600 outfitted with aerials on the roof, slid up the drive. The meta-diplomat descended. A driver jumped out to open the back door. McEwen nodded a greeting in the direction of the chauffeur and sank like a potentate into the car. The door shut with a gentle thud. Passers-by looked on. Silly oglers, he thought, presenting them with a serene silhouette.

Orders in the vocabulary of the Gestapo filled the air at the Pullach gate. McEwen closed his eyes. One would think, he thought, they would recognize him by now. But no, papers were checked before the gate opened. The system functioned, but only barely, he concluded. If opening a gate took time, imagine how the rest was functioning. As the car moved deep into the complex, he rehearsed his opening remarks. *Read the Jahn columns, Alexander? Bozodom! Close to the bone, don't you think? Is it around? Lurking? Do you expect the latest Constitution will be*

354

up to handling it – you know – in the event there's another outbreak?

McEwen imagined Graf Bornhof's silky reply in an outrageously perfect Oxford accent. His face went askew. It became so contorted that the chauffeur, examining him in the mirror, momentarily thought the passenger was going into a seizure. But the fit passed. Waiting in the silence of the meeting room McEwen closed his eyes. From long experience he knew it would be more effective if rage didn't show.

"Randolph, I am terribly pleased to see you!" Graf Bornhof entered with companionable energy. "Short notice, I know. Had a good flight?" He held out one hand and placed the other on McEwen's shoulder to welcome a colleague, a partner, a friend.

"A trifle bumpy on the way down, Alex. But charming otherwise. I was wonderfully entertained."

"Really? Tell me. Sit down. Sit down. You do look well."

"Just us two today?"

"Indeed. We're off record, Randolph. Gives us a chance to talk as friends."

"Jolly good. How's Anne?"

"In the UK at the moment. Family visit plus some research. Well, I'm in suspense. You are a bachelor. Who was beside you on the airplane?"

"I can't recall actually. I entertained myself. I skimmed through the Jahn columns. Part of the landscape for our case. I'm sure your people have made a detailed analysis. Have you read them?"

The graf shook his head. "I have read *of* them. How shall I put it? Not flattering, I suppose, the whole subject."

"Quite right. An unflattering century. We have an expression, Alex. *Call a spade a spade.* I think she did that. Courageous girl. Most commendable." McEwen's hands, finger tips touching, were held just beneath his chin. Smirking like an oil sheik, he gazed at Graf Bornhof over his half glasses. "She has little good to say about the brown shirts.

And the red socks don't fare much better. Anything comparable on the horizon today? What's your view? Green shorts perhaps?"

Graf Bornhof adopted a wholesome smile. "Your sense of humour, Randolph. It reminds me of Anne's brother. Why can't more people have it? I was referring to commentators not having much positive to say about *her*. One of them suggested she engages in a populist form of journalism unbecoming for a serious paper. Another said she doesn't go deep enough and her style has perhaps too much innuendo. One of my colleagues claims she's just another whining Ossi. I personally don't know. I stay away from the media." The graf with his intelligent eyes looked steadily at McEwen.

"You ought to pay attention to the Ossis, Alex. Frontier people. Impulses from the frontier always stir up established power centres. We have experience with that over *several* centuries, I can tell you. Still, a number of interesting suggestions emerge in her columns. The Steamroller notion. Something I would worry about. People who feel pushed around react unpredictably."

"But Randolph," Graf Bornhof said soothingly, reaching for a thermos of coffee, "we're sending two hundred billion marks – *billion*, Randolph – their way each year. Forty years of development are being squeezed into perhaps five. I wouldn't call that a Steamroller. Cash Dispenser would be better. Coffee? White?" He placed a cup and saucer before McEwen and poured slowly.

"My reading of the columns is different, Alex. Something is unsettling on the left."

"Not unsettling so much as still settling out. Former apparatchiks have little to do but preach nostalgia. That will fizzle. Personally, I would be more worried about the right. It is scarcely possible to overestimate the danger there."

McEwen gave a short, high-pitched laugh, a kind of squeal. "That's in the columns too. *Bozodom*!" He took out a handkerchief to blow his nose. "She seems to think the German tribe *needs* an intrusive state apparatus. She argues one exists today. Could it be your constitution is nothing more than a pretty wrapping hiding that?" McEwen took off his glasses and held them up to the light to see if they needed a polish.

"We can be a little top heavy," agreed Graf Bornhof pleasantly. "But the second half of the century is different from the first. Our constitution is the divide."

"That is most reassuring." McEwen began to wipe his glasses with the lower part of his tie. "Yes, well, Gundula Jahn. We both know she is part of something nasty. Fine writer, I think, but not so expert at the other things." McEwen's voice changed. "What's your cover name for the operation, Alex?" he said coldly. "I thought of *Sherwood Forest* – you know, all three of them, Robin Hood, Maid Marian and Little John. How ought we to manage it? Have your people thought of timing?"

"I'm sorry, Randolph. You've left me," a mystified Graf Bornhof said. "I don't recall an operation called Sherwood Forest in your case files."

"The twenty-four-seven operation. The consul in Berlin." McEwen said impatiently. "We are to deal with the results, informally, off-the-record. Correct?"

"Yes. Of course. I am sorry. I wasn't quite sure what you meant."

"You *are* keeping me on edge, Alex. What is the news? I *presume* it is good."

Graf Bornhof opened a thin binder. "I believe so, Randolph. The enforcers went in. An expensive operation." Graf Bornhof looked at the top page of the report. Six people, three weeks. A considerable amount of overtime. But worth it, I suppose. Consul Hanbury is clean. We're very pleased. It restored our confidence in diplomats from the Commonwealth."

The meta-diplomat sat passively. Some of the most sulphurous eggs in the world had been laid in the Commonwealth and if one person knew that, it was him. McEwen looked at Graf Bornhof. He looked at the binder. "May I have a peek?" he whispered. "Is everything there? Three weeks, did you say? Had we not agreed on two months?"

"I obtained approval for four weeks, but after three Cologne cut the operation. Zero yield. Missing a week of zero yield is not a loss," he explained calmly. "Do have a look." He pushed the binder towards McEwen.

McEwen regarded Bornhof's slender binder with suspicion. Out of a jacket pocket he produced his notebook, then the stubby pencil. And from the secure briefcase with the scruffy corners emerged a thick folder held together with a ribbon. Resorting to a ritual developed over decades, he placed his folder methodically on the table to the side. As the muted cuckoo clock ticked, McEwen began paging with slow deliberation through Bornhof's binder. The Graf silently observed. He watched his visitor turn the pages, forwards, backwards, forwards again, occasionally licking his pencil. Graf Bornhof left the room, returned and re-assumed his patient pose. McEwen, immersed in study, acknowledged neither departures nor arrivals, until at last he spoke.

"Well. Yes. Indeed." He expelled a long breath of air. "Fascinating material. May I ask two or three tiny questions on mechanics?"

"Of course, Randolph."

"Observations commenced on December 23. The consul is at work that day, has lunch with his staff and subsequently goes to Tegel Airport. No observations are made inside the terminal, but he emerges shortly afterwards with a woman." McEwen's voice was soft.

"That is correct."

"I notice she is nowhere identified."

"Indeed."

"She spends three days and nights with the consul, shares his bed, then disappears as if from start to finish she was nothing but an apparition. Yet all the agents saw her. One of them managed, early one morning as I understand, to get a glimpse of her in full carnal integrity. Yet she could not be identified?" McEwen asked this genially, consulting his notebook closely and flipping the binder in an exaggerated show of searching.

"That is correct," repeated Graf Bornhof.

"Thank God, I suppose, that they were sure she was indeed a woman. I don't see the passenger manifests of the incoming flights on December 23 in the binder."

"On December 23, Randolph, in the afternoon, there were fifty-seven arriving flights in Berlin bringing in over eight thousand passengers. I know what you are thinking. A computer matching with passengers on departing flights on December 26 would narrow her down. But she didn't leave by air. She departed by train."

"Yes," mused McEwen. "I did see a reference to a railway station. But I notice a *departure* is not confirmed. She was last seen emerging from a taxi next to Bahnhof Zoo. She was not sighted going into any train. She *might* have taken public transport to the airport. Was no computer match considered, just to be on the safe side? Excuse my pedantry. Let's not stumble. Another tiny issue. Curious, don't you think, how the consul and his concubine appear each morning, manage to escape surveillance early in the day, then reappear at home late at night. Might there have been a purpose to such controlled disappearing and appearing? Were they *playing* with enforcement? Do tell me the agents' names. Maxi, Wolfi, possibly Heini?"

"It's a big, busy, complicated city, Randolph," said Graf Bornhof, gazing steadily at McEwen.

"To be sure, Alex. I live there." McEwen looked tired, nearly apathetic. "Forgive me. I was being niggling. One last trifling question. The listening devices in the house. The dailies are remarkably empty. Only some fragments of conversation are transcribed. A technical problem?"

"Only partially. Consul Hanbury is a music lover, Randolph. The blanks show he was listening to music. It seems that's mostly what he does."

McEwen nodded his understanding. "They didn't place the listening devices directionally, to minimize stereophonic interference? A standard element in the art."

"Of course," Graf Bornhof patiently replied. "But it seems he suddenly changed the furniture around and adjusted the direction of the speakers. As a result the music got aimed at the table lamp where the bug was placed." The graf switched to a personal tone and lowered his voice. "Randolph, look at it from a different perspective. A woman arrives to spend Christmas with a man. They go sightseeing. They listen to music. They go to bed. They go for a winter walk in the forest. All of it normal. Most people at one time or another spend a few days like that. Haven't you?"

McEwen nodded again, more wearily this time, not to agree that he once had his share of women who were casual about sex, but as a personal recognition that in Pullach things were far worse than he had imagined. His eyelids sank until they nearly shut. As on the train the previous day, he experienced a surge of empathy with the seeing eye of Gregor and the pertinent questions Gregor asked. Too bad, McEwen thought, that Gundula Jahn was part of Sherwood Forest. If she were clean – *if only she were clean!* – he would recruit her on the spot. He would arrange a short assignment. He saw it clearly. Place her strategically inside Pullach. Not that she would learn much that was useful, McEwen was sure of that. But it would provide good copy for more columns. She could publish another diary. *My Errant Ways: by Uncle Teut.* With a melancholy smile McEwen massaged one hand with the other, his habit for keeping rage bottled up. "Perhaps the consul is not quite as innocent as you think," he said slowly. "I have taken a few facts down from your material, Alex. May I read them to you? I also have here a few facts of my own." He patted the thick folder held together by a ribbon.

Graf Bornhof, without expression, nodded to McEwen.

"Fact one. The consul perceives he's under observation almost from the moment it commences. Does he show he knows that? Does he panic? No. He has a *textbook* response. As I was trained. You too. Look at the dailies. Take any one, Alex. Let's take day two on the Ku'damm. He and the woman stop walking. Here, read it." McEwen pushed Graf Bornhof's thin binder over. "He acts as a tourist but scans the scene without moving his head, as in Volume One, page one, of *The Polished Agent* – available in eighteen languages, including Russian. *Evidently* he knows Heini is on duty and wants a fix on Heini's coordinates. Then comes evasive action, standard behaviour. Page two of the manual. Into the subway, onto a train, to the next station, into another train, out again as the doors close. Heini – poor Heini – is forced to take the rest of the day off. Beautifully described by Heini by the way. A succinct style of writing. Each day the consul finds a way to get beyond his prying eyes. Rather odd, I'd say. The simple question is, why?

"And let us have a peek at fragments of speech recorded in between symphonic sounds by Heini's well-placed bugs." McEwen consulted his notebook, then paged through the binder. "Ah, here we are. What words do we find? *…nuclear weapon grade material…Russia…*There's a reference to a market too. Might the consul and his lady have been discussing business? Some deal on dangerous commodities? Russian plutonium perhaps? Oughtn't that to be worth a moment or two of close attention?

"Next, we note the mystery lady is slightly coloured. A touch of Asian blood? Heini isn't sure, although he lyrically describes the beauty of the unclothed form he observes one morning through a window. Which countries are interested in illicit plutonium, Alex? May I guess? Countries that produce sultry women inside lovely amber skins?"

Graf Bornhof sat without expression. In Pullach they had been through all this and drawn negative conclusions. He didn't mind the sarcasm, nor the venom. He liked McEwen's Englishness. His principal challenge, Graf knew, was to coax the old warrior into retirement, to convince him to begin it sooner. In The Lake District perhaps, or Kent, or the Cotswolds? The Cotswolds! Graf Bornhof loved the Cotswolds. He was younger than McEwen, though not by many years. He and Anne had made their retirement preparations. They had their Cotswolds cottage. Long walks after breakfast each day in the English countryside. The prospect inspired Bornhof. Why did McEwen not live in such happy anticipation? He was already a living legend. What drove the man? Why this lamentable insistence on breathing life into a stillborn case?

"That is in *your* binder, Alex," McEwen summarized frostily. "It has no insight whether the dark lady came to buy or sell plutonium, but I know that. She came to *acquire* it. Would you be interested in knowing why I know that?"

Graf Bornhof continued to look at his guest with bemused kindness.

McEwen's quick fingers then undid the ribbon. His voice became a little sharper, the movements of his hands a little crisper, as he pushed document upon document crammed full of facts towards Graf Bornhof, who examined a page here, a page there, stacking the documents neatly in a rising pile before him. "Sherwood Forest!" McEwen revealed with a flourish. "Let's focus on Maid Marian first." McEwen described how Gundula Jahn had been checked out by both Moscow and Kiev Stations and the resulting information was conclusive. "One of her former lovers, a certain Vassiliev – extract seven before you, Alex – manages a nuclear reprocessing plant in the Ukraine. He has plutonium coming out of his ears. It's rather informative to read the letters he wrote her. Extract eight." McEwen pointed at the impressive pile. "*What an irony it is*, Vassiliev writes, *that we have great wealth all around us, but we can't sell it to meet our needs. We are counting on your help*. That, or something like it, is in several of the letters. Vassiliev wants Gundula to organize a sale. And since Gundula is on the sales side, we can conclude the Asian lady came to buy."

Graf Bornhof flipped through the photocopied letters, stopping to read several. "Part Russian, part broken German, Randolph," he said. "I read Russian. Do you? The references to commodities for sale sound more like a description of the local economy. Vassiliev may be meaning vegetables for all we know. Carrots. Turnips. It sounds to me he wants Germany to help them get a distribution system going."

"Much too charitable, Alex," McEwen countered. "Our responsibility is to think worst case scenarios. These are clever people. They know how to lull authorities. Don't fall into that trap." Lines on the graf's mouth tightened. He waited for the old man to go on.

McEwen was turning the pages of his notebook with more ceremony. "How far have we come? We have a seller of plutonium; we have a buyer. Missing only is a centre." With scarcely concealed triumph he pushed a last document forwards. "This, Alex, is the centre." A tolerant Graf Bornhof took a dozen, hand-written, stapled sheets, rifled through and placed them on the others. McEwen observed the disinterested nonchalance. "Then I shall tell you the contents." He described a conversation overheard by one of his last spectators in East Berlin. "Picture Sherwood Forest, Alex, a dark place, a cellar in Prenzlauerberg. Who should be waiting there with open arms for Robin Hood and Maid Marian to come along? Little John is waiting. Do you remember Günther Rauch?"

"Quite well," Graf Bornhof replied. He did not hide a first hint of irritation. "We checked him out. Not much there. A misguided, bitter Ossi who has a problem with the past, the present *and* the future. He is quite harmless."

"You may not have checked with adequate thoroughness," McEwen said coldly. "Knowing what transpired in that cellar would put most people on alert. There was a long political discussion with a great deal of love expressed for Marx. Marxists are bad at many things, but at one thing they excel. They know how to hijack constitutions. And Little John, I'm afraid, wants yours. He merely needs a little money. So Robin Hood comes onto the scene to help. Read what the consul says: *A couple of phone calls and you'll all be in power*. It's there, Alex, black on white. All one needs do is read it."

But Graf Bornhof had become inscrutable. "Randolph," he said quietly at last. "Randolph, really."

McEwen turned one more page in his notebook. He was icy calm. "I shall summarize," he said. "The consul is a lifelong Marxist – we know that from his Berlin student days. For years, he bides his time and develops wonderful cover. An opportunity to return comes just as his old friend Günther Rauch is planning a new left wing movement. All he needs is cash to get it going. The consul meanwhile has developed exquisite connections to the international nuclear weapons scene through his work on disarmament issues. He is informed Gundula Jahn will be the go-between. He looks her up under the guise of routine diplomacy. He knows the buyers too. A mystery lady comes to talk business. If the consul brokers a deal, Günther Rauch's finances will be secure forever." The meta-diplomat pushed what was left of his folder, an empty shell, towards Graf Bornhof and as an afterthought flicked him the ribbon through the air. "Sherwood Forest. Time to send the bailiff in."

The mechanism pushing the voiceless cuckoo out whirred. McEwen smoothed his white moustache. Graf Bornhof studied the stack of paper. They sat like gamblers, each confident of having better cards. Graf Bornhof knew it was his turn. Call? Raise the ante? Or make it look that he was folding? He had called McEwen to Pullach to inform him that his transferred networks were not working out. They were promising on paper, yes, but when touched they collapsed, like cardboard structures. And now this irrational vendetta against a consul in Berlin? Another flimsy construction rising up from baseless conjectures. How, Graf Bornhof asked himself, might McEwen be neutralized? How to end the game? "More coffee, Randolph?" he asked. "And a biscuit?" He poured from the thermos and slipped him a tray. "Compelling material," he said thoughtfully. "I suppose we ought to call the bailiff."

"That would be most wise," McEwen said.

"We will want to check out some small points first, but I doubt it will take long."

"Prudence can be beneficial," agreed McEwen, smiling kindly. "How do you expect Sherwood Forest will end? A triple arrest? Robin Hood declared *persona non grata*?"

"Possibly. It might go in one of a dozen ways," Graf Bornhof said evasively, paging through the Sherwood Forest dossier. "We'll do the right thing. I assure you."

The business done, talk turned to retirement. Where would McEwen settle? Yorkshire, he answered. He planned to buy a farm. Graf Bornhof described his cottage. Anne wanted to go back to her roots and spend their golden years close to Oxford. "When we've settled in, I shall visit you in Yorkshire," he said.

"It would be my pleasure," McEwen replied, munching on a cookie.

※

From the rear seat of the Mercedes, McEwen did not salute the guards. They had a brief glimpse of a tranquil figure lost in thought. Outside the gate, the car accelerated smoothly and took the road to Munich. On the train back to Berlin McEwen ran out of things to read and spent time staring out the window. Graf Bornhof's last words, like a recording, began playing in his head. *We'll do the right thing.* Fuzzy words. What did they mean? Can any Hun be trusted if he says he'll do the right thing? Suddenly the Cold War warrior stiffened. Why hadn't Graf Bornhof asked for his remaining networks, his pipeline into the diplomatic scene? Had he been suckered into playing a part in a despicably elaborate Pullach game? Did Sherwood Forest now rest in the hands of an untrustworthy man? McEwen's instincts told him something was amiss. A new bout of spite set in, but quickly it transformed as an empathy for the Beavers came on strong. The Beavers were dependable, partners in the great days of empire, cut from the same stock. Thinking of the Beavers soothed the master meta-diplomat. He resolved the moment he was back in Berlin to make a transatlantic call. It was never a bad idea to anticipate perfidy, to take out some insurance against the Hun.

McEwen reached for his briefcase. He had an urge to spend the remainder of the journey with Maid Marian. Hauling out the sheaf of clippings, he began once more to read the earliest letters from Gregor to his mother. As the train neared Berlin, an old man's nostalgia hit. Why couldn't he have run into someone like Gundula years before? Taking a folded photo from his wallet, he fixed his eyes on her.

CHOPIN PLAYS ON THE TITANIC

ix time zones apart, Anthony Hanbury and Irving Heywood were in a concurrent rush. The consul was absorbed in late-afternoon final preparations for what was to have been a cosy housewarming party, but somehow turned into a great feast staged by Gifford. Even the invitations had a special aura – society watchers sensed it – that the event would be the diplomatic season's highlight. Florists, caterers, waiters, musicians – all were arriving on the consul's front steps more or less at once. All wanted to know from whom they should be taking orders. As Hanbury stood in the swelling confusion and nervous countdown that precedes large parties, Heywood was unceremoniously puffing his way down a corridor towards a lift. It would raise him eight stories, then eject him into the high priest's ante-chamber. The high priest was new, and rumoured to be mean.

"Is this Irving Heywood?" the high priest had said with a voice drawn from high grade tensile steel. "Yes it is," Heywood growled back. The caller identified himself. "Sir!" Heywood said with a changed tone.

"Welcome. We are proud you were appointed to lead the Service."

The new high priest was not *of* the Service. He had been parachuted in after a stay with the Tithe Collectors across town. The reputation he earned there was fearsome. Naturally, the Service rank and file sniggered when he came up in conversation. Sniggering was habitual; it accompanied all the stories of the exploits of the senior men. This time too, in the cafeteria, or on the evening busses delivering the working levels back to waiting families in the suburbs, there was buzz about the new high priest. But the tittering he brought on was different from the others. It was shallower and short-lived. Plaintive silence hung between the bursts of gossip. The high priest's mandate, rumour had it, was to decimate the Service. Heywood had heard it too. At his age, he knew, he was especially vulnerable.

Heywood, though assertive on the phone, was actually overcome by an unpleasant sensation. Physically, his innards began roiling; mentally, he felt small. "Irv," said the high priest icily. "Gotta see you fast. Get your ass up here." "Yessir." The telephone went dead.

Heywood thought feverishly about reasons for the call. He had just completed the annual Investitures task of drawing up new ambassadorial nominations. A secret memorandum had been sent to the high priest, but had brought no echo. A problem with the list? Seen as too conservative? True, it did read as a kind of Who's Who of Old Farts. But they were Heywood's friends. If any one of them had become Investitures priest instead of him, he, most assuredly, would not have been forgotten and would have his place on the list that matched men with plums. The priestly conspiracy demanded it. Heywood suddenly turned suspicious. Had someone blown the whistle? Had ambitious young bucks approached the high priest? Heywood knew about the previous year's complaint, of the unruly talk that there was incest within the senior ranks. The high priest's tone had not been reassuring. Heywood grabbed a copy of his memorandum and hurried off. "Mr.

Heywood," cried one of the girls, "can I get a signature? It's really urgent!" "Sorry," the Investitures priest called back over his shoulder. "The high priest is waiting." Half a dozen underlings looked up. They witnessed an unstately departure down the hallway – a quivering rear end of many pounds trudging off without a single ounce of grace.

In the high priest's ante-chamber, sweat formed as Heywood waited. He dabbed his brow with a tissue. "It won't be much longer," soothed the receptionist. "He's on the phone. It's like this all the time. On the phone. On the phone. On the phone. It never stops." A loud roar of laughter rose on the other side of the door, then subsided. There was some shouting, more laughing and garbled loud talking. The Investitures priest began to review his memorandum. It was a defensible list, for the most part, he consoled himself. What else can be done with the twilight generation of the Service except make them ambassadors? Headquarters was no place for them. It wasn't a geriatric ward. These men no longer had the strength for bone-crunching, never-ending hours. That was the underlying purpose of the list, to offer a solution. What would the Service be without the safety valve of the annual ambassadorial rite?

The door flung open. A tall, slim-hipped, wide-shouldered figure fixed aggressively on Heywood. The belt sported a wide buckle and the shirt – two breast pockets closed with flaps – had a subtle western look; the necktie was a strip of leather. Meet Bo Bilinski, the second son in a cow-punching family that owned a spread in Alberta's Buffalo Head Hills. Because the business hadn't been big enough for three grown men with egos, Bo gravitated East when he was young, where his government career advanced meteorically. Bilinski had learned a few tricks before he turned his back on steers. And so it was that in no time at all he punched the country's economic policies from the left end of the spectrum over to the right. When he roped in the industrial subsidies, he set a new world record. Then he turned to the toughest steer he ever wrestled – bureaucratic waste – and laid it low. And now he was beginning a wild ride on a heaving bull – running the country's foreign service. Everyone knew Bilinski had strength, but the unanswered question was, did he have a quick-enough response? Could he stay on the shifty beast for the distance? Or would he be thrown and trampled like others before him? The stands were packed to watch the great event.

Bilinski scowled at Heywood. "You Irv?"

"I am," Heywood said, rising.

"Elma. No calls." He beckoned Heywood with a finger. Inside his office he pointed at a chair while he went to a far corner where glass panels went from floor to ceiling. Bilinski stood for a bit, seemingly lost in thought. The view was north-facing. The frozen river below was covered with snow. Lit up in the morning sun, it resembled an immaculate avenue defined by patches of black wintering trees along the banks reaching east to Montreal. In the distance beyond Hull rose the Gatineaus, magnificently textured hills speckled black and white and, on this day, looking soft and downy. The early spring light attacked the snow, which sent it flying back, making the view blinding.

Why was Bilinski lost in thought? Heywood convinced himself the high priest was experiencing a silent exultation over the inspiring landscape. Before Bilinski earned this office – the inner sanctum, the best part of the tabernacle – he would have had a standard cell across town, one of those colourless cubicles in a jungle of government concrete. Heywood once saw an office there and he had shuddered. "Lovely scene," he offered. "The nicest of any foreign ministry in the world. I have a cottage in those hills. Knowing it was there kept us sane through many a hardship assignment."

"That's nice," Bilinski said with the tone of, *Who cares?* Threateningly he turned around. "Tell me Irv, who the hell is Anthony Hanbury?"

Heywood, surprised, shifted on the leather chair. "Hanbury? Why, he's on assignment in Berlin."

"That, Irv, I had figured out. Jesus! What I mean is, what kind of asshole is he?" Bilinski had the hooked nose and slicked-back hair look of a professional wrestler.

"I know him somewhat," Heywood said, sucking in his breath. Bilinski had moved to stand in front of him, the prominent belt buckle not too far from his forehead. "Tony is quiet, unassuming," Heywood said. He looked straight ahead, then quickly upwards. "Not the type to put the world on fire, but not unsuitable for some assignments. He seems to be settling down in Berlin. He wrote us a charming note before Christmas."

"Is that so? And do you know Harry Manteaux?"

"Oh yes. We work closely with his people. Their intelligence assessments may be somewhat...well...alarmist, but still, they identified some Soviet agents back then, when there were agents. Some of Manteaux's people are under the same roof as us abroad."

"Don't bullshit, Irv. I want you to know something. I hate Harry's fucking guts."

"I see," said Heywood.

"Spent two weeks with Harry years ago. One of those bullshit courses for senior pencil-pushers. Hated every minute of it. Manteaux was the pedant in the crowd, a son-of-a-bitch of a whiner. It disturbed me. He's pissing me off all over again just thinking about it." Bilinski moved back to the window. All Heywood saw was the broad back, narrow waist and long athletic legs. "So Harry phones. Like an idiot I take the call. He wants to discuss *my* man in Berlin. I tell you Irv, a cock and bull story. A pain in the ass. A goddamn waste of time. So when he said I should terminate some joker called Hanbury, I told Harry to screw himself. High time someone told him that. What it was about, I can't figure out. Some shitty problem with reporting from Berlin.

Reporting! Christ! Who needs reporting? We've got to shut the thousands of report scribbling bureaucrats off, Irv, not turn 'em on."

"We share most of our reports with Manteaux's people," Heywood said, trying to be helpful.

"Well, Irv, I tell you, I don't give a goddamn about that. What I want you to do is phone that fairy in Berlin and tell him I don't like being called by Harry or any of the other spooks. I never want to hear Harry's goddamn voice again and if it takes a report or two to do that – if that's the problem – I'm prepared to bend my principles. Tell that shithead Hanbury to send the spooks a couple of reports. OK?"

"Of course."

Bilinski turned around. "So, whatcha waiting for?" He gestured to the door.

The Investitures priest fingered the secret memorandum. "Sir," he said, "could we quickly go over this year's Head-of-Mission proposals? I sent you a note a few days ago."

"Never saw it." The high priest looked accusingly at the top of his vast black desk. The only things on it were a fountain pen in a stand and a photograph of a smiling wife hovering over three radiant children. "Wait." He picked up his phone and jabbed a button. "Robbie? You got something there from someone called Heywood? Yeah? Bring it in won't you?" Bilinski pushed a palm towards Heywood. "Stay. This'll take thirty seconds flat. Heads of mission, that's them pampered ambassadors. Am I right?"

"It is important to name experienced people," Heywood said. "With the wrong man in charge, an embassy goes off the rails in no time." Bilinski was silent. Heywood felt relieved. No young buck had got to the high priest. The door opened silently and a young woman slipped in.

"Robbie," Bilinski said. "Met Irv yet?"

"No! High time I did. Hi Irv." The high priest's executive assistant was a lovely creature. She lowered herself into the chair opposite Heywood and crossed her legs.

"So, we're about to decide who becomes ambassador, right?" Bilinski said, setting out some ground rules. "Have you read Irv's piece of paper, Robbie? Can I have a peek?" Robbie gave the secret memorandum to the High Priest. "Why these guys, Irv?" Bilinski asked matter-of-factly.

"Can I say something, Bo?" Robbie said, cutting Heywood off with a smile.

"Shoot."

"We should freeze the list. There's heaps of time. It's only March. Changes don't take effect until summer."

"Well just a second," Heywood interjected robustly. "These aren't high school drop-outs. They're senior people. They need time to prepare themselves."

Bilinski looked at Robbie. He looked at Heywood. With the way he moved his head, he transmogrified in that instant into a mountain hawk, about to swoop and dig talons into quarry.

"That's the problem with the list," said Robbie sweetly. She wore a fluffy white blouse done up to the neck and expensively tailored black pants. "The list isn't intergenerational."

"Is that true Irv?" Bilinski demanded with suspicion.

Heywood saw the writing on the wall. The young bucks hadn't got to the high priest: they got to Robbie. They must have smelled her from afar. Never underestimate the rutting that takes place in the hallways. He also knew, given Robbie's comment, that he had no more than two seconds – maybe only one – if he wanted to survive as priest. "I wouldn't exactly say it isn't intergenerational," the Investitures priest said slowly, to gain precious milliseconds, "but Robbie has put her finger on a problem. We have a lot of senior people, sir. Maybe the list isn't an ideal way to solve it."

"Goddamn right, it isn't," the high priest said.

"That was going to be my next point," Robbie said. "I'm just thinking out loud, Bo, but maybe this is the time to get *Bitrap* going. Get that done before we think about new ambassadors."

Bilinski returned to the tall glass panels to observe the splendid hills. Too bad all that was park, he thought. Too bad he couldn't start a ranch there. The kids were growing up and he feared they were turning into eastern softies. The other day it was minus twenty and they complained about the cold. Shit, up in the Buffalo Head Hills, minus forty was considered balmy. The time was coming to get back to the open spaces. He owed it to the kids. But some things needed doing first. *Get on with it*, Bilinski urged himself, in the way he always did before his other superhuman feats. Was Irv the man for *Bitrap*? Bilinski wasn't sure. Irv had put his finger on a problem all right. Allowing old shitters to spread their fat fannies on expensive crappers all over the world was no way to solve the population problem. Irv looked like a softy, but you never knew. Some damn good wranglers came out of the east. Son-of-a-bitch. Go for broke. He turned back from the window.

"Irv," he said, "know what a trapezoid is?"

"I believe so. Geometry I think."

"Right on. Good thinking. A trapezoid is like this." The high priest drew an airy figure, a horizontal line, two sides sloping outward and then the broader base. "That's this organization, Irv. It's gone trapezoidal. It's fat. That ain't right. We gotta fix it. Out of the trapezoid we gotta get a pyramid. My solution, Irv, is to draw a line from the corner upper left down to the corner bottom right." He traced the slanting line with an ominously pointed finger. "That, Irv, is a bisection. If everything above that line disappears," – he waved half the trapezoid away – "you tell me what's left. Bloody right. Bureaucratic perfection. The goddamn dip list isn't the way to solve the population problem. *Bitrap* is. I'd like you to work on that for a few weeks. You know, bisect the trapezoid, get it done. When it's finished, come back with a new list. Robbie will work with you, provide cover. We know from other places how everybody suddenly starts shooting if things gotta change. Your backside isn't tiny, but don't worry about it getting hit. No one slaps the projectile stuff back faster than Robbie. Okay? Thanks. Come back in two weeks."

The Investitures priest sputtered, which made the high priest look severe, so then Heywood nodded. Bilinski smiled and made a gracious gesture to the door. "I've got some ideas on how to announce this, Irv," Robbie said helpfully preceding Heywood out. "I'll pop down to your place after lunch."

The underlings in Investitures noticed a leadenness in Irving Heywood's pace when he returned. In one hand he held a crumpled sheet of paper. "Broken by the high priest," an observant young thing whispered. With his head held low, Heywood really did resemble a tired rodeo horse that had been outlasted by a champion rider.

Suppose we bisect, who'll do all the work, Heywood had asked Robbie when they left the ante-chamber. "Irv," she had said, "Irv, come into the modern era. Join us! The empirical evidence is in. Productivity increases are a function of the inverse of the reduction in the size of an organization. Across town that theorem is an absolute truth now. Cut an organization in half and the output quadruples. It's been proven." Robbie had smiled at the older man. Heywood had asked, *if you cut the organization to a third, does that mean productivity goes up by nine?* Robbie had taken it as a serious question. She had said that for the government sector the evidence was not yet in, but the betting of the gurus was that proof would be available next year. "Anyway for the economy as a whole, the answer is likely to be a clear yes. Cutting one job creates two, maybe three, maybe even four." "Miraculous,"

Heywood had said. His mouth was dry and he tried hard to stop his stomach from rebelling.

In his office Heywood organized his thoughts and made another list, not of ambassadors, but of things to do. The ability to think fast even when someone had him in the wringer once elevated Heywood into the ranks of priests; within five minutes a plan existed. *Easy, Irving,* he then calmed himself. First things first. Get rid of the undergrowth. Deal with the Hanbury problem, then tackle the bigger job. The Hanbury issue sounded trivial enough. Heywood dialled Manteaux's number, but Manteaux had just left for Canberra for a conference on post Cold War intelligence challenges. *Could it wait two weeks?* the secretary asked. "Not really," growled Heywood.

He demanded to speak to Manteaux's executive assistant. No, the EA knew nothing about a reporting problem with Berlin. "You know there's two types of reporting from diplomatic missions," the fresh assistant informed the Investitures priest. "There's substantive reports – like stuff that's in the papers, only better, you know, the inside dope. Then there's the contact reports – about brushes with security agents from the other side." Concerning which of these two kinds of reporting, the EA wanted to know, was there a problem in Berlin? "I'm vaguely aware of the distinction," Heywood sighed. "Listen. Harry initiated this. He knows, I assume, which reporting is the problem. Which is why I'm asking you. Are you his EA or what? Don't you know what's on his mind?"

"Mr. Manteaux keeps things close to his chest. I'm afraid I can't help you."

Then stick your finger up your ass, thought Heywood, taking a cue on management style from the high priest.

He turned to his computer. Contact reporting could *not* be the problem, Heywood reasoned. The Wall was down, the Warsaw Pact finished. East and West were friends. The spies had left Berlin for Baghdad and Tehran. The complaint must be over-substantive reporting. Had Tony done some lunatic scribbling? Typical of Tony, to try to do the right thing, but miss the target. Heywood remembered only too well the near fiasco in Vienna over the PM's speech.

The computer booted, Heywood clicked in the archives code and called up the index to the general files. *Search?* appeared on a menu. Heywood typed *Berlin*. A new menu unfolded on the screen. *Berlin -Admin, -Consular, -Culture, -Reporting, -Staffing.* Heywood clicked *Reporting*. He scrolled through *economic, political, social, commercial,* one after the other. Each category was blank. That's it, crowed Heywood. No wonder Manteaux complained. Tony had filed no reports, not even translations of newspaper articles. Naughty, naughty Tony, spending all his time tomcatting around Berlin. But Heywood was cautious. Easy, Irving, he counselled, easy. Cover all the bases. Lack of substantive reporting from Berlin is *probably* the answer, *but check it out.*

Heywood phoned the European zealots and asked for the woman who good-humouredly bore the nickname Krauthilda. "Mr. Heywood!" she cried. "This is unexpected!" She was friendly. He remembered she had written him a memo asking for re-assignment to Rome.

"What's your view of Hanbury in Berlin," he asked. "How's the reporting?"

"Great," she said enthusiastically.

"Yeah? Where is it? No trace in the archives."

"That's the point. He doesn't do any. I told him that. It's the way we want it. We get all the information we need from the wires. We don't need reports from Berlin."

"You're in tune with the times, I'll say that much."

"Thanks," purred Krauthilda. "By the way, Mr. Heywood, I'm taking Italian in my spare time. You should know that."

"That will be helpful. I'm boning up on geometry myself."

"Oh wow!" Krauthilda cried. She assumed the Investitures priest was angling to become Ambassador to the United Nations – circular arguments, elliptical interventions, global problems that zip out to infinity faster than a parabola. "Enjoy!" she sang.

That settled it. *Substantive* reporting was the problem. The zealots wanted none; the spooks, as usual, were hooked like junkies. And an unsuspecting man stood in the middle. Poor Tony. Heywood felt a sudden priestly warmth. The short note last Christmas, Zella showed it to him before she left. Tony wrote some decent things. *Tell Heywood I appreciate the burden leadership brings.* Heywood's eyes turned dewy. Helping time for Tony, he thought. He looked up the Berlin number, dialled, but got no answer. Of course not. It would be evening in Berlin. First thing in the morning then. The Investitures priest assumed the consul could hang on that long.

The niggling reporting problem dealt with, Heywood turned his attention to the bigger challenge. He reviewed his plan once more, then called Spinks in Superannuation, Ashbalm in Continuing Training, Leclerc in Tax Planning, Litbarskow in Financial Inducements, Duhaene in External Placements, as well as Madame Tassé, the busy counsellor for the Service's despondent souls. A crisis session began one hour later.

"I've received guidance from the high priest," began Heywood in a stentorian voice. He had regrouped. "*Operation Bitrap.*" Heywood's hands were planted wide on the table. Madame Tassé, observing the investitures priest with narrowing eyes, was the only one who noticed something vulnerable clung to him. A moral lapse? A fermenting conscience? A fallen priest?

Heywood outlined his plan. The experts whistled through their teeth. "My intent, at least for once, is that the bottom ranks won't bear the brunt," the Investitures priest sermonized.

In retrospect, this became a defining moment. When Bilinski's demand for the trapezoidal bisection was eventually met, Heywood was acclaimed by the survivors as hero. The generous remark concerning the bottom ranks did not go unnoticed. It forced the nimble Madame Tassé to change her view on the spot. *Not* a fallen priest! Before her sat a man capable of high moral choices, a man prepared to break with tradition, a man willing to rise to defend the little guy. She made a quick notation. *The rank and file will not carry the brunt.* In the weeks that followed she showed this pad to everyone. The page took on a spiritual quality. It became an icon. The words echoed in the corridors, flashed through the cafeteria, were born outward on the evening busses, penetrating deep into the suburbs. Small children, once the Irving Heywood story had been narrated at the family dinner table, insisted that it be told once more when they snuggled down in bed. With some embellishments it turned into a legend. Heywood had bucked and thrown the high priest, the worst ride the bronco-buster ever had. In fact the high priest got thrown so high that when he finally landed, he was back out West.

But that was in the future. In the present there was work to do. "Twice daily meetings, at eight and one," Heywood decided. "The task is tough, but I believe together we can do it. This will be the war room."

❦

Hanbury had spent time sitting in a kind of war room too, the alcove off the office hallway, a nerve centre for purposeful planning. It consisted of two rickety bridge tables placed together with sagging armchairs jammed around. "Perhaps I should invite some people to celebrate after I move in," the consul had mused when his new residence was nearly ready.

"Excellent idea, Tony," replied Gifford. "The funds are there. Shall I draw up a party concept?"

"Why not? Yes Earl. Please. If you could."

This casual remark sparked things off. Gifford's zeal, as always, was like the crest of a wave surging forward. Planning the party took three weeks. Gifford, like Heywood, ran daily sessions. The consul sat in once a week. The computer generated a critical path with key dates in bold letters. Progress was rigorously monitored. Gifford was on the lookout for the trivial oversights that turn parties into calamities faster than fingers snap. Tasks were divvied up. Frau Carstens: guest list and tracking acceptances and regrets. Frau von Ruppin: flowers and decorations. Frau Köhler: printing, publicity, interviews. Sturm: parking, police liaison, driver control. Gifford had responsibility for food and drink, plus channelling Herr Neumeister's creative input. The latter insisted on having a hand in the party's design, offering the service cost-free because, he said, the event would be living art. The consul contributed too, meeting twice with a renowned string quartet, *The Whisperers*, to discuss the musical programme.

"What's your estimate," Gifford asked Frau Carstens at the second planning session, "a thirty percent acceptance rate?"

"Depending on whether the Federal President is in or out of town, it could go slightly higher. Possibly thirty-five," she answered with authority.

Gifford wanted the Federal President's schedule checked. He would be away. "Important information," Gifford said on day three. "We want about a hundred and fifty, so we'll need a list of about four to five hundred." Given the size of the consul's stable of contacts, Frau Carstens had to prioritize. She asked him for his preferences; he replied he wanted to think it over. That evening, at a gala opening of the Bolshoi Ballet, Hanbury consulted von Helmholtz at intermission. The latter responded with a handwritten list the next day containing two dozen more names, recent, prominent arrivals in the city. *Useful to invite.* The CEO of German Railways, the Superintendent of Public Television, a banker with a national profile fresh from the top floor of the highest office tower in Frankfurt, architects from London, Paris and Rome setting up offices in Berlin, three new filmmakers attracted by subsidies at the Babelsberg studios in Potsdam, an American Nobel Prize winner in economics now at the Free University and studying post-communist consumer behaviour. Frau Carstens recognized that von Helmholtz's proposals should take precedence, but over whom? "The dips?" Hanbury asked innocently.

"Do you think so?" she asked with initial horror. "Do you really *think* so?" A little girl's smile spread over her face, so wicked was the idea behind the consul's question.

"Why not?" he replied casually.

With a strange, almost vengeful delight, Frau Carstens activated her computer's delete command. Erasing so many diplomats at once gave her a queer, nearly sexual delight.

Day four. The printed invitation cards went out. When no one looked, Hanbury pinched one and addressed it to Gundula. Enclosed was a note urging her to come. *To make amends for my poor behaviour after the Press Ball.*

Day ten. The task force confronted a problem. Acceptances were outnumbering regrets five to one. Gifford did a quick extrapolation. The estimate: possibly four hundred guests. Anxiety descended, Sturm being the exception. He looked forward to hosting every chauffeur in town. Gifford scratched his neck. "The residence is big enough, I guess," he thought aloud. "Neumeister was hoping to contain the party to the dining room and the salon. But if we open the doors to the music room, the tea alcove, the library and the conservatory, we might get by without too much discomfort." The question was whether these parts of the mansion would be ready. It meant accelerating the purchase of a grand piano, several dozen large oriental vases, a couple of thousand leather-bound books and a small forest of potted palms and fig trees. "We have no choice," Gifford concluded.

On the phone that day he puffed, cajoled and threatened. Neumeister helped. He identified a Steinway in London and snapped up a collection of nineteenth-century books from a Russian dealer, payment to go into a Channel Island bank account.

Day fifteen. The consul was relocated to the Greco-Roman mansion. Hanbury's few personal belongings – clothing, the stereo and four big boxes of compact discs – were picked up by a moving company. Departing from the little bungalow one last time, Sturm drove solemnly, as if to a higher calling. But an event marred the journey to Dahlem.

As he drove, Sturm was describing his latest observation of the once divided city. Birds, he claimed, were happier in the East. Pigeons, sparrows, chickadees and the like – they weren't afraid to get close to people in the East. No bird in the West had ever been seen to do that. Sturm reasoned it was because people in the West snarled. "Everything that lives gets hissed at. Birds too." The birds, he theorized, developed accordingly. But in the East, evolution created a different, a more trusting bird. He noticed it on the sidewalks. A pigeon once walked through his legs on Lenin Platz. A sparrow nearly did the same. "Something's causing that," he speculated. "I doubt it's behavioural. Maybe it was once, but no longer. Trust. It's got into their genes."

That's when the trip became blemished. They were at a spacious traffic junction called Roseneck making a left turn to Dahlem. A Jaguar driven by a woman with striking auburn hair and dressed in a jacket that was once the skin of a Himalayan tiger came from the opposite direction, also turning left. A moment of confusion as Sturm and the woman tried to gauge whether they would pass in front or around each other. The result was the Opel and the Jag in a nose to nose confrontation. "Back off, lady," Sturm muttered, waving patronizingly as in the days when he drove Lord Halcourt's Bentley. A window lowered. A lovely head came out. "Get that tin can out of the way!"

In Sturm's estimation this was slander directed at a sovereign government. He rolled his window down and cried, "Why don't you prove your bucket's got a reverse!"

"I never back away from loudmouths!" she threatened.

"You're a monkey in a tiger suit," roared Sturm, "and that cage you're in is ready for the zoo!"

"*Halt die Fresse, Schlappschwanz!*" she shouted. She called him a limp prick and told him to shut his trap.

"*Pissnelke!*" Sturm roared.

"Sturm," the consul ventured gently from the rear seat. "Don't rile her. She looks like a nice lady."

"Sure. A loving mother of three kids. Lord Halcourt said *all* Jag drivers are upstarts. I never knew him to be wrong."

As the traffic lights clicked into a new cycle, car horns sounded all over Roseneck. Sturm in the middle, with a patrician's calm, continued shooing the Jag off, as he might a fly in a kitchen. The woman lost her nerve and reversed a couple of meters. Sturm threw his wheel and eased by. She gave him the finger, saw an opening in the traffic, gunned the engine and produced two smoking strips of rubber. Hanbury turned around to see her lurch into Hagenstrasse where, he supposed, she would probably touch a hundred and fifty. Sturm sat out the cycle like a meditating Buddha, then ambled towards Dahlem without a worry in the world. "It proves my point, Herr Konsul," he remarked. "About the pigeons. You see why in this part of town they stay away from people."

Gifford and Neumeister, hands behind their back, were waiting at the top of the steps. Hanbury ascended to meet them. Neumeister couldn't have been more excited if the Chancellor's wife had commissioned him to redesign her boudoir. He gave the consul a frenetic tour, breathlessly detailing the work still to be done before the party. Hanbury mostly nodded. From time to time he turned around and spoke to a trailing Gifford. "Excellent," he said. "Good. I think that's fine." Gifford looked upon the residence as his life's work also, and was elated it brought praise. One day, when the consul was away on vacation, he would show the place to Frieda. He imagined her reclining in progressive stages of undress on each of the eight splendid sofas. Afterwards, in the conservatory amongst the fig trees she could act out the role of Eve.

Gifford and Neumeister left. Towards the end of the afternoon, the consul departed for a reception and was back at nine. The mansion sounded hollow. Hanbury discovered the stereo had been set up in the salon. He rummaged through a packing case of discs, deciding on the New World Symphony by Dvorak. The salon had wonderful acoustics. Hanbury turned the volume up, then up some more, until the music reverberated. He sat down in a deep chair in a corner, but had difficulty concentrating on the sound. Impatiently he jerked himself back on his feet and began wandering from room to room. He ascended the stairs to his private apartment, then up another narrower one to empty rooms underneath the roof where normally servants would be housed. Everywhere he switched on lights.

A night pedestrian would have taken notice. Scintillating reflections jumped off Neumeister's multi-coloured walls and loud music reached out the windows. A glittering effect, a royal vessel of merriment on a nocturnal cruise. But had the solitary occupant been seen wandering from room to room staring at lifeless objects, the observer would have changed his mind. He would have thought the lit-up scene, the incongruously cheerful notes sent into the frigid Dahlem night, was not a merry barque at all. The conclusion would have been that the mansion was more like a ship of doom, a Titanic, all lights ablaze and with the pathos of a thousand voices singing hymns as it went down.

※

D-day. Four hundred and thirty-two guests were on the list.

At the very moment that Heywood began his sonorous sermon to the

Bitrap task force, Hanbury in formal dress was pacing in the vestibule and tugging at his shirt cuffs. Frau von Ruppin and Frau Köhler stood at the ready in the cloak room; Frau Carstens hovered by the guest book; a sweating Gifford was checking details in the kitchen; and Sturm was outside directing traffic. In the salon, two rows of waiters stood at attention holding trays of briskly effervescing, chilled champagne. The salon looked exquisite with paintings capturing the light and mood of the nineteenth-century Mediterranean. They were in a mystical style which Neumeister called neo-ambrosial, explaining they were so evocative they even aroused his sense of smell. Their pastels matched the curtains which hung from solid brass rods and were gathered at the sides by sashes. These, close observers at the party would eventually ascertain, were custom-made in a velvet that had tiny red maple leaves woven into a white background – a subtle Neumeister touch. Three great chandeliers dominated the salon. The floors were covered by thick Persian carpets.

Double oak doors to the dining-room stood half open, entry teasingly prevented by a velour cord. Inside, softly illuminated by indirect rose-tinted lighting, five silver candelabra each supporting five blood-red burning candles stood on a long table. Spread around the candelabra were trays laden with the finest delicacies from the Frozen North – slices of marinated bison meat, tiny pancakes of Indian corn flour covered with strips of Arctic char, breast of Canada goose and Manitoba mallard, smoked British Columbia sockeye salmon, Quebec elk filet, Davis Bay caviar, cubes of peppered Alberta grain-fed beef, all of it surrounded by Nova Scotia fiddleheads and Saskatchewan wild rice salads. And numerous desserts: Ontario maple-syrup sauces, pastries filled with hand-picked Newfoundland blueberries, thick cream whipped up in fine New Brunswick dairies. The culinary art was by two internationally decorated chefs flown in from Winnipeg. Deeper in the mansion, in the region near the music room, the instruments of *The Whisperers* were being tuned.

In the vestibule, the air prickled with an onset of panic. Despite all the acceptances, might no one come? Impossible. But who would break the ice? It turned out to be the banker newly sent from Frankfurt. His Mercedes entered the driveway silent as a shark. He was deposited at the bottom of the steps. The car moved on. Sturm, waving flashlights, directed it to the camouflaged parking lot.

In the marble vestibule, the consul greeted the banker warmly. "I'm pleased you found it possible to come," he said. "Your reputation preceded you."

The banker bowed. "Oh, am I the first? My deep apologies." He forced a short laugh. His gaze roamed up the vestibule's Ionic columns. He noticed the opulence of the salon. "Yes, a step up from the consular corps in Frankfurt," he said. "I heard it would be like this in Berlin."

Berlin's Senator for Culture came next, a bear of a man with white hair layered like a wig. "Herr Konsul," said the senator, "a good idea, having a party at this time of year." Hanbury introduced him to the banker. The two soon guffawed. A pointed remark from the senator on extravagant bank profits had been countered effortlessly by the banker with a call for better tax breaks on donations to the arts. They moved into the salon.

Neumeister was an early arrival also. He wore a cape slung from his neck and a wide-brimmed floppy hat. Using a diamond-studded cane he immediately began pointing out to guests the meaning of the swirling stucco patterns on the ceilings.

The trickle of guests turned into a flood. A line formed at the door, snaked down the steps and out along the driveway. Nervously, expectantly, enviously, one couple after another squeezed into the crowded vestibule, removed coat and hat and waited to greet their host.

A lovely house.

A jewel.

Very, very tasteful.

Superb, really quite superb.

I always imagined life in Canada would be this good.

Hanbury accepted the compliments with grace. He nodded when the speaker of Berlin's parliament said the residence symbolized national glory. The commanding general of the German army (recently moved back into Berlin after a half-century absence) rhapsodized that it represented a country with pedigree and not burdened by history. The consul, on behalf of thirty million countrymen, gratefully squeezed the general's hand.

The line continued moving. Frau Carstens made check marks on her list. Outside, Sturm waved his flashlights. When von Helmholtz reached Hanbury, he apologized. He could not stay long. "A dinner commitment, Tony, but I wanted to see your new residence. You've set the future standard. That's obvious." He leaned forward to whisper a confidence. The consul turned to Frau Carstens. "Can I commit myself for four o'clock tomorrow afternoon for a quarter of an hour?" he asked. "Tomorrow? Yes," she replied crisply. "I'll expect you then," said the Chief of Protocol. Von Helmholtz entering the salon set off a wave of social energy which surged throughout the mansion. A momentary pause in the decibel level of hundreds of voices recognized that the best-known man in Berlin was amongst them. Did this, or the consul's subsequent short speech, constitute the evening's finest moment?

Somewhere among the arrivals, Gundula slipped by Frau Carstens and stood before the consul. She wore a tight dress, black and short, like her hair. Men glanced at her with concealed admiration; women ignored her with cold envy. The consul held her hand fractionally too long. "I'll catch up with you later," he said. "Okay, boss," she teased, withdrawing her hand.

When the arrivals thinned, the consul joined the squeeze in the salon. Guests had spilled into the other rooms to admire colour schemes and tapestries, hand-carved woodwork and Gobelins furniture. *The Whisperers* pumped out Mozart. Waiters, possessing their profession's most esoteric secret – how to make matter pass through matter – moved through the crowd with trays of drinks held high. At the location where the salon opened to the south wing a sound system had been set up around a small podium. Speakers had been placed everywhere, including in Sturm's domain below. The consul made his way to the podium. "May I have your attention please," he said modestly several times into the microphone until the chatter died away. He had polished some welcoming remarks, but with several hundred faces focussed on him, a tiny quiver crept into his voice.

Hanbury described the reason for the party. *Since my arrival in Berlin I have been a guest so often, I was worried if I didn't offer some hospitality in return the Chief of Protocol would soon ask me to leave town.* Low decibel laughter, everyone looking in the direction of von Helmholtz smiling. The consul said it had at last proved possible to move into a residence that *allowed* a party. He described the search for a suitable place, making a light remark about viewing a neo-gothic mansion in Babelsberg built by a film tycoon. *Just getting it fixed up would have been a horror movie!* A generalized, broad grin. The state of the Babelsberg mansions was well known; no one had difficulty visualizing the devastation left behind by the Russians. The consul mentioned the genius of Herr Neumeister. *He's like a master gunsmith. He arms diplomats with the weapons they need to achieve victory in gruelling campaigns.* More polite laughter and a frantic, appreciative flopping of a wide-brimmed hat.

Hanbury noticed Gundula at this point. She was on the left side, leaning against a tapestry. Their eyes met for an instant. He saw a disbelieving smirk. The curved-up corners of her mouth formulated a question. Why the performance, Gundula was asking. Why was he having them on? The consul pressed forward. He made a few obligatory statements about Berlin's future as a pivot for East and West, the rejuvenated heart beating loud at the centre of Europe. Appropriate clichés. Coming from an outsider, however, they took on a different light, appearing sharper, truer, more absolute, and he received sustained applause. Then came a kind of coup. Hanbury thanked his staff and, after that, the drivers. *The men who fight to get us through!* A pause before a muffled hurrah reverberated from below. At last the consul declared the buffet open. On cue, Gifford removed the velour cord. *The Whisperers* started afresh with new energy drawn from Gershwin, Mancini, the Beatles and Scott Joplin.

Hanbury began to look for Gundula, but guests attached themselves to him like snails. They seemed to want to leave their shimmering trail somewhere on the inside of his thoughts. Sometimes he had three conversations going at once. He got close to Gundula at one point. An arts magazine editor invited by Frau Carstens, a certain Heinrich Fest, a fat man shoe-horned into a tight, dark-purple velvet suit, was drawing Gundula into his orbit. The consul laboured in their direction. He assumed Fest wanted her to write for him, but his leaning towards Gundula was obscene. As Hanbury neared, Gundula's eyes locked on his. She winked, as if to say this party was just fine. Her plate of blueberries and whipped cream was a last but vanishing barrier between her and the editor. Hanbury wanted to say something to Gundula – *stay on a bit after the party* – but an elderly lady, an influential benefactress to the world of opera, intervened and insisted on a tour. Leading her away, Hanbury caught the eye of Gifford, who in turn went looking for the master of interior decoration. Neumeister arrived in minutes, unlocked the benefactress's clasp on the consul's arm and entwined it in his. Waving the cane, carefully in step, he moved off with the fragile woman. When Hanbury returned to where he last saw Gundula she was gone. Fest too had disappeared.

The orchestra was popular. The party became ever louder and more gay. A carpet in the salon was rolled back. Some couples tangoed. Eventually everybody danced. The consul spent an hour at the door waving guests off. When, past midnight, *The Whisperers* began to dismantle, the last ones leaked away. The kitchen staff had cleaned up. The mansion was empty. Only Gifford remained.

"A night cap?" Hanbury asked.

"Oh no. Thank you, but no. Tomorrow is a working day."

"A happy troop tonight."

Gifford's face lit up. "The music did it, Tony. Your show."

"The arrangements were impeccable, Earl. Superb food. First class catering."

"Thank you," beamed Gifford.

Hanbury watched him leave too. The driveway was deserted. No Trabi in sight. He closed the door and surveyed the mansion's after-party state. The salon had come through more or less unscathed. In the kitchen he discovered an open bottle of champagne. He poured a glass, drank it, and poured another. In the drawing room, Hanbury turned the stereo on, rummaged through some boxes and picked out a disc called *Harlem Soul*. Decompression time. He sank into a chair, sipped from the glass and concentrated on the music. Although the first piece was slow and calming, it did not erase malevolent images of Fest. During a pause between tracks he heard a footstep. Hanbury twisted in the chair. Gundula, wearing a rescuer's grin, was standing in the doorway. "Well boss," she mocked, "more orders?"

Hanbury jumped up. "Gundula! I thought you had left! Where were you?"

"Hiding in your palm forest from the awful people at your party."

"You mean Fest. I'm sorry about him. I didn't put him on the invitation list."

"He was not the worst."

"I tried to get to you all evening. I've never experienced anything like it. A straightjacket. I couldn't move."

"You were a busy boy. Everybody wanted to either kiss or lick you."

"Can I get you some champagne?"

Gundula nodded yes and watched him disappear in the direction of the kitchen. She knelt down before the box of CDs on the floor and began to flip through. Hanbury returned with a fresh bottle in a bucket. "I don't think this house is quite you," Gundula said absent-mindedly, fingering the discs, studying them front and back. "I don't think the party was either."

"No?" Hanbury said, popping the cork. "The house is all right. It'll do. Good acoustics. What's me? What's your opinion?"

"Not Soul, but I see you go for it all the same. I don't know what is you. You seem part cowboy, part European effete." The consul handed her a glass. They clinked.

"Don't think about it too hard," he said.

Gundula nodded distantly. "You never said you were a fan of Soul."

"I wasn't, but you are. I began listening to it after the ball. I'm acquiring a taste."

"Because of me? All that?" She gestured towards the box. There must have been six or seven dozen discs in it.

"I was advised it was a cross-section."

"Most is bad."

Hanbury shrugged. "I can't tell the difference yet, but I'll get there."

"Maybe *that's* you," she said, eyes teasing. "The pursuit of achievable aims. So tell me, what kind of music did you listen to before you wasted all that money?" Hanbury answered the classics were his forte. He slid a large packing box filled with CDs out of a closet. Then another, and another. Gundula was puzzled. Thousands of discs. "That's not a forte," she said. "That's an obsession."

The consul explained his collection. One series was by composer. Another by conductor – all the recorded works of Furtwängler, Klemperer, Solti – and so on. Artists were a further grouping, then one by instruments. Everything was a little mixed up now as a result of the move. Gundula remained skeptical. The point of music is to listen to it, she said, implying his was packed away in boxes. But he claimed he did. Sometimes, on a weekend, he might go through thirty discs. Gundula shook her head, saying it confirmed he had an obsession. "Well," Hanbury inquired, "what's yours?"

They fenced pleasantly like this through eight more tracks of Harlem Soul. The consul refilled the glasses. Gundula asked if she could see the rest of the house, laughingly adding to skip the conservatory which she had seen plenty of already. In the music room Gundula was arrested by the gleaming grand piano. "Yours?" she asked, lifting the cover and allowing her fingers to walk over three or four keys.

"Oh no! Part of the house. You're not holding your fingers quite right when you do that, Gundula. That's a fairly harsh tap, tap, tap...like a frightened kitten. Try drifting your hand; let the fingers caress." Hanbury with one hand dazzled off a shower of delicate notes. It was the first time that evening Gundula's eyes stopped mocking. The upturned corners of her mouth dropped. *How did you do that!* her body language demanded.

"I'll show you the Chinese vases in the tea room," he said casually, moving off.

Gundula pulled him back. "Do that again!"

"Oh no," Hanbury said, dismissing the suggestion. "I don't play. Not anymore."

"That was your left hand. Can you do it with your right?" She placed it on the keyboard. "Let me see." Hanbury danced off a dozen virtuoso chords. Gundula forced him to sit down on the bench and joined him. "All right," she said. I'll take your advice. My hands will drift and my fingers will caress. If it's that easy, I should be able to do it." A few partial notes were plunked out. "Modern music," she laughed. Hanbury took her hands and slid them back and forth, hitting keys with his own little fingers. He made it add up to a reduced version of the German national anthem. Gundula loved it. "Do the East German one!" she cried. "I haven't heard it for a while." The consul didn't know it. "Pretend you're Chopin," she urged. "Impress me."

Hanbury eased a few more notes out of the piano, bits of melodies, excerpts from well known concert favourites: *Pictures at an Exhibition, Swan Lake, Peter and the Wolf.* He halted and studied the keys for a while, as if making a decision. Gundula thought he was taking the measure of the instrument. With a deep breath Hanbury began the opening passages of a Rachmaninov piano concerto. The instrument was good; it had a solid sound. The opening bars of the concerto, deep, powerful Russian notes filled the room. Hanbury skipped to other parts of the concerto, making the pieces add up to a coherent extract, as if practised for weeks. His swaying torso pressed against Gundula. "I don't actually like Rachmaninov," he said, stopping in the middle and snapping the keyboard cover shut. "He drenches things with emotion. Anyway," he shrugged, "I'm out of practice."

Gundula was annoyed he had cut Rachmaninov off in mid-stream. Sarcastically she said, "So, where did you pick that up? Sitting around a campfire?"

"I love it when you talk like that," Hanbury said. He slipped an arm through hers.

"And you?" she said bitingly. "This act of yours. Sailing through life like a prince. Making genial speeches. Deploying perfect camouflage."

Hanbury laughed with astonishment. "Gundula," he said, "what do you mean?"

"Listen, Chopin, we've had this conversation before." The same vague tone of accusation coloured her voice, as during the evening in Prenzlauerberg. Hanbury ceased laughing. Gundula pushed on, frustration building. "Why am I here?" she demanded. "What are we doing?" Hanbury looked down with deepening worry. "We're sitting on a piano stool," she continued, "thigh to thigh." For emphasis, she gave him a shove. "We may sit like this until the sun comes up." No reaction from the consul. "What was that nice sentence you wrote on the invitation?"

"I wanted to make amends," Hanbury said quietly.

"Well...?" she urged. When he continued to look blank, Gundula shook her head in disbelief. Then she regained her smile, but it was shallow, resigned. "You really are the diplomat. No move unless it's been agreed to in a treaty, initialled, signed and ratified by an assembly."

"What I meant," the consul said with effort, "was that I hoped we could redo the scene outside your apartment."

"Then we ought to get going. It's an hour's drive." The sarcasm was back too.

"I mean here. We could redo it here."

"We could redo the whole Press Ball here. There's enough room."

Hanbury began to laugh. "The quickstep? Again?" Gundula began to say something, but he told her to wait. "Stay here tonight."

"At last!" Gundula clapped and took her champagne glass. "*Prost!* To a great artist at work. Genius proceeding slowly." She smiled winningly. Hanbury wanted to kiss her, but they clinked glasses instead.

On the long, curving stairway to his private chambers, Hanbury held Gundula's arm. She said, in a big mansion like this, you had to be in shape to get to bed. He replied the stairs were designed to be a warm-up. In the bedroom they embraced and kissed. She began undoing his clothes but had difficulty with the studs on the formal shirt. Bow tie, cuff links, cummerbund: more complicated than women's wear and Gundula complained about it. To prove a point, she slipped out of her clothes so fast a horde of angels must have helped. The consul inelegantly shed socks before they embraced again. "I suppose you have a condom?" Gundula whispered.

"Oh God!"

"I knew it," Gundula murmured, biting his ear. "Cowboy habits. Don't worry. I thought of it."

He massaged the nape of her neck. "You know what they call it?"

"What?"

"Out on the range. They have an expression." Hanbury switched to English. *Riding bareback.* He gave a dirty chuckle. Gundula wanted to know what it meant. "Nothing between you and the horse. Something like that."

"No doubt the highest form of cowboy pleasure," she said. The condoms were in her purse by the piano, so Hanbury trundled off.

A consul without clothes is a comical sight, hurrying down a flight of stairs with his penis flopping up and down. Hanbury was grateful Gundula wasn't there to see it. What would she have called the apparition? *A cowboy's flaccid weapon? A diplomatic tail?* With Gundula everything was possible and he loved her for it.

Gundula had slid between the covers. He handed her the purse; she took a package. Hanbury ran a hand along the outline of her body. She had small breasts, gentle elevations, culminating in hard nipples. "Laying claim to new territory?" she murmured.

The next hours were repetitive: bouts of intensity, quiet talk in the spaces between. The hues of love subtly woven into a tartan. Hanbury asked Gundula to tell him more about the time before she joined the paper. She described Schwerin, a place she never fitted in. She always wanted to travel, but the only place she ever got to was Ukraine. She had propped herself up on an elbow, a leg swung over him. He asked about the paper. Gundula said the atmosphere was changing. Gregor Donner Reich had been fun, but it backfired. She was now assigned to reporting on trivial stories, crime in the eastern streets. She'd been shunted aside. "Funny isn't it. I didn't fit in then. I don't think I fit in now."

Why didn't she turn to foreign issues, he asked. Foreign issues were safe. Domestic readers never react badly to criticism of another country. She said she lacked the confidence, not having done enough travelling, not having the language skills. Gundula began to rub his body. "Chopin," she whispered. "Ready for an encore?" It took longer to finish. They lay still for a while. Gundula moved on to another square of the night's rich tartan. She asked how he came to be so skilful on the piano.

"Prairie air," he joked.

"Seriously."

"I practised."

"You practised a lot."

"When I grew up, that's all there was."

"Why didn't you stick with it?"

"I guess, like you, some things didn't fit."

A long silence set in, a dark stripe in the tartan. Gundula whispered there was a final condom, but the consul's breathing was deep and regular. For a while she watched him sleep, got up, adjusted the cover, gathered her clothes and slipped away into a night as dark as the one that sank the Titanic. The next morning Hanbury found the condom package spread out on the night table. A scribbled sentence on it read, *Vielen Dank Chopin. Es war herrlich.* Thanks Chopin; it was lovely. The third condom, still immaculate, lay beside it as a gift.

PLANNING A VOYAGE OF DISCOVERY

*T*he headline on the society page the next morning was big and bold. **DIPLOMATIC GLAMOUR RETURNS TO BERLIN**. The caption identified a bemused Consul Hanbury standing between an aging Heidemarie Gräfin Krauch von Hugenberg, whose great uncle had been ambassador for Bismarck, and a rotund Sigmund Prinz von Lippert, member of the board of directors of a private bank. His great grandfather had been a leading member of the German delegation at the famous conference in 1906 in Algeciras – where the German delegation (supported by Austria) took on France (with Britain on its side) in a tussle over Morocco, was quickly outmanoeuvred by Britain (who else?), and returned home in a fit.

This judgement of history was omitted in the article; it was the pedigree of *Prinz Sig* that mattered. A full paragraph was devoted to the intensity of Berlin diplomatic life pre-1914. The last sentence concluded that the consul, through the rich feast in his residence, had kicked off a new era and that the presence of the *Gräfin* and the *Prinz* proved it would be anchored to the legendary past, before the century had delivered its regrettable disruptions.

⁂

Schwartz read the article while drinking morning coffee in his university office. He called Hanbury immediately. "Herr Konsul," he mocked. "You surprise me. I had no idea you've become friends with Heidi and Sig." Hanbury replied he felt he had been adopted by the scions of Prussia. Schwartz reverted to a first-name basis. They talked easily, like two long-time drinking pals who know a thing or two about life's stormy seas. They had been doing this for weeks. Since the success at Geissler's, the professor often called to suggest a drink. Whenever they talked politics over a beer, Schwartz would observe the consul's carefully crafted presence: an agreeableness mixed with restraint, plus an undercurrent of managed innocence. Acquired behaviour, he assumed, learned in diplomatic school. But the consul's reserve also provoked. Why hadn't he said something about his new residence, or the party, or the swarm of invited elites listed in the paper? Schwartz was piqued when he saw the picture, and now, on the phone, he made a pointed remark about being left out.

"It was an official event," Hanbury hastily explained. "I didn't want to mix in the personal side. I want you and Sabine to come over another time, for Sunday coffee and cake. Bring Nicholas. And a soccer ball. There's acres of room in the garden." He added, "I didn't know you're on close terms with the Duchess and the Prince."

"Friends of my mother's family. Well, never mind all that. Sabine and I want to invite you too, for dinner. Has she said anything? And there's something else I want to ask." Hanbury said he would drop everything at any time to have dinner with them. What else did Schwartz want to know? Not on the phone, the professor said conspiratorially. A beer? This evening? The consul said that would be fine.

Schwartz wasn't the only one who called. All morning the office phone ran hot. Frau Carstens took most of the calls. One thank-you after another for the fabulous party. She was radiant, as if she'd won an Oscar for best supporting actress. Actually, with the newspaper publicity, the whole staff basked in a scintillating aura. Sturm strutted about with new authority. *Two hundred eleven cars!* He repeated the words again and again. He got them in and he got them out. Lord Halcourt, now resting for eternity in a granite sarcophagus in the abbey near his manor, would have been pleased, had he been informed of his chauffeur's Berlin feat. Sturm was sure of it.

The phone in Gundula's office rang too. The night had been too short. She felt a pressure behind her eyes. Mauve bags clung to the lower lids. But the dullness was worth it. Such nights are always worth it. Unfortunately she now faced a deadline for an article – a crime wave by North Vietnamese migrants in East Berlin – and the story wasn't clicking. She was attacking it with an axe rather than her customary chisel.

"Jahn," she said into the phone closing her eyes and massaging her forehead.

"Trabi got you home all right?"

"Chopin!" She had been waiting for this call.

"Thanks for the note. And the present."

"No cowboy should leave home without one."

"I enjoyed last night, Gundula."

"I thought that. You fell asleep so peacefully."

"Sorry."

"Thank *you* too. The party wasn't my cup of tea, but the concert afterwards was lovely. Sometime you'll have to show me what else is in your repertoire." A dirty, little chuckle arrived through the phone. "I'm talking about the piano," she said.

"If you come, will you bring Trabi?"

Gundula paused. "To where? Your music room?"

"I looked for Trabi last night after everyone was gone. I wanted to see how he would look, parked in the driveway."

"I parked a block over." He asked why. "That was one of the things wrong with your party. It looked as if you have something against Trabi owners."

"That's not true. There were several former Trabi owners there. I like Trabis. You can park yours at the foot of my front steps anytime."

"A fetish?" Gundula asked. "Like bare shoulders?" She still saw the sleeping consul. More than just bare shoulders. The memory helped lift the heaviness around her eyes. "Or are you looking for a marker?" she teased. "As when the flag flies on the President's palace to show he's in."

The phone line brought a sigh – the sound of someone making no headway. The same sigh was stamped on the night before, in the music room, before she forced things. He struggled when she teased him. She knew it. But he was charming when he struggled. Manoeuvring him into apparent inner anguish wasn't something she planned. It happened by itself, spontaneously, the result of psychic waves. She got him into a corner and there he stood, defenceless, eyes pleading. *Why are you doing this?* But tiny wrinkles on his face signalled he was loving it. Something about all that was alluring.

He asked outright when they could get together again. Gundula almost said, *tonight*, but checked herself. She took time to think about it, claiming she was looking in her diary for an opening. Finally she answered, "Next week Wednesday?"

"That's fine. Super," the ardent consul said. "I'm looking forward to it." They could go to a pub of her choosing on a street where Trabi would blend in. And, if she liked, they could run a test: had the cowboy left his homestead well-enough prepared? The offer was punctuated with a renewed chuckle.

"Chopin," she said lightly, "stick to what you're good at. Your music moved me."

"As you wish. We shall sit at the piano until the sun comes up."

Gundula laughed and hung up. When she refocused on the article, the heaviness had disappeared. The axe was now a chisel. The piece emerged quickly. Once it was dispatched to editing, she had time to think.

She kicked herself. Wednesday was six days away. *Super*, he said. Why wasn't he irritated? Why hadn't he howled? *Next Wednesday? By then I'll have forgotten what you look like!* But no, no howl. The consul was polite, happy as a choirboy. In some ways he resembled Vassiliev. Vassiliev often behaved as if he could do without her. Too late she realized it was because he didn't wish to own her. *What's best for you*, Vassiliev habitually replied when she asked him what he wanted. But what sort of love is that? He could have hollered, *Gundula! Stay! And if you do, I swear I'll make you happy!* But no, no demands. She misread the signals and left Kiev. He slipped away to marry someone else. Vassiliev hadn't been the owning type and Tony wasn't either. Something to keep in mind. But damn his patience all the same. Six days!

The next to strike by telephone was Irving Heywood. From a snow-surrounded tabernacle radiant in a morning sun, he got through to the consul as light was ebbing from the Berlin afternoon and the consul was about to depart for his appointment with von Helmholtz. "Recognize the voice?" the Investitures priest asked playfully. The line went still. Heywood thought the connection had been broken. "It's Irving," he revealed. "Tony, how are you? Hiding your light under a bushel?" Another pause, then Hanbury's voice. "Enjoying Investitures?" "You have no idea," said Heywood.

In truth, Bitrap was the opposite of Heywood's idea of a good time. He was sick of soul and needed to confide in someone. But whom? Not Hannah. She would use it as pretext to urge him to take the same golden handshake he was offering everyone else. But suppose he did that, suppose he grabbed the money and left the tabernacle – forever – in an unseemly rush. What then? Days of staring at the empty crescent on which they lived waiting for the excitement of the mailman to come by? Sure, in summer, retirement might work. He would enjoy the cottage porch. He could watch the wind play in the trees and listen to loons rule the lake. But in winter? Four months when nothing stirred save a snowplough exploding into the crescent to administer two minutes of mayhem before roaring out. No thanks. Bitrap was awful, but retirement was worse. All the same, shoving his own generation over the edge was a dreadful act and he desired intimacy with someone on whom he could unburden his plight.

"And you, Tony?" Heywood asked sweetly, "enjoying Berlin?" The Investitures priest thought he sensed a tightening on the other end. It happened all the time. No one believed a call from Investitures was ever innocent.

"Some days are better than others," was the reply from Berlin.

Tony, Heywood knew, never wasted words. Tony was a listener. Would he be willing to listen now? Would Tony be prepared to share a confidence about the reasons for his torment? Heywood wasn't sure. Prolong the pleasantries, he thought, get a better feel.

"You must be settled in pretty well by now," he ventured.

"I know my way around."

"Busy?"

"Overwhelming some days."

"Good staff?"

"Cast in solid gold."

"Wonderful, Tony. Sounds like you hit the jackpot. I knew you would. You deserved it after the Priory. The years were harrowing, I know." Heywood went through a pulpy moment recalling the fabulous days of the Cold War. The jobs in the Priory had been real. A pressure cooker, sure, but no pain then such as he had now.

"A wonderful gang we were. Everyone has drifted off. One by one. Did you know that?" Heywood experienced a surge of affection – for the Priory, for Hanbury, for the past. "The Priory was my high water mark, Tony. Yours too?"

"I learned a lot," the former Priory deputy replied.

"I appreciate that, Tony. Thank you for saying it. Well, you know, I did my best. What more can one do?" Heywood's voice, like a teddy-bear's, was furry and soft.

"Not much," said the consul.

Heywood hoped Hanbury would say more, provide stronger hints of telephone companionship. He wanted to confess his anguish more than ever. But the Berlin end stayed silent. Heywood sighed inwardly and carried on. "I know you must be wondering why I'm calling. I couldn't get through yesterday. I guess I tried a bit late."

"I was flying the flag. Hosting a reception."

"Went well?"

"A line or two in the gossip column."

"No one could ask for more," Heywood said gravely. Another pause, each waiting for the other. The Investitures priest cleared his throat. "The reason for my call…how shall I put it…Look, Tony, we know each other. I'll blurt it out. Something isn't right. There's a few people here, they want more reporting from Berlin. Wait…I know. It sounds odd. But you know me. I won't pussyfoot around. I'm telling you straight that's the verdict. I know there's a good reason for not reporting. I know you're damn busy. But I thought, at least, you and I, we should talk about it."

The line once more seemed dead.

"Hullo?" Heywood sang. The priest made it sound expectant, like calling into a burial cave to determine if a resurrection has occurred.

"I'm here."

Hanbury's calm voice was so near he could have been sitting inside Heywood's ear. "Tony. Don't misinterpret this."

"Why would I?" The voice was precise. "The Zealots didn't want me to report. There was a broomstick of a girl. Very smart young lady. Slim hips. Keen on Italians."

"Krauthilda?"

"That's it."

"I knew it. Her days are numbered. As Krauthilda I mean. I'm sending her to Rome. Tony, listen, I know the Zealots told you that. Fair game. It's transpired, though, that others in town are taking an interest. Gently, nicely – I have to say that – nicely it was asked if once in a while you could, you know, send in a piece on what's happening there. If I recall, you did a bang-up job reporting in Kuala Lumpur. It's your reputation. A reputation doesn't just disappear. So there's an expectation."

"Send in a piece on what?"

"Whatever you think is important. Whatever local fragrances tickle your nose."

Fragrances. Heywood realized all the more that his task that day would have a putrid stench. In two hours, in his war council, the Investitures priest would perform a ceremony. With a knife that would turn horribly bloody he would cut the Service body in half. The hideousness of the looming act contrasted with the easy pleasure of ruminating with Tony. And Tony was saying if that was wanted he would try his hand at reporting. Anthony Hanbury, salt of the earth, *summa cum laude* graduate from the Heywood school of positive thinking. The Investitures priest could have bussed the consul. Heywood began formulating a glowing report to the high priest. *Sir, that little hiccup in Berlin. It's solved.* His mind wandered to the inner sanctum. The high priest would ask about Bitrap and he would have to confirm it, too, was done. Fucking good job Irv, would be the answer. Thinking this made Heywood blush. "I wish the damn pond weren't between us, Tony," a mushy Heywood said. "The years we spent in the Priory. We didn't get to know each other well enough. Too damn much work, I guess. Still, we were always there, I like to think, you know, when the other needed a boost. Do you look at it that way too?"

"There was no place like the Priory," were the clipped words coming through the phone line.

Heywood took a deep breath. He was about to say, *Tony, just between the two of us, something truly awful's about to happen*, but the connection went dead, a cable cut by a submarine, or a satellite hit by a meteor. Heywood thought of redialling, but you can't restore the magic of a conversation that's been ripped apart. He consoled himself; he had confided enough. He had almost shared his burden. Tony would have listened. Words of support, *It's a test, Irving, your toughest. I admire you for facing it full square*, had *nearly* been expressed. Gratitude, a volcano of affection, erupted inside Heywood and he resolved that when he came to draw the Bitrap line, no matter the arguments from others, the consul in Berlin would have redemption. He owed him that.

The phones in the Rote Rathaus were also ringing. Most calls were standard fare – ambassadors claiming to have important instructions from imperious officials in capitals about planned visits by heads of state and demanding to speak to the Chief of Protocol. Such calls were shunted off to subordinates for rehearsed answers. *Of course the limo will be bullet proof. Yes, a masseuse will be on standby in the suite. Thank you, it's vital to know tomato soup causes the great man indigestion.* Important details, the nuts and bolts of protocol. But the call from Pullach, von Helmholtz took himself. Graf Bornhof inquired whether the consul had been in yet. "In about an hour," the Chief of Protocol replied.

"Sorry to be pushy, but Randolph McEwen is calling daily."

"It will be casually staged. I'll keep a lid on it."

"I'm sure. I don't need much. Confirmation that you've read the riot act will be enough. With that I'll stare McEwen down."

"He's done this before. He sees demons under his own pillow. I don't admire witch-hunts."

"You don't have to convince me. He'll be retired in a few months. Let's coddle him that long."

"I'll call you when I've spoken with him."

The Chief of Protocol hung up. He shook his head. He had never heard a more ridiculous story. Plutonium smuggling! McEwen was old and eccentric and becoming deranged.

※

When Hanbury entered, Von Helmholtz was standing by the balcony doors, attention fixed on the skyline. With a slight head movement he bade the consul to join him before opening a door and stepping out. Traffic noise drifted up. The narrow balcony was wet from a rainshower. An upward draught transformed their breath into mist. "What will this look like in ten years?" von Helmholtz reflected. "The cranes spin their cocoons. I suppose we're optimistic something beautiful will burst out."

"The process is extraordinary," Hanbury said carefully.

"Without parallel. Is it happening too fast?" Jack hammers in the distance sounded like an artillery platoon. "Well, I didn't ask you here to listen to me speculate." Von Helmholtz closed the door to his office behind them. "Thank you for last night's party," he said. "I'm sorry I was unable to stay long." The two men on the balcony stood surrounded by the city's dull roar. A new movement of air brought a drizzle so fine it didn't fall; it attached itself as a thin, damp veil to solid objects. "We're outside to avoid the risk of our conversation being overheard." Von Helmholtz said this casually. Hanbury answered with a light remark about Berlin's traditions, but von Helmholtz ignored it. "Tell me about Günther Rauch," he said. A moment passed. Von Helmholtz saw the consul keep his eyes on the skyline, eventually shifting his gaze to him, then back to the skyline. His expression skewed into a question mark.

"Has Gundula talked to you about him?" Hanbury asked. "Is she in difficulty over her columns?" A question answered by a question, thought von Helmholtz. He knew about the evening in *Friedensdorf*. He knew more about it than he wanted. When Pullach suggested the consul should be told to leave, he put his foot down and rejected the wishy-washy case. He told Graf Bornhof he would agree to nothing without seeing details. A thick file was rushed up in which he read the biographies of three people. The two he knew something about had been twisted beyond recognition. "No, it's nothing to do with Gundula's columns," von Helmholtz said. "I know you two went to see him. Tell me about your interest in Günther Rauch." The consul shrugged. "There isn't much to say. I met him years ago, not long after the Wall went up. I wanted to see him again. Gundula located him. We went to a pub he uses. He hasn't changed."

Going through the thick file, von Helmholtz read about all three. He skimmed reports from around the world by Warsaw Pact embassies on Hanbury the diplomat. He glanced through confidential personnel records on Hanbury the bureaucrat. He saw a photograph of a naked woman behind the window of the consul's house, proving Hanbury had loved. The part of the file that chronicled the life of Gundula Jahn had sickened him. But the account of the *Friedensdorf* evening with Günther Rauch he had read very closely, because the whole case hinged on that.

"Do you plan to see him again?" von Helmholtz asked.

"Probably yes. Why not?"

"Stay away from him," von Helmholtz advised. He observed Hanbury grip the balcony railing. *I need an explanation for that one*, the body language said. "You were overheard in *Friedensdorf*," the Chief of Protocol continued. "Günther Rauch talked about a new political party. He asked you to help with money." From the beginning, despite all he had read, von Helmholtz had planned to say no more than this. "My

God!" Hanbury cried. "That was in jest. Günther Rauch was spinning a vision. He did that twenty-five years ago too. Who would take it seriously?"

"The Stasi did. He spent years in jail."

"It was harmless then. It's harmless now. And the Stasi don't exist anymore."

Von Helmholtz had not previously seen the consul so assertive. If you find yourself fencing with a diplomat, the Chief of Protocol once advised a trainee, feint as much as he does. "Our preference," he said carefully, "is not to have more Stalinists on our hands."

"Günther Rauch's a Marxist, not a Stalinist."

"One turns into the other."

The consul scowled. "In Günther Rauch's case that's rubbish." A pause, then, "Can I ask something?" Von Helmholtz nodded. "Do you check the Stasi files for people like me?"

"Of course not."

"I have a Stasi file. I came across it by chance." Hanbury described it. For a long time von Helmholtz listened to what he already knew. Why the file was started; how reports continued to be added. "Someone looked into it recently. Somebody checked me. If it isn't a standing procedure, then who would do that, and why?"

"I don't know," von Helmholtz answered as if the subject annoyed him. How far from, or close to a lie is a denial of knowledge? Von Helmholtz had never found a satisfactory answer. He took only the slightest comfort from the fact that he was now denying things he knew to protect the consul's peace of mind.

"Was that file search connected to being overheard in *Friedensdorf*?" Hanbury pressed. "Is the Cold War still on?" he said sarcastically. "Are the spies still out?"

Von Helmholtz didn't like the questioning. He might endlessly have to repeat, *I don't know, I don't know, I don't know.* Suppose Hanbury asked about the twenty-four-seven operation? Suppose he explored the link to Gundula and learned of the theory that she was acting on behalf of a former lover in charge of a nuclear plant in the Ukraine, and that Hanbury stood accused of abetting plutonium trafficking? Denying he knew all this, denying he'd read it in a file – it would be like repudiating honour.

The consul was thinking many questions. Von Helmholtz could tell. It was obvious from the way he gripped the railing with growing agitation. To forestall them, he said quietly, "You may be right in part. Remnants of that period are still about. There's people who can't let the past go. In six months it will be different. Leave Günther Rauch alone for half a year. Can you do that?" He met Hanbury's stare and knew that somewhere in the middle of a further stretch of silence he obtained consent.

"He'll think I betrayed him," Hanbury said at last. "Gundula predicted it would happen. She thinks making and dropping friends is something I do for a living."

"Then don't drop her," von Helmholtz advised. He steered the consul back into his office. "Do you still have a few minutes? I'm worried about her."

Sitting on the two leather sofas at right angles in the poise of statesmen, they talked about her as if she was their ward. The Gregor Donner Reich columns *had* damaged Gundula, von Helmholtz feared. Her new work lacked fire. She needed a fresh challenge, something that played to her strengths. With her special style and ability to breathe life into complex issues, she should become a foreign correspondent. But to get started she needed help. Hanbury was a friend. Had he discussed it with her? Von Helmholtz recalled having once or twice suggested he do so. Could the consul work on it? "You'll be with us for a few years yet...unless you have other plans." Hanbury's careful smile said, *I hope to stay forever.* The Chief of Protocol rose. At the door the consul impishly said, "Let me know when the Cold War leftovers are in the garbage." The Chief of Protocol laughed. An agile performance, he thought, right down to the witty end.

⁂

An hour later Schwartz entered *Das Klecksel* where a miasma of tar and nicotine seeped out of the walls and curtains. But what public house doesn't reek of cigarettes, stale air and yesterday's grease smoking off the oven? Despite the mingling of disagreeable odours, the professor and consul were regulars because Hanbury liked the place. Schwartz wondered whether it was because of the pub's name. *Das Klecksel.* All newcomers were taken by it.

Some said the name was homage to Wilhelm Busch, poet and caricaturist, who created an epic work in 1884 about a delinquent student of art called *Maler Klecksel.* The pub went back to 1885. The dates meshed. Others said the name was a Berlinerization. What would a Berliner do with the word *Klecks,* a blotch, or stain? He would corrupt it, into *Klecksel,* a term for a minor stain, or disfigurement, something misbegotten. The pub's name, by this analysis, was chosen to capture the essential nature of the lives of its clients. Did not each of them have a reputation that was smudged? Did they not all have consciences as convoluted as blots in a Rorschach test? A variant to this approach was that the pub's founder, through the name, had wanted to draw attention to the fact that each of the regulars was no more than a speck of colour, a dreary little blotch on the complex canvas of Berlin life.

The first time Schwartz and Hanbury drank in *Das Klecksel,* the waiter, a fill-in, a student, eloquently presented the theories of the origin of the name. Once finished, he said he could do it in English too, for the place was often full of tourists. The professor popped him a five-mark piece for the effort and waved him off. From that point on the consul loved the place. It possessed something special, as had *The Tankard*.

Schwartz slid behind a table with a view of the door. The plank floor made a hollow sound whenever someone entered, like jackboots on a wooden bridge. But this was audible only in the early evening. Later a cannon would have to go off to rise above the tumult. Or a bomb. The current owner swore that happened once in '45. A forty-pounder sliced through the building's upper floors, going off the moment it came to rest next to the piano. The player, as well as the current owner's mamma and papa behind the bar, along with a few dozen regulars, all of them defying the screaming air raid sirens, were instantly ripped apart.

A few years later, human stains duly scrubbed away, *Das Klecksel* was restored, as was the clientele. The piano again punched out songs worshipping Berlin's air, the cafés on the Ku'damm and the seduction of Emma on a bench by the Krumme Lanke. Once more the floor looked as if for centuries it had been absorbing gobs of mustard, portions of sauerkraut and spilt beer. And the walls sported the same mixture of Berlin memorabilia that graced them prior to the blast: photographs of city life in the 1890's, assorted Prussian military decorations, random newspaper headlines from all the decades, drawings by Busch of *Max und Moritz* and prints of the rawer strata of society by Heinrich Zille. For the regulars, *Klecksel* history was world history and it came to be divided into two main epochs, pre- and post-big bang. Only the erection of the Wall in '61 was grudgingly admitted as also epoch-defining.

The woman tending the bar this evening was a direct import from one of Zille's seamy drawings: a busty, big-boned, round-bottomed creature, with rapacious lips and a crude tongue. Schwartz occasionally listened to her. How Berliners love to belittle, he thought, and how readily they move to other arts they keep well-polished, those of berating, humiliating, moralizing. How the city functioned at all was an enduring mystery for the professor. Take something basic, take a saleslady whose job it should be to talk sweetly to customers. In Berlin she would normally begin with a reproach – that her attention was being sought – following up with a show of high frustration that a customer had dared enter the store. Rudeness next, especially if the customer asked to look at something on a shelf. It was no different in the banks, the post office, the car repair depots, the hospitals, the police. The Police! Try phoning them! *A car theft? I don't do car thefts. Colleague Horst does; he's away at a spa recovering from stress. Call back the day after tomorrow. Even better, try next week.* Is it any wonder, Schwartz reflected, that after listening to the standard early morning rebukes, the first one from a bus driver, followed by one at the post office, and then from a teller at the bank, that people feel anger stirring? Is it any wonder their aggravation gets transferred, first to other customers in the queue, then to people on the street? And doesn't it stand to reason that they react in kind? Doesn't that explain why every day the whole city starts to snarl? Schwartz visualized how a thousand epicentres of aggression each sent out pugnacious waves that soon engulfed the city. Even the caring souls, who really did begin the day intending to treat the world with charity, would join the ranks of the haranguing. In such circumstances, how does anything positive get done? The energy was there, but the aggression misdirected. The professor considered it a monumental waste. What was needed was discipline, a finer sense of order. "What d'yuh want?" glowered the barmaid. "A beer," said Schwartz. "Really? Now *that's* different." She plodded back to the bar.

The professor looked at his watch. Where was the consul? Five minutes late was usual, but fifteen was pushing it. The article on the social page had been a surprise, Schwartz admitted it. It showed he and the consul were not as friendly as he believed. He needed to get closer still. What bargain could they make? What might Hanbury accept in return for Schwartz's use of the consul's access to places from which he was barred? Schwartz wasn't sure. Perhaps an outright request for a favour, as with Geissler's book, was best. Some people enjoy doing other people favours. Hanbury arrived the moment the barmaid banged a glass down on the table. "Another," Schwartz told her. She huffed. Couldn't he have ordered two at the start? Schwartz observed that Hanbury, easing onto the bench against the wall, was preoccupied and for a while the conversation was all one way. *A fine splash this morning, in the paper. A brilliant party you had. You're on the map now. Part of the landscape. You must be pleased.*

The professor dropped compliments in a steady rhythm, but the consul was unresponsive. He actually seemed melancholy. Schwartz finally inquired if anything was wrong. "It's been a rough day." "A pressure cooker?" Schwartz inquired. Why wouldn't the consul's staff go easy on him after a large party? It's human to need time to recuperate. "Oh, that wasn't the problem," Hanbury said listlessly. Schwartz asked more questions and offered understanding. Meeting people all day long must be tiring. No, not too many at all, not really, not today. Of course, nothing is more tedious than staff problems. In the university the academics are like dogs going for each other's throats. Was that a problem? Not at all. Far from it. Today, in fact, the staff was in high spirits. Perhaps the mail. A heavy burden. Letter upon letter. All wanting something. There were some letters, yes. Mostly invitations. Four out of five had to be regretted. The usual. Not so challenging. Isn't the telephone miserable? An invasion of privacy, the bearer of bad news.

"You can say that again," said the consul with undisguised disgust, adding that transatlantic calls were the worst. "It got so bad today I threw the receiver down."

"Family?" Schwartz wondered, to keep momentum going.

"Not family. Headquarters. Monstrous people."

A little more coaxing and the main features of Heywood's call came out. "Why don't you do some reporting then?" Schwartz said.

"I can't compete with the wire services. Heywood knows that. He's setting me up, but for what?" The consul, obviously rattled, was drinking fast. For Schwartz, Hanbury's crisis as it unfolded was like a gift being unwrapped. But he was amused too. He had never seen anyone so upset by the need to do some writing. "Maybe you can't compete in speed," Schwartz said encouragingly, "but in sensitivity, depth, accuracy...you could beat the wire services every time. Wire services don't think."

Hanbury laughed darkly. "I did political reporting in Kuala Lumpur. The ambassador went through bottles of red ink improving my drafts. It's true. I admit it. I don't have a knack for it, not for writing. My mind doesn't work that way. Not like yours. You have a talent for thinking things through."

Schwartz bowed cordially. "But you're the diplomat. You have the better position." He lifted his glass. "Well, to our respective strengths." Their glasses clinked. "You're too hard on yourself," he added. Hanbury shrugged. What's there to report on, he asked. What subjects could he write about that would interest headquarters? "Why don't we pool our strengths?" Schwartz suggested. He began to develop a line of thought. "If I were in your shoes, knowing what I know, what would I report?" Hanbury said he'd like to know that too.

A slight sneer formed on the edge of Schwartz's steady gaze. "In your shoes, I would report on Germany's prospects. First set the scene; a look back; what has shaped the Germans? Then an analysis of where they are today; are they fulfilling themselves as a nation? Finally, the future. What's Germany's destiny? Fifteen, perhaps eighteen reports. Your foreign policy makers ought to value work like that."

"I doubt I could do it."

"That's the point. I'm the academic. You're the man of action. I work with you; you assist me. We both gain." The consul, continuing to grip his glass, wanted to know what he could bring to a process like that. "Several things," Schwartz said easily. "A perspective for one. What do you consider important? Historians don't think like diplomats. Also, you have access to influential people. You could explore their thinking. That would help me. I've been asked to give some lectures in this area next year; I'm working on them now. As I said, we pool strengths."

"Well, eighteen is too many. I doubt headquarters could cope with six."

"We'll cut the sail to fit the cloth. Let's outline a few." Schwartz located a ballpoint inside his sweater. "We need some paper."

Taking their order for more beer, the barmaid regarded them as raving lunatics when she was asked for paper. She didn't answer. She just trudged off tapping the side of her head. Hanbury reached into a pocket and took out his program. It had blank back pages. They set to work, leaning over the paper on the rough oak table, becoming absorbed, paying no attention to the regulars arriving. Some looked sideways at them with disgust. Schwartz's movements were concise, his script small and elegant. The notes were practical. No woolly theories of history; only simple truths. He sensed Hanbury was warming up. "Yes," the consul repeatedly said, "That's a good point. That's absolutely true." Germany's romantic and brooding soul: *Das Deutsche Volk*. Its sense of being special; its need for order and authority; its abhorrence of defeat; the current urge to make no move save through consensus. All this, in the professor's neat writing, found a place on the back of the consul's program. Analytical notes were added too. *A conservative nation. Individualism is disliked. Guided by group instincts – different from the Anglo-Saxon tradition.*

Schwartz's scribbling scarcely kept pace with his thinking. Germany's problem, he said, was an incompatibility between an American implanted constitution steeped in the liberal tradition of transparency and openness, and the German cultural urge to manipulate the affairs of state behind the scenes. Liberalism, the professor argued, is anathema for the average German. Their penchant is for heavy bureaucracy and state control, no different than in ancient Prussia. Hanbury asked where all this was leading. The three pages had filled up with orderly columns of points to be grouped and developed. Schwartz sat back looking satisfied. He lifted his glass. "Review the outline," he said, as if to a graduate student. "If you're comfortable, we'll take it further next week." The consul refolded the program along the crease and slipped it back into his jacket. He seemed relieved. "It's like starting a voyage of discovery," he said.

"You still haven't told me about your party," Schwartz remarked casually. "The paper reported everybody was there. Is that true? Did Kurt Stobbe go? Do you see much of him?"

"Only that time he showed me the Stasi files."

"We may need him for our project. At one stage we'll have to focus on the trauma of the divided German nation. Some research in his archives will be essential. And we have to keep Nazi war criminals in mind."

Hanbury, once more his relaxed self, believed that would be no problem.

"It proves my point," said Schwartz. "I have access to the past. You have access to the present. An ideal combination."

"I'll drink to that," the consul said.

ACROSS THE DIVIDE

"I've read about events like this, but to be inside, taking part..." Sabine's voice trailed off. She was dressed formally in a black narrow-cut skirt suit. The tailoring set off her figure, the black colour brought out the arresting blondness of her hair. The Reichstag was filling fast. The galleries were loaded with TV cameras. In one corner, members of the Berlin Philharmonic were taking their position. The section reserved for diplomats, close to the front, was just behind the political elite. A by-invitation-only ceremony with tight security. More Berlin history in the making.

"I'm glad you asked me to come." Sabine's voice – a tremor hinted at inner excitement – was at odds with her stiff posture. Hanbury noticed it. "I'm glad you came," he replied. He was in the royal pose, one leg crossed over the other, hands resting on a knee. On the podium von Helmholtz was giving directions. His idea, the consul supposed, a ceremony in Berlin for Mikhail Gorbachev and Ronald Reagan. Who else would have conceived it?

"Mein Kollege." A voice nearby. Hanbury half-turned. It was the Argentine consul, a short, stocky man with thick lips and eyes sad as a Saint Bernard's. Hanbury tried to recall his name. *"Darf ich Ihnen Frau Schwartz vorstellen?"* he said, politely offering to introduce his companion. "But of course. But of course," said Argentina. Sabine offered a hand. Argentina took it, bent forward and pressed his mouth against it. A slobbering Saint Bernard. A long, probing Latin look into her eyes sought a reaction, but Sabine turned away. Argentina made small talk. He had information Reagan would not be coming. "But Gorbachev will." Another passionate glance at Sabine. "Gorbachev is reliable." Hanbury shrugged, as if to say, *Win some, lose some.* Argentina wandered off. "What a preposterous little man," Sabine said. "A colleague? Are they all like that?"

"They vary."

Sabine could see that for herself. Others were arriving. Hanbury greeted them with perfunctory nods. Some came over to shake hands. The affable Finn lingered. Hanbury told him he had heard Reagan might not be coming. "No? That would be a pity. But I compliment you. As always, you are so well informed." Hanbury indicated he heard this from Argentina. "Exactly. Both of you. You are both always so well informed." Finland moved on too.

The Berlin diplomatic corps, with its morbid desire to spend time in the vault of democratic horrors, always turned out in numbers for Reichstag functions. The consul and his escort observed the influx.

It had been like this for weeks. The more Hanbury saw of Sabine's husband, the more he saw of her. He normally approached Schwartz first. His polite suggestions amounted essentially to a question that would have sounded crude: *Can I borrow your wife?* The answer from the husband was steadily affirmative: *It's good for Sabine to get out.* Then he'd go to *Bücher Geissler* to ask Sabine if she'd like to join him. She replied she'd check at home, to avoid overlapping social obligations.

There never were any. In this way, Sabine began attending functions she never knew existed.

Hanbury suspected she enjoyed them even if it didn't show. In public, such as now in the Reichstag, they behaved as a couple that's been together so long there's little left to say. Their mutual nonchalance towards one another confused the consul's colleagues. *Who is the elegant lady*, they wondered, *and why does Canada treat her with such indifference?* Sabine was becoming a fringe topic on the cocktail circuit. The diplomatic corps speculated that if Canada had hidden this beauty for so long, he might well be hiding more.

Argentina was right. The Old Gipper had decided not to come. Gorbachev alone would have the limelight. The packed Reichstag erupted into sustained applause as the Chief of Protocol led Mikhail and Raisa to their places.

The program started. The Berlin Philharmonic played a solemn Beethoven movement. Speeches followed, each one about the last half-century of German penance. Then a video: the Soviet military driving through the Brandenburg gate on May Day '45; footage of post-war street signs some months later – *You Are Now Leaving the American Sector* – and of Soviet and American tanks staring each other down at Checkpoint Charlie; the Wall rising in '61; Kennedy there in '63; Ronald Reagan ascending a platform in '87 with the Wall behind him and behind it, two steps inside East Berlin, the Brandenburg Gate. Berlin celebrating its 750th birthday that year and Reagan putting on a show. The video shows him challenging the President of the Soviet Union: *Mr. Gorbachev! Open this gate! Mr. Gorbachev! Tear down this Wall!*

Hanbury could see Gorbachev at the front. He and Raisa were listening to the Russian soundtrack through earphones. Gorbachev was studiously impassive, watching the Hollywood President.

The video moved on: September '89, the fortieth anniversary of the

East German communist dictatorship; Gorbachev joins the celebrations in East Berlin and kisses Honecker; Honecker claims his totalitarian paradise will last forever; Gorbachev – studiously impassive then too – listens; later, he walks in East Berlin and mingles with the people; they want to know what he thinks of a regime that denies its people foreign travel. The camera zooms in. Gorbachev speaks calmly: *History punishes those who act too late.* Translation: Honecker is on his own, because Soviet tanks won't roll again against the people, not like in '53. With that remark the rug is pulled out from under forty years of German Communism. Two months later the regime is swept aside. Trabis invade West Berlin; Ossis and Wessis kiss and embrace.

The video over, after more speeches, Gorbachev (with Reagan in absentia) joined Bismarck as Honourary Citizen of Berlin. At a reception in the foyer, Sabine stood in a circle with Gorbachev who answered questions through an interpreter. She was ambivalent. She could not forgive the Communists for walling off her city. On the other hand, with his dancing eyes and dark spot on his forehead, he was a fascinating man. Upon leaving the Reichstag she described to Hanbury what she felt. "It was a remarkable event," he agreed.

Sipping a hot drink in the Opera Café, they still talked about the ceremony. It symbolised a wrapping up of a chunk of world history that coincided with their lifetimes. They talked about the feel of the period when they lived together and the changes since. Sabine then casually asked what Tony and her husband did when they went drinking. He explained they were collaborating on a project. "It's working out well," he said. The dialogue paused. Sabine studied the enlarged reproductions of old Berlin prints on the walls. They portrayed a quiet, uncomplicated, orderly Unter den Linden a century and a half before. Something about that time was right, but something about the last few months was right too. She mused aloud that no one could have predicted a day would come when she and Tony would be going out like this. Or that Tony and Werner would become collaborators on a project. She told the latest stories of Nicholas who enjoyed sport, like her father. She switched to her work, talking of friends who dropped by the store, Tony now one of them.

Hanbury listened. He liked it when Sabine talked. Publicly she said little, but privately she didn't stop. It was this way whenever they were together, she drawing him into a world where cold professional contacts had no standing, but where simpler things did.

❦

More than the deepening friendship with Sabine was making the weeks special. The consul felt embraced by the city. He absorbed its moods, its sunny and its dark sides. He breathed the air of expectation and acceleration. He listened to the cacophony of renewal. Berlin was making up for lost time and Hanbury sensed that he, too, was on a forced march into a shimmering future.

It was the process of becoming. But becoming what? It was impossible to know. He believed that a kind of height of land had been crossed, that he was moving with the current now, not against it. An anticipation for a destination gripped him. He tried to put his finger on the moment when he crossed the divide. Was the party in his residence the turning point? He remembered the hours as if they had been filmed – the night with Gundula and the continuation the next day of the mood of fulfilment. But the afternoon – talking to Irving Heywood and seeing von Helmholtz – brought setbacks. Yet, during the evening's drink with Schwartz some lost ground was recouped. After that day, his assignment in Berlin was different. He was coasting. Everything was working out.

The call from Heywood had been disturbing. Unctuousness traversed the ocean through the phone line and Heywood's words jolted loose a sense of foreboding. The feeling had remained with him even as he stood next to von Helmholtz on the balcony, where it was replaced by something worse. The Chief of Protocol had been dignified. Hanbury recognized he had a crude task to perform for unknown others. Hanbury restrained himself so as not to make the situation more difficult. Upon leaving city hall, Hanbury had racked his brains to see a context for what von Helmholtz had said. Was Günther Rauch really the focus? Was being spied on in *Friedensdorf* a unique event, or was it part of something bigger? He thought back to Zella's visit, her phantoms, his dismissing them. Was that part of it? Or the notation on his Stasi file? Where in all of it did that fit? And what about the timing of Heywood's ingratiating call and the vague reference to some people having an expectation? Was all this coincidental, or was it linked? And, if so, was there a centre? Hanbury couldn't get the pieces to add up. The end effect was that he had a sense of having been invaded, that something was at work intending to take him apart.

How ironic then that that same evening there was relief. And that Heywood's request for reports was part of it. When Hanbury entered *Das Klecksel*, not wanting to talk to Schwartz about Günther Rauch, or about feeling invaded by unseen forces, he got Heywood's remarks off his chest instead. The professor's offer of assistance with political reporting helped focus his thoughts away from the balcony talk and onto something do-able. Von Helmholtz's suggestion to stay away from Günther Rauch for a few months occasionally crossed his mind, but, Hanbury reasoned, the time would go by fast enough and in the interim, collaborating with Schwartz on the reporting project was proving satisfying and productive.

Hanbury made careful notes at all the *Klecksel* sessions. The professor talked; the consul wrote. Subject: *the Nazis and the Modern German*. Main Points: *– lay bare the excesses; – describe the legacy; – address responsibility and objectify guilt; – draw out aspects of the national socialist agenda which could have been positive had the leadership been less parochial; – set out the main elements of a neo-conservative platform which Germans intuitively want*. In a slow, sure voice Schwartz summarized books, described learned articles, drew irresistible conclusions. Afterwards, at his office computer, the consul fleshed out the notes and reconstructed the professor's encyclopaedic verbal essays. He didn't find the going easy. Sometimes one hour produced one sentence. He pursued the subjects elsewhere. Schwartz suggested he talk to politicians, journalists, essayists, a slice of the intelligentsia. Frau Carstens arranged appointments. When a report was done, once it had been revised, tightened and discussed one last time with the professor before the final polish, it would be dispatched with pride to the tabernacle readership.

Productive personal relations, productive professional deeds. The consul was riding high. Even the weather was collaborating. The winter gloom was lifting. The sun had delivered spring's delights. A million snow drops stood in his garden; ten thousand blue and yellow crocuses flooded the lawn; a band of daffodils, a bar of solid gold along one side, was arrestingly beautiful.

The light worked other wonders. Sturm arrived at the residence early each morning to inspect the garden's delights. From the breakfast nook Hanbury saw him strolling along the paths, bending over to study a flower, or lifting his head to the sound of frantic birds. *Good morning, Sturm. Guten Morgen, Herr Konsul. Everything fine with the world? As good as it was in Oxfordshire, Herr Konsul.* On the way to the office, Sturm contemplated the wonders of biology. Why do some birds have a happy song, others a plaintive one and still others squawk? Sturm's theory was socialization. The least aggressive birds sing the happiest, most beautiful songs. "You'll find it's that way with labourers in the East," Sturm said. "I've walked up and down the streets and listened to the sound of renovation. Workers in the East are happy warblers. In the West, they're like crows. They screech."

Beyond the resurgent vitality of spring, the consul also benefited from routine. Once a week now he had a formal evening in the residence. Guests chosen by Frau Carstens were bundled around a theme: the visual arts, the performing arts, film, literature, science or technology, third-world economics. She lifted the themes from feature sections in the paper, searched out the personalities, sent out invitations, worked with chefs on menus and arranged for after-dinner entertainment such as opera singers, instrumental soloists, or theatre personalities who would read from Goethe. The consul's job was to smile, ask stimulating questions, charm the guests and raise his glass in a toast – to the House of Windsor, to the House that Adenauer built, and to the future of Berlin.

Visits to *Bücher Geissler* were part of Hanbury's routine. Herr Geissler would be waiting. Once the doorbell finished clanging, he advanced in his awkward shuffle. *Herzlich willkommen, Herr Konsul. Guten Tag, Herr Geissler. Guten Tag, Frau Schwartz. Guten Tag, Herr Hanbury.* Sunny smiles all around. Geissler would drag him into an aisle, pull books off the shelf to watch the consul handle them with admiration. Afterwards at lunch, Tony and Sabine conspired about the next museum.

He continued with his walking too, supplementing it with S-Bahn rides. The bewitching inner city trains, he thought, snaked through Berlin like through a permanent exhibition. On them he often played a game. Spot the political era. Start with train design. The age of the swastika built robust carriages, first used to carry passengers to the '36 Olympics on slatted wooden seats. Even today they were going strong. Wagons made during the period of the hammer and sickle were easily identified: tacky designs, plastic interiors, sticking doors. The new Berlin appeared infrequently on the tracks. These trains swooped in silently; their doors opened reliably with a convincing soft hydraulic swoosh. Only the ancient, worn-out trains plied the tracks from Alexanderplatz to Bahnhof Zoo. The consul liked this stretch from the centre of the East to the heart of the West and rode it whenever he had a chance. It was an incomparable inner-city experience, a journey in a time-machine, travellers moving from one world to another. Hanbury sometimes thought the trip should be slowed down to a snail's pace – to allow the concentrated experience to be savoured fully. *All aboard! S5 departing Alexanderplatz for Friedrichstrasse, Lehrter Bahnhof and the fleshpots of the West.*

The train, shuddering as brakes release, creaks into motion. On board with the consul is a motley crowd: some winos, a few students, a sprinkling of pensioners out for an afternoon of Western shopping. As always, the consul sits at the end of the carriage on a bench with his back to the direction of motion. It enhances the element of surprise.

No sooner have the doors slammed shut than a beggar speaks. *My name is Jochen. Three years ago I was infected with HIV and was laid off. Without a job I lost my apartment. Without an apartment I can't get a job. My disease is coming out of dormancy. I need drugs. The Sozialamt's pfennigs don't pay for what's needed. A small contribution for my condition would be helpful and I would be thankful too.* Jochen does indeed look as if he's ravaged by an early form of AIDS. Or is it make-up? He collects his pfennigs – mostly from the students because the Eastern pensioners are shivering in their seats. It has to be said – Jochen at this point is only warming up. The lucrative S-Bahn stretches are in Charlottenburg, Grunewald, the Westend. There his voice will have tremors of drama. The consul knows Jochen by now. He knows each word in Jochen's speech. Their S-Bahn paths cross every week.

First stop, Hackescher Markt. Jochen gets off to rehearse in another carriage. The expanse of socialist heaven at Alexanderplatz has transformed into narrow streets with crumbling buildings. Everything is in scaffolding; everything has to be propped up. Too few travellers know that nearby, in Rosenthaler Strasse, the central committee of the Communist party was headquartered in the twenties. More old politics in the opposite direction, the improvised SS detention centre on Rosenstrasse. In '43, 5000 Jewish men (with Aryan wives) were locked up here awaiting a decision to send them to the concentration camps. Their enraged spouses, devoted Berlin women, began demonstrating outside. What could the SS do to racially pure German women except yield?

Destination Auschwitz cancelled for the husbands.

The next stretch of track borders a park named after an eighteenth century palace, Monbijou. When it stood, it really was a jewel, but the Communists blew it up after the war. They didn't like the fact that the aristocracy used to dance there. Beyond the trees is the golden dome of the restored Synagogue, rising over its surroundings like a beacon. The S-Bahn would have to come to a stop for several hours to allow its story to be told, even if restricted only to *Kristallnacht*.

Communists. Fascists. Scenes of rampage and destruction. The S-Bahn weaves its way through history.

It crosses the river onto the island. The benefit of sitting with your back to the direction of motion now becomes apparent. The island is dotted with museums and the elevated S-Bahn pursues a narrow course between them. Were the track displaced a mere few metres to the south, the train would be creeping through the Pergamon itself, through the lovely, multi-storied temple altar from Asia Minor and the lovely friezes of gods fighting giants. Enlightenment struggling with tyranny in the centre of Berlin. As the train rumbles off Museum Island the beauty of classical antiquity recedes.

The traveller arrives in Bahnhof Friedrichstrasse, a Cold War border crossing, a place for interrogations and detention and now a cold dose of contemporary Berlin. Fifty years of soot, physically and symbolically, cling to the roof. Outside, skinheads, punks and drunks in full regalia hang around as if in permanent detention, while all around the nimble North Vietnamese peddle smuggled cigarettes.

The train moves on into a landscape with all the charm and colour of the moon. Square, brown-black elevations totter on the edge of ruin like rocks on rims of lunar craters. An earthliness returns, however, as the track begins to parallel the north bank of the Spree. Squatting opposite is the Reichstag. The Wall ran into the river here and continued on the opposite side. At first, Easterners tried to swim out through the watery opening. Good shooting practice for Communist border patrols: a decent distance, a target that moves, though not too fast. On the south bank by the Reichstag the West kept score. Dozens of white crosses sprouted up.

A barren emptiness that was once a thriving neighbourhood persists from the Reichstag to Lehrter Bahnhof. What's Lehrter Bahnhof? It's a little local station which sits there like a pauper. But it has a princely future. When the Tiergarten Tunnel is finished, the heap of bricks will be transformed into a shiny European crossroads. Maybe into the greatest railway station in the world. By then today's rheumatic trains may be extinct. The tracks curve south, past Schloss Bellevue. The flag flaps on the roof: the President is in. Quick views of Golden Ilse high up on her column with her spread wings angelically protecting Sturm's ghosts in the park below. She may be praying. *May they never again experience carpet bombing and be allowed to haunt this arboreal peace forever, amen.* Finally, brakes squealing, asbestos smelling, S5 pulls into Bahnhof Zoo. Another trans-epochal journey successfully completed. Loudspeakers scream out information on connecting trains. One announcement is prominently missing: *Keep your hands on your wallets! Con artists enjoy the freedom of the city in this place.* It's true. The police have given up on the many pickpockets and bag-snatchers in Bahnhof Zoo. Having flooded in from eastern Europe, they face no restrictions. And since Western police precincts inherited Trabis from the East's *Volkspolizei* and Western officers now drive around in tinny little cars, the thieves in BMWs outrun them easily. Cops and robbers Berlin style.

❧

Dapper police Trabis with hectic little engines bravely racing around Bahnhof Zoo always made Hanbury think of Gundula pushing hers to the limit. She had a new bumper sticker: *My other car is a Rolls Royce*. Sturm once told the consul a Trabi joke based on the text of the German constitution: *The dignity of a Trabi is inviolable.* He tried it out on her. They were bouncing along a cobblestoned East Berlin street after an evening of cabaret. Gundula loved it. She shot right back: *And all Trabis are created equal.* Gundula knew about constitutions. She was also up on the latest Trabi jokes. *Every Trabi has the right to exist in top condition*, Sturm had quoted and Hanbury repeated it to Gundula. *To respect, protect and maintain Trabis is the highest duty of the state*, she glibly replied. Never mind a Charter of Rights for Trabis. These days Gundula's Trabi had one sole purpose: putting in long hours late at night going back and forth between Dahlem and Marzahn. "He sounds happy," the consul often said. "I hope he'll hang in." "I don't see an alternative," she remarked.

If Gundula didn't see one, Hanbury didn't want one. Sabine by day; Gundula by night. Part of the weekly routine. Gundula would wait a discreet distance from the diplomatic functions. When the consul came out whistling with freedom it was off to her part of town, her pubs and off-beat galleries and halls of cabaret. Fifty years of prohibition on freedom was over and the East was jumping with the kinetic energy of a spring. She, child of the latest German revolution, owned this scene. She was the celebrity here and the consul the after-thought, the tag-along.

Very late, another long haul for Trabi, back to the Greco-Roman villa in Dahlem. Inside, music might emerge from the grand piano. Then the chandeliers dim, the action moving up a floor. Somewhere near day break more commotion as Gundula departs, rousing Trabi, humming happily to herself the whole way back to Marzahn.

A closer look at the congenial hours in the mansion.

Arriving from their midnight dinner, Gundula and the consul proceed to the cosy confines of the music room. Teasingly she gets him to sit at the huge piano. Reluctantly he puts a finger to the keyboard. Pieces of music follow, an étude, a polonaise, a slavonic dance or two. Once he gets going, he keeps going, closing his eyes, swaying with the music. Concentration is written on the furrows of his brow. Sometimes his upper body rises – or collapses – depending on the passage he's playing. Gundula in an armchair is concentrating too. He's giving; she's receiving. They are physically apart, but the music is a bond.

One evening Tony was playing a longer piece. Gundula rose from the chair and walked to the window where she stood in a thoughtful pose, one arm across her body under her breasts, the palm supporting the elbow of the other. With the free hand she sensually stroked her neck. Her body rocked a little. Hanbury opened his eyes as he ascended with the music and looked at Gundula. At the moment of eye contact his face transformed. She saw it fill with horror. Abruptly he ceased playing, jumped to his feet – so fast the piano stool went flying – and slammed the keyboard lid down. Two giant strides and he had left the room. "What's happening?" she called after him.

Gundula righted the stool and caught up with him in the kitchen where he was undoing a whiskey bottle. He poured himself a shot and emptied it. Perspiration trickled down his temples. She asked if he was all right.

"Oh yes."

"What happened?"

"Nothing. I shouldn't play. Really, I shouldn't."

"Why? You played last week and the week before. Why a heart attack today?"

Hanbury wiped his forehead with a dishtowel. "No heart attack."

"You're dripping with sweat."

"I'm fine," said Tony. "Never been in better shape. I'll prove it. Race you to the bedroom. Last one to have an orgasm is a rotten egg." He broke into a crooked grin.

Gundula insisted on an explanation. When Hanbury shrugged as if there was nothing more to say, her eyes flashed with anger. "We've been sleeping together for two months. Don't I have the right to know what's bothering you?"

"Nothing's bothering me. Everything's fine. Let's go upstairs."

Gundula took a glass, snapped it onto the counter, poured herself some rye and drank it in one go. "Your turn," she said thrusting the bottle back. Hanbury didn't move. "We'll take turns," she said, still white hot, "until one of us pours his heart out. I predict it won't be me." She tipped the bottle over his glass until it held three fingers of undiluted liquor. "You're next." A hollow look developed around Hanbury's eyes. He emptied it with two hard gulps. Gundula poured once more for herself.

"This is ridiculous," he said. "We'll get sick. I didn't feel like playing anymore."

Gundula knocked back her glass in one smooth motion and refilled his. "I want to know." She thrust a third whiskey tumbler at him.

"You reminded me of my mother," he said. A sudden admission.

"I don't believe you. You jumped up like you saw a ghost."

"I thought I had."

"I don't believe you. Drink," she ordered.

Hanbury took the bottle and the glasses. He said, "Let's go up. I'll tell you there."

The tumblers on the night table remained untouched. At first there was very little talking. Gundula lay astride Tony. Under the covers he ran his hand along her back. "I can't believe I remind you of your mother," she said.

"You don't," he said in a whisper. "Of course you don't. For a moment only, the way you stood at the window touching your face. She used to stand like that. I spent years practising with her in that pose. She was making mental notes. Afterwards she explained how I should improve."

Gundula laid her fingertips against the side of Tony's head. "Mothers teach their children," she said. "No need to get jumpy about it forty years later."

"She went mad. She wasted away. I shouldn't play. I really shouldn't."

"Why did she go mad?" whispered Gundula.

"The doctor said she had an illness."

"I hope, Chopin, that when you play now you're playing for me, not her." Gundula shifted her weight. Her hand slipped from his temple and continued a journey down. "An interesting idea you had in the kitchen, having a race."

"I love competition," he said into her ear.

"Ready for the starting signal?"

"Don't forget the condom," cautioned Tony.

"Damn the condom," replied Gundula, emboldened by the whiskey.

❧

The hours the consul spent with his day- and night-time women were blanks on the official program and Frau Carstens viewed them with suspicion. She tried tenaciously to fill them, but an equally determined Hanbury resisted. She pondered this. Was he attending secret functions? Were important contacts being allowed to slip away?

Actually, in those easy, happy downhill months Hanbury kept much of what he did to himself. Such as the long-promised dinner on Fasanenstrasse. Being a casual affair, informally staged, it would in any case have been unsuitable for inclusion in a diplomatic program. It seemed to be an innocent enough evening. Only later, when deciphering numerous inter-connected strands, did Hanbury realize it too contributed to the unceremonious ending of his Berlin career.

It was a dinner without five courses. The food was put out in advance. Neither host nor hostess got up to serve. Baskets of bread and bowls of salads stood down the middle of a table. Surrounding them were plates of cheeses, hams, salamis, smoked fish and patés. The guests took and ate and took some more. The drink was beer. Sabine and her husband had each invited two friends plus consorts. Hanbury came at the invitation of both and was seated in the middle, halfway between the host and hostess at the ends. Schwartz's friends – two professors with earnest wives – were on the consul's right, Sabine's on his left. One was Martina, still going out with Professor Kraft, the other Lisa who had dragged her husband with her. All evening long, when Hanbury looked up, he was confronted by a knowing smile from Martina. If he turned his head right Schwartz winked encouragement at him, and when his gaze wandered left, he saw a radiant Sabine listening carefully to the learned anecdotes of Kraft. Confronted with so much friendship and good will, Hanbury drank quietly.

Lisa's husband Ulrich, a mathematics teacher, was drinking faster than the others. Stray locks of thick hair fell over heavy glasses and a walrus moustache got wiped dry each time he quaffed. Lisa watched him like a hawk. Initially Ulrich looked glum, but slowly he came forward on his chair, as if the beer was helping him out of a chrysalis. Eventually he was leaning forward on the table and mumbled something which made Kraft giggle.

"What did he say?" Lisa asked Sabine.

"I don't know. It was in Latin."

"He only knows two Latin words," Lisa scowled. "*Pi* and *Theta*."

A resigned Ulrich shook his black-maned head. "That's Greek," he said sadly to his wife.

"*Ut multus e visceribus sanguis exeat*," Kraft spouted effortlessly. "Ciceros's Disputations. We were talking about East Berliners."

"What about them?" demanded Lisa.

"*From the flesh much blood pours forth,*" translated Kraft.

Lisa thought about this. Ulrich continued the hushed exchange with Kraft. "I don't think that's suitable for East Berliners," said Lisa. "That's West Berliners. We're the ones bleeding." Suddenly there was a yelp from Ulrich. He raised a bottle. "To mistresses," he shouted. He had just learned that Martina and Professor Kraft were unmarried. The academic end of the table fell silent. All eyes were on Ulrich who tipped the bottle so that beer flowed freely down his throat. "And to the men that love them," Martina added warmly. She lifted her glass too. Ulrich turned to her. "Madam, you deserve to be kissed." The edges of his words were becoming slightly indistinct. "Ulli," Lisa threatened. "You don't have one?" Kraft asked, egging Ulrich on. "Of course," Ulrich continued, his pouchy black eyes more resigned than ever. "Berlin is my mistress. She's not beautiful, but she is intense." "Stop it, Ulli," Lisa said. "She is inspiring," Ulli continued, now viewing his wife. "And she's always there."

The other end of the table had been shifting in their seats. Something Ulrich said touched one of the professors. He admitted he didn't know much about it – he could only make assumptions about what it was like to have a mistress – but if they were moody and fickle and different every day, he would have to agree with Ulrich's vision of Berlin. "Right now, though, she's getting her plumbing readjusted," he added, smirking.

"A temporary stay in the intensive care unit only,"proclaimed Ulrich with authority. "When she's out, she'll be more licentious than ever." Here and there a titter could be heard around the table.

Martina, with eyes not quite synchronized, asked Hanbury a direct question. "Do you agree with that, Herr Konsul?" Attention around the table shifted to the consul as if a piece of exotica had been discovered.

"What fascinates me is to see the two halves coming together," he said blandly.

"Exactly!" said Ulrich with triumph. "Berlin is coupling." He held his bottle towards the consul in salute.

Professor Kraft was quick to pick up. "And what fascinates *me*," he said, once again giggling, "is that it's impossible to know which side is getting screwed." Ulrich began to shake and Sabine, her husband and even the two professors' wives were now laughing. Only Lisa remained stern.

One of Schwartz's professor friends said he'd heard a joke about the East-West cleft. "Tell us," commanded Ulrich.

"An Ossi and a Wessi meet under the Brandenburg Gate right after reunification. The Wall is gone. They look past each other into the other part of the city. The Ossi says: *Isn't it wonderful? We're one People again.* The Wessi replies: *I'm so happy for you. That's what we are too.*" Kraft loved it and Ulrich clapped before he grabbed another beer. "You've had enough, Ulli," said Lisa. "It's good beer," he told her. Kraft said, "We had some good stories in East Germany, but telling them was a crime." "Tell the one about God, Helmut," Martina prompted. "I'm not good at it," Kraft protested. But Schwartz from the far end demanded to know about God and the GDR.

Kraft relented. He described a scene where the heads of state of the USA, the USSR and the GDR – Reagan, Gorbachev and Honecker – were having a summit with God. Each asked God about his country's prospects for the next millennium. "Ah, yes," said God, "early in the next millennium the USA will become socialist." Reagan, dumbstruck, turned around, covered his face with his hands and cried. "And what will happen to the Soviet Union?" Gorbachev wanted to know. God sighed. "It won't exist anymore." Gorbachev's head sank, also unable to keep his tears from flowing. Now it was Honecker's turn. He asked what was in store for the GDR. God was silent for a moment, then turned away and wept.

Ulrich hooted. With his shoulders shaking he began polishing his glasses with his serviette. Everyone, even the two earnest wives, loved Kraft's story. Kraft said he had one more. "Honecker is visiting the Kremlin," began Kraft. "He sees a black telephone next to the famous red one and immediately inquires what it's for. A direct line to Hell, is the explanation. Honecker wants to try it, but is advised not to speak long – the call costs 100 rubles per minute. Back in East Berlin, Honecker insists a phone just like it be installed at his desk. Once hooked up he wants to try it. He asks about the cost. The reply, fifteen pfennigs a minute. So cheap? he asks, adding in Moscow it was 100 rubles. A pause, then the answer: *Here it's a local call.*"

When laughter subsided a second time, Martina said, "You see, Herr Hanbury, how preoccupied we are with ourselves. Is it like this in your country? Do you endlessly analyse yourselves too?" Hanbury smiled evasively. "Tell us a Canadian story," cried Ulrich, his black hair ever wilder, his glasses askew. "Lift us out of navel-gazing." Hanbury caught Sabine's look. She signalled him part apology for what was being done to him and part encouragement to bear it.

"We don't have too many good ones," said Hanbury.

"A bad one will do," said Ulrich impatiently.

"A Berliner's addiction," explained Lisa.

"I heard one from an academic once," Hanbury said.

"His field?" asked one of the wives who believed it mattered.

"Philosophy," Hanbury replied.

"Escape artists, every one of them," growled Ulrich. "I bet it's an escape story."

"Sort of," Hanbury said carefully. "Imagine the French Revolution. It's in full swing. Citizens' committees are in charge. They have taken the law into their hands."

"Sounds familiar," sniggered Ulrich. "Come around to our apartment when Lisa has her meetings."

"Shh," said Lisa.

"Three men are arrested," continued Hanbury, "an American, a German and a Canadian. They're accused of spying, tried, found guilty and sentenced: death by guillotine. In the market square, thousands looking on, each is allowed a final statement."

"Mercy in my apartment would be no better," Ulrich said, but this time Sabine motioned that he remain quiet.

"The American stands tall on the platform, steps forward, rests his eyes on the crowd and shouts: *Motherhood, Baseball and Apple Pie!* He goes to the guillotine and puts his neck on the edge. The instrument of death sparkles in the sunlight. The blade swishes down. Miraculously, it halts just above the neck. There is a cry in the crowd: A sign! He's innocent! Let him go! So the American goes free.

"The German is next. He comes forward, slightly dazed because everything's been happening fast. His last chance to speak. With glazed eyes he recites: *Sauerkraut, The Beer Purity Law, No Speed Limits on the Autobahn.* He shuffles to the guillotine. The blade speeds down. Again, it stops just short. The German too is free."

"Bad news," mumbled Ulrich.

"The crowd – one last chance for blood – concentrates on the Canadian. He comes forward thoughtfully, as if working through a problem, his attention fixed on the upper part of the death machine. He begins to nod and points at the mechanism. *I think I've figured it out, he says. If you give that screw up there a quarter turn...*"

Ulrich was the first to laugh. He couldn't stop; tears rolled down his cheeks; he wiped his mustache without interruption. Others grinned. "Good," said Kraft. "Admirable. What a culture. What a national type!" "Are you really like that?" asked one of the wives from down the table. "Selfless white knights, all of us. The truth first, self-preservation second," responded Hanbury. "It doesn't surprise me," said Martina, "with your spectacular gene pool." "A country of uncommon wealth," the consul affirmed. "I do hope you're taking steps to share them," said Martina.

After more anecdotes, the dinner party settled into a quieter phase. Ulrich seemed to go to sleep. The academics complained about university administration. The consul was entertained with stories about the days when Sabine, Lisa, and Martina were girls. Schwartz brought out a bottle of schnapps. Sabine brought in coffee and herbal tea for Lisa. One by one, the couples produced reasons to depart. Only Lisa, who was with Sabine in the kitchen, and a quietly snoring Ulrich were left. Schwartz refilled Hanbury's glass. "Sorry to talk business, Tony, but I've studied the material you obtained the other day. Fascinating. Did it take long?"

"It was slow going..." Hanbury admitted.

"I hope it isn't an imposition. I know you're busy."

"Oh no. After what you've done for me, I'm happy to do it."

"I appreciate it." They clinked glasses.

Hanbury described the latest afternoon he spent in the Normannenstrasse complex searching through the files. The main problem was scheduling enough time away from the office. Schwartz said the information dug out by Hanbury contained new leads. With Stobbe's people focussing solely on screening public figures for their Stasi links, requests like Schwartz's for historical research wouldn't get attention for years. "The potential information on Nazi war criminals is rich. I'd like more digging on that."

Hanbury said it would be difficult to schedule more than an afternoon a week for the files. How long might it take to pursue all the leads?

"Full time, maybe a week."

"I'll take a vacation," said Hanbury. When Schwartz protested that was going too far, Hanbury dismissed it. "I haven't had a day off since I got here," he said. "Anyway, it's amusing in there. It's sort of like exploring."

Sabine and Lisa returned from the kitchen and brought Ulrich back to life. He stared at Hanbury. "The handyman," he mumbled, rising onto unsteady feet. "What a story."

"It was good," said Sabine warmly. She stood with an arm through her husband's.

"I'll help you get him down," Hanbury said to Lisa.

He held a swaying Ulrich firmly for two flights of stairs. "You were the life of the party," Hanbury said.

"One day I'm going to visit America..." slurred Ulrich.

"You'd enjoy it."

"...and get picked up for drunken driving."

"Not that."

"They'd put me in an electric chair."

"Unlikely."

"They would. A quick end. But first, Handyman, I'd want you to check the wiring."

Outside, the midnight hum from the Ku'damm funnelled down Fasanenstrasse. Hanbury accompanied Lisa and her husband as far as the next U-Bahn station. "I suppose you have a gas guzzler parked somewhere," she said severely. "North Americans are the worst in the world for energy waste and garbage production." "He'll fix that soon enough," said Ulrich with conviction. "No car," said Hanbury. "I like walking." "See!" said Ulrich to his wife as arm in arm they disappeared.

Hanbury began the trek to Dahlem along the Ku'damm. A store window with trinkets brought him to a halt; the kind of place that would have excited Zella. Further along, a Trabi clattered by, reminding him that he was in love with Gundula's sharp tongue. A tenderly linked couple stood waiting at a taxi stand. Sabine and her husband were like that at the door when they waved their guests goodbye – a liberating sight. All along the Ku'damm Hanbury received life's signals and each one was set on green. Nothing held him back. The path before him had an easy downward slope and, on auto pilot, all he had to do was coast.

A BERLIN VACATION

he vacation Earl had promised Frieda was not far off. They were finished forever, he told her, with organized bus tours to Bavaria. From now on their annual outing would be five-star: grand hotels in Liechtenstein, or in the Engadin in Switzerland, or on the Côte d'Azur. To prove he meant it, he chartered a yacht for this year's holiday, a sixty-footer out of Monaco with a crew of four and a luxury apartment for them. She asked Earl to determine if their quarters would be soundproof. Frieda was not so concerned about hearing a bit of muffled engine noise, but she would be squeamish about the captain hearing *her*, when Earl made love. Earl checked. On a boat like that, he said, naturally she needn't worry.

Gifford wheeled his Mercedes into the club. By the time he was back from his vacation McEwen would have left. Retired. The car's climate control was on low, the June weather being spectacular. The air was light, easy to breathe, the sky a pristine window on the universe. The azaleas and rhododendrons had bloomed and Berlin's wide, tree-lined avenues had disappeared under heavy foliage. The city was green. Green, green, green. The greenest city in the world. The Tiergarten was once more a paradise and boats with tourists on the upper decks drinking Berliner Weisse plied the Havel. The pleasantness was so intense it seemed it was never different before and would be forever thus. Which was how Gifford felt about his own existence.

In an urgent duck-walk, impressive hams shaking, he entered the club, a thick envelope squeezed under an arm. Something to share with McEwen. Gifford had suggested this rendezvous; the initiative was his. "Why Earl," McEwen had said on the phone, "of course I have time. A few more weeks and I shall be history. Yes, yes. Do come down. We shall enjoy a pint. Been having them alone these past few months. Queer, how one gets used to it."

The last time they tipped one, months before, the meta-diplomat had been embittered. He sat still then, teeth clenched. He spoke in high-pitched, nasal bursts. The newsy, nosy drinking companion, the confident wizard with unusual recipes for acquiring information, the serene uncle bringing wandering children back, was no more. All that was left of the old McEwen was restraint. Gifford had recognized this when the meta-diplomat admitted he was disappointed. Disappointed? Yes, with Uncle Teut of course, though rather more so with the Beavers.

"They went to sleep, Earl. With Uncle Teut I suppose it was to be expected. But the Beavers? What has happened to the propitious influence of the Crown? In earlier days half the evidence we had on Friend Tony would have triggered a full-scale, secret government inquiry. I can give you ten examples. Customarily there would have been de-indoctrination, re-indoctrination, possibly incarceration, certainly dismissal." McEwen's pitch went up as he recalled an age when friend and foe were well-defined. He took a long gulp of his bitter. "And what happens in today's age of confusion? Uncle Teut requests Friend Tony to stay away from *Friedensdorf.* As if a tiny breach of etiquette occurred. And the Beavers hide behind an instruction that their man in Berlin become more careful in reporting his questionable contacts." The meta-diplomat's composure broke down for a moment, because he gave an impromptu, emotional little squeal. It was, Gifford assumed, his way of despairing. Gifford remembered he was uncomfortable at this point. He wanted to be done with the business. He wanted out.

"Less than a rap on the knuckles, Earl," McEwen had gloomily continued. "I cannot fathom it. Can you?" Gifford had shaken a commiserating head at the stupidity and the injustice and kept his drinking in pace with McEwen's to show solidarity. Since then, no contact. No pints, no lunches, no gossip. The silence, Gifford had assumed, meant McEwen was arranging his affairs. Everybody at the end deserves some quiet to review mementos, some time to decide to throw everything out.

Gifford passing through reception saw McEwen was already at their table. "A splendid gesture, Earl," a subdued McEwen said, rising, laying a hand on Gifford's shoulder. "Take a seat, take a seat. I was sitting here reflecting and it dawned on me that loyalty is the highest virtue. Your call made me realize that. We did well over the years. I won't forget you came to say good bye." The once proud master of Berlin Station had shrivelled. Mustache untrimmed, eyes pushed back in lamp-black sockets, thin strands of white hair straggling down his forehead, cheek bones ready to break through sagging skin. Signs of age, if not insanity.

"Almost out to pasture, Earl," McEwen said with senile optimism. "Already am, really. Things haven't quite turned out. No blaze of glory at the end. Still, I suppose I had my innings. Thank you for coming. Your pint is on the way." With a doting grin he studied Earl's envelope. He assumed it contained a present. A plaque, perhaps. He began to describe Yorkshire and his new status: gentleman farmer. What was Earl's opinion of that? "Take a vacation first," Earl advised. He, himself, was planning a proper break, he said. "You and Frieda? How splendid. Where?" "We've always been fond of Bavaria. But this year there's a departure. A cruise. Frieda is becoming adventurous, more worldly." "A sign of a mature woman, Earl. You're most fortunate."

Gifford shifted on his great hams. He saw Frieda modelling the bikinis she was shopping for, putting them on and taking them off. Thin laces disappeared into the deep folds of her flesh. The vision stirred him, but he shook it. "I have something for you, Randy." Gifford patted the envelope, as McEwen used to, before handing it over.

"Really? How unexpected." A contented McEwen, the very picture of a patriarch, took a table knife and sliced it open. "How deeply mysterious," he murmured happily. "Whatever could this be?"

"I looked in on Friend Tony's C-drive the other day." Gifford said harshly. "Out of habit. That's what I found." Gifford's tone shattered McEwen's mellow state of mind. He sipped his pint, but a change came over him. It was noticeable in the setting of his eyes. Sentimentality seeped out; a focus, an interest, a resilience flooded in. He explored the thickness of the emerging sheaf with a rifling thumb. "I thought it might interest you," Gifford added. "Over eighty pages. He's been busy writing."

"Writing?" McEwen said suspiciously. "Isn't that odd? Was he a bard before?"

"Certainly not," confirmed Gifford.

"What, one wonders, has Friend Tony been writing?" McEwen studied some pages. An energy was being generated deep inside, for his forehead wrinkled and the stubby pencil came out. He wetted it with his tongue and began jotting in the margins.

Gifford drank patiently, one pint, another, watching a transformation, seeing McEwen's eyes begin to dance. His own thoughts drifted to the yacht. The brochure had a picture of the principals' bedroom. It brought him a new vision: Frieda on her back on the circular bed, rotating her hips, staring at her nakedness in a ceiling mirror.

"I don't know what to make of it," McEwen said. "Political reports.

Bloody good actually. I've intercepted a few in my day and can tell. Have you read them?"

"No. I didn't discover them until yesterday. They date back months."

"I see," McEwen said slowly. "Why has he turned commentator, Earl? He never was before. Another attribute he kept hidden."

Gifford shrugged. "He's been talking to many people. I asked him about it. *Just obtaining other points of view,* he said. That's fair, I thought. That's why the world has diplomats. Here's the list of people he's been seeing. Thought you might like it."

"Ah, thank you, Earl. Good work. Let's see who he's been courting." McEwen alternately hummed approval and shook his head. His attention returned to the reports. "Admirable objectivity," he said, "presenting all sides of complex issues. Take this one on the Oder-Neisse line. Good arguments why the current border with Poland will never satisfy the Germans, why they will never stop looking for ways to get their eastern territories back. Then comes a contrary position: western-minded Germany has lost its territorial ambitions. And yet another view: German business heading east is finishing what Hitler's armies started. Territory is not important: control of markets is. Well argued, if you want my opinion."

"You're right," said Gifford.

"Oh, Earl," cooed McEwen, "here's a good one. Listen. *Germany is an uneasy nation. It vacillates between extremes, between too little democracy and too much. Deep down, Germans don't want too much democracy. They desire strong government, clear decisions and, if necessary, the rule of an elite. Deep down they worry that pluralism slows them down.* Hear, hear! I wish I had written that. And here is the contrary position. *Historically Germans have achieved a high standard of humanism. Kant, Beethoven, Schiller, Goethe, they define the German nation, not Friedrich Nietzsche, Guido von List or Adolf Hitler. And the best Germany has historically offered is once more ascendant.* Do you believe that, Earl?

Poppycock, if you ask me. Ah, a word about you and me and the consul too. *Germans don't like foreigners. Foreigners erode tradition; they destroy the psychic immediacy of being German. The virtues of patriotism, duty, constancy and purity of blood are seen as being watered down by strangers. They want foreigners fenced-out, and fenced-in, to avoid dilution.* But we turn the page and suddenly the picture is not so clear. *Few countries are more tolerant than Germany. Refugees and asylum seekers flood in by the thousands. They are housed, fed, put on welfare. Other countries would long ago have closed the borders.*"

McEwen quoted more passages with the delight of someone reading another's mail. But Gifford scarcely listened. He had decided the material on the consul's C-drive amounted to kilobytes of rubbish. His focus was on real-world challenges, such as managing money and looking after Frieda. Once more he saw her on the bed. Its circularity meant he could creep at and slide over her from all directions.

"Remarkable material, Earl. I'll want to study it more closely." McEwen was business-like. "A fine present. And otherwise? How has he behaved?"

"Close to normal, Randy. Devoted to his work. Punctual with his appointments. Responsible in his formal entertaining. Crisp with his consular responsibilities, although continuing to be away on certain afternoons. In addition to that…" Gifford searched for words that would appeal to McEwen, "…he has produced these respectable reports."

"Quite, Earl. Quite. A good word. Respectable. But the afternoons off, for what purpose? Any clarity on that."

"Not sure. It'll be more than that soon. For a start, next week he's taking the whole week off. A vacation. Mine begins after he returns. It's closely coordinated."

"I suppose after so much scribbling he's tired. Going to a south sea island?"

"I asked him. He's staying put. I asked why. He said he wants to look into something. Museums I suppose. He's been visiting museums regularly. He talks about them constantly."

"How odd. He wants to look into something? He wants to do that at a museum?" McEwen raised a skeptical eyebrow. "And during his vacation? If he treats museums as part of his work, why would he visit them on his time off?"

"Perhaps not museums then," said Gifford casually. "He said, above all, he wanted to be on his own."

"On his own? How most curious."

Gifford left and McEwen spent the afternoon studying the papers. He made a detailed list of subjects treated. Then he juxtaposed the list of people the consul had been meeting with those whose views were quoted. He struck off a name each time he matched it with a paragraph. After several hours, the names had entirely disappeared into the essays on the Germanic soul. Most of the material was attributable to specific sources. McEwen went through the reports once more, this time circling paragraphs without a source. Whose views, he wondered, did they portray? The question sustained McEwen through the weekend. He read the reports again, and again. He closed his eyes and meditated, seeking a template that would give sense to the paragraphs that had no attribution. The meta-diplomat was convinced the consul had not done the writing, not on his own. The break with his record was too severe. But who would have held the pen? Theory after theory crashed on the shores of things unknown.

If you look at mysteries long enough, McEwen knew, answers eventually jump out. So he studied and dissected and on cue, on Sunday afternoon it happened. When he regrouped the passages without attribution, when they were stripped of qualifications and reduced to simple thoughts, they added up. He reduced the sentences further, down to bare phrases. Eighty pages were distilled into a mere few dozen lines. Staring McEwen in the face was an outline of a political agenda.

> *Create myths – to shape public attitudes; manipulate social impulses – into a drive for nationalism; revise history – present Germany as a country being held back; vest authority in a few – with sufficient Will to force recognition that Germany must take its rightful seat at the table reserved for the world's two or three pre-eminent nations.*

For some time McEwen was immobile. Who was the consul getting this from? The origin and purpose of this thinking was wrapped up inside multiple shrouds and McEwen saw it as his duty to peel away the layers. Sitting trance-like in a high-backed chair, head slanted forwards, McEwen drove his mind into a fever. His operational capacity was gone. Uncle Teut would be a hindrance. A few loyal spectators remained, listening and observing for old time's sake, but they were unsuitable for what needed doing. McEwen concluded that a final unmasking of Friend Tony lay ahead, and the task would be his alone. Instincts told him to start with the Berlin vacation. McEwen went to bed but lay awake for hours. The excitement of becoming operational once more, the prospect of field work kept his mind churning. He always loved field work best. His career commenced as a field man. How fitting that it would end as one. When sleep eventually came, it was regular and deep.

The next morning, armed with sandwiches and a thermos of coffee, he set out for Dahlem. Fifty yards from the consul's mansion he parked his compact to begin a patient wait. The street was leafy, quiet, pleasant. The house had palatial beauty, McEwen admitted to himself. In the bright light, it looked dignified, clean, wholesome, but in its dark recesses lurked Friend Tony, ensconced, now as always, in multiple layers of pretence. McEwen ate two sandwiches at lunch and gulped two more several hours later. By six the thermos with its sweet black brew was empty. Still no sign of life in the vicinity of the mansion. By eight he was tiring and permitted himself a snooze, only to wake up to a barking dog. It was on a leash held by a lady who regarded him with cold suspicion. McEwen huffily drove home, to rest and generate fresh determination.

Next day the field man took up his post earlier. On the Dahlem street the morning activities were in full swing. A postman on his rounds. Garbage being collected with some banging. No one, not even a consul, McEwen was sure, could sleep through that. A street-cleaning vehicle came up from behind. The brushes loosened debris from between the cobblestones and sent it shooting into a collecting tank with the pinging sound of bullets. The machine made a detour around McEwen's car. The cleaned track lay there like a ribbon of good order, but with a kinky deviation. He watched the street sink into unbroken somnolence. Dahlem as Dahlem was meant to be. The sun rose, went through its zenith, then traced an arc back down. No sign of Friend Tony. When the early evening dog-walking began, a stiff-limbed, sullen McEwen concluded Gifford had given him bad information. The consul wasn't in town. He wasn't delving into the charms of local museums or anything else. He was pursuing other pleasures, maybe scuba diving off the Great Barrier Reef. McEwen drove off, leaving behind a small island of uncleanliness on the carefully scrubbed street.

"Nobody home, Earl," he said into the phone. "I've been watching. From early morning to late in the evening, nothing. He's gone. He's had you on." Gifford said he'd check. The next day, mid-morning, he called McEwen back. The information was accurate. The consul was not away; he was simply up and at it very early. Out of the house at seven-fifteen. Gifford read from his notes. "He said he's never felt more virtuous. He then asked me, *What's up?* He wanted to know why I was calling at 6:30 am on the third day of his vacation. I said, *Any objection if I send window cleaners round tomorrow?* I had to make up a reason for calling."

"Of course," said McEwen. "And then?"

"He said, *Thanks, Earl. Don't know where I'd be without you.* You're laughing, Randy. Why?"

"He is most extraordinarily devious. Go on."

"He said, *I'll be out tomorrow. The place is yours.* That was it."

"Quarter past seven, you said. That's frightfully early."

"Yes," said Gifford, "especially on a vacation."

"My very point."

On Thursday, the field man was rewarded. The consul emerged from the mansion punctually at seven-fifteen carrying a thin portfolio and when he turned the corner at the end of the block, McEwen's car surged. Restraining excitement, he caught up, drove by, turned onto a side street, eased into an opening, side mirror trained on the intersection. He observed the consul merrily swinging the portfolio leave the curb with a light, half jump and continue as before. McEwen did a three-point turn. Back at the intersection he surveyed the avenue and saw the distant U-bahn sign. He waited. Sure enough, the consul disappeared. McEwen raced to the station, slammed on the brakes, rammed the car up a curb. A train was coming in. Hurrying down, he heard doors opening, the shuffling sound of many feet, the station attendant's warning to stay clear. *Zu-u-rück blei-ei-ben!* But by the time his stiff-legged run brought him to the platform, the carriage doors were slamming shut. McEwen hastened on with one hand in the air, wanting to take hold of the train and keep it back. With disbelief, he watched it trundle off. The platform emptied, except for the attendant. The man tried to be helpful. "*Der nächste geht in vier Minuten.*" The next one leaves in four minutes. "Regrettable development," McEwen muttered. "Most unfortunate."

"*Amerikaner?*" the chatty attendant asked.

On the final day of the vacation, McEwen adopted a procedure that always brought an all-or-nothing thrill. He pulled away as the consul left the mansion and preceded him to the station. It triggered the same heart-stopping, breathless anticipation he experienced during his very first operation four decades earlier in Istanbul. He bet everything then – his whole future, really – on the Bosporous ferry to Asia. The Cambridge don arrived as McEwen's instincts said he would. During the crossing he took damning photos of the effete man in intimate conversation with a muscular, blond Slav youth. It clinched his supposition: top secret advances in solid-state physics being exchanged for homoerotic love.

On the U-bahn platform McEwen studied a map of the public transport system, felt his target coming down the stairs, and in the glass watched a transient reflection pass. No different than in Peking. That's how he'd once kept an eye on the Aussie woman. The consul drifted towards the far end of the platform and the field man, a few nonchalant steps at a time, gravitated in that direction too. A train rolled in. A group of students disembarked, and in the crowd the master of Berlin station lost his man. He hurried forward. *Zu-u-rück blei-ei-ben!* warned the attendant through the platform speakers. McEwen slipped into the front carriage just as the doors were closing. The compartment was fairly crowded, two rows of indifferent faces swaying with the acceleration of the train. McEwen took a place and sat there brooding with the best of them. He stole glances at the consul who studied posters above the windows. In a screaming red-checked sport shirt he was difficult to overlook. It reminded McEwen of Miss Australia in China, who had a similar casual approach to fashion, except – as he had had several occasions to observe – she loved to shed her clothing, doing so in the company of an overtly luckless Arab trader who covertly was in China's service. Post-coitus she talked like a waterfall. McEwen recorded every word. Impressive really, her total recall of shared intelligence assessments of China, which as registry clerk she had the duty to file. Well, Canberra yanked her out fast, the master of Berlin Station recalled with an inner squeeze of pleasure.

More commuter bodies crammed in as the train neared the centre of West Berlin. Calcutta. It reminded McEwen of the masses of Calcutta. Through a gap, he saw the consul readying himself to get off. Uncanny, really, how he resembled that little Californian who had filled a briefcase with certain English drawings of a new Rolls-Royce jet engine, quit his position at a San Diego aerospace company, and departed for Calcutta. McEwen loved recalling how over a three-week period he had tightened a net and hauled him in – just before a rendezvous with commercial attachés from the local Soviet consulate. And today another net was tightening. Good, basic field work. Nothing was sweeter.

At Wittenbergplatz the crowd rushed to other connecting lines. The consul slipped smoothly to another platform where a new train arrived in seconds. The field man slid in behind. Potsdamer Platz, Stadtmitte, Spittelmarkt – deeper into East Berlin. McEwen casually studied progress on a map pasted on the ceiling, but his instinct was screaming. This was it! The consul sitting there so naturally, so tranquilly, in such simplicity. Down here in the bowels of the city on this, the ultimate of rides, sharing it with a cunning target, while above lay a realm where every telephone, every mail room, every club and school and church bore Stasi scars – the experience thrilled McEwen. He admitted it. Deep down he always admired the Stasi. Few organizations had been more formidable. Better than the KGB. Better cover. Perfect cover really, the way they turned into West Germans. What a stupendous infestation they had managed! He remembered the anecdote shared by both sides in the business: *When in Bonn the chancellor farted, Honecker in East Berlin fanned the smell away.* The pipeline had been that wide open.

Stop by stop the train emptied. The consul got out at Alexanderplatz. On a new platform he paced up and down. McEwen assumed a low profile behind an advertising sign. With the chase momentarily paused, a fresh wave of nostalgia hit the field man. His whole career, a long parade of accomplishments, passed before his eyes. Passport corruption in Hong Kong; money laundering in Singapore; arms deals in South Africa; the lively trade in military secrets in Vienna. He had seen it all. How fortunate he was to have this final journey in Berlin. No other city in the world could generate a happier conjunction of place, persons and perfidy.

A train clattered in and the consul boarded. McEwen slithered into the far end of the same carriage, where he sat with his back turned. Deeper and deeper into the East. At this rate they'd soon be in Poland, McEwen mused happily. At Magdalenenstrasse, the consul got out once more. McEwen's instincts roared with fresh conviction. He suppressed an urge to jump up. But he remained seated for a moment and lingered on the platform, to allow a tracking distance to develop. At ground level the field man noted the city was broken up and bleak.

The consul was a practised walker. His pace was brisk and McEwen, on stiff legs, broke into a half-run to keep up. Something about the area was familiar. A neighbourhood in Moscow? Or was it that adrenaline-filled outing he once had in Bucharest? The consul turned left. At the corner McEwen glanced up at the street sign. *Normannenstrasse*. At that moment multiple conjectures fell away. The field man knew this place. He knew what the lifeblood of this street once was and what went on behind the walls that he now reached out to touch. He steadied himself. His brain was beginning to whirl so fast it nearly spun apart and, as excitement at the discovery grew, he was momentarily overwhelmed by dizziness. Recovering, he observed that down the street the consul waved to a guard at a gate in a most personable way and, just as remarkably, the guard congenially waved back.

That was because the guard was used to seeing this visitor by now. Nor was the guard alone. Most of Stobbe's people treated the consul like one of them. A bright thumbs-up good morning at the gate would be followed by light bantering inside the complex. Hanbury looked the veteran by now, the way he went up and down the aisles, a finger running along the markings until he found a file. With an archivist's touch, he eased folders out of shelf slots and deftly slipped them back. Everyone in the place shared light moments to relieve the oppressive atmosphere. *Whose soul is being bared today?* a post-doc in library science would ask. *The Werewolf? The Raven?* Hanbury would respond: *Not the Raven. Not the Werewolf. Not today. Today I'm going after infernal Lucifer himself.* The deep and dreary catacomb would resound with peals of laughter.

Raven. Werewolf. Cover names appropriate for Nazi war criminals. After their service to the Third Reich, many became useful to the Stasi, and somewhere in Stobbe's archival jungle a fertile relationship between men who once wore brown shirts and those who preferred red socks – to use a Gregor Donner Reich distinction – lay waiting to be found. Although the paths were cleverly concealed, Hanbury *had* unmasked a Werewolf, *and* a Lucifer, and spent hours searching out Satan, Serpent, the Prince of Darkness and others of that ilk.

Obtaining the pass had been straightforward. He reintroduced himself to Frau Rommelsberger at the front desk. She had forgotten his visit, but after some coaxing plus a show of his calling card identical to the one she eventually pulled from a drawer, her memory came back. "*Natürlich erinnere ich mich,*" she said, her perky eyes wondering why he asked. "Naturally I remember. I wouldn't forget a consul. I wrote your name on the back of your calling card. You see. Here it is. Herr Stobbe wanted you to join us." Hanbury handed her a completed form and two photos. She prepared an identity card and plasticized it with a heat-treatment machine. The machine reminded her, she said, of her old iron.

"I did a lot of ironing in my day." "Some skills are forever useful," the consul said agreeably. She pinned the badge on his jacket. "Now you're one of us," she said.

The number of researchers in the labyrinth had increased and he joined the busy seekers. Their mammoth task was to identify every informant, each double agent, all the hundreds of thousands of Stasi collaborators in the GDR. To warm up for his own exploration, Hanbury retraced the steps he took with Stobbe months before. He poked around the various index rooms, F16, F17, F22, F77, F78, and wandered through the caverns with the neatly ordered rows of files. Then he got down to business.

In F16, the master index with its sly, phonetic approach to ordering six million names, he looked for himself first. Nothing had changed. He was there, forever slotted in between Bruno Hähn and Wilhelm Hähne. What wrong had they committed? Maybe having been overheard listening to pop songs on West Berlin radio? Hanbury would never know. He was there to research other personae. Schwartz had provided him with half a dozen cards, each with a name neatly printed in the top left hand corner: **Grassinger**, Alwin P; **Richter**, Johann Georg; **Winterstein**, Reinhardt: **Böckel**, Julius Arthur; **Reuss**, Ernst Wilhelm; **Woltmann**, Karl.

That first time in F16, Hanbury searched them out. He found three and transcribed details from the index onto Schwartz's cards. Winterstein was the easiest. Grassinger was more difficult because he had been filed with only one s. Eventually Hanbury came up with Woltmann too, at least he believed he did, if a Karl amongst the Wohltmanns was the right one. With Richter, Böckel and Reuss he had no luck.

Later, in *Das Klecksel*, Hanbury pulled out the meagre harvest. Schwartz took the cards eagerly. "I'm surprised these three drew a blank," he said. For some reason he believed all six would have Stasi records.

"I ran out of time. They might be there, but the filing is bizarre. Look at Grassinger and Woltmann." Hanbury pointed at the arbitrary changes.

Schwartz thought about this and added other possible names to the three cards. To Böckel, he added Bokel, Bockal and Böcal. Similar variations were put on the cards of Richter and Reuss. They turned to the three names Hanbury located. "What are those numbers?" Schwartz asked.

"They tell you where to look in F22, the procedures index. No names there, only numbers. For example, my F22 card shows my file can be located using the foreign enemy index, F17."

"Can you tell anything from these F22 notations?"

"No, except that two are in the F47 index and one is F56. Next time in I'll take a look."

Schwartz then handed Hanbury twelve more cards with names.

Hanbury checked each one out. With practice it went faster and Schwartz passed him more cards, so that by the time his Berlin vacation began he was working on more than fifty names. One by one he traced them deep into the files. Some names, after complicated cross-references had been tracked down, pointed to a file location called *DDB*. Hanbury eventually located a small room in a remote corner of the complex with a card thumb-tacked to the door showing these three letters. The files in *DDB* were meagre compilations, a few sheets of notations that were very difficult to decipher. The information seemed meaningless to him. But once Hanbury had jotted it down and brought it out, Schwartz was excited. "Fascinating," he muttered. "Rich material. More research in that area will be essential. See this..." He pointed at a word.

"Tristan," said Hanbury.

"Remember two days ago? Isolde? And the file on Karel Neumann mentioned a Parsival, also with a reference to *DDB*. We'll keep looking for references like that. Some kind of group existed with cover names borrowed from Wagner."

"A special class of informants?"

"Possibly. Possibly something else. And there's another category that's fascinating. Leopard, Grizzly, Scorpion. Dangerous creatures. Are they connected? And these others – Herald, Incubus, Charlemagne. There must be information on them somewhere. If only we could find a way to match cover names with real ones."

"I could try tracing them in reverse. References to cover names always come at the end of searches through the substantive files. Suppose I start with the cover names index tomorrow and see where trails go then?" Schwartz agreed and prepared a fresh pile of cards, this time with cover names in the upper left hand corner.

Thus began the productive final two days. Thursday morning, promptly at 8:30, in F77 – the index to the cover names – Hanbury searched out Dragon, King of Fear, Black Queen, Cactus, Spear, Minuteman, Saturn, Chairman, Northern Lights, Poison and so on and so forth. The index pointed to many file locations. Not infrequently, there was a link to F47, the Stasi control officer index. Going into F47 through this back door provided still more trails, which took him into parts of the complex he had not visited before.

The summer weather that evening was at its finest when the professor and the consul met in the *Klecksel* garden under an enormous oak. As daylight faded, small oil lamps on the tables flickered in the darkness; the tree above was an impenetrable dome. Schwartz picked slowly through the latest cards. Remarkable, he kept muttering. Remarkable. "Last day tomorrow," he said. "Concentrate on *DDB*. We're near a breakthrough."

Hanbury spent the final day in the small back room looking for answers to Schwartz's questions. On Friday night a rich pile of cards, each one covered with precise notations, lay before Schwartz on the *Klecksel* garden table. The professor was calm, but it was a forced calm. The day's haul excited him as none before had. "*Jawohl*," he said several times. "Yes. Indeed yes. This fits." A few cards later, he sucked in his breath. "A surprise. Truly a surprise."

"After yesterday and today, I'm no longer so sure all this is purely Nazi war criminal material," Hanbury broke in.

"What makes you say that?" Schwartz asked carefully. He continued studying the cards. "If not Nazis, then what? What's your guess?"

"Most of the information you're looking at has an F47 connection. At first, I assumed these people were Stasi agents since we knew they were not Stasi targets. But taking the names back to the main index, F16, and from there to F22, they didn't lead me back to F47 as should have happened had they been agents. Many led to F59 instead. That's the index on economic operations. So, these people are neither targets, nor agents, nor informants. They're a different class. These were people who cooperated with the Stasi in other ways. If you take for example the economic sector's cover names, Panther, Leopard, Stinger and the others, and check them out through F77, the cover name index, the file numbers you get there are different again. It's not a circle. These cover names take you in all kinds of directions, except most of the time there's the *DDB* hint. And when I went after those hints in *DDB*, as you can see here and here too, you get German names, foreign names and cover names, plus a recurrence of the acronym, *BKK*. What's *BKK*? Financial information is often associated with it, sometimes in DM, often US dollars. So I doubt it has anything to do with the Nazis. *BKK* seems like a commercial entity, maybe engaged in weapons sales, or something like that." Hanbury was pointing at words and numbers on the cards. "Furthermore, these others – Joker, King of Fear, Superman – these individuals are not that old, not old enough to have been active Nazis. Interestingly, they travelled to international conferences. These scribbles seem to be shorthand reports on meetings with personae who carried cover names based on ancient philosophers – Democritus, Epicurus, Socrates, Aristotle. What might those meetings have been about? Philosophy? I doubt it. What would the King of Fear have in common with Socrates? Mind-expanding drugs? And this is an interesting grouping too. Shakespeare, Titian, Paganini. People buying or selling art?"

"What about linking cover names with real names?" asked Schwartz. "What would you say about that?"

"There's nothing direct, but I'm pretty sure Leopard was, or is, someone called Hans-Detlef Weisshagel. They appear in similar contexts several times. He in turn was closely associated with Reusch, who you thought at the start was Reuss. Joker seems almost certainly to have been a certain Burkhard Wegener…"

"Go on."

Hanbury flipped through more cards, linking cover names and their activities with names of persons. Schwartz took all this down. "And this is based on *DDB* files?" he asked again, to be certain. "It's all *DDB*. That's where real names and cover names become nearly directly linked. Most of the documents have a reference to *BKK*. What does it mean?"

"*BKK* stands for *Bereich Kommerzielle Koordinierung*," Schwartz said. "It was a wing of the Stasi that bought and sold goods on world markets, sometimes illicitly." He said this as if it were widely known. "Fine work, Tony. It goes without saying there's a good report in this for you and a monograph or two for me. A productive week." Schwartz rifled through the cards with his thumb.

Reports! Hanbury thought about slaving over yet another one. It gave him no enthusiasm. His life had been ruled by reports. Admittedly, they had caused a stir. Krauthilda had phoned to say her last act as a Zealot was to let him know a rumour was circulating that the high priest wanted the Berlin reports used as a model. "You should also know," she had announced, "that Krauthilda is history. Starting Monday I'm first political secretary in Rome. I hope I get on with Italians as well as you do with Germans."

And now, under the *Klecksel* oak, recalling the phone call, Hanbury shook his head. What report with what kind of theme would do justice to the information he had lifted out of that strange *DDB* room? Who could possibly be interested? In his last report he had explored the skinhead phenomenon. Schwartz had labelled them directionless creatures lacking a spiritual framework, but possessing enormous reservoirs of energy. Would the Stasi's Scorpions, Stingers, Jokers, Supermen, whoever they were, be treated by Schwartz in a similar way? Misfits with unused potential? Hanbury was curious. "What monographs?" he asked. "What would you write about? What do you think all this information means?"

The professor studied the consul. "It's too early to say," he said. "It's good to know what's in the *DDB* room, but I'll need outside corroboration to see what it adds up to."

"Tell me, this *DDB* crowd, are they a sociological phenomenon like the skinheads?"

"I'll know more in a few weeks," Schwartz replied evasively. "I doubt direct comparisons can be made. What makes you ask?"

"The last report we did on the neo-Nazi movement. You suggested the members were in search of spiritual roots. Remember, you said if they were handled properly they could make a contribution. I'm wondering whether the *DDB* crowd is like that, whether they have that potential. My impression is they're more likely to be criminals."

"Some of them may be," the professor said.

Hanbury laughed. "That would be quite a monograph, sketching out a spiritual rationale for the *DDB* crowd of criminals. You know, I've seen skinheads hanging out around railway stations begging for coins. They're not great advertising. I personally think it would be a hard row making them productive." He made more light jokes about the thin parallel between Stasi-linked criminals and neo-Nazi rowdies. "If the former deserve no respect, then why the optimism about the potential of the latter?" he asked.

"You haven't seen them in their element," said Schwartz. He looked at the consul for a long time, seemingly making a decision. "It's Friday evening," he taunted. "Are you free? Shall I show you something?"

Hanbury shrugged. "Why not? I'm on vacation."

❧

The destination, Hanbury learned, was Potsdam. In Schwartz's car he asked what was there. "I'm doing something I normally wouldn't," Schwartz replied, refusing to say more. The route took them through Wannsee. The sinking sun had set the sailboats out on the water ablaze and in the light the lake's surface was a sheet of platinum. Crossing the Glienicker Bridge into Potsdam, the professor joked about the brisk East-West trade in spies once staged there. "Of course, only the important ones came through here," he added. "The small fry were swapped on the S-bahn." On the Potsdam side the road was rough and Schwartz reduced speed. The houses were monstrously run down. Always into a different world, wherever, whenever a crossing into the East is made. The Russians, he remarked, reduced Potsdam to crumbling outer shells. The professor knew his way here. At Cecilienhof he turned right, to the river, and then left on a track that took them into a forest. The sun's final rays of the day came in below the crowns of trees. Schwartz said he loved this sylvan way – *Ich liebe diesen Holzweg* – adding that it provided a sense of nearness to the stirring Germanic feat 2000 years ago of vanquishing the Roman legions in forest warfare and driving them back to the other side of the Rhine. The path continued over little rises and around massive trees. Here and there the wood thickened into a tangle of luxuriant creeping green, then opened into stands of beeches, or groves of massive oaks with gnarled boughs reaching out. "It seems untouched for centuries," said Hanbury, inspired by the peace and the smell of rich, dark humus. He was ever more intrigued about their final destination. "A place to feel religion," Schwartz confirmed.

They came to a clearing. On one side ran a stockade and behind it stood a fading sandstone building, the remains of an old *Waldschloss,* an aristocrat's forest hideaway. The stone was discoloured with lichen and decorative elements were breaking off. Vines crept up the sides and pushed through the roof. Nature doing its reclaiming. But the stockade was recent, and newer still were black pig heads stuck on pointed poles next to the entrance. Eyes had been gouged out; flies clustered in the cavities. "How welcoming," said Hanbury. He viewed the pig heads with suspicion.

"It's not the Potsdam Rotary Club," Schwartz sneered. "*Weiter gehen?*" Continue?

"We've come this far." Occasionally Gundula would dare him with the same words – *Weiter gehen?* – just before entering another of her East Berlin dives. We've come this far, he always said. But here he was less nonchalant. Schwartz didn't have Gundula's light-hearted, peppy way.

Inside the stockade patches of earth were scarred where fires had burned. Schwartz went to a side door and tapped out a complicated pattern. A small shutter slid aside, then the door opened. "*Ein Gast,*" Schwartz said quietly. He led his guest into a narrow passage to the main hall of the house. An oak staircase was in near collapse. In the muted light Hanbury saw rough planks had been hammered over missing steps. Schwartz followed his gaze. "The Russians," he said. "They used it last."

Thick candles marked a passage down another hallway. A pounding noise grew louder as they went. When Schwartz opened a heavy door the sound instantly converted into wild, driving music which seemed to jump at them. Hanbury stood still, thinking maybe it was better to turn back now, but Schwartz motioned and he followed, down narrow stone steps to a cellar. The music was an assault on more than the ears. It created a black, disorienting pressure. Pushing forward, Hanbury had trouble with his breathing. Finally the professor parted a curtain and preceded him into a cavern where more candles flickered. The consul recoiled. This time the assault was on his eyes. On low stools, around slices of tree trunks serving as tables, swaying to the driving beat, sat a pack of drinking, smoking warriors. Most heads were shaven, others had tails growing out the back. Army fatigues, chains draped over bare chests, swastikas tattooed on upper arms, army belts with bayonets in sheaths, jackboots laced up to the knees. Was this the corked-up creativity which Schwartz declared was being wasted?

One glance was enough. Hanbury wanted out. He had a sickening sensation that if he went one step further, this sullen pack would rip him apart. But Schwartz continued in, raising a palm in greeting to a nearby table, giving a finger salute to others. Hanbury followed against his will, as if caught in a slipstream. At a vacant chunk of tree they sank down on stools. The professor pointed two fingers at a figure draped with cartridge belts who snapped an index finger back and soon brought them each a beer.

The loudspeakers fell silent; the grotto calmed. In a corner a video began playing on a large screen. Nazis marching at the Nuremberg rallies; tanks rolling; dictators making rousing speeches; footage of crosses burning in the presence of the Ku-Klux-Klan. Random fascist images. There was little talk. The warriors smoked and drank and watched the video. Hanbury saw one with an Iroquois swath of hair growing from his forehead, over his scalp and down his neck, who operated a Polaroid. He was in demand, the pictures coming out setting off little eddies of manly giggling. "Well?" the professor challenged. "Do they look like beggars?" Hanbury shrugged. "Good local colour," he said non-committally, masking a deep foreboding. He noticed Schwartz was different here. The academic arrogance was gone. A severity, a deadly lack of humour had replaced it. "I understand what you meant about the pent-up energy. It's powerful," Hanbury added, wanting to be conciliatory. "I thought you would," said Schwartz with cold triumph. He looked in the direction of the video which showed brownshirts smashing Jewish windows.

Hanbury wanted to remark he didn't need to stay longer, but the skinhead operating the Polaroid came over. Without warning the flash went. Schwartz was instantly annoyed. "*Franz! Nein. Das will ich nicht.*" I don't want that. "It's a Polaroid, Herr Professor," the skinhead smiled. "If you don't like the picture, throw it away." Franz lifted the photo off the back. Before their eyes, it formed. The consul looked lost; the professor stared out of the picture with hatred. The back of a warrior at the next table, naked from the waist up, was on the picture's edge and hieroglyphic markings on the wall behind seemed to spring out of their heads. "It's yours," Franz said to Schwartz, "or yours," to the guest. He continued to the next table. "I don't like my picture being taken," Schwartz muttered.

Hanbury studied the photo, then turned around to look at the markings on the wall. "What's that?"

"Symbols of an ancient Aryan cosmogony," Schwartz said, taking the photo from Hanbury and putting it in his pocket. "They depict fire, air, earth and water." He pointed at several specific symbols. Hanbury asked about the others. Schwartz explained that a symbol with three curved hooks joined at the centre portrayed the swirling fire whisk from which the universe was born. Inverted triangles and anti-clockwise markings including the swastika – he called them triskelions – symbolized stages in cosmic evolution. Such portrayals, he said, had developed over time into the Maltese cross, which in turn was the basis for the iron cross with its Prussian importance. "I did research into ancient Nordic runes years ago," continued Schwartz. "I explained the meanings to these boys. They wanted to believe in them. One might say, they felt it pointed them towards a divinity that was uniquely theirs. The book you got from Geissler improved my understanding. It revealed pictograms I hadn't seen before. It had quite an impact here, as if their version of the Dead Sea scrolls had been found. Well, now they have the full spiritual vocabulary of the ancients. So they painted the signs on the wall. This space is their temple."

Hanbury was incredulous. And what are you doing here? he almost cried. Where do you fit in all of this? But the video was over and the music restarted. Schwartz's spiritual horde began their motionless contemplation once more. As the pain of the eardrum-cracking beat became unbearable, he shouted into Schwartz's ear that he wished to go. The professor nodded. It was too loud for him too. In the upstairs hallway Schwartz took the photo from his pocket, stuck it in a candle and held the burning picture by a corner until it was gone. "Visits here do not take place," he said. "We did not come. Agreed?" The cold severity was gone. The customary arrogance was back. "Sure," Hanbury replied meekly. Schwartz broke into grin. "It would take too long to explain to Sabine."

Reappearing in the easy evening air was like awakening from a disturbing dream. Hanbury now asked his question. "How did you get involved with them?"

"Research," Schwartz answered smugly. "A historian needs to understand the present to interpret the past as much as he studies the past to shed light on the present."

"And you were comfortable there?" Hanbury probed. "I wasn't. I admit it. That was a brutal video."

"There are no restrictions, no taboos in my work. That video tells us about power and how it is manipulated. The Nazis had good insight into power, but they set themselves poor objectives. Imagine what could have been achieved with better goals."

Hanbury thought about this. He might have asked more questions. Why furnish neo-Nazis with the spiritual vocabulary of ancient Aryans? Or, was there a link between this and the information he had dug out of the Stasi archives? But Hanbury didn't ask his questions. He didn't want to know the answers. *Visits here do not take place.* He agreed with that. As Schwartz's car rolled and pitched out of the forest, he tried to purge his mind of what he'd seen. He wanted to get back to the beginning, to the time before he and Schwartz began collaborating. He wanted to get back to simplicity and innocence, to his sanctuary in Dahlem, where Gundula sat next to him at the piano and afterwards they went onto the terrace to drink champagne, looking at the treetops silhouetted against the stars, until a nudge from her said it was time to go inside, and holding hands to ascend the stairs.

SUMMER DOLDRUMS

"My dear Alex, if you really want to know more," McEwen was telling Graf Bornhof on the phone, "do come to Berlin."

The graf had called McEwen to thank him for the photo. He had examined it, he said, and had some questions. McEwen, picking up signals of worry behind the graf's casual tone, pressed his advantage. Graf Bornhof paused, then said he'd be on a plane the next day.

A picture is not only worth a thousand words, McEwen thought as he rang off, a picture concentrates the mind, even the Hun's.

He was quite a picture himself, a perfect picture of a merry uncle. McEwen was engaged, as he liked to say, in pleasurable, last minute, pre-retirement planning. And with Graf Bornhof consenting to visit, the send-off would be grand. McEwen sang a *Tra-la-la*, until his crusty vocal chords tightened up and the notes flipped into a squeal. *That* made him giggle. The new file – his final file – had been thickening nicely. He was undecided on one point only: whether to put the photograph from a last and loyal spectator in Potsdam on the front cover as a stirring opening, or at the very back, as a finale. Technology nowadays, thought McEwen. Remarkable how little cameras take pictures from inside big cameras. He sat at his kitchen table paging through the dossier with an avuncular air, feeling good towards Graf Bornhof, overcome with anticipation for the Yorkshire farm, indescribably thankful to the consul for being more duplicitous than could ever have been imagined and, not least, giving way to a feeling of magnanimity towards the Hun. When you're about to leave a land forever and are swollen with success, the locals, McEwen grudgingly admitted, deserve a modicum of credit.

❧

The joy filling McEwen's apartment was matched by a carefree exultation on the streets. Berlin was devoting itself to pleasure. As the summer's intensity grew and temperatures notched up ever higher, life in the bars and cafés spilled into the open, and bathers clogged the beaches around the city's delightful forest lakes.

Gundula's apartment in the concrete jungle of Marzahn had become unbearable. The scorched fields of concrete scarcely cooled at night. The pre-fab cages there were like ovens getting hotter by the day. Gundula, accustomed to spending nights in the consul's villa with its high-ceilinged rooms and liveable temperatures, accepted his suggestion to move in. During the days they went their separate ways. But with the consul's social obligations also having hit the summer doldrums, they whiled away the evenings on the terrace. The first hour was spent catching up on reading and then, outside speakers activated, they listened to Gundula's favourite tracks of Soul.

It was somewhere in the middle of that lazy summer period, spending so much time together, that Gundula began to wonder about something. At first she attributed it to the heat, which could do funny things to the imagination, then to the leisurely pace of the days, which freed the mind. Then she realized her preoccupation with Tony had nothing to do with either. The thought was slowly crystallizing that she was with him all the time, yet scarcely knew him. When she thought about it, in her mind he mostly added up to a collection of negations. He was, to start with, not like other men she'd known. Most were intent on treating women as creatures to be steered towards self-improvement. Nor was he anything like the Russian swimmers she knew when she was a girl. They had a dark side to their passion. She recalled they would speculate for hours about the spiritual dimensions of a man and woman having been united in sex. It had strained her patience to the limit. But Hanbury didn't go in for exploring mystical meaning. Once or twice she actually tried to find out what he thought about their steady sex. He said he looked upon it as a wonderful prelude – to a glass of chilled champagne – adding he was off to get some. She couldn't be too vexed, because he was right: chilled champagne after making love on warm nights was a high. No, he wasn't ponderously self-important like her German men, nor spiritually moody like the Russian ones. Nor was he much of a cowboy – even if she still occasionally called him that – because, really, he lacked swagger. And, despite his talent for the piano, she'd also stopped calling him Chopin. Missing entirely was a volatile artistic temperament. For a while, she teasingly called him Casanova, but Casanova petered out. He was no commanding officer, neither in bed, nor out. He was no intellectual, but not a fool. He wasn't decisive. He wasn't stubborn. He wasn't almost anything. So, other than being pleasant and accommodating, what was he?

The fuzziness of his persona made Gundula recall a saying she some-times heard her grandmother use: things vague when they begin show purpose when they end. Did this apply to Hanbury? Did it apply to them? She also wondered if it applied to her career. Her purpose at the paper was on hold. Having been relegated to the back pages, her assignment now was cabaret reviews. How would that end? She and Tony talked about it once on the terrace. He listened attentively and made a suggestion. He probably meant it well, but it wasn't carefully thought through. "International relations, Gundula," he said. "Write about that. You'd be a good foreign correspondent."

"A foreign correspondent for whom?"

"Your paper."

"I happen to live *here*."

"You'd have to do some travelling."

"The only other language I speak is Russian. Sorry, I'm not interested in going there."

"Go back to school. Learn English. You could practice on me."

"You make it sound so effortless. It don't think it would be easy."

Given the precarious situation at the paper, any hint to management that she was interested in training could mean them easing her out permanently. No, she had to tough it out, spend time camouflaging her talent, put up with writing for the popular culture section, and re-establish credentials.

"If you decided to do it, you'd be successful. I'm sure of it." Hanbury told her. Although Gundula wouldn't admit it, she had once or twice considered, purely in the abstract, what Tony suggested. Gerhard von Helmholtz had hinted she should be doing that too. The problem with their line of thought was that it didn't clarify her career outlook. If anything, it made the future even hazier.

One Saturday morning after breakfast, both of them with their noses in the paper, Hanbury raised the subject once more. He read aloud a headline from the foreign section. "Isn't it interesting what's going on in Papua New Guinea?" he said. Holding his part of the paper between them like a barrier, he then asked for her opinion.

The question irritated her. "I don't know a thing about Papua New Guinea. Do you? Are you planning to become ambassador there?"

"I'm not making any plans. I've learned to keep a low profile." A voice of unconcern spoke from behind a wall of paper.

She could have given a stinging reply to that! She could have speculated that must be why men turn into consuls: because they want no profile. But she didn't. It was simply another case of him being a non-thing. Naturally he wasn't making any plans. He spurned every hint of planning. She didn't consider herself a particularly strong planner either, but all the same she did more of it than him. She was planning a holiday on the Baltic coast to coincide with one her family would be taking. She was hoping he would take a train up for one of the weekends. But when she hinted at it, he was non-committal. Non-planning, non-committing, non everything. She let it pass and instead read to him from the Saturday feature section. "It says here the Russians are beginning to depart. Six hundred thousand of them. Imagine the logistics."

"One of the all-time great military retreats."

Gundula suggested a drive to the Oder River. Perhaps they would see Russians abandoning German soil. Afterwards they could have a picnic.

"If you think Trabi is up to it," he said.

❦

I'm not making any plans. An innocent enough remark. But for Hanbury it went deeper than being disinterested in an ambassadorship in Papua New Guinea. He had a problem Gundula knew nothing about. It originated with Sabine. She had made a proposal that had been gnawing at him these past few days. It occupied his thoughts even as he agreed with Gundula to go look for Russians. By mutual consent, given the fine weather, he and Sabine no longer visited museums. They went walking in the Grunewald instead. A few days before, as usual, Hanbury arrived at *Bücher Geissler* for the outing, but the front door was locked. The lights in the store were off. He rattled the door to see if it might spring open. He pressed his face against the glass and cut off reflections with cupped hands. No sign of life. A grey eminence, someone picking a living off the street, came hobbling by. When the consul began rapping on the glass, he stopped to lick the stubble around his mouth. "Knock as hard as you want," he said. "It won't bring 'im back. He's dead." "Who's dead?" Hanbury asked the scruffy guardian of the street. "Who do you think? The stinker that lived there. He wasn't even that old." The scrawny Methuselah seemed proud he had outlived yet another human being.

The door opened. Sabine, looking grave, motioned Hanbury to enter. The grey eminence spat and shuffled off. "Is it true?" he asked anxiously. "Has Herr Geissler passed away?" She relocked the door, nodding a quick affirmation. He followed her to the rear. "When? How?"

"Yesterday morning. He didn't come down. I called the police. They broke into his apartment on the top floor. He was lying on the floor. A stroke."

"Sabine, how awful for you. I'm so sorry."

"He wasn't well. Something could have happened any time." She tried hard to stay objective, but a tear slid down her cheek.

Hanbury took her by the shoulders and she began to cry, burying her face against his chest. Hanbury tried to give support. A bad patch, he said. It would pass. She had her family, her friends. "I don't know why I'm upset," Sabine blurted. She took out a handkerchief to blow her nose. "I didn't particularly like him. But the last months – after you started coming by – he was different. You meant a lot to him. He's left me the store, the apartments, the whole building. I don't deserve it. I don't like it when people die."

"Wash your face. We'll talk about it over lunch."

They found a table in deep shade under an awning in a nearby restaurant. Hanbury listened to the details. Sabine was well along in making arrangements. Once an ambulance had removed the body, she contacted an undertaker who arrived within an hour. Any next of kin, the undertaker asked? No one she knew about. Was there a will? he next inquired. Occasionally the deceased left instructions for their final ceremony. Sabine replied Geissler had never said anything about a will, although he had recently muttered he was ordering his papers. Check the desk, the undertaker advised. They went into Geissler's office and found an envelope addressed to her with several papers in it, including a handwritten will. "Does it say it's a will?" the undertaker asked. Sabine confirmed it did, but there were no funeral instructions. After the undertaker left, she read the will carefully and called her husband who left his institute immediately. Once he too had read the will, he made an urgent appointment with a notary. Completely genuine, the notary said: Sabine was the beneficiary of everything. They returned to *Bücher Geissler* where a bewildered Sabine began ordering the office and an eager Schwartz descended into the cellar.

"Werner believes the books in the cellar alone are worth a fortune if marketed properly," she told Hanbury.

He had been listening patiently. "I'm glad Geissler left you the store. You deserve it."

"It's exciting. But it frightens me too."

After lunch Sabine claimed she had too much work now for strolling in the Grunewald. Walking back to the store, she said casually, "A note from Herr Geissler mentioned you." Hanbury stopped. "He suggested you become a partner in the store. He wrote he trusted you with the books." Hanbury was speechless. The overall situation with Geissler having died was serious, but the notion of him becoming a clerk in a bookstore was too absurd. Restraining himself from saying anything rash, he stared at Sabine and stayed silent. She wanted to know what he thought about it. She and Werner had discussed it and Werner believed it would work. "I'll need help running the store. It would be wonderful if you decided to settle in Berlin. You say you feel at home here and you're practically a member of the family."

"I don't know anything about books."

"You have a way with books. Herr Geissler noticed it. What you don't know you'd learn. I can't imagine a better business partner. I plan to modernize the store, go upscale." They were back at the *Bücher Geissler* storefront. "Anyway, there's time to think about it." Sabine suddenly had an objective tone, the bearing of a manager. "We can talk about it more next week. Don't feel you have to decide right away." Hanbury nodded. "I'll think it over." Sabine kissed him lightly on both cheeks and disappeared into her new world.

※

The proposal had been preying on him ever since. Gundula would divert his thoughts, but before long it crept back, stalking him, creating an unease, a sense of something slipping out of control, a fear that the uncomplicated mid-week hours with Sabine would end. It was almost perverse, he thought. The last time he saw her husband, when they went to Potsdam, he came away with foreboding. And now for different reasons, Sabine filled him with apprehension too. Could he seriously contemplate spending the years beside her at a sales counter, as if in their advancing age this would correct the failed partnership of their youth?

Even now, heading towards the Oder River, when he should be concentrating on Gundula in her skimpy summer dress, and teasing her for pushing Trabi beyond his limit, Sabine's proposal was with him. The simple thing would be to tell her no, but confronting her made him feel ill at ease. It affected his conscience. His staying would mean much to her. *You're practically a member of the family.* How could he turn that down? How could he reject Sabine a second time? On the other hand, he turned white with fear imagining himself spending decades standing in a store. In comparison to that suffocating vision, the whining and vibrating confines of Trabi seemed like a huge wide open space with plenty of room left to grow.

"Trabi is really flying," he yelled at Gundula, forcing himself back to the present. Her farewell dress for the Russians was all-white with a V-cut plunging front and back. A few grams of silk, no more. A political provocation. "Let's hope he doesn't overheat," Gundula shouted back. The noise level approached that of an open cockpit in a biplane. The exhilaration of flying along in Trabi, always on the edge of mechanical breakdown, must be, Hanbury speculated, the same as the early pilots experienced in their rickety test machines. "Think we'll see some Russians?" he yelled once more, as if they really were in a plane, flying low, maybe over the African savannah, as if in search of elephants. "They're around." Gundula yelled at the top of her lungs, radiating a pilot's confidence.

Hanbury's thoughts, wretchedly stuck for days on selling books, now skipped to another possible future, the one that posed the question of where Gundula fit in his life. Suppose he decided to stay and sell books, how would Gundula react? Badly, he was sure. She would never be part of something which implied that kind of static permanence. A bookstore future, he was convinced, would not have Gundula anywhere near it.

Were there other possibilities? Take the current situation. He and Gundula on the move. Suppose *it* were permanent. He could see Gundula focussed and determined to get them where they planned to go, Gundula finding the solutions to life's labyrinths, Gundula being saucy, Gundula teasing, Gundula punching hole after hole into diplomacy's staidness, Gundula at night, immodest, insatiable and tender. Was a future *without* Gundula imaginable? Hanbury concluded it was not. He had come to love her. She had come in through his front door and taken over. But a precondition for this future, both of them on the move together, was her leaving the paper, which he knew she never would. Whenever he raised the subject, she posed objection after objection, steering the suggestion – and their future – into a swamp where it sank from sight.

A lose-lose situation. If he decided to settle in Berlin Gundula would be scared off, while continuing the affair required subtle assurances that one day it would end. The only way to keep her was one day to leave her. But, if Gundula could not figure in his future, why not stay to sell books? Whichever way he looked at it, his prospects sent shivers up and down his back.

"Russians!" the pilot cried triumphantly. Ahead on the autobahn a long column of military vehicles, camouflaged trucks transporting artillery pieces darkened the right lane. Some kilometres later, they hit a more menacing column: three hundred armoured personnel carriers and heavy, self-propelled, wheeled guns, perfect for manoeuvring in cities, indispensable for suppressing revolution. "Imagine how nervous everybody would get if this were going the other way," Hanbury said.

"What do you know about it? Was your country occupied by Russians?"

"It's our pleasure to have the Yanks close by."

"You can't compare them." In Gundula's opinion Russians were charming individually, but brutal as an army. Americans were the other way around.

Ten minutes later, a third column. This one had stalled. Stretching down the autobahn was an endless gypsy caravan. Trucks filled with civilian goods and hundreds of private vehicles – Ladas, Skodas, Trabis, Wartburgs – half of them in tow. The cars were stacked as full as the trucks. Cardboard boxes, piles of clothing, jerry cans, old radios and TVs, bits of furniture, heaps of random junk. The feared Russian army departing German soil was a rag-tag band on the move. Gundula said there was a rumour that they were even lifting runways off military airfields, carting the concrete slabs home.

They'd seen enough of the humiliation. Gundula swung off the autobahn. She knew an area to the south with lakes. They would picnic there. Half an hour later she drove into a thicket. Once Trabi was parked, Hanbury took the picnic bag and followed Gundula down a trail. The innocent summer sound of people frolicking on a beach drifted at them through the trees.

"In luck," Gundula said. She had spotted a shady area on the forest edge and marched there through loose sand. Hanbury put the picnic bag down. The reflection of the sun off the water blinded him. Shading his eyes he turned to Gundula, who was removing her sneakers. He was about to tell her the spot was well-chosen when, with an easy movement, she raised her dress up over her head and draped it across the picnic bag. Just as fast she stepped out of her panties. Gundula was lovely anytime and especially when naked, but her stripping down to nothing in the open astonished him.

"Gundula, what are you doing!"

"Take your clothes off," she said with a daring smile.

"It's a *public* beach!" Guiltily he scanned the area. Then he saw she wasn't the only one naked.

"Is this a nudist beach?" he asked suspiciously.

"Just a beach. Let's swim."

"I don't have a bathing suit along."

"People wear bathing suits where you come from?"

"In public, actually, yes."

"How silly." Gundula took an aggressive stance. "Start with your T-shirt," she ordered.

Hanbury slipped it over his head, then undid his sandals. Gundula waited for him to go on, but he hesitated. He closed his eyes to let a strange sensation pass. Gundula continued taunting. "Don't be prudish. You'll be noticed only if you swim in walking shorts."

"Why go swimming at all?" he asked defiantly, but it was a last line of defense.

"Tony!" Gundula said impatiently. Reluctantly he unzipped his shorts and stepped out. The underwear was next, whereupon she sweetly took his hand and led him to the water.

The lake was refreshing. They swam out in the direction of the sun, then back. Coming in with the light behind, Hanbury made stealthy observations. Unclothed, overweight bodies lay on the beach like walruses sunning. Others were playful, taut, lithe and heathen. Gundula caught him staring. "Anyone you particularly admire?" she inquired. He said he would rather look at her, but most of her was under water. *Voyeur*, she said. *Human*, he rebutted. *You?* was the reply.

For the picnic Hanbury carried the provisions to an inconspicuous area under a low-branched tree. Away from the water's edge, passing a wine bottle back and forth, eating bread and fruit, they joked about the Russians struggling with the autobahn heat. "A scorched-earth policy in reverse," Hanbury declared. Gundula said she felt sorry for them. If things had worked out differently she might now be living in the Ukraine, she said. She told Tony about Vassiliev. "I was in love with him. I thought I'd marry him. I went to see him in Kiev." "And?" Hanbury asked, drinking wine directly from the bottle. "I wasn't sure it would work. I needed to think about it and left. Not long afterwards he married someone else. But we stayed on good terms. He sends me pictures of his children." Gundula stretched out on the sand, clasped her hands under the back of her head and closed her eyes. Feeling the wine, Hanbury languidly took time to do two things: he reflected on what Gundula had just said *and* practised voyeurism. He studied the wet hair clinging to her head; he scanned the neck, the small breasts – dark, perky, pointy nipples – the belly and its undulating contours funnelling down to a jet-black crop of hair. From here the legs began a lovely journey to the feet. Intoxicated – by the wine, but more so by her beauty – he flipped onto a side, leaning on an elbow and thought. Gundula had almost married?

With eyes closed, she wanted to talk. She described her family in Schwerin, the brother seeking asylum in Vienna, a father refusing to continue with Olympic doping, the Stasi targeting her family. Things she had not talked about before. She was serious and reflective and it reminded Hanbury of her best columns. This was the other Gundula speaking, the one he once despaired he'd ever get to know. "For some reason we never talk about ourselves," she continued. "Why is that, Tony?" She didn't often call him by his first name. He would be *Cowboy* (if he showed chivalry), *Your Excellency* (when he wore a suit), *Superman* (if changed a light bulb) or, when he returned to bed with chilled champagne, *Herr Bacchus*. He presumed *Voyeur* would now be added to the list. Today, she had called him Tony several times. What was happening? He didn't answer her question. Instead he said something he had long wanted to share. "I've got a Stasi file too."

"I don't believe you."

"It's true." He told her how he had discovered it, that it got started because of Günther Rauch. What was in it? Well, once the system started on him it seemed incapable of stopping. It kept track of him for decades. Trivia. Masses of it. And what was his reaction when he looked into it? "A sense of being taking apart, a sense that little pieces of me were being studied. My life reduced to something like a shop floor manual. At the time I thought you ought to write a column about it."

"You should have said something. I might have. Today I could only touch the subject if it were expressed as cabaret." Hanbury thought he detected a bitter note, but it passed and her humour came on. "Diplomats as shop floor manuals," she said impishly. "Good cabaret potential. Let's think of a title." From her prone position she looked up. "How about, *Consul ex machina*."

After a pause he replied drily, "Why not, *Consul machina est?*"

"Also very good. We could have two pieces. Maybe more. You have so many sides." She became serious again. "We have more in common than I thought. Tell me how you got to be Chopin? You never told me that."

The uncomplicated banter was comfortable, almost therapeutic. Was it the effect of the sun and the wine? Or, having bared his body, had he become less hesitant to bare his soul? Whatever the reason, Hanbury was not inclined to be evasive, not this time. "Got an hour?" he asked.

"Until dawn, if you need it."

Hanbury told Gundula the story of Claudette Cadieux, a talented music student who made the serious mistake of falling in love with Hanbury's father. He was from Moose Jaw, she from Montreal, meeting when they were both students at McGill. What could they possibly have seen in each other? Was it Harold's self-assurance that impressed Claudette? Did she believe him when he said no place on earth was more beautiful than the prairies? Who knows? The end result was marriage and they headed west. A position waited for him at the experimental farm in Indian Head. "She didn't know what she was being taken to. She had no idea what it would be like." Gundula said she knew all about that. It was no different when she travelled to Kiev.

Hanbury elaborated. Claudette had no inkling she was going into a desert. It wasn't the countryside that struck her that way when they arrived. Summer rain had fallen; the land was green. Her first impression of the prairie was its melancholy. But no, the desert wasn't in the land-scape. It was something she felt in her heart. After a year or two, Claudette could rattle off the components of this inner desert: an incomprehension that someone from Montreal might speak a different language; little appreciation for the arts – concerts, theatre, exhibitions – things she liked to have around her; no cosy tea houses or specialty stores with stylish clothes; no animated summer gatherings on neighbourhood sidewalks; no night life; no tree-lined streets with tasteful villas; no cathedral; no majestic river spanned by equally majestic bridges. Moving to Indian Head, Claudette convinced herself, was like moving to nothing. When she tried to share this view with Harold, he said she was going about it the wrong way. She should stop comparing, he said. His culture, he argued, was subtler than Montreal's and she should open up to it. He left her alone to do so, because already in the early years he was preoccupied with the daily ritual of warfare, combatting the drifting off of soil. Into this situation, Hanbury told Gundula, he, Anthony Ernest – *Antoine* to his mother – was born.

Claudette focussed on him in the same way her husband did on prairie dirt. She wanted her son to become what she might have been: a concert pianist. He had her talent and every day, every week, every month she worked on Antoine's piano future. He gave concerts in school auditoriums, church basements, community halls. She organized a recital in Regina attended by two hundred people. He accepted the regime. After all, he and his mother were two bodies suffused by a single soul. Everyday she told him that.

Doubt about this did not arise until he was in his teens, when he became convinced he wanted to be normal and not treated like a freak. He was tired of not being allowed to play basketball because he might break a finger, of not touching a hockey stick because it could stiffen his wrists, of not hanging out around the curling rink because throwing a stone might cause a shoulder dislocation. Tensions grew. The unitary soul was being pried apart. It culminated in a tearful session with Antoine uttering cruel oaths that he would never again touch a piano. He left for Saskatoon to study political theory. Could anyone be more normal than that? After eighteen years, Claudette's desert now rolled in with a vengeance. She went from one nervous breakdown to the next. "She was less coherent all the time. In the end she wasted away. There was some gossip that my father and I neglected her. That that's what killed her." The descending sun was reaching forward under the low-hanging branches. As he talked, Hanbury had watched the edge of the tree's shadow steadily recede up Gundula's body until she lay entirely illuminated, as if she were in a spotlight on a stage.

"That was unfair," Gundula said. A slow stretch ended with a lazy twist onto her side.

"What was?" The light had reached him too, but he was oblivious to it.

"Being held responsible for your mother dying."

"It was just gossip."

"You dismissed the accusation?"

"Yes."

Thinking back, he believed he began distancing himself from certain things at an early age. The more his mother forced him into the margins, the more he wanted to be mainstream. "Something in me began rejecting her early on." "A habit you haven't shaken," Gundula said casually. She was playing with the sand, taking a handful and allowing it to slip out of her fist as if through an hourglass. "Wanting to be normal?" "No. Rejecting people. Keeping them distant." When Hanbury didn't reply, Gundula ceased playing with the sand. She looked directly at him, but he was as expressionless as ever. He stared at the picnic bag for a while, then he shifted his gaze towards the water. He seemed to want to see beyond the sun. "Oh, I don't know," he said with a slight hesitation. "I don't think so. I don't know of anyone I do that to."

❧

After midnight in the Greco-Roman villa, Tony beside her breathing in a steady rhythm, Gundula reviewed the day's events. Twice they made love – the moment they were back from the beach, and again just now, pushing the consul into his peaceful sleep. The love-making was good, but better still had been his suggestion that he take a train next weekend to the Baltic coast to join her and her parents. It signified more to Gundula than she had expressed. Suppose you lose your way? she had asked. You'll find me, he had answered. Why the change? Was it because of the quarrel they had on the beach, the catharsis that took place, because they had, so to speak, cleaned themselves out? Had that rendered them different? Had things *permanently* changed?

Tony's non-response to her assertion that he tended to reject people was totally infuriating. Another example of masterful evasion. He was always steering normal subjects for discussion into a quicksand from which nothing emerged. She told him that. The vehemence surprised him. Pardon? he said with wide-open, innocent eyes. What exactly did she mean? Could she run all that by him once more? She took him back to the evening when he had a breakdown at the piano. "Remember?" Gundula asked severely. "You were unwell because I reminded you of your mother. We drank too much whiskey. Remember? You never did answer my question." The consul lost composure. Callously he wanted to know what *that* evening had to do with *this* picnic, which he had been finding very pleasant. "Everything," Gundula replied. "Because it's taken until now for me to get a simple answer. But even so, there's more of the same. All the time. We live together, but you won't open up. We seldom talk."

That's when the altercation began. Accusations and counter-accusations. Gundula learned some important things. He agreed, yes, that their easy-going domesticity was superficial, but that was because *she* wanted it that way. What? she said with disbelief. He admitted it suited him too. Why? Because, first, he had serious misgivings about the long term viability of two cultures mixing, and after today she should understand that. Second, there was the complicating factor that one day he would leave. *Let's not hide our heads in the sand!* He said this so loud he almost shouted. Her non-reaction, he claimed, to his suggestions that she pursue other journalistic avenues made him assume she would stay in Berlin. Always. Forever. And he respected that. But in those circumstances, since they had no future, he wondered rhetorically, what was the best course? Go deep, or stay on the surface? He answered his own question with an answer which came out as a kind neo-epicurean *cri de coeur: Let's just enjoy the present!*

His assumption was wrong, she said, deeply stung. Wretchedly wrong. She had thought about becoming a foreign correspondent more often than he could know. She had also contemplated learning English. She had even considered free-lancing if the paper were to decide not to keep her. But none of that would work if he didn't want it to. Hanbury's mouth fell open so wide she had nearly asked him to close it. *I had no idea. Really, I didn't. Gundula, that's terrific.*

Another revelation followed. Since she had told him about her Russian boyfriend, he wanted to tell her about a liaison he once had, at the same time he got to know Günther Rauch. The story was somewhat long. By the time he finished it the sun had dipped below the trees on the far shore. He admitted he should have told her earlier. His panicky flight from Berlin, he took pains to point out, was not a rejection of Sabine. He had merely been afraid of a repetition of the disastrous marriage of Harold and Claudette. He wanted Gundula to know that. Gundula said she left Kiev in circumstances that were not too different. Such things happen when you're young, she added, putting it into a broad perspective. After this unburdening, the consul was a different man. Gundula, let's go home, he said, which was a far cry from, *Shall we go to my place?*

It was when Trabi clattered back to Berlin that he sprung the surprise, the one that thrilled her. "I'm not doing anything next weekend," he said. "I could take a train to the Baltic. You could introduce me to your folks." Scarcely suppressing her excitement, Gundula teased him to travel light. "Leave your bathing suit at home. Up there, textiles are optional." Once the front door of the mansion shut behind them, they turned on each other with passion and made love, first standing up, then half-crouching on the landing. After showering they retired to the terrace. She picked out the music; he fetched a tray of food and a bottle of champagne. The disc she chose was by the band that played at the Ball. "Remember the diplomatic shuffle?" Gundula asked, laughing. "All I remember about that night is that you were annoyed I didn't right away hustle you into bed." He shook his head recalling the depravity. "Also, you promised to teach me the quickstep. And where is it?" "By next season I'll have you doing the quickstep and the tango." He said, since this was her favourite music, they could start with a little shuffling now. In the night air on the terrace they danced to Soul and in the middle of it he whispered that he loved her. "I see," she murmured back, almost adding, *I'd like that on paper, signed by a head of state and ratified by a Parliament.* But a long kiss substituted for all of it.

The second round of love lasted longer than the one on the landing. The smell of it lingered. As long as it did, Gundula didn't want to sleep. She lay wide awake, thinking of the future. Once the summer was finished, her evenings would again be spent in the halls of cabaret, and the mornings doing the reviews. But the afternoons would be used for learning English. And the words she learned she would practice on the consul after he came home at night. The whole time she was awake she thought forward to preparing for a great experiment. It was hours before she slept.

PATERFAMILIAS II

o Bilinski, like a caged Rocky Mountain cougar, was pacing back and forth along the bank of windows in his office. Elma was having trouble placing a call. The delay had brought him close to boiling. This day, like the ones before, had started well enough. For a few weeks now Bilinski had been enjoying an inner peace he hadn't known for years. The fact was, he had bought a ranch. Because of that he was now spending a good part of each day before the windows, studying the distant Gatineaus, thinking quietly of the future. Earlier this afternoon, he had slipped once more into a meditation. The Gatineaus didn't exactly remind him of the Alberta foothills. They were not as big, not rugged, certainly not dangerous. They lacked a spectacular unbroken mountain wall as soaring backdrop. But all the same, if he looked at them long enough – and made an imaginative jump – he could picture them as being emptier and wilder than they were. Which made him think of home. Here in the east, Sharon, the children, the whole family had bobbed on the surface of things too long. The little skiff that was their life had been battered by the unclean Eastern sea. He was glad to be getting back to the West, back to purity and peace.

Bo had confided to Sharon that during the second half of his earthly existence he wanted to be surrounded by real things: open country, horses, cattle, the annual noise and dust of roundups. He went so far as to tell her that the years in government had made him feel polluted. It was because of Policy. Suppose, he asked her, that Policy's intangibility were transformed into some form of matter – what would it be? Festering mucous? Pus itself? And the nightmares hadn't helped. In them, he experienced a slimy substance oozing from his pores. "The crap of government," he whispered to his wife during the hours of insomnia, "I tell you, Sharon, it's like sitting in a vat of goddamn filth." Bo Bilinski cracked his knuckles as he recalled the fateful confession. The next day Sharon left for Calgary to find a ranch.

The Service had been the final straw. With it the nightmares began. All along Bilinski had known that work in government could make you walk and talk and smell like Policy, if you weren't careful. But he had always managed to outrun its peculiar fetor. Hadn't he shot Tax Policy to pieces without being corrupted? And blown Competition Policy apart with his swagger undiminished? Even a thorough evisceration of Industrial Policy hadn't threatened his survival as a human being. But running Foreign Policy forced him to the conclusion it was time to quit. Foreign Policy was inconstant, a moving target, weaving and ducking, all the time. Even if he happened to land a blow it seemed he had only punched a bog, because foul vapours were suddenly released. Bo Bilinski swore that Foreign Policy sucked at him, drew him in, and the harder he struggled, the faster he got pulled down.

Sharon's resolve saved him. The end of *all* Policy was in sight. Thumbs stuck in his belt, meditating by the windows, motionless as a medicine man on an outcrop over the Great Plains, Bo thought of spiritual cleansing on his new Bo-Bil Ranch, and of the buffer – three hours hard riding – to the next-nearest sprinkling of civilization. His final weeks as high priest were characterized by one simple instruction to Elma. *No goddamn calls.*

But today, in the middle of the afternoon, during a reverie which had him doing an easy gallop through a gully, he suddenly got bushwhacked. He was instantly so fucking mad he wanted to quick-lynch the assailant. That son-of-a-bitch Manteaux was calling. *Tell him to bugger off*, Bilinski yelled at Elma through the intercom. Having to listen to Manteaux was worse than to coyotes howling. But Harry Manteaux was insistent, threatening to go higher.

"What do you want, Harry?" Bilinski finally snarled into the phone. "I'm pretty damn busy. I'm gonna put you on the speaker 'cause I've got urgent papers to sign. So, what'cha waiting for? Get on with it, goddammit."

Bilinski heard Manteaux's excruciating voice through the speaker. Manteaux, Bilinski suspected, was a pervert because he sounded like one. He had a high, nasal voice which revved up like a siren. But this time, although Manteaux was whining, he was ordering too. He gave a speech full of orders. It made Bilinski listen. He stopped looking at the Gatineaus. "I gave explicit instructions to someone to tell that asshole to behave," Bilinski yelled back at last in the direction of his desk. But the argument had no impact. Manteaux kept coming, kept jabbing through the phone, and Bilinski began hurting. He finally went to his desk, grabbed the mouthpiece and hissed. "Keep your paws off. He's my guy. I decide what happens. Not you. And not some dumb Kraut in Munich either. I'll have this fixed in half an hour. Somebody'll let you know. Bugger off, Harry." Bilinski slammed the phone down. "Elma," he ordered through the intercom, "get me that son-of-a-bitch Hanbury in Berlin."

In Berlin, the phone rang and rang. Bilinski opened the door to the ante-chamber. "Well?" he barked. "No answer yet," Elma sang brightly. But just as she was about to stop trying, the instrument in Berlin clicked. "Consul Hanbury?" Elma asked. "Yes? Thank goodness you're there. Please stand by for Mr. Bilinski." Bilinski closed his door and took the phone. "Hanbury?" he threatened. "Where the hell were you?" Bilinski listened to a few words from the other end. He tensed. "You wanna know who I am?" he said with disbelief. "Oh Holy Jesus! Look in the goddamn phone book. Page one. At the top. The very top. Now listen, you've destroyed some of my time today, so what I'm gonna say is short and sweet. One ground rule. You listen. No questions, no rebuttals. You do as I tell you and you'll do it smartly. Understand? Tomorrow, Consul Hanbury, you'll be on a plane. I don't know which plane. I don't know where it'll take you. One thing is sure. It's gonna take you far away. After it leaves you're never gonna set foot in crappy Berlin again. Got that?" The high priest waited for an answer. "Got that?" he repeated. "Well good. In half an hour someone will call to tell you all you need to know. That's it. I'll share a personal comment. You screwed up a couple of months ago. Recall that? You've done it again. That's not good. If I didn't hate a certain pervert across town, you'd be out on your ass. If you wanna keep your job, watch yourself from now on. Okay? That's free advice." Bilinski put the phone down. He buzzed Elma. "Get me Irving Heywood."

The Investitures priest was used to the urgent calls. Bilinski kept in touch throughout Bitrap and Heywood came to believe that although rock hard on the outside the high priest was a squishy noodle, a kind of dreamer, underneath. At key moments his eyes would turn glassy and he didn't seem to hear. Heywood also concluded Bilinski hated being in the East, which, in his developing theory of causes and effects, might be the reason why Bilinski's mouth was so foul. On his home turf he might be chatty, even witty, a man with rough but charming edges. Heywood liked to think this was true of himself too – tough as nails on the outside, but piloted by a caring soul. Realizing they had things in common gave Heywood a feeling of kinship with Bilinski.

"Good afternoon, Sir," he said pleasantly when Elma put him through.

"Hi, Irv. How are you."

"Very well, Sir. Thank you. How are Sharon and the children?"

"Good, Irv. Pretty damn fine."

Bitrap from Heywood's perspective had been a wild success. As with any mass public execution, the first chop caused squeamishness to ripple through the Service. The second wasn't quite so bad, and the third easier still. From then on, the slaughter was routine. The old hands were soon gone. One reason why Bitrap's virulence played out so fast was Robbie. How she silenced the snipers! Too bad, Heywood had thought in the middle of the massacre, that Hannah had never borne him a daughter. She would have been like Robbie, he was sure. The diplomatic list was through too. With Robbie's help he had created a model of inter-generational correctness. Fresh-faced boys and girls were heading out into the world to play ambassador. The dip list through, Bitrap done: the Investitures priest believed there were good reasons for him and the high priest to be chummy.

"Irv, listen," the high priest continued. "There's a job for you. Remember that fairy in Berlin? What's his name?" "Anthony Hanbury," Heywood said crisply. "Right. Just talked to the son-of-a-bitch. Told him he's out." "Sir!" Heywood exclaimed. "Whatever for? If it has to do with that problem of reporting, I had a good chat with him back then. He's been producing marvellous material." "Irv, listen." Bilinski lowered his voice, an invitation to participate in a secret. Heywood loved it when the high priest did that. "I've got nothing against your buddy in Berlin. I want you to know it's that sodomite Manteaux again. Remember? He tried to bugger me that other time." "I do," said Heywood solemnly. "Are you sure he's a sodomite?" "Sure. His type, you know, spooks, they fuck the world in the strangest places." "Well, yes," Heywood half agreed, though he would have put it differently.

"This is what you gotta do. The longer we talk, the less time you got. By my watch there's twenty-five minutes left. You go through your bag of tricks and find your pal a new assignment. Not here. Somewhere out there. Phone him. Tell him where he's going. Get him booked on an airplane leaving Berlin tomorrow…"

"Sir! Tomorrow. That's impos…"

"*Irv*," the high priest reprimanded, "don't interrupt. I haven't goddamn well finished."

Bilinski continued his precise instructions. "Hanbury leaves Berlin tomorrow. Arrange it. Don't be sneaky about it, Irv. Send him some place. Far from here. Okay? After you've done it, get your secretary to phone Manteaux's lady. Don't do it yourself. Got that? We're not on speaking terms with buggerers. Not me. Not you. Not anybody who's got rank. So, your secretary tells the other one that our man in Berlin has new instructions. She phones once more later to pass on information on tomorrow's flights. That's it Irv. A half-hour. Not difficult. When it's done, relax. Forget it happened." The high priest put the phone down.

A late afternoon mood was settling over the hills outside Bilinski's windows. His mind was back to where it was before, except he saw himself coming out of the gully. He had roped the bushwhacker, tied him to a tree. A pretty mountain valley stretched before him with light hard as a diamond and air clean as glacial ice.

Heywood dropped his head. His great frame heaved in a tearless sobbing. But he regrouped. If he had one strength, he liked to think, it was bouncing back. With a push of his feet, he rolled his chair to the computer. He scrolled through the list of diplomatic missions where staff openings had existed, not expecting much of a harvest. The annual assignment changes had all fallen into place. He had one hope, a position where the new incumbent hadn't yet left town. The Investitures priest checked dozens and found one. His first thought was that it was too good, *too senior* for Tony, but hang it, the situation wasn't ordinary. Besides, the Berlin reports had raised Tony's trading value. Resolved to do the high priest's will, he phoned Robert Etchley in the Asian Temple who, Heywood knew, had a wife, two children and a large debt on a new house in the suburbs.

"Bob?" Heywood said in a no-nonsense voice, a mimic of Bilinski's. "Irving Heywood. Bad news. Your assignment's off." A pause, then excitement and much hand wringing. "Sorry. That's the way it is. Nothing's ever certain. You know that." A long, emotional confession, Etchley revealing he could not *afford* headquarters any longer. His debts were mounting. Also, the wife and children were set to go. The garage sale was over, the kids' bikes sold, the house rented. "Too bad about all that," said Heywood. Swearing came next. The Investitures priest listened patiently, but ignored the demand for an explanation. "Bob," Irving said finally, "you'll be at the top of the list next year. I promise. We'll talk about it soon." The Investitures priest hung up, leaving Etchley the task of breaking the news to his wife. Service experience showed, Heywood knew, that she was suddenly predestined to have an immediate and total breakdown.

Ten minutes were already gone. He next called South Africa. Luck was holding. Ambassador Lecurier was not yet in bed.

"Irving, how absolutely delightful to hear from you," the ambassador exclaimed. "When are you coming this way? Make up a reason, then combine it with a holiday."

"Hannah would love to get back to Africa, Jacques. Our second boy was born there. Did you know that?"

"It's a wonderful continent for making children," the ambassador agreed.

"Jacques, listen, I'm a little pressed. We'll chat another time. I had to cancel Etchley. I'm sending you Anthony Hanbury instead. He'll be arriving tomorrow or the day after. I guess that's all right?"

"That's a bombshell," said the ambassador calmly. "I was looking forward to Bob. He has a delightful wife. Ever met her?"

No, thought the Investitures priest, but I expect soon to hear her primordial scream penetrating all this way from the suburbs. "Haven't had the pleasure, Jacques."

"Not being married myself, it helps if the number two has a presentable wife. Hanbury's wife – what's she like?"

"Hasn't got one."

"Oh my! Another bachelor. Well, someone to take prowling." The ambassador seemed tickled by the thought.

"You're both adults," Heywood said gruffly. "You two can prowl to your hearts' content. What do you say, Jacques? A green light?"

"I don't know Hanbury," the ambassador said cautiously. "Could he handle it here? The post-apartheid world is demanding."

"He's more than up to it, Jacques. He worked for me. Best deputy I ever had. Before that he did a bang-up job in Kuala Lumpur as number two, and this last year he ran the office in Berlin. He's done wonderful work there. Superb reports, approaching the quality of yours when you were in your prime."

"And when was that?"

"Peking, I'd say."

"Thank you. That's right. And why is he leaving Berlin? He's been there one year, you say?" Lecurier looked for a hidden angle.

"Boredom."

"Ah, a sapping disease. He'd be cured quickly here. Well, I suppose it's fine. After the gentle pleasures of Asia and the rigours of the German way, experiencing Africa's earthiness should round him out nicely."

"I'm sure you'll broaden his horizons," Heywood said and hung up. Five more minutes gone. The clock was ticking. He instructed an underling to begin flight reservations. Next, the Investitures priest dialled Berlin.

Hanbury picked up the phone before the first ring finished.

"Yes?" he said urgently.

"Tony, hello. Irving Heywood here. Everything fine?"

"Irving! What the hell is going on?" Hanbury jumped at Heywood through the phone line like a wild man.

"Your boat's sprung a little leak, Tony. Nothing I can't fix," soothed Heywood.

"Why did the high priest call me?"

"What did he say? Tell me."

The reply to this was shouted back with such force that Heywood had to hold the phone away from his ear. But despite the volume there was no insight. Heywood wondered who was more upset, Hanbury or Etchley. Most upset of all, he imagined, would be *Mrs.* Etchley. "Settle down, Tony," he counselled. "It's not the end of the world. I've found you a new spot. Right up your alley. You'll be working with the most wonderful ambassador we have. The pair of you will see eye to eye on everything. That's my feeling."

"I want to know what's happening!"

"I was hoping you would tell me," Heywood probed once more.

"Who's put you up to this?"

"Bilinski wants it. Arnold's booking your flight."

"There *has* to be an explanation. It makes no sense. I'm just beginning to hit my stride here. You wanted reports; I did them. Krauthilda called and said they were fine. I plan to keep doing them. Why change things?"

"The reports were first class. Everyone agrees, the high priest included." Heywood fished a last time. "The spooks are involved. Did you know that? Once your situation is rearranged, we're to let them know it's done. Any idea why? Any odd experiences lately?"

Heywood received a loud and foul reply. He sighed. "Look at your new assignment as an improvement, Tony. You'll be front and centre again, like in the Priory." More deep, profanely uttered despondency from Berlin came at the priest. He decided to make it short. "Pretoria. Number two. Lecurier is waiting for you with open arms." The voice in Berlin now asked specific questions. "Arnold is making the arrangements. He'll phone in minutes. You know, you and Lecurier, two bachelors, you'll have quite a time. Makes us married folks wonder if we made the right decision." When Hanbury remained silent, Heywood said, "Give me a call when you're there, Tony. Let's stay in touch." Then he put the phone down. Three minutes were left.

The Investitures priest rose. "Call Mr. Manteaux's office," he ordered his secretary. "Confirm Berlin has been vacated." He continued down the hall to check on Arnold's progress. The voice in Berlin had been belligerent, even ungrateful. A side to Tony he hadn't seen before. Heywood shook his head with sadness. Next time they talked he'd raise it.

Throughout the night the consul wandered in a daze, back and forth through his mansion. Arnold rang first. He was followed by another, an unknown caller who informed him he would be escorted to the airport in the morning. No indication exactly when or by whom. Somewhere in the night Hanbury packed a bag. As the hours passed, in a tangle of contradictory emotions, he fixed again and again on two cryptic remarks. *You screwed up twice*, according to the high priest; *It's the spooks* came courtesy of Heywood. There had to be a misunderstanding, a big one, something truly grotesque, but what? His mind jumped crazily, from aimless reasoning to revisiting all that happened since arriving in Berlin. He had to contact Gundula – she had to know – but Gundula was not reachable. He visualized her on a railway platform in three days time, waiting for him, waiting until the train emptied, afterwards driving off, her worst fears confirmed. He ought to phone Sabine, but tell her what? I'll be off in the morning. Good luck with the store. Impossible. Why the spooks? All night the same question. Why the spooks? And if this was a second time, when was the first? The time he stood with von Helmholtz on his balcony?

All night Hanbury stalked what he couldn't see and pursued thoughts that led nowhere. Pacing without pause, considering one stillborn theory after another, his torment mounted. In the early morning, emptied out, incapable of thinking clearly about what was and about what might be, he went onto the terrace. The sun was just up; the lit edges of the trees seemed to be burning. He and Gundula had seen it often enough. The doorbell sounded. Gundula? He waited. But there was no second ring in quick succession, no rescuer's grin waiting for him on the doorstep. The bell sounded again, longer, insistent. He pulled himself together. Whoever it was would see him leave with dignity. But his composure fell apart.

"Gerhard!"

"Ready to go?" the Chief of Protocol asked.

Hanbury looked past him. Two vehicles were in the driveway, von Helmholtz's stretch Mercedes and a fast BMW. Three men, humourless barons wearing loose jackets, were planted between the cars. "Who are they?" he asked. "Representatives of agencies interested in your departure. You have some explaining to do. Are you packed?" The Chief of Protocol was impatient. "I have to explain?" the consul said with a bitter laugh. "Is that your luggage?" Von Helmholtz pointed at a suitcase.

The barons watched the consul pull the front door shut, descend the steps and heave the bag into the Mercedes trunk. "*Zum Flughafen*," the Chief of Protocol ordered. The motorcade pulled out the driveway, the trio in the BMW riding guard. "I have no idea why this is happening." Hanbury protested from deep in the back seat. "Somebody's made a big mistake."

Von Helmholtz didn't reply. He saw Hanbury was agitated, even bewildered. Despite his own outward calm, von Helmholtz was not at ease either. He'd slept no more than the consul. Half the night was spent studying a file, the other half he was on the phone. At times it had been tense. *Another witchhunt!* he claimed angrily at the beginning. But supporting information began arriving by fax. Von Helmholtz stood at the machine. Page after page streamed in, a flood of supporting information. He studied the material, then called Graf Bornhof back. *Preposterous!* he barked, though he was less sure than he sounded. In the early hours he had to yield, in part because the proof was unassailable, in part because confirmation came that the consul's own people wanted him out. Very well, he agreed, he would see to it that Consul Hanbury had an orderly departure. Graf Bornhof informed him the situation was more complex. Other agencies besides his now had the file. The protectors of the constitution as well as the law's enforcers, both had decided they had a stake. They insisted on witnessing that the consul got on a plane. Von Helmholtz shook his head, but acquiesced. He was too tired for turf wars.

The night's drama had lengthened because of negotiations with Ottawa. Pullach, Graf Bornhof confided, wanted him declared *persona non grata* and, initially, on the other side of the Atlantic they agreed. Then came a change of mind. *Put everything on hold. Do nothing for half an hour.* A counter-proposal was made. Make the departure look routine. Avoid adverse publicity. Present it as a diplomatic reassignment. Pullach was against it, until von Helmholtz weighed in. He ruled a quiet removal would be in everyone's interest.

Now, as the Mercedes sped along the quiet Dahlem avenues, von Helmholtz glanced at the collapsed figure next to him. The posture was at odds with the evidence. "I was on the phone all night because of you."

From somewhere behind a pathetic and defeated face came lingering defiance. "What for? Why didn't you call me?"

"Know somebody called Schwartz?"

The consul almost taunted him. "Schwartz? Of course."

"Tell me about him."

"Nothing to tell. A professional acquaintance, pure and simple."

"You never suspected he might be...questionable?"

Just another professional acquaintance, was the answer, like dozens, amongst whom was a Chief of Protocol as well. All above board. The voice trailed off in disgust.

"If what I've seen is true, you've betrayed the trust of many people. On my side they wanted you declared *persona non grata* for what you and Schwartz were up to, but someone on your side put a foot down. *Persona non grata.* It would have been quite an achievement." An exclamation of more defiance was followed by an expression of utter disbelief. Von Helmholtz decided to administer shock. "You may be the most two-faced person I have ever met." As the consul digested this, von Helmholtz continued. "Why did you take up with Schwartz? I'd like your version."

Hanbury's voice dropped. Some of the fight was coming out. There wasn't much to say. He occasionally had a drink with Schwartz to talk about their work. He once located a rare book for him at Geissler's. When headquarters demanded reports, Schwartz helped with analysis and background, a favour in return for finding him the book. But the information could have come from anyone, from the Chief of Protocol, for example.

"I read the reports," von Helmholtz said. "Clever documents. Penetrating. But ideologically disturbing in spots." The information faxed by Graf Bornhof had taken hours to absorb. "I don't think you're admitting everything you know," von Helmholtz said. "You didn't suspect anything? You never worried what Schwartz might be?"

The consul shook his head. Schwartz was the husband of a friend and that was all.

"There's more to it than that." In a dull tone, like someone reciting lottery numbers, von Helmholtz described Schwartz as a leading figure in a small organization with questionable political objectives. They wanted a halt to what they saw as a slide to political weakness, to an enfeeblement of the state. The members were well-placed and well-to-do. Schwartz was the thinker, the ideologue. His task was to draw up a political platform and action plan that would look reasonable and doable.

Hanbury, recognizing some of the language, stiffened.

The Chief of Protocol continued. "They have an extreme, conservative agenda, ultra-right, but it's cunningly presented. Some people would see it as far-sighted. Such thinking touches tender nerves, Tony. It's unclear how far Schwartz and his clique would be prepared to go. I'm informed that some time ago he began cultivating the neo-Nazi scene. So, once more, for my own peace of mind, tell me about your role? Are you a closet neo-fascist."

"A closet neo-fascist! Gerhard! For God's sake!"

The Mercedes had turned onto the autobahn and was accelerating to the airport. Von Helmholtz recalled the other time he and Graf Bornhof had discussed a file. That time, they agreed it drew absurd conclusions. This time, Graf Bornhof said the material was not conjectural; it was irrefutable. The consul had to go. But von Helmholtz had doubts, and Hanbury's reaction sowed more doubt. He decided to test him further. "The irony is," von Helmholtz said calmly, "that not long ago certain people tried to convince me you were a neo-communist. Remember our talk about Günther Rauch?"

The consul made silent gestures. His disbelief was so colossal that he was barely capable of finding words. "Idiotic," he said at last. "I'm not a neo-fascist. I'm not a neo-communist. I'm not a neo-anything."

"Certain people think there's a connection of sorts between Günther Rauch and Schwartz."

The material from Graf Bornhof setting out a conspiracy theory linked the early period of the consul's activities in Berlin to what he did in the last months. For von Helmholtz this had been the least acceptable part of the new file. *Facts twisted to support a pre-conceived idea*, he had said. *It destroys the credibility of the argument.* Graf Bornhof quickly backed off. The new file stood on its own, he claimed. It didn't need to be linked to anything. But von Helmholtz put the connection to the consul all the same, to see the reaction. "Certain people," he said, as vaguely as before, "think you took up with Günther Rauch to lay a smokescreen. They believe you wanted to create an impression of being connected to the far left to hide your real intention – which is to advance the interests of the far right. Your reports have been interpreted as hiding a neo-fascist agenda. Did you really come to Berlin to help Schwartz lay his hands on politically destructive information?"

Hanbury could take no more. "It is utterly ridiculous," he said meekly.

"That may be, but some people don't think so." Von Helmholtz was still unsure. Why didn't the consul open up? As blandly as before, he turned the tourniquet still tighter. "Most of what I know is not ridiculous at all. You've been seen – photographed in fact – with Schwartz in some kind of neo-Nazi club. More damning is what you did for him in the Stasi files. What can you tell me about that?"

Hanbury's head sank into his hands. An urgent, broken whispering began. The rear seat became a confessional. Yes, he worked the Stasi files. Schwartz was doing a monograph on Nazi war criminals. Cooperation between former Nazis and the Stasi would be one dimension. He asked for help. And why not? Revelations from the files were in the papers every day. Access to the Normannenstrasse complex was no problem. But the idea from the beginning was to look for former Nazis, not abet the far right. And, yes, there was an outing to Potsdam. An unguarded remark about skinheads had been taken by Schwartz as a challenge. "I was there for twenty minutes, Gerhard. I wasn't comfortable. I never want to go near a place like that again."

Stacked against all that emotion, von Helmholtz knew, were hard facts. He did not relent. "You spent a week doing Schwartz's bidding in the Stasi files to flesh out a paragraph or two for a monograph?" he said incredulously. "A whole week?" Hanbury now let all he knew flow. He described the process, Schwartz providing names, he tracking them down, going ever deeper into the files.

"You found what Schwartz wanted?"

"Yes."

"Schwartz was happy?"

Hanbury nodded.

"And you were convinced you were looking for Nazi war criminals."

"At the end I suspected some of them were not."

"Why?"

"I found a room. *DDB.* The files there referred to people too young to have been Nazis and they didn't seem involved with Nazi things – the death camps, extermination of the Jews, all those things. But most of the information I took out made little sense to me."

"It did to Schwartz?"

"It seemed to."

Von Helmholtz had the full picture now. He felt tired. Throughout the night he pressed Graf Bornhof to provide *all* the information, not just carefully chosen pieces. After a further stream of faxes, a few pieces began to fit. The constitution's protectors had tried to trace Hanbury's paths criss-crossing through the files, but failed. He had handled too many indices; the routes were too random. So law enforcement got involved and broke into Schwartz's university office, where they found neatly ordered bundles of cards covered front and back with notes in the consul's handwriting.

"You were not looking for old Nazis, Tony," von Helmholtz said wearily. "You were picking out Stasi collaborators in the west. *DDB: Deutsch-Deutsche Beziehungen.* Inner German Relations, that's what you were looking at. Dozens of West Germans, well-known and in high places. You were handing Schwartz one political time bomb after another."

Hanbury, spirit crushed and in a hoarse voice, said he didn't know, he really didn't.

"Politicians, senior government officials, journalists, scientists, businessmen, artists, entertainers. That's what you found in *DDB.* Some were simply paid spies, but others traded in controlled technologies, handled stolen works of art, siphoned off private money transfers from West to East, or supported terrorists. Schwartz planned to leak the information little by little. He wanted to create an atmosphere of the established elites everywhere being morally bankrupt and corrupt. Schwartz's group would then agitate – in the media, on the opinion pages, through publishing houses – for a clean-up of all the elements that cooperated with the East German regime over the years. Eventually, who knows, an investigation, maybe a parliamentary committee might have been struck. In a situation like that, a fresh political movement with a clear direction and no links to the Communists, embodying the old Prussian virtue of order might do well. As for the skinheads – I don't know – perhaps he saw them as having potential to become the movement's workers after some indoctrination. Would it have worked? Perhaps. Perhaps not."

The Mercedes arrived at the airport. Hanbury sat transfixed. He asked who found out, who recognized him on the photo, but he met a wall of silence. At the terminal the barons spilled out of the BMW. Von Helmholtz went to talk to them and came back with one. "Horst here will take your luggage and check you in. We've got twenty minutes. Let's walk a bit."

"Who recognized me on the photo?" Hanbury repeated. "Who knew I was working on the files? Is Kurt Stobbe part of it?"

Von Helmholtz nudged Hanbury to start walking. "No," he said. "Not Stobbe."

"Did our spooks feed yours? Is that how you got my reports?"

"No."

"So your side fed my side."

"Not my side, Tony. Information has been coming to us."

Hanbury did a mental check. "The Yanks," he said.

"Not necessarily, Tony," von Helmholtz said. "Not them."

All the questions that plagued Hanbury throughout the night came gushing out. If not the Yanks, then who? Who checked his Stasi file? Who organized the Christmas phantoms? Who was listening in *Friedensdorf*? Who got hold of his reports? Who observed him in the Stasi complex? And why was a photographer handy in Potsdam? Hanbury beat his forehead with a palm. "I've had all night to think about it. It's systematic, but I can't see any links. Is Gundula part of it? Is she working for them?"

"Not Gundula." Von Helmholtz's eyes bored ahead, like someone wanting no distraction, someone wanting to forget. "You don't want to know," he advised curtly. "Take my word for it."

"I may keep trying to figure it out all the same," Hanbury said bitterly. He took a deep breath. "Well, I'm paying for my mistakes. What's happening to Schwartz?"

Von Helmholtz was severe. "Your judgement, to say the least, was poor. You're getting off mild. Keep that in mind. As for Schwartz, he's been questioned. I'm told he was composed. Since he no longer had your material stashed away in some hiding place he lacked bargaining chips. I suppose he weighed the pros and cons. Did he want a leaked picture of him on the front page identifying him as a suspected right-wing extremist? Did he want the same leaked story to say that he might soon face investigative custody of indefinite length. I'm sure he thought about it and saw reasons to cooperate. I understand he did. In return..." A resignation came over von Helmholtz. "...he will continue a quiet academic life."

"Hushed up," The consul concluded. Von Helmholtz looked neither right nor left. "He hasn't, strictly speaking, broken any laws."

"And the Stasi collaborators in West Germany?"

Von Helmholtz didn't reply.

"Hushed up too?"

"It's too early to be sure. I understand you matched cover names with real names on the basis of intuition. So far there's no direct evidence that the pack – the Scorpions and Midnight Angels – are the personalities you assumed they were. They may eventually be identified, after due process."

"No one called to account..." Hanbury said.

"It's not something we are traditionally good at."

"...except me, and in half an hour it will be as if I've never been here either."

"You'll be better off in South Africa."

They were half-way around the airport's inner circuit. With the time left shrunk to minutes, Hanbury denied this. He seemed set vehemently to contradict it, but after a pause he became thoughtful instead. This was the one place in the world he might have stayed, he said, to have been somehow part of it.

"Gundula?" Von Helmholtz asked. He finally glanced sideways at the consul and saw him nod. "It would be a mistake to stay because of her. I would advise against it." Fresh bafflement formulated on Hanbury's face. "I mean," von Helmholtz said, "Gundula's staying would be a mistake. She has no future here. Your places – South Africa, Brazil, India – that's where her future lies."

"When she finds out why I left, it's not too likely she'll want to have much to do with me. Closet neo-fascists aren't her cup of tea. Simpletons and dupes don't rank high either." The Chief of Protocol muttered regret, but had he understood right? She didn't know he was leaving? He hadn't called her? Hanbury said he didn't know where she was, only that she was somewhere on the Baltic coast with her family. In three days she would be on a railway platform forming the conclusion he'd run out on her.

"You underestimate her."

"I haven't handed her too many reasons for having a high opinion of me."

"Write her," Von Helmholtz commanded. "Do it fast. Send it off quick. Invite her to South Africa. I'll explain to her you were caught up in things not of your doing."

Hanbury remained doubtful, but the Chief of Protocol was insistent. He belaboured his point until Hanbury acquiesced. They were back at the entrance to the terminal. "Does Schwartz's wife know?"

Hanbury then asked. This irritated von Helmholtz. "I doubt it. Is it important?"

"She inherited Geissler's bookstore. She offered me a partnership."

"In that case, it's a very good thing you're leaving."

Hanbury thought about this. He stood for fifteen, perhaps twenty seconds, looking at the Chief of Protocol, realizing he would need longer to think that through. Horst was motioning. "Visit me, Gerhard."

The Chief of Protocol looked stern, then broke into a thin smile. "I will, but not until Gundula is there." The agency reps came up, tugged at the consul, and led him away.

Von Helmholtz got back into his limousine. Before he was outside the terminal his office had patched him through to the police chief in Schwerin and before they were at the first traffic light he had issued an order. "I need to know where somebody called Dieter Jahn is," he instructed. "He's on vacation somewhere on the Baltic coast." Within the hour, von Helmholtz was dialling an obscure guest house on the northern tip of the island Rügen. "*Haus Kap Arkona,*" a crackly voice said. "Gundula Jahn, please," the Chief of Protocol replied with sonorous importance. When Gundula heard what had happened, she told von Helmholtz he needn't bother with arrangements for forwarding mail from Tony. "Think it over," he cautioned. "Don't make a rash decision." "Too late." Gundula said. "I've made up my mind. I'm going back to Berlin now. I'll wait there for his letter."

⚜

The former consul couldn't complain about Arnold's arrangements. He had the last seat on the plane, first class, all the way to Jo'burg. The journey began with champagne. Calmer now – internal reparations ongoing – he gathered his thoughts, about the place he was leaving, and where he was heading. Sporadic questions crowded in. If not the Yanks, then who? Who intercepted his reports? *You don't want to know.* But he did. Someone he knew?

A change of thought.

Your places – that's where Gundula's future lies. Von Helmholtz the optimist. The irony was that Gundula's career as a journalist died with Gregor Reich, whereas his stay ended on account of Schwartz. Gregor searched for truth; Schwartz planned to abuse truth. Both of them, he and Gundula, had dabbled in truth, and it did them in. *More champagne?* an attendant asked. *Yes please. Leave the bottle. Thank you.*

The letter to Gundula, he ought to do it before he reached the bottom of the bottle. He needed to be careful. He didn't want to be known as *Goethe* for the remainder of his days. *Dear Gundula.* Too trite. *Dearest Gundula.* She would break down with laughter. Something impertinent? Impertinence worked for Gundula, but with him it would sound contrived. He had no choice but to send her one line only: *Gundula, please, please come.*

He wrote a short note to Sabine too. The explanation – that he had been reassigned quite suddenly – came easily, but the ending was lame. How could he write her that her husband was the cause? So he wrote that in his career change was a fact of life. But this time, he promised, he would regularly write.

He came back to a pressing question. Who was behind it? Someone local? Someone he knew? A member of the staff? Frau Carstens? She had access to his reports. No, not Frau Carstens. The other ladies? Sturm? Rule them out too. Gifford? Hard working, pious, sweating, earnest Earl, always ready with bags of money to do anything for the consul? British Council Gifford. Was he the front man for an unseen universe? It had to be Gifford.

Knowing this made Hanbury feel strangely better. He extended the seat to its full length; the cabin attendant supplied a blanket; the world closed in. Comfortable now, he saw Gundula. She was at the wheel of a

Jeep Grand Cherokee powered by a smooth engine with the kind of size that she deserved. The vehicle was in four wheel drive and a determined Gundula, handling the gearbox flawlessly – as if she had never driven anything else – was bouncing across the South African veldt. He was strapped into the seat beside her studying a map and reading a compass and trying to figure out where she was going. And in the back, holding on for dear life, was a vacationing Chief of Protocol, sun-burned, wind-ravaged, eager eyes under the broad brim of his safari hat, taking in every square inch of the magnificent landscape.

Somewhere over the sands of northern Africa, with this peaceful preview of the future, the former consul fell asleep.

❧

That same morning the news hit the yacht. Earl and Frieda had just finished making love and lay on the circular bed studying the ceiling mirror. Frieda, satisfied by Earl, was stroking her belly. Earl was watching her every movement with a bird-like stare.

A loud knock was followed by sheets of paper shoved in under the stateroom door. The intrusion hit like a thunderclap. "*Ach, nein,*" Frieda complained. She wanted no disturbances. He grunted, swung his legs into a sitting position and hobbled over to the papers. "A fax from Frau Carstens," he announced. He didn't mind. Faxes with **URGENT** big and black at the top gave an impression that in his job he had to keep the world spinning. But, as Earl scanned the pages he swore and Frieda stopped playing with her body. "*Liebster!*" she said. Earl frantically wrapped a towel around his waist – it didn't entirely make it, so he bridged two corners with a fist – and ran out the cabin. "Captain!" he yelled, stumbling up the steps to the back deck where the luncheon table was already set. "*Capitaine!*"

The captain, relaxing at the controls on the upper deck, took a Gauloise from his mouth and turned to the huffing client. *"Monsieur?"* he asked, wondering why the ceremony with the towel. Most guests on the open sea were so taken by the beauty of his boat and the spiced artistry of the ship's cuisine that they soon discarded their clothing. But this pair was different, reserved, always in their cabin. New money, he had concluded. Upstarts too up-tight to do their fornicating on the back deck in the open like the guests with established wealth. "Turn around!" the client shouted. With a free arm and an index finger he began to draw large urgent circles in the air.

"Retournez. Vite. Maintenant."

"Immédiatement? A Monaco?"

"Oui. Oui," Earl said.

The captain stuck the cigarette back between his teeth, shrugged and spun the wheel. The ship's lurch made Gifford lose his balance. He grabbed a railing with both hands. The towel dropped. The steward, walking down the gangway to see if lunch was to be served, bent down to pick it up. Helpfully he returned it. *"Monsieur,"* he said.

In the state room Frieda had begun to paint her toes. Gifford studied the fax. Seven sheets, the first three pages being an emotional outpouring from Frau Carstens. Who gives a fart, Gifford thought, what Frau Carstens felt when Sturm phoned from the mansion to say the consul was gone, maybe abducted. There was paragraph upon paragraph of brooding self-examination and thoughts about why she never learned to cope with the unknown. Only when Frau von Ruppin checked the fax machine where she found a message from someone called Arnold, did they stop fearing the worst. However, they remained anxious and decided to contact Gifford to ask for guidance on what should happen next.

Gifford scanned Arnold's pages. The first, a copy of a message addressed to a certain Ambassador Lecurier in Pretoria, confirmed a flight from Berlin to Johannesburg for Mr. A. E. Hanbury. Gifford checked his watch. He would be over the Mediterranean by now, maybe directly overhead. The second, to Johannesburg, asked for a hotel reservation for one night, onward travel to Pretoria the next morning. The third was actioned to Berlin, copied to Pretoria, instructing the office to pack up and ship the consul's things. The fourth, a head-quarters message issued by Arnold under authority of somebody called Heywood, said no information could be given yet about the arrival of a replacement consul. There was a shortage nowadays of qualified personnel. Gifford grunted.

"What's the panic, *Liebster*?" asked Frieda. She had shifted her attention from her toes to her fingers. "An urgent development at the office. We've got to get back." "Ach nein!" Frieda protested again. She had just begun to like the yacht. Earl started to massage her shoulders. If he acted quickly, they could soon buy the yacht, he explained, and the crew too. Affectionately he rubbed and stroked until she whimpered and agreed that whatever he decided would be best. Earl began to work the phone to charter a jet from Monaco to Berlin. Time was of the essence. He had a mansion to get onto the market and he had to find a cozy little bungalow for the next man.

❦

As for Irving Heywood, give him his due, he kept his promise to Etchley. When the next assignment cycle started, the Investitures priest asked him to come by. "You know, Bob," Heywood began, "I liked the way you handled yourself last year. I know losing Pretoria was tough, but you didn't let it get you down. The wife's recovered?"

Etchley replied Judy was a trooper. She had picked herself up and kept on going. "Good, good," nodded Heywood. "What's your wish, Bob?

I'm moving a couple of dozen people at your level and you're first."

Etchley told Heywood his situation had changed. Last year he couldn't afford to stay; this year he couldn't afford to move. Once Judy got over the shock they did a frank assessment. "She's from Newfoundland, you know," Etchley confided.

"No! I'm from Atlantic Canada too." Heywood was inspired.

"Coming from Newfoundland, she knows about adversity."

"Tell me about it! All of us from there do."

Etchley said his wife, once their problem had been talked through, decided to find a job to help meet the payments on the house. The kids weren't babies any longer, she argued. Her working would be tough on all of them, but what's a family for if not for facing tough times together. She found a position as *Coordinator, Anti-racism Programs* in a bank. "Now she makes more than I do," explained Etchley.

"That's wonderful," replied the Investitures priest. "That is truly wonderful. I'd like to meet your wife. Why don't you bring her to the cottage. Hannah would love to meet her too, plus of course your little girls."

This was how Heywood fell into reminiscing on the porch. It was a lovely summer day with a light air that made breathing effortless. Bob was drinking beer; Irving, thermos in hand, sipped whiskey. The two Etchley girls splashed happily in the water below. Hannah and Judy had sneaked off to a boutique in a nearby, restored mill. "You know, I never thanked you for your confidence in me last year when you rearranged the Service," Etchley was saying. "You don't know how proud it made me – Judy too – that I wasn't cut, that I was able to stay on."

"You were easy, Bobby," Heywood said with pride. "Your reputation was sky high. You've done wonderful things over the years. Yes, yes. Bitrap…" Heywood sighed. "It brings back memories."

He thought of Bo Bilinski and gulped more whiskey. Bilinski had sent a Christmas card. Who would have expected it? A photo had been enclosed. Bilinski in western drag: a towering Stetson, buckskin jacket with fringes, a revolver on his hip and flaring rawhide breeches. He stood next to a great palomino stallion. Lovely mountain ashes in their brilliant autumn colour framed him on both sides. Behind, dusted by the first snow of the season, rose the Rockies. Bilinski looked into the camera with a steady, questioning, yet peaceful stare.

"Well, thanks all the same," Bob Etchley continued. "Tell me, Mr. Heywood..."

"Irving, Bobby. Out here it's Irving. I don't like inter-generational barriers."

"Thanks, Irving..."

"Irv's okay too."

"Sure. You know, I shouldn't ask this, but since I didn't get Pretoria, can you tell me what really happened last year in Berlin?"

Heywood filled his great chest full of air. The air went in until it seemed he'd burst. He was leaning dangerously backwards by the time a slow exhalation started. He began to shake his head. "I don't know, Bobby. Really I don't. I'd tell you if I did. The high priest did that one on his own. He got a phone call from the spooks. Then he took out his great sacrificial knife and plunged it into Tony like a lamb on an altar. I swear, that's all I know."

"Jesus Christ," said Etchley. "That's pretty scary."

"You said it." Heywood shook his patriarchal head. "I was pretty close to the high priest, but he never told me a thing. I checked the file too. Everyday I looked, hoping something would come from somewhere, but nothing ever did. The spooks were involved. Maybe it had to do with his reports. Maybe his assessments were at odds with the stuff coming from Washington. Maybe he got caught in some kind of crossfire. He was doing marvellous reporting from Berlin. The best ever. Everybody said so."

"I heard that too," Bob Etchley confirmed.

"Sure you did," Heywood agreed. "And you know, it wasn't just Berlin. He's still going strong. Between you and me, Bobby, I always thought you were best for Pretoria. You've got a presentable wife. Lecurier wanted you badly. I had my doubts about Tony. Pretoria is a big job. But he's doing fine. Poor Lecurier having that safari accident, the rhino puncturing his right lung. Suddenly Tony's running the embassy. He's got a woman helping him. From Berlin. She did a great job organizing the funeral. Turned the residence into a youth hostel for Lecurier's children. Dozens came, from every corner of the world. Apparently everybody loves her on sight. She's like your Judy, Bobby. A doer. And his political reports continue to be marvellous. He's way out front of the papers. The European Zealots did a study last month. One of them reads the German press. There's a rag there called Dee Seit, something like that." "*Die Zeit.*" Etchley knew the international papers. "Yeah. That one. The stuff on South Africa in that paper has been remarkably good lately. Better than in *Le Figaro.* Better even than in the *New York Times.* And, get this, the study showed the stories in Dee… whatever…they confirm Tony's reports down to the details. But because of Tony, we know about what's going on a couple of weeks before the Krauts. In anybody's book, that's great work."

Heywood turned nostalgic. "I have to tell you, I look forward to seeing him again. We've been through a lot." He suppressed a whiskey-induced sniffle and pulled his jersey up, using the lower part to dab his eyes. "The ladies will be back soon. What do you say? Time for a dip? Let's splash around with your lovely babies for a while." Lumbering to the dock, Heywood slung an arm over Etchley's shoulders. "I'm glad you came to visit, Bobby," he said. "You know, you, Tony, some of the others, next to Hannah and the family, you're all I've got."